PRAISE FOR *POOR LIT*

'Bold, brash, whiplash fast -
Jackie Collins' *Marie Claire*

'Ah Jackie, just as the wind ... and the autumn days seem a bit dreary, here she comes with another sun-soaked dose of steamy Hollywood intrigue' *Daily Telegraph*

'Jackie Collins is an undisputed genius . . . Sex, money, power, murder, betrayal, true love – it's all here in vintage Collins style. Collins's plots are always a fabulously involved, intricate affair, and this does not disappoint. Also, brilliantly for those of us who miss them like they're our own family, various members of the Santangelo clan make an appearance. Hurrah' *Daily Mail*

'Panic not, Jackie fans, because the illustrious Santangelo family are back to fight another day . . . A whole lot of satisfaction for the millions who worship at the temple of La Collins' *Scottish Daily Record*

'Whether you read the book with a straight face, or enjoy its tongue-in-cheek subtext, Collins remains mistress of her own genre of Hollywood bonkbuster-cum-crime thriller' *Independent*

'Collins doesn't just keep coming up with the goods, she explores with humour and intelligence the shallow lives of the uber-privileged. Driving it all are beauty, betrayal and three real divas' *Mirror*

'Ridiculously addictive' *Metro*

'Secrets, sex and lies abound in this steamy tale of friendship and jealousy from the queen of racy reads' *Woman*

'If you're in the mood for some scandalous escapism, who better to turn to than Jackie Collins. The best-selling author's brilliant new novel offers a tantalising mix of affairs, murder, drugs and money, and is a certain page-turner with a riveting storyline. Simply spectacular fiction' *Closer*

'Vintage Jackie Collins that exposes the seamy side of Hollywood' *Woman's Own*

'Another romping great read from Collins . . . with all the twists and turns you will be taken on a journey of deceit, money, secrets and lust' *Scottish Daily Record*

Also by Jackie Collins

Married Lovers
Lovers & Players
Deadly Embrace
Hollywood Wives – The New Generation
Lethal Seduction
Thrill!
L.A. Connections – Power, Obsession, Murder, Revenge
Hollywood Kids
American Star
Rock Star
Hollywood Husbands
Lovers & Gamblers
Hollywood Wives
The World Is Full Of Divorced Women
The Love Killers
Sinners
The Bitch
The Stud
The World Is Full Of Married Men
Hollywood Divorces

THE SANTANGELO NOVELS

Drop Dead Beautiful
Dangerous Kiss
Vendetta: Lucky's Revenge
Lady Boss
Lucky
Chances

Jackie Collins

Poor Little Bitch Girl

POCKET BOOKS

LONDON • SYDNEY • NEW YORK • TORONTO

First published in Great Britain by Simon & Schuster UK Ltd, 2009
First published by Pocket Books UK, 2010
An imprint of Simon & Schuster UK Ltd
A CBS COMPANY

1 3 5 7 9 10 8 6 4 2

Simon & Schuster UK Ltd
1st Floor
222 Gray's Inn Road
London WC1X 8HB

www.simonandschuster.co.uk

Simon & Schuster Australia
Sydney

A CIP catalogue record for this book is available from the British Library

ISBN 978-1-84983-441-4

Printed by CPI Cox & Wyman, Reading, Bekshire RG1 8EX

For family and friends.
You are the best!
&
For my three incredible
Amazing daughters.
Talented, smart and caring.
I love you all so much.

Chapter One

Annabelle

Belle Svetlana surveyed her nude image in a full-length mirror, readying herself for a thirty-thousand-dollar-an-hour sexual encounter with the fifteen-year-old son of an Arab oil tycoon.

Belle knew she was a beauty. What the hell, enough money had been spent along the way to make sure she was beautiful. A nose job ordered by her mother when she was a mere fourteen, a boob job shortly after – that was *her* decision. And then later, liposuction when needed, lip enhancement, regular facials and skin lasering treatments to make certain her skin remained the milky white she'd worked so hard to achieve (getting rid of her freckles had been a bitch, but she'd done it).

Ever since her teenage years Belle had strived for perfection, and now she'd gotten pretty damn close. Her hair was a pale golden-red, shoulder-length and wavy. Her eyes were a spectacular emerald green. Her body – a playground of delights.

Yes, she thought, staring intently at her unabashed nakedness, *I am worth every cent of the thirty thousand dollars cash already neatly stashed in my safe.*

Usually she did not go out on "dates" herself, but Sharif Rani – the oil tycoon – had insisted that it was she who should teach his youngest son the joys of the flesh. So, for a princely sum, she'd finally agreed.

Reaching for a peach slip of a dress, she stepped into it, powdered, perfumed and ready for action.

Thirty thousand an hour, not bad for a job which would probably take her no more than fifteen minutes to complete.

Of course, she could have turned the job down and suggested one of her twenty-thousand-an-hour girls, but sometimes it was fun to play – especially as she could pick and choose amongst her roster of rich, powerful and famous clients, which included everyone from Hollywood's biggest stars to several princes, more than one captain of industry, a few superstar rappers, dozens of sports heroes, and too many politicians to count.

Yes, Belle Svetlana – née Annabelle Maestro – ran *the* most exclusive, expensive call-girl business in town – the town being New York as opposed to Los Angeles, the city she'd grown up in, surrounded by luxury and all the opulence two movie-star parents could buy.

Thank God she'd escaped those two egomaniacs – Mom, the ethereal queen of quality independents – and Dad, the macho king of big-budget schlock. What a horror show, having *them* as parents.

When she'd dropped out of college in Boston and settled in New York, neither of her loving parents had given a rat's ass. Admitting to a grown daughter did nothing to enhance their public images, so they'd arranged to send her a monthly allowance, blithely told her to follow her dreams, and left her to her own devices.

Annabelle was no slouch when it came to following her dreams. She'd soon found herself caught up in the club and party scene – a lifestyle that had satisfied her for a while, until one night she'd been introduced to Frankie Romano – a popular deejay who worked private parties and the occasional hot club. One look at him and it was lust at first sight.

Originally from Chicago, Frankie was quirky and attractive in a Michael Imperioli kind of way. Fast-talking and edgy, he had longish dark hair, ice-chip blue eyes, and sharp features.

The trouble with Frankie was that he was usually broke, this on account of the fact that he was a dedicated coke-head, and whatever money came his way went straight up his nose.

Annabelle fell hard, for in spite of Frankie's drug use it turned out that he was a star in bed – whenever he wasn't too coked out to perform. She didn't know anything about his background, and she didn't care. As far as she was concerned, they were soulmates.

After a few weeks of crazy togetherness, Frankie had moved into her SoHo loft. Annabelle hadn't objected. The only downer was that she'd found herself spending her entire allowance keeping him in drugs, so it wasn't long before – at Frankie's urging – she'd called her dad in L.A. and requested that her allowance be increased.

Ralph Maestro, the self-made son of a Brooklyn butcher – a man who'd gotten shot by a robber when Ralph was twelve – told her no way. "I made it on my own without two cents to rub together," he had sternly informed her. "We've already given you a head start. If you want more money, I suggest you go out and find yourself a job."

Annabelle was furious. Her parents raked in millions, and Daddy Movie Star was telling her to get a job! Screw them! It was increasingly obvious that they didn't give a damn about her.

A couple of weeks later, she and Frankie had come up with a masterplan. They'd been lying in bed reading the lurid headlines about a married politician who'd recently gotten caught having sex with a series of high-priced call girls.

"How stupid is he?" Frankie had ruminated, scratching his skinny butt. "The dumb asshole should've paid cash. That way nobody gets busted, an' everyone goes home happy."

"Cash is good," Annabelle had agreed. "For special girls only."

"Yeah," Frankie had said half-jokingly. "Not some mouthy skank who's gonna sell her story, but *very* special girls. Y'know the kinda babes I mean. Models, actresses – they're always on the lookout for an extra score. An' here's the sweet part of the deal – we know 'em all."

"We sure do."

"So . . ." Frankie had said after a thoughtful few minutes. "You thinkin' what *I'm* thinkin'?"

She was indeed. And so their adventure had begun.

At first they'd both considered it a lark, but after a few months it had turned into one of the most successful call-girl businesses in town.

Flushed with success, Annabelle had soon created two identities for herself. As Annabelle Maestro, she was a girl struggling to make it in the fashion industry as a sometime designer. As Belle Svetlana (she got off on the exotic sound of the Russian surname), she was a woman of mystery who was able to supply the right girl to satisfy any man's fantasy.

For a price.

A hefty price, depending on what was required.

Annabelle's girls were not hookers. They were stylish, good-looking career women who enjoyed the extra income. Models, actresses, singers, designers, all classy, smart and discreet, and some of them quite well-known.

It was Annabelle's idea that the girls they recruited should wear masks when they went on jobs, to hide their identities. She was sure that the men would get off on the mystery, and the girls were happy too, imagining that wearing masks would conceal their true identities.

Finding the right girls was no problem. Frankie, a major cocksman before hooking up with Annabelle, knew them all, and he used his considerable way with words to talk them into anything.

A shitload of untaxable cash income was the big temptation, and as Frankie pointed out, since most of the girls were fucking for nothing, what was the big deal if they did it and got handsomely paid? Especially if they were able to remain anonymous.

Frankie vetted all their would-be clients, while Annabelle liaised with the girls and arranged the appointments. Between them they pocketed 60 per cent of every assignation, and it didn't take long before they were rolling in cash. It was always cash, no paper-trails involved.

Now they'd been doing it for almost a year, and what a sweet money-making business it had turned out to be. Neither Annabelle nor Frankie had any complaints – that is, until they both realized they needed help.

After thinking about it for a while, Frankie had recruited Janey Bonafacio, one of his many cousins who lived in Brooklyn and worked as a bookkeeper. He'd asked her if she'd be interested in working for him, and since she'd always harbored a huge crush on Cousin Frankie, she'd immediately quit her job and was hired to take care of the phones and schedule the girls' appointments.

Janey, a 275-pound unmarried mother with a nineteen-year-old son, Chip, was delighted to get the job. Worshipping her cousin from afar was one thing, but actually working for him was a dream come true, even if the business he ran with his snooty girlfriend was fairly dubious.

Annabelle trusted Janey, but she wasn't so sure when it came to Chip – a surly slacker with way too much attitude and a complaining disposition. Annabelle regarded him as a not-so-charming Frankie in training. They used him to run errands and drive the car.

"At least they're family," Frankie had assured her. "They'll never screw us."

"Don't be so naïve," she'd retorted. "When it comes to money, everyone has an agenda."

"Hey!" Frankie had said. "We're payin' Janey plenty to make

sure they stay discreet. An' remember this – Janey's got a thing for me. She'd never do anythin' to hurt me."

Annabelle was not so sure.

* * *

After making certain that she looked her most seductive, Annabelle buzzed downstairs to check that her car was waiting. Her main residence was a Park Avenue penthouse where she and Frankie spent most of their time, but she still kept the SoHo loft; it was the place where her parents and old friends could contact her. Not that her parents ever did – she heard from them maybe once every few weeks. As for her old friends, she was not interested in them; she had a new life now, and in her new life very few people knew who her parents were and where she came from. That's the way she liked it.

Earlier in the day, Frankie had driven to Atlantic City to spend the weekend with a couple of his guy friends, Bobby Santangelo Stanislopoulos, and Bobby's business partner, M.J. Annabelle knew both Bobby and M.J. from way back when they'd all attended the same high school in Beverly Hills. Yeah, fun times. Bobby and M.J. were a grade ahead of her, but she'd never forgotten the infamous prom night when the three of them had hung out, gotten totally high, and on a dare she'd ended up making out with the two of them.

Hmm . . . just one of those crazy, out-of-control teenage escapades, although it was quite a memorable experience. Neither Bobby, M.J. nor she had ever mentioned it again. It was a no-go zone.

Then one night, years later, after she'd moved to New York, she'd walked into *Mood* and there they were – Bobby and M.J. At first it was quite a shock seeing them, but they'd soon got to talking and catching up on old times. In fact, it was M.J. who'd introduced her to Frankie.

She'd never told Frankie about her one night of lust with his two best friends, since some things were best left in the past. Besides, she didn't imagine he'd be too thrilled if he ever found out – and when pushed, Frankie had a vicious temper.

Since gambling seemed to be Frankie's new passion, she hadn't objected to him taking off. Her live-in boyfriend was a handful and then some, so she didn't mind the occasional night on her own. Chilling out without Frankie would allow her a pleasant break.

The desk porter informed her that her driver was indeed parked outside.

Picking up her Chanel purse, she headed for the door.

As she stepped outside, the phone began to ring. She chose to ignore it; she had a thing about phones, hated answering them. Whoever it was could leave a message.

She left the apartment and descended in the elevator, quite psyched about the prospect of inducting an innocent young man into the joys of sex. His father, Sharif Rani, was one of their biggest customers. Sharif required a different girl several times a week, and he always came back for more. Annabelle considered Sharif Rani to be a primo client, along with the Hollywood movie star who was an insatiable pussy-hound, and the Hall of Fame rock 'n' roller with the nine-inch cock and a penchant for girls who would agree to indulge in bathroom activities all over his craggy face.

"Good afternoon, Miss Svetlana," the desk porter said, moving out from behind the long marble counter, rubbing his palms together in anticipation of a large tip.

Annabelle discreetly slipped him a twenty. She'd learned early on that it was smart to keep everyone happy.

The desk porter tried not to stare at her. She was a beauty, with her pale red hair and slinky body. She was also quite mysterious. Nobody in the building knew what she or her boyfriend did, just that they were young and rich and that they had plenty of good-looking friends.

Annabelle walked outside, slid onto the back seat of the Mercedes they'd recently purchased, and settled back against the plush leather. She was glad this was an afternoon assignation, because after educating the boy she'd decided to pop into Saks and buy herself the new patent-leather Prada purse she'd seen in the catalogue. And since Frankie was not big on buying her gifts, maybe she'd even treat herself to a David Yurman piece of jewelry.

Yes, that's what I'll do, she thought dreamily. *I'll reward myself for five minutes of not so hard work. I deserve it.*

"Hey there," Chip said, glancing in the rear-view mirror, his narrow eyes busily checking her out. "How's it goin'?"

"I'm not in the mood for conversation, Chip," she said crisply, tuning him out because he bothered her, he always had. There was just something about him . . .

"'Scuse me for existing," he muttered.

Damn! She decided then and there that Chip had to go. And the sooner the better.

Chapter Two

Denver

My name is Denver Jones and I am a twenty-five-year-old so-called hot-shot attorney, an attorney summoned to be part of the defense team being put together to save Ralph Maestro – a mega-famous action movie star – from a murder rap, should he be arrested.

His beautiful wife – also a movie star, Gemma Summer Maestro – is dead. Shot in the face, her ethereal beauty no more.

It is early December, and in spite of the blazing California sun, the fake snow is already neatly stacked along the Maestro driveway as I make my way up it. It doesn't surprise me as I have been here before, many years ago when I was a scrawny twelve year old attempting to curry favor with the most popular girl in school, Annabelle Maestro.

"Fake snow!" I remember exclaiming the first time I'd visited the Maestro mansion. "You mean your parents have fake snow brought in and pile it all along your driveway?" I'd stared at my new best friend in disbelief.

Twelve-year-old Annabelle Maestro had stared back at me defiantly. "Denver Jones," she'd said, wrinkling her freckled nose, the braces on her teeth catching the afternoon sunlight, "you are *sooo* dumb! This is Beverly Hills, stupid. We don't *have* real snow in Beverly Hills."

"You don't?" I'd mumbled, fresh out of Chicago with my not-so-normal parents. Dad, a maverick lawyer, Mom, a political activist and sometime homemaker.

"No way!" Annabella had huffed, as if I was the town idiot. "You're so dense!"

"Sorry," I'd muttered, although I'd had no clue what I was supposed to be apologizing for.

Annabelle had picked up a fistful of fake snow and pitched it forcefully into my face. It felt like cotton candy.

"Come on," she'd said, her long legs racing up the snow-covered driveway. "I'm starving!"

I'd trailed behind her, brushing the fake snow off my face and out of my hair.

That was then, and this is now, and I am no longer that naïve twelve-year-old girl, but I'll never forget Annabelle and her freckles and the way she used to wrinkle her nose. I haven't seen her in years. We lost touch right after high school, then later I heard she'd left L.A. to attend college in Boston, and after dropping out she'd apparently moved to New York where she was doing something involving fashion.

I wondered where Annabelle was now and if I'd run into her. We hadn't stayed friends for long. I was never cool enough for her – too work-oriented and different for her tastes. Her deal was trolling up and down Melrose Avenue and Robertson Boulevard searching for the new hot bag or the latest cool jeans, and that was hardly my scene. Even if I'd wanted to, I certainly wouldn't have been able to afford the Maestro Princess lifestyle. In fact, it was a relief when Annabelle had started ignoring me and hanging out with a group of similarly rich girls with equally famous parents.

Losing Annabelle's friendship was no big deal. My mom was relieved; she'd never much liked Annabelle or all the things her family represented. Fame. Vast wealth. The full Beverly Hills scene. Mom was happier when I teamed up with Carolyn Henderson – a brainy kid whose father was a plastic surgeon, and whose mother worked in real estate. As soon as Carolyn graduated college she scored a job as an intern in Washington. She is currently personal assistant to Senator Gregory Stoneman. We are still close friends, even though we live in different cities. We keep in touch on a regular basis, although it isn't always easy as we're both major busy. Thank God for e-mailing and texting.

This year, Carolyn has promised to make it out to L.A. for Christmas, in spite of a workload that makes *me* look like a slacker, and believe me, I am no slouch.

I can't wait to spend time with her, especially as we both recently broke up with our significant others, which means we'll have plenty to talk about. Carolyn dumped her boyfriend, Matt, because she caught him cheating – which came as no surprise to anyone. Matt was an up-and-coming political journalist who everyone (except apparently Carolyn) knew had a major zipper problem.

My break-up was a different story. Josh – a successful sports doctor – left *me*. He complained that I put work first and that he'd had it with always coming second.

On reflection I have to admit that he was right, or maybe I simply didn't love him enough.

Josh and I were together three years, so the break-up came as kind of a jolt, but I'm not heartbroken. I have to admit that I do miss our Sundays devouring the newspapers in our sweats, taking long vigorous hikes up Malibu Canyon, watching *Entourage* and *Dexter* on TV, and gorging on my favorite Chinese food straight from the cartons.

I do *not* miss the sex. Like most relationships it started off incredibly raunchy and hot, but after six months it had turned into kind of boring comfortable sex.

Where did all the passion go? Hey, I'm no expert, but I did

experience a couple of sizzling affairs in college – one with a married professor, and one with a major jock. Both times the sex was mind-blowing, so I certainly know the difference. Although sleeping with a married man on the side is not for me. Too many lies and complications.

Sometimes I think our dog, Amy Winehouse, misses Josh more than I do. We came across Amy – a mixed breed – wandering on Venice Beach, lost and filthy, so we took her home and named her after my favorite singer because of her throaty growl that emulated Amy's lowdown, sexy voice.

When Josh left, I inherited Amy. "No visitation rights," I informed him coldly, although what I really wanted to say was, "Piss off, asshole, *you're* dumping *me*."

Josh gave me attitude about the dog – but hey, if he wanted out that's exactly what he'd get. Out. Gone. History. I don't believe in dragging things along; when something's over, it's best to make a clean break.

This time, my mom was not happy. She was fond of Josh, as were the rest of my family, especially my three older brothers.

Too bad. Josh was likeable as a friend, but he certainly wasn't the man with whom I planned on spending the rest of my life.

And who might that man be? Truth is, I haven't found him yet, and the prospects in L.A. are hardly promising. The only men I meet are clients, and they're usually married or gay. Then there's the slick lawyers who drive gleaming Porsches or Mercedes and favor twenty-year-old nubile blonde models or actresses with all the attributes.

Not that I'm a dud, lookswise. If I didn't live in L.A. I guess I'd be considered extremely attractive. I have long, chestnut-brown hair with natural golden highlights, wide hazel eyes, I'm five foot seven and I take a size eight dress (large by Beverly Hills standards – small for the rest of the country!).

Okay, so I'm no Pamela Anderson, but believe me – I have

no desire to be. Fake anything grosses me out – lips, breasts, cheekbones and chins. Ugh!! What are these women *thinking*?!

The truth is that if Josh hadn't broken up with me I would have eventually dumped *him*, because comfortable is great for a while, but passion is definitely lurking out there somewhere, and I *do* intend to find it. That's when I have time, 'cause as I might have mentioned before, I'm a dedicated workaholic.

This all happened three months ago, and word is that Josh has hooked up with a new girlfriend – some blonde, anorexic stylist to the stars that he picked up in a club.

Hmm . . . talk about not waiting around. Anyway, good luck to him, I couldn't care less.

I myself am a little more discerning. Right now I'm not interested in anything permanent. I've decided that I should have some fun while I'm waiting for Mister Right to put in an appearance.

"You're late," my boss scolded, greeting me at the door.

My boss, Felix Saunders – or Mister Shark Teeth as he is known around the office, on account of the fact that he recently had his teeth re-crowned, and they shine like a row of dazzling white beacons – is ready for action. Felix is an imposing-looking man with a sharp Roman nose and a shock of crazy silver hair that stands on end, making him kind of resemble a white Don King. He also has a penchant for light-colored Brioni suits, colorful shirts and pointy-toed lizard shoes dyed in a variety of outrageous colors. Most people regard him as quite a character.

Saunders, Fields, Simmons & Johnson is the name of the law firm I work for. I started out clerking for them while still in law school, then after I passed the bar they hired me as an associate. Within three years I was promoted to senior associate.

I hate to sound immodest – well, not really! – but I am good, very good, and I think that Mister Shark Teeth loves me. Not as a woman, but as his right hand – a hand he knows he can always depend on. The man is a brilliant lawyer with a killer mind, so over the years I studiously ignored the whiter than white teeth, the out-of-control hair and the overly expensive suits, and learned everything I could from him. He is an excellent teacher and I'm a quick study, so it's turned out aces for both of us. Soon I expect to be promoted to junior partner.

I guess Josh is correct. I do put work first, and right now I have no reason not to.

I consulted my watch – a Cartier – a birthday present from Mister Shark Teeth. Personally I'm not into labels, but other people seem to hold them in high regard, especially in Beverly Hills.

"Two minutes hardly counts as late," I said crisply.

Felix Saunders raised a bushy eyebrow. "Always an argument," he said, verging on irritable.

"Facts are facts," I responded.

"The girl who always sees things in black and white," he said dryly, tapping his chin with his slightly crooked index finger.

"Nothing wrong with *that*," I countered. Getting in the last word is one of my habits that drives people crazy. I don't give a crap, I *enjoy* having the last word. Besides, again, I don't wish to sound immodest, but I'm usually right.

"Follow me," he said. "We have work to do."

I am considered a hot-shot attorney because in the past eighteen months I have defended two high-profile men with great success. Client number one was a well-known studio executive accused of rape by a TV star whose career was on the downslide. The upcoming trial hit the front pages for months, culminating in a fast five days in court.

The actress was not a popular woman; she'd portrayed a bitch on TV for several years. It wasn't difficult for me to convince the jury that her role on TV came naturally to her, while also playing up the studio executive's happy family angle, pointing out that as far as he was concerned, the one night of sex was consensual, he loved his wife and family, and that he deeply regretted the entire incident. Then I emphasized how much the actress needed – in fact, *craved* – the headlines of her past stellar career. And how she'd gone after Mr Big Studio Executive with a vengeance.

"You saw the Beyoncé movie *Obsessed*," I dramatically stated in my closing argument, fixing the jurors with my wide hazel eyes, which I've been told can be quite hypnotic. "Then may I suggest that you consider this as the real-life version. Put yourselves in this man's position."

A long pause for effect.

"Yes, it's true, my client cheated on his wife, but he's never claimed to be a saint. And that's *all* he did. One night of weakness with a seductive actress determined to get her career back on track. So . . . because of one lapse, and a fading actress who feels she's been rejected, is this innocent man supposed to lose everything?"

Another long pregnant pause. More deep eye-contact.

"I don't think so. Do *you*?"

The jury were sold.

Result. A big victory.

Everyone at the firm was more than pleased with the way I handled myself in court, and within six months I was handed another big newsworthy case. This time it was a beloved comedian accused of exposing himself to children in public places. I painted him squeaky clean. He had a family who was dear to his heart. A wife he doted over. Children of his own that he adored.

Then I gave the impassioned closing argument about how this man – this *gentle* man who had raised so much money for children's charities – would *never* harm a child or even think of doing so.

Once again we won.

Now this. A murder case. Although nobody had actually accused Ralph Maestro of killing his wife.

Yet.

"I think you'd better fill me in," I said to Mister Shark Teeth as I followed him inside the Maestros' imposing mansion.

Felix stopped and patted me on the shoulder, while whispering confidentially in my ear.

"Ralph Maestro is a very big movie star." He paused to reconsider his words for a moment. "I mean, he *was* the biggest. Not so much today. But once a movie star it sticks, whether you're still pulling in the big bucks or not."

"And is he?" I asked curiously.

"Is he what?"

"Still pulling in the big bucks?"

"That's irrelevant," Felix said testily.

I wondered if now was the time to tell him that I knew the Maestro family, had indeed attended school with their daughter. Then I decided it wasn't necessary – they wouldn't remember me anyway.

Felix proceeded to tell me what had taken place. Apparently the Maestros had attended a major fundraiser the previous evening at the Beverly Wilshire Hotel, returning to their home at eleven. Gemma Summer Maestro had gone straight upstairs to her bedroom, while Ralph had stayed downstairs watching TV and enjoying one of his expensive and most likely illegal Cuban cigars. Later, he'd walked outside to visit with his dogs – two fierce pit bulls who were not allowed inside the mansion.

Around one a.m. he'd gone upstairs to his bedroom – the Maestros kept separate bedrooms – not unusual amongst affluent celebrity couples. There he'd watched more TV until finally he'd fallen asleep around three. When he'd awoken at six in the morning he'd gone straight to his private gym in the back of the house, and it wasn't until their Guatemalan housekeeper, Lupe, discovered Gemma's body – shot while lying in her bed – that Ralph realized anything was amiss.

I quickly fired off a few relevant questions. "Have the police found the murder weapon?"

"No."

"Any sign of a break-in?"

"No."

"Were the Maestros getting along?"

Felix shook his head. "Who knows? But once I shift the detectives out of here, we'll soon find out."

There were two investigating detectives and a legion of cops crawling all over the house.

The housekeeper, Lupe, was in the kitchen making wailing noises.

Gemma Summer's body was still upstairs in her bed, while the police photographer was on his way downstairs.

I started talking to one of the detectives, an African-American guy with an older Will Smith look. My imagination told me that he'd come to Hollywood hoping to be discovered, and ended up becoming a detective. That seems to be most people's stories. He was Detective Preston; his partner, an Asian woman, was Detective Lee.

I wondered if either of them had called Annabelle and told her the devastating news.

Suddenly I experienced a sick feeling in the pit of my stomach. How does anyone make that call?

"*Good afternoon, Miss Maestro. This is the Beverly Hills Police Department. Your mother's dead, shot in the head. Your father is the prime suspect. Oh yes, and may I take this opportunity to wish you a very Merry Christmas.*"

"What's the matter?" Felix growled. He expected my full attention at all times; a wandering mind didn't do it for him.

"Has their daughter been notified?" I asked.

Felix narrowed his eyes. "How do you know they have a daughter?"

"It's general knowledge," I answered quickly, still not prepared to reveal my connection to the Maestro family.

"As far as I know, nobody's been notified yet," Felix said,

groping for a box of extra-strong breath mints in his jacket pocket. Without offering me one he popped a couple in his mouth before putting the packet away. "Do you have any idea how the press are going to bite into this one?" he said, minty breath wafting in the air. "It'll make the Phil Spector and Robert Blake cases look like goddamn picnics."

"Do you think the police are planning on arresting Ralph Maestro?" I asked curiously.

"Not if *I* have anything to do with it," he answered, full of his usual unshakeable confidence. "There is absolutely no evidence that Ralph did it, none at all."

"*Did he?*" I was dying to ask.

But I refrained from doing so. Sometimes you learn more by saying nothing.

Chapter Three

Carolyn

"You told me you were going to leave your wife," Carolyn Henderson said, her pale-blue eyes filling with tears as she confronted her boss, her lover, the man who had promised her everything and delivered nothing. "You faithfully promised it would happen before Christmas."

Senator Gregory Stoneman paced around his office, unable to look at the pretty girl with the honey-colored bob and the tears in her eyes. He was a tall man of fifty, with a thick head of greying hair, a sharp aquiline profile, and a politician's ready smile.

"Listen to me, sweetie," he cajoled. "You must—"

"I *have* been listening to you," Carolyn interrupted, her voice rising. "I've listened to you non-stop for the last two years." She stared at him accusingly. "You swore to me that we'd be together this Christmas. You promised you'd leave her."

"I know, but—"

"You lied to me, Gregory," she continued, her voice rising. "You *still* haven't told her about us, have you?"

Tears began to course down her cheeks in an uncontrollable torrent.

Gregory Stoneman frowned; there was nothing more irritating

than a crying female. Bad enough that he had to put up with it from his wife on occasion, now this one was starting to become extremely demanding. He didn't need this kind of nonsense. Besides, he'd recently met a British journalist, the London correspondent for an up-market English newspaper. The girl was young and fresh, and looks-wise she put Carolyn to shame, although he had to admit that Carolyn did have a sensational body – great tits – which was one of the reasons he'd strung her along with all the false proclamations that one day he was definitely going to divorce his wife.

As if.

There was a game in Washington. And the game had stringent rules. An affair was an affair, and it *never* interfered with a marriage. Everyone who cared to play should learn to abide by the rules.

"Hush," he said soothingly.

"Screw hush!" she shouted.

"After Christmas—" he began.

"No!" she shrieked. "You promised. And I expect you to keep that promise, or . . ."

"Or what?" he asked ominously.

"Or *I'm* telling your wife about us, since you can't seem to do it."

Her words hung between them like a dark curtain.

Gregory's frown deepened. If only her boyfriend, Matt, had stayed around, this wouldn't be happening. But no – Matt had made an abrupt exit. And where did that leave him? Stuck with a clinging girl who was starting to make demands he had no intention of meeting. And if that wasn't bad enough, now she was making threats. Threatening *him* – Senator Gregory Stoneman – an upstanding member of the Senate with an unsullied reputation and a solid twenty-year marriage.

Her behavior was unacceptable and he was not about to stand for it.

"Kindly do not do this in my office," he said, glancing agitatedly at the closed door.

"Why not?" she demanded, her face reddening. "Everyone will know soon enough."

"No, they won't."

"Oh yes they will."

He was getting severely fed up with her attitude. Who the hell did she think she was?

"And how's that?" he asked coldly.

"Because *I'm* going to tell them," she answered defiantly. "Your wife first, and then everyone else."

He caught hold of her arm in a vice-like grip. "No, you are not," he said, his voice turning into a strict command. "Do not even think about it."

"Try stopping me," she responded, determined to go through with this.

"Why?" he asked, making a stringent effort to control his anger. "Why, after all this time, are you doing this to me now?"

Carolyn stared at him, her lower lip quivering, hands shaking. She hadn't wanted it to come out like this, but he had to know.

Her words were slow and halting. "I'm pregnant," she said at last.

"*What?*" he said, visibly blanching as he took a step back.

"Pregnant," she repeated, delighted that she finally had his full attention.

"That's impossible," he snapped, refusing to entertain the idea. "You're on the pill."

"Mistakes happen," she muttered.

"What *are* you talking about?" he said brusquely.

"The pill doesn't always work," she explained. "It happens, you know."

"Christ!" he exploded.

"So, you see," she said, beginning to feel a lot calmer now

that she'd told him, "it's time for us to come out in the open. We have to."

He paced up and down for a moment or two before turning toward her with an accusatory expression. "What makes you think it's mine?" he said harshly.

She'd known he'd say something like that. It pained her, but she understood Gregory's weaknesses only too well, and when it came to confrontations he always tried to dodge the blame, exactly as he did in his political career.

And yet . . . she loved him. Couldn't help herself.

Now she had his child growing inside her, and she wanted to be with him more than ever.

"It's definitely yours," she said quietly. "There's no doubt."

"It could be Matt's," he argued, furious that he was caught in the oldest trap known to man.

"It's yours," she repeated.

"How can you be so sure?" he insisted.

Oh God! He was making her feel like such a loser. And it simply wasn't fair. She loved him so much, she always had.

"Because I haven't slept with Matt in over three months," she said in a low voice. "This baby is yours, Gregory, face up to it."

"Christ!" he exclaimed for the second time. "Why did you do this?"

"Why did *I* do this?" she responded with a sudden flash of anger. "If I remember correctly, it's ***you*** who comes to my apartment twice a week all ready to fuck my brains out."

"Don't be so damn crude," he said, throwing her a disgusted look. "It doesn't suit you."

This wasn't turning out the way she'd planned. She'd wanted him to say, "You're right, this is wonderful news. We should be together. I'll divorce my wife immediately."

Yeah. Sure. In her dreams.

Deep down she'd had a hunch his reaction would be pure crap.

She sighed, and wished she had someone to confide in. But right from the beginning of their affair he'd sworn her to absolute secrecy, so she hadn't even told Denver, her best friend who lived in L.A. As far as Denver knew, she'd been in a loving relationship with Matt until they broke up.

Ah Matt, even *he* had never suspected what was going on. They'd kept separate apartments, and he'd rarely stayed over at hers, so she'd been able to keep her affair with Gregory secret.

Now all she wanted to do was tell the world, and she especially wanted to tell Gregory Stoneman's wife, Evelyn – who, according to Gregory, was a cold, domineering woman who refused to give him any sex. It was one of the reasons Carolyn had never felt guilty about sleeping with a married man. He needed her. She needed him. They shared an extremely close bond.

Gregory walked over to the window and stared out, his back to her.

"So . . ." she ventured, hoping his attitude was about to change and soften, "I think this means you have no choice. Either you tell your wife, or I do."

He turned around, a strange look in his eyes. "Is that what you think will happen?" he said, his tone icy.

"Yes, Gregory," she answered bravely. "This time I really mean it."

"Do you?"

"Yes."

His expression was thoughtful. She took this as a positive sign; it was better than listening to him rant.

There was a long silence, and then he said, "You shouldn't have told me here. This is something we need to talk about in private."

"I agree," she said, relieved that it seemed he was finally accepting the news.

"And you have to give me a couple of weeks to work this

out," he added, staring at her intently. "I cannot perform miracles overnight."

"I can do that," she said quickly.

"As you know only too well," he continued, biting on his lower lip, "it's very, very complicated. There's my wife, and my children to consider . . ."

"Yes," she said obediently. "I understand that it won't be easy."

"You bet it won't," he said, a sharp edge to his voice.

"But the thing is, we can do it together," she added soothingly. "It'll all work out, and then we'll have each other."

He shot her a wary look. "You haven't told anyone, have you?" he demanded.

"Of course not," she assured him.

"You're absolutely certain?"

"Why would I? It's our secret."

"People tell secrets."

"Not me."

He began pacing, not looking at her.

She took a deep breath and waited for his next words.

"How pregnant are you?" he asked.

"Seven or eight weeks. I'm not sure."

"Have you seen a doctor?"

"I made an appointment with my gyno for next week," she answered, encouraged that he was taking an interest.

"Cancel it," he stated abruptly. "I want only the best for our baby. I'll arrange for you to see someone."

Our baby. How intoxicating were those words coming from Gregory. *Her* Gregory. She thought about the time two months ago when his wife and children were out of town and he'd taken her to his house. They'd spent a magical few hours together, he'd been so loving and so had she. That must have been the day she'd become pregnant.

Filled with a sudden rush of affection, she moved toward

him, impulsively throwing her arms around his neck. "I'm so sorry," she whispered, nuzzling close and inhaling his masculine smell. "I didn't mean for this to happen. But now that it has, I think it was meant to be. You do know how much I love you, and how I'll always be here for you."

"Yes, I know," he said, his mind racing in a hundred different directions, none of them pleasant.

"It'll be such a relief when we can come out in the open," she said, imagining herself accompanying him to important Washington events and glittering dinner-parties. "You'll see."

"Yes," he said slowly. "Only you must allow me to handle things my way."

"I will," she promised.

"You cannot say a word to anyone," he reminded her. "That's imperative. Do you understand?"

"Yes, of course I do," she said, kissing him, her tongue darting in and out of his mouth.

In spite of himself he was aware of a familiar stirring in his pants.

He felt angry, cornered and threatened, yet the conniving bitch could still give him a hard-on.

Placing his hands on her breasts he began tweaking her nipples through her blouse.

"Lock the door," he muttered after a few moments, his voice suddenly thick with lust. "Then take off your top, get down on your knees and do that thing with your tongue you do so well. We'll call it a celebration."

"Yes, Gregory," she murmured, thoroughly grateful that everything was going to be all right. "Whatever you want."

Chapter Four

Bobby

When Bobby Santangelo Stanislopoulos walked into a room, women took notice, for not only was he over six feet tall, in his mid-twenties, and undeniably hot, he possessed great style. With his longish jet hair, intense black-as-night eyes, Greek nose and strong jawline, he drove women a little bit crazy. And it wasn't about being incredibly good-looking – which he was. Nor was it about being the heir to a major fortune – which he also was. No, it was just a certain something. A mix of the young John Kennedy Jr., a touch of the Ashton Kutcher edge, and the mysterious allure of a Robert Pattinson.

Bobby's Greek billionaire father, the late Dimitri Stanislopoulos, had been a powerful man, a true force in the business world of shipping and commerce. Bobby had never harbored any desire to follow in his father's footsteps – that kind of business was not for him. Nor did he wish to emulate his mother's successes. The wildly beautiful Lucky Santangelo had always done things her way – including building several Las Vegas luxury hotels, and running and owning Panther Movie Studios for several years. Bobby had always been surrounded by high achievers. Apart from his parents there was his stepfather – Lennie Golden – a former comedian/movie star, who now wrote and directed highly successful independent films, and his maternal grandfather, the inimitable Gino Santangelo.

So . . . what was a young college guy supposed to do to make his own mark in the world?

Fortunately, Bobby had big ideas of his own, and without asking anyone's permission or opinion, he'd dropped out of college, headed for New York with his best friend, M.J., the African-American son of a renowned neurosurgeon, and the two of them had put together a group of investors, enabling them to open *Mood*, a private club, which after a few months had taken off and become *the* late-night place of choice.

Bobby was a hybrid of both parents. He'd inherited Dimitri's dominant personality, along with his acute business savvy, and he possessed Lucky's addictive charm, stubborn ways and strength of character. Not a bad combination.

Everyone wanted to be Bobby's friend, but Lucky had taught him at an early age that when it came to friends and acquaintances he had to be extremely discerning. "People will want things from you because of who you are," she'd warned him. "Money always manages to attract the wrong people. Look at Brigette and the series of losers who've latched onto her along the way. She's fortunate to have survived."

Brigette Stanislopoulos was Bobby's niece, even though she was almost a decade older than him. Brigette was the daughter of Olympia – Bobby's deceased half-sister – and the granddaughter of the long-dead Dimitri.

It seemed there were a lot of deaths on the Stanislopoulos side of the family. Bobby always kept the belief that he was more of a Santangelo.

He was extremely fond of Brigette, but from the stories he'd heard it seemed that she'd always fallen for the wrong men, and as a result she'd paid the price over and over again.

Because of Brigette's example Bobby trod a wary path, especially with women.

He'd had many girlfriends, not one of them serious, all of them incredibly beautiful. Society girls, models, actresses. They came, they went. He enjoyed himself. Why wouldn't he?

But none of them had meant anything, apart from Serenity – a woman he'd been hung up on eighteen months ago until she'd dumped him, had a one-nighter with his friend, Frankie Romano, then mysteriously vanished with her Russian husband to God knew where.

And then along came Zeena, a singing star known by one name. Zeena was the wrong side of forty with a body like Madonna, a bad girl attitude, and a cult-like following.

The woman was something else. An exotic beauty – half-Brazilian, half-American-Indian – she sashayed into *Mood* with her adoring entourage at least twice a week, always with a different young guy in tow, and yet somehow or other – much to Bobby's extreme irritation – she usually managed to either flirt with or totally ignore him.

Zeena's switches in temperament were driving him a little bit nuts. It was a miracle that he was keeping his infatuation to himself and not confiding in M.J. or Frankie – especially Frankie – who deejayed at the club, and was Annabelle Maestro's boyfriend.

There were times Bobby couldn't help wondering why he and Frankie were such close friends; they were so different it was ridiculous.

Frankie was into doing coke and getting high.

Bobby wasn't.

Frankie was into cheating on Annabelle.

Bobby believed in monogamous relationships.

Frankie had an aversion to real work.

Bobby got off on making deals. Together with M.J. he was currently planning a franchise to open branches of *Mood* in Miami, London, and maybe Moscow.

In spite of their differences, Bobby liked to think that

Frankie would always have his support and vice versa. Besides, they had a history together, and that would be Serenity, the beautiful Slovakian model who'd slept with both of them and then taken off.

Bobby still felt the sting of Serenity's rejection.

Wisely, he chose not to trust either M.J. or Frankie with his latest obsession. If he told them about his thing for Zeena, they'd plague him to death with smart-ass remarks and sarcastic jibes; better he stay silent.

That didn't mean that he couldn't help having an urge to talk to someone about her – get an unbiased take on the situation.

Was she into him? Or did she get off on torturing him? Because she sure as hell knew how to do that.

He often wondered why the women he was most attracted to were the ones who rejected him. Lucky's best friend, Venus – who'd treated him like a kid. Serenity – who'd treated him like an annoying lapdog. And now Zeena – what did *she* have in store for him? And why did he want her so much?

A shrink could go to town on *that* one.

To get his mind off Miz Superstar, he decided to take the weekend off and go on a trip to Atlantic City with Frankie and M.J. Frankie had been bugging him about it for weeks, so why not indulge in a little R&R?

Perhaps Zeena would miss not having him around, although being the woman she was, she probably wouldn't even notice he was gone.

* * *

The drive to Atlantic City went by quickly. Frankie had been desperate to take his new red Ferrari, but as M.J. had rightfully pointed out, there was hardly room for two, let alone three inside it, so they'd ended up taking Bobby's black BMW sedan instead. Bobby could've easily bought himself the latest Lamborghini or Porsche, but keeping a low profile was more his style, especially as on his twenty-fifth birthday he'd inherited the lion's share of his late father's estate – making him even richer.

Frankie and he never discussed money. It was one of those taboo subjects that neither of them ventured near, ever since Frankie had requested a loan early on in their friendship, and Bobby had turned him down flat. There was no way he was financing Frankie's coke habit. Besides, Lucky had taught him that it was a big mistake to lend money. "You'll lose a friend who'll end up resenting you," she'd explained. "So either give them the money and expect nothing back, or simply say no." It was excellent advice.

Apart from deejaying, Frankie had recently gotten what he claimed was an investment business going on the side – something that he and Annabelle had gone into together.

Bobby and M.J. knew exactly what Frankie was up to – girls talked. But they'd decided to wait until he told them himself. Business must be booming, because Frankie's latest acquisition – the red Ferrari – spelled out that whatever he was into was making him plenty of big bucks.

Before they left, Bobby got on the phone to Lucky. She divided her time between Vegas, L.A., and wherever her husband Lennie happened to be on location shooting one of his movies.

He reached her in Vegas, where she was keeping a sharp eye on The Keys, her latest creation – a magnificent hotel/apartment complex. Only open a couple of years, The Keys was already a major success.

No surprise there – everything Lucky did always turned to gold. Being her son, Bobby had a lot to live up to – and didn't he know it. It was one of the reasons he'd taken off for New York and done his own thing. No competition.

Thank God it had all worked out. He had a successful club,

with more on the way. A great apartment on the West Side. Friends. A crazy social life. And a mom, stepfather, two half-siblings, and various other family members he loved. Especially as they mostly lived in California and he was firmly settled in New York.

As far as his inheritance was concerned, it was a huge responsibility – and instead of dipping into it, he'd decided not to touch it until he was older and wiser. Right now he was almost twenty-six and making it on his own. That was enough for him to feel damn good about himself. His inheritance could just sit there earning interest. It was far more rewarding and a hell of a lot better for his ego to live off the money he made himself.

"Hey!" Lucky said over the phone, sounding delighted to hear from him. "What's going on with my number one son?"

"Number one son is on his way to Atlantic City for twenty-four hours of debauchery and sex," he answered lightly.

"Just like your grandfather!" Lucky responded. And he could imagine her smiling when she said it.

"Seriously," he added. "I'm taking off with M.J. and Frankie. Turning my phone to dead."

"I wish you wouldn't," Lucky said. "I hate it when I can't reach you."

"Twenty-four hours, Mom."

"Fine," she said with a dramatic sigh. "I won't worry."

"Yeah, like *you* worry. Not!"

Lucky laughed. "The only one I worry about is Brigette. Have you seen her lately?"

"Called her a couple of days ago. She seems okay."

"You're her uncle," Lucky scolded. "I wish you'd stay in touch."

"Yeah, an uncle who happens to be ten years younger than her," Bobby pointed out. "It's not like we have a lot in common."

"Doesn't matter. You know she's a magnet for losers. Someone has to watch out for her, and I'm not there."

"Got it," Bobby said, scrawling Brigette's name on a pad by the phone so he wouldn't forget. "I'll call her again when I get back."

"Thank you," Lucky said briskly. "Oh, and give my love to M.J. When are you two coming to spend a weekend at the hotel? I'm very fond of M.J."

"Yeah, M.J.'s cool," Bobby agreed, thinking how far back they went. High school. College. Opening *Mood* together. They shared many a fine memory. And since they both came from money, they'd never wanted anything from each other – only friendship.

"Speaking of the hotel, how's everything going?" Bobby asked, glancing at his watch, thinking it was time to hit the road.

"Thriving. We're completely booked out. Even Gino gets off on visiting, so I've allotted him his own special suite. You should see him, Bobby. That man is king of the pool – everyone loves him. Men, women – *especially* women – he's such a dog."

Grandfather Gino Santangelo. Once a notorious figure in Las Vegas back in the Meyer Lansky, Bugsy Siegal days when Vegas was just beginning. Gino who'd built major hotels, fought off vicious rivals, bedded hundreds of women, and created an empire. Now he was ninety-seven years old and still active, with a much younger wife (his fourth) and a true zest for living.

"Tell him hi from me," Bobby said. He was quite in awe of his amazing grandfather. Gino Santangelo was a force of nature.

"Tell him yourself," Lucky responded. "The old man's planning a trip to New York."

"No kidding? Jeez – I'd better start lining up a shitload of action. Strippers . . . hookers . . ."

"Paige will be thrilled to hear how excited you are," Lucky said dryly, mentioning Gino's current wife.

They both laughed.

"By the way," Lucky added, "Max is desperate to talk to you."

"Where is Little Sis?"

"Max is not so little any more, Bobby."

"Yeah, I can believe that."

"And right now she's probably out with yet another horny boyfriend."

"How many horny boyfriends does she have?" he asked, amused.

"As many as she can get," Lucky replied with a resigned sigh.

"Okay, so I'll give her a call later."

"Do that. I have a feeling she's ready to take off on her own, and there's no way I can stop her. She's saying a flat-out no to college and anything else we suggest."

"Face it, Mom, she's a wild one, exactly like you."

"I had to fight for *my* survival," Lucky said, frowning at the memory.

"Heard it all before. I'll definitely call Max. You stay out of trouble."

"Shouldn't I be saying that to you?"

"Yeah, yeah. Stay cool, Mom."

"Yes, Bobby," Lucky drawled sarcastically. "Whatever you say."

Bobby grinned. His mom was something else. Still insanely beautiful and ready to take on anybody and anything. Lucky walked through life her way, and woe betide anyone who tried to stop her.

Max, his about-to-be eighteen-year-old half-sister, was the mirror-image of Lucky. A straight-talking beauty, unafraid of anything, she was bold, sassy, and kind of street smart. Even though Lucky and Lennie had tried to protect her, she'd never allowed herself to be fenced in, not even after a life-changing kidnapping a couple of years ago when she was only sixteen. Like Lucky, Max took no prisoners.

Bobby knew that she was desperate to come to New York and move in with him – she'd dropped enough hints. But he wasn't looking for a room-mate. And he certainly had no intention of being responsible for her. Little Sis was too much like hard work.

She'd visited him a year earlier, a few weeks after graduating high school. She'd arrived all set to party – a total wild thing. He shuddered at the memories. Every guy in the club had started checking her out – especially Frankie. Bobby had soon found himself desperate to ship her back to L.A. before she got herself into real trouble.

Yeah – a repeat performance was not on his agenda. Babysitting a teenager was hardly his thing.

Still . . . Max was an extraordinary girl, very special. And he had to admit that he did miss her. On occasion . . .

Chapter Five

Annabelle

Assignation: Teenage boy
Time: 4:00 p.m.
Place: The Four Seasons
Room: Penthouse suite
Boy's name: Omar

On the way up in the elevator, Annabelle smoothed down the bottom half of her silk dress. The material felt sensuous and rich against her skin. She wore no undergarments – just the slip of a dress, her honey-colored fox-fur coat, and spike-heeled Christian Louboutin short boots.

Before arriving at the door to the boy's suite she slipped on a satin eye-mask, the trademark move of all her girls. Not that she was a recognizable face like most of the girls who worked for her, but she'd soon realized that mystery was everything.

The moment she placed the mask over her eyes it transported her to another zone – an exciting place where she became Belle Svetlana – a woman with no history, a woman who was light years away from Annabelle Maestro, the unknown and unnoticed daughter of two famous movie stars.

The door to the suite was flung open by a twenty-something fat creature wearing baggy rapper clothes with multiple gold and diamond chains hanging from his neck, sinister oblique wrap-around shades, diamond stud earrings and an elaborate tattoo of a dragon covering his forearm.

Annabelle was thrown. There was not supposed to be anyone else present, she'd made that perfectly clear to Sharif Rani.

"Omar is expecting me," she said, imagining that this creature must be the boy's bodyguard.

"I know," the man cackled. "I *am* Omar."

"That's impossible," she said, somewhat nonplussed. "There's no way you're fifteen."

Letting forth another manic cackle, he reached forward, grabbed her wrist and hauled her into the suite, almost knocking her off-balance.

"Fifteen an' way ready for some hot steamy action," he guffawed, kicking the door shut with his Nike-clad foot. "We're gonna get it on, *beeitch.* I bin waitin' all day."

* * *

If there was one thing Frankie Romano knew about his girlfriend, Annabelle, it was that she hated cell phones, always had. In fact, she hated phones altogether. It bothered her that with a phone in her purse, anyone could reach her at any time. Frankie often told her that she was crazy, since he was never without his iPhone and his BlackBerry – both of which he used constantly. But Annabelle was adamant. No cell phone for her, she preferred voice mail, on her home phone, which she hardly ever checked.

"What if there's an emergency?" Frankie often asked.

"Then I'll deal with it when I get home," she always replied.

So after Frankie checked into the hotel and caught the news

of Gemma Summer's murder on TV, there was no way he could reach Annabelle. She was locked away somewhere with a fifteen-year-old Arab kid teaching him the joys of sex. Meanwhile her mother had been shot to death in L.A.

This was obviously the emergency he'd always worried about.

Damn Annabelle for refusing to carry a phone. She was a stubborn one, always insisting that she wanted things her way. Usually he didn't object, but today was something else.

He tried to remember if she'd mentioned where the assignation was taking place, but they'd both been joking about it so much that he couldn't recall. All he could remember was that they were pocketing thirty thousand dollars for her to have a quick sex romp with a teenager which would probably last all of three minutes.

"Find out if he's got a sister," Frankie had quipped. "I'll do her for the same price."

"You will *so* not!" Annabelle had retaliated, exhibiting her fiery jealous streak. As far as she was concerned it was okay for her to service a client or two if they paid enough, but Frankie with another woman? No way.

Frankie was well aware of the house rules, therefore he never pushed it. Why rock the latest Ferrari he'd recently purchased?

"Shit!" he muttered. What exactly was he supposed to do? He was in Atlantic City with the guys, and he knew that if he reached Annabelle with the news, she'd expect him to rush right home.

Not that he wasn't into her – she was the greatest. How many other women would embrace the business they'd embarked on with such unbridled enthusiasm? *And* participate when the money was right?

But he was on a fun trip, and it wasn't as if Annabelle was close to her mom. In fact, from the few times she'd mentioned her famous mother it was quite the opposite.

It occurred to him that since Gemma Summer's untimely death was all over the TV, he didn't have to be the one to tell her. She'd find out soon enough, and when she finally called him, he could make out that he hadn't heard.

Yeah, that would work. Especially if he turned off his phone for a while so that he could at least enjoy a few hours of freedom.

Frankie always had an answer for everything.

Determined to put the news from L.A. out of his mind, he rejoined M.J. and Bobby in the casino.

"Where were you, man?" M.J. asked, indicating an empty seat at the blackjack table.

With his shaved head, dazzling white teeth and friendly brown eyes, women found M.J. irresistible, even though he was on the short side. They all wanted to mother him – although once he got them into bed, mothering him was the last thing on their minds. M.J. had hidden talents.

"Takin' a crap," Frankie announced, eliciting a disapproving glare from an elderly woman at the far end of the table.

"I'm losing my ass, while Bobby's cleanin' up," M.J. griped.

"Bobby always cleans up," Frankie grumbled, sitting down at the table. "It's in his genes."

Taking his eyes off the dealer's cards for one swift moment, Bobby shot Frankie a devastating grin. "Sit. Play," he commanded. "I need someone at this table who knows what he's doing."

"Jeez!" M.J. complained, rolling his eyes. "I'm tryin' to work it here, an' that's the thanks I get?"

Frankie passed money to the dealer in exchange for chips. "I'm in," he muttered.

Bobby shot him another look. "Wipe your nose," he said, *sotto voce*. "You look like you fell into a vat of baby powder. I don't get why you're so into that shit."

Automatically Frankie ran his hand across his nose. It pissed him off big-time that Bobby refused to indulge. Without the coke to keep him elevated, Frankie himself simply couldn't function.

He'd started hanging out with Bobby and M.J. when he'd deejayed at their club a year ago. M.J. had hired him to work several private parties, and it didn't take long before he and Bobby discovered they happened to be sleeping with the same girl – Serenity – a sleek and overly confident bitch. She'd thought she was playing them, but when they'd discovered they were both in bed with her, they'd bonded – even though they hailed from totally different backgrounds.

Bobby came from money, money, money, while Frankie was the son of a timid mother and a tough Italian Chicago union boss who used to beat the crap out of both of them, until, at the age of fifteen he'd tried to defend his mom, and his dad had beaten him so badly he'd had to be taken to the hospital. Two weeks later, he'd said goodbye to his mother, made a midnight run for freedom with seventy bucks in his pocket, and headed straight for New York. He'd never looked back, although he often fantasized about returning home and putting a bullet right between his dad's eyes. He might seem cool on the outside, but within Frankie lurked a simmering deadly anger.

"This game is shit," he complained after losing four times in a row.

M.J. agreed, he wasn't doing well either, while Bobby was continuing to rake it in.

"Hey," Bobby said, tossing the dealer a generous hundred-dollar chip. "If you guys aren't into it, let's split. I got no problem with that."

"Finally!" Frankie exclaimed, pushing his chair away from the table, feeling only vaguely guilty that he wasn't on a fast track back to New York to be by Annabelle's side.

What the hell – he wasn't about to give up a night out with the guys. And maybe a girl or two, because when Annabelle wasn't around . . . who knew what the evening would bring.

* * *

Annabelle was overcome with feelings of deep apprehension. This huge sweating hulk in the would-be rap-star outfit and insane tattoo was hardly the young innocent Arab boy she'd been expecting. He wasn't Middle Eastern, he was all American. And he *certainly* wasn't fifteen.

She did not appreciate the way he hauled her into the suite and almost threw her down onto a large couch.

"You can't possibly be Sharif Rani's son," she said, gathering her composure, while in her mind she was busy planning a fast exit. *No sex with this big lout. No sirree.*

"You doubtin' me, *beeitch*?" he shot back belligerently, planting himself in front of her, massive legs widely spread. "My old man paid you up front, an' he dint pay you to ask no dumb questions. So get your fuckin' clothes off an' let's get it on."

"There's been a very big mistake," she said, managing to keep her cool.

"What fuckin' mistake would that be?" he snarled, folding his arms across his burly chest. "You got your money, didntcha?"

Yes, she had gotten the stacks of cash delivered early that morning by one of Sharif Rani's minions. The money was even now inside her safe.

"I said there's been a mistake," she repeated. "I need to speak to your . . . uh . . . father."

"Y'know what?" he said, smirking lustfully. "Soon's we get it on, *beeitch*, y'can talk all ya want."

And with those words he dropped his pants, revealing multiple rolls of dimpled white fat around his middle, and lower down, a small, angry, uncircumcised penis pointed in her direction.

Annabelle had never been caught in a situation like this before, although sometimes she'd heard stories of bad behavior from her girls. There was the family TV star who was into strangulation and nearly went all the way with one unfortunate girl. There was the rock star with a sudden urge to inflict extreme pain. There was the soul singer who attempted to involve a child before his "date" walked out on him. Oh yes, she'd heard many things, but she'd never personally experienced a difficult situation.

Now that situation was here, and how was she supposed to handle it?

"Suck my dick," Omar commanded, thrusting his penis toward her. "Suck it hard."

"Oh no," she said firmly, struggling to get up from the couch. "This is *not* going to happen."

"That's what *you* think!" he roared. And before she could get to her feet, he fell on top of her, jamming his penis into her mouth, at the same time ripping the front of her dress and exposing her breasts.

She would've screamed if it was possible. But it wasn't.

Omar was on a roll, and he obviously had no intention of backing off.

Chapter Six

Denver

Shaking hands with Ralph Maestro was not a pleasant experience, since his hand was big, meaty and slick with sweat.

Not a flicker of recognition crossed his big bland face as he shook my hand. But why should it? There's no reason he'd remember me. After all, why would a big movie star like Ralph Maestro remember a scrawny little kid from Chicago who'd hung out with his daughter many years ago?

"Sorry for your loss," I murmured respectfully. Hey – whether he'd done it or not, as part of his future defense team I had to hope he was innocent.

"Thanks," he muttered, practically ignoring me as he turned quickly to Felix. "Is this your secretary?" he asked, cracking his knuckles.

"No," Felix answered patiently. "Denver is my colleague. She's an excellent and accomplished associate, and I can personally assure you that she's a brilliant girl who has done some outstanding work for our firm."

Brilliant, ***outstanding***! I preened a little. This was the first time I've heard such a positive statement of my talents coming from my boss, although I'm not thrilled that he referred to me as a "girl." Surely "woman" is more appropriate?

Ralph Maestro was unimpressed. "She looks awfully young," he grumbled, hardly a man bent double with grief. "And what kind of name is Denver?"

It's my *name, asshole. So don't even go there.*

He didn't, and neither did Felix, who knew better than to do so. We'd had the name discussion a few months after I'd joined the firm. "Maybe you should change your name to something less strange," Felix had suggested.

Strange? I'd never considered Denver strange. In fact, I was very fond of my name. According to my parents I'd been named for the city I was conceived in, and Denver suited me just fine.

The two detectives had left the room, but they remained in the house, huddling in the front hallway, no doubt trying to decide their next move. To arrest or not to arrest. That was the question.

No weapon. No apparent motive. No witnesses.

My guess was that they wouldn't risk it. Ralph Maestro is famous. He has clout. He knows all the right people. And in Beverly Hills having connections means everything.

"Nothing wrong with being young," I said brightly, which was probably not a wise thing to say, because after that Mr Maestro froze me out and spoke only to Felix, even when *I* asked the questions.

If there's one thing I can't stand it's a big fat chauvinist, and even though Ralph Maestro is not fat – still surprisingly buff, actually – he's an obvious chauvinist.

I started wondering if he'd done it. Shot his beautiful wife in the face. Killed her beauty and her future.

Bang. Bang. You're dead.

He'd always had a thing about guns. I can recall Annabelle dragging me down to the basement one day where there was a locked room dedicated to his gun collection. Naturally Annabelle was adept at picking the flimsy lock; she was one of those girls who did anything she wanted and always got away with it. And on that particular day she'd been intent on showing off her famous dad's gun collection.

I decided it was time to jog Mr Maestro's memory. What the hell, *I* certainly had nothing to lose.

"Uh, Mr Maestro," I ventured. "Or do you mind if I call you Ralph?"

He threw me a baleful glance. Yes, he minded, it was written all over his movie-star face.

"Do you still have your gun room downstairs?" I continued.

"Huh?" Felix said, quite startled.

"Excuse me?" said Ralph, also somewhat surprised.

"Your gun room," I repeated.

"What gun room?" interrupted Felix, almost spitting out a mint.

"How do you know about that room?" Ralph demanded, shooting me a very action movie-star-ish suspicious look.

At least I finally had his attention. "Your daughter Annabelle and I used to be friends," I volunteered. "We were at school together."

Now it was Felix's turn to shoot me a look – a look that said, *"How come I'm only just finding this out?"*

"You and Anna were friends?" Ralph asked as if to say, *"How is that possible?"*

"Yes, we hung out for a short time."

"And you came to my house?"

I noticed he said "my house," not "our house." Interesting.

"That's right," I said, feeling that *I* was the one being questioned.

"So you're saying that my daughter took you into my private gun room?" he went on, his tone verging on outraged that she would do such a thing.

"She was probably showing off on your behalf," I answered. "You know how kids are."

Ralph shook his head as if he still couldn't quite believe it.

I took the time to study his face. It was definitely a face meant for the big screen. Larger than life and craggy, with a strong jawline and enormous white teeth. Ralph Maestro was handsome in that older action movie-star kind of way. He possessed a Harrison Ford, Bruce Willis vibe. Kind of sexy if you're into older dudes. Actually I'm not. I prefer them young and way hotter than this old guy.

"Showing off on my behalf, huh?" Ralph said at last.

"Well . . ." I ventured. "Like I said – you know how kids are."

"No, I don't," he sneered, curling his lip. "How are they?"

Ralph Maestro was being facetious. His beautiful wife was lying dead upstairs, and he was behaving like a major asshole without anything on his mind except being pissed at a couple of kids who'd invaded his privacy years ago.

I shut up, because I knew if I said anything more I'd be history. And I wanted to be involved in this case – it had major potential.

Later in the day, the press descended. Not that they could get in the house or even up the long, winding, fake-snow-decorated driveway. But the security cameras showed that they were out on the street with a vengeance. TV camera trucks, on-air talent with hand-held microphones and plenty of pissy attitude, paparazzi darting around like a trail of furtive ants, with their long-lens cameras at the ready.

Bad news travels fast, and this happened to be a juicy story. A brutal shooting of a beautiful woman. Two mega movie stars. Money. Fame. Hollywood. Oh yeah – this one's a surefire headline grabber.

I'd better remember to call my parents. There is nothing they like less than catching a glimpse of me on the TV news without fair warning. My dad was horrified when I became a highly paid defense attorney. He thinks I should have followed the path of righteous prosecutor and eventually become a D.A.

I obviously didn't agree with him.

Defending people is a challenge, and I always get off on challenges. Besides, my dad is a civil prosecutor – an excellent one – so when I decided to study law I did not want the comparison. There is nothing more soul-destroying than attempting to follow a member of one's family into the same profession.

The thing is, I love my dad – but doing the same thing? No way.

As we walked down the winding driveway on our way out, Felix gave me one of his long penetrating looks. "Well?" he asked, clearing his throat. "I always rely on your intuition. What do you think, Denver? Did he do it or did he not?"

I took my time answering because I honestly wasn't sure. And whether or not Ralph Maestro *had* killed his wife really didn't matter, since we were the defense team; we had a job to do, and that was to protect Ralph Maestro at all costs.

"I'm not sure," I answered hesitantly. "He certainly doesn't seem at all broken up."

Felix popped another mint, still not bothering to offer me one.

"They won't arrest him," he said knowingly. "Too many connections."

"*She* must've had connections too," I pointed out.

"Ah, but *she's* dead."

Oh really, who would've guessed?

"We'll keep a sharp watch on this one," Felix added. "Be on alert. I gave Ralph your cell-phone number. Told him he can reach you at any time of the day or night."

Thanks a lot! Why am I *on call? What's wrong with* your *cell phone?*

"The press'll go to town on this one," Felix continued. "But I can guarantee that Ralph won't be arrested."

Note to self: *If I ever decide to murder someone I must first*

become famous, then make sure to commit the crime in Beverly Hills. Movie stars can get away with anything. Or so it seems.

The crowd of press people jumped when they spotted us emerging through the imposing wrought-iron gates. Felix is well-known to the media, and since my two high-profile cases, I like to think that I am too. However, I always follow my boss's lead, and his lead is to hold up a firm hand and announce in sonorous tones, "No comment, people. Kindly back up."

I know it's shallow, but I kind of get off on seeing my photo in the newspapers.

"Hey, Denver," one of the on-air reporters called out. "What's *your* opinion on this?"

I did a fast double-take. I'd been checking this guy out on TV for the past few weeks. He was new to the L.A. job from a popular news show in San Diego. Now here he was in the flesh. And I have to admit that the flesh was quite tempting for a girl who's been on a sex-starvation diet. He's Latino with a buff bod, smoky eyes and a cocksure grin. Even better, he felt comfortable enough to use my name – and that boosted my ever-needy ego.

I decided that he's probably great in bed. Latino men usually are – or so I've heard.

Hmm . . . perhaps the time has come to put it to the test.

"Sorry, I don't have a take yet," I replied, incurring a disapproving glance from Felix, who would prefer me to stay silent.

"When you do, how about giving me a call?" suggested Mr Latino, swiftly handing me his card.

We'd reached Felix's car, a conservative black Bentley. My boss got in, and with a terse, "See you back at the office," he took off.

I turned around and headed for my four-year-old silver Camero, a twenty-first birthday present from my parents.

"Nice wheels," Mr Latino murmured, trailing me curbside.

I took a surreptitious glance at his card. *Mario Riviera.* Quite a memorable name.

I couldn't help wondering if there was anything else about him that was memorable, what with sex being on the missing list and all.

I think I need it – in fact, I damn well *know* I do.

"Thanks," I said casually, aware that he smelled of grass and sweat, a potent combination. I imagined that he must've been running or lifting weights when he was called to work, and he'd not taken the time to shower.

The very thought turned me on.

"How about we get together for a drink later," Mario suggested, moving closer. Obviously he was as into me as I was to him.

Hmm . . . a drink – isn't that a euphemism for sex and "Let's get it on"?

Of course it was – so why not? Because I am certainly ready, especially as Josh has moved on like a freaking express train, and here *I* am fast becoming a nun!

Enough is enough. I'm ready for action, and plenty of it. So bring it on, Mister Reporter.

"Sure," I answered casually, thinking, *He's way hot, I'm horny, and we're both available.*

Or are we?

I quickly checked his hand. No ring.

Okay then – as far as I'm concerned it's a done deal.

Chapter Seven

Carolyn

Carolyn Henderson drove to her apartment in a happy daze. She'd told him. She'd actually told him.

It was such a relief. And the greatest news of all was that Gregory had agreed with her that it was for the best and that he would finally inform his wife of their affair – an affair that would eventually culminate in marriage!

Well . . . he hadn't actually mentioned marriage, but she was sure that when his divorce came through, and he was a free man, and their baby was born . . . that yes, marriage was definitely in their future.

She smiled to herself, almost running a red light.

God! She was so excited. She'd been sleeping with this man for over a year, and during that time he'd made countless promises to leave his wife, never keeping one of them. Soon it was about to happen, and she was dizzy with anticipation.

Of course, she wasn't naïve, there was always the possibility that he could break his promise yet again.

But this time she was positive he wouldn't. This time there was a baby to consider, and the fact that she was carrying his child made all the difference.

This time she was home free.

* * *

"Fucking devious cunt!" Gregory Stoneman muttered under his breath as he got into his dark-blue Lexus and set off on his drive home. Did Carolyn honestly believe he would leave a woman like Evelyn for a snip of a girl like her? She might possess a great set of tits, but Carolyn Henderson was a nobody, a nothing – whereas Evelyn was cultured, a woman of great style, a well-established Washington hostess, and even more important, she hailed from a powerful and extremely affluent family, the Bamberrys.

Evelyn's father was a Judge, her mother the heiress to a textile fortune. The Bamberrys represented old money and excellent breeding.

Gregory would never give that up, especially as he came from more modest stock. His father was a car salesman, and his mother was a former nurse. Quite frankly he regarded his family as an embarrassment, and the less he saw of them the better.

Meeting and marrying Evelyn had boosted his political career no end, allowing him to move into social circles that before Evelyn had been beyond his reach.

Apart from that, he had his children to consider – eleven-year-old Clarence and seven-year-old Miranda. The two shining stars in his otherwise complicated life.

Well . . . only complicated because of his needy assistant pulling the oldest stunt in the business. "I'm pregnant," she'd said – the words no man wants to hear from a woman he's banging on the side.

What to do now?

Offer her money for an abortion?

No, he understood Carolyn well enough to know that she would never agree to an abortion.

Set her up in an apartment, wait until she gave birth, and have the baby adopted?

No way would she accept adoption.

What then?

Carolyn Henderson wanted him to leave Evelyn and marry *her*. He had no doubt that was exactly what she expected him to do.

She'd maneuvered him into a corner and now there was no escape.

Or was there . . .

* * *

"Hi," Kerri Tyson called out as Carolyn passed by on the way to her apartment.

Carolyn stopped short. She was so caught up in her thoughts that she hadn't noticed her neighbor emerging from the apartment opposite hers.

Kerri was half-African-American and half-Asian. Plump and pretty with short curly hair and an appealing personality, she was a legal secretary who went through boyfriends, most of whom she found on-line, at an alarming rate.

"You look as if you just won the lottery," Kerri remarked. "Either that or you're getting royally laid."

As Carolyn considered her answer, she wished she could tell Kerri everything. They were friends – not close – but they'd been out to dinner a few times, hit a couple of bars, exchanged ex-boyfriend horror stories.

"Wouldn't *that* be nice," Carolyn sighed. "But unfortunately, it's not true."

Kerri raised an eyebrow. "No new stud on the horizon?" she inquired. "'Cause you got the glow goin'."

"It must be my new make-up," Carolyn answered modestly. "NARS Blush. It's called Orgasm. It's obviously working."

"You bet your ass it is," Kerri giggled. "Got to grab me some of that. If you're free tomorrow, maybe we can hit the mall. Whaddya think?"

"I'll have to let you know," Carolyn replied, stalling. Now that she'd told Gregory she was carrying his baby, she expected things to change. Even if he didn't tell his wife immediately, he would probably want to spend more time with her.

"Call me," Kerri said, heading for the stairs to the street. "I'll be home later."

"I will," Carolyn said, unlocking the door to her apartment.

God! She was so excited, she had to tell *someone*. But whom could she trust? Not her mother, who wouldn't approve. Certainly not her father, who'd be shocked and disappointed in his little girl.

Then how about Denver, her best friend since school?

Unlike most people, Denver could keep a secret, and she'd be totally thrilled, although she'd also be major surprised since Carolyn had never mentioned that she was involved in a hot and heavy affair with the Senator.

Oh my God! Carolyn thought excitedly. *I cannot keep it to myself any longer! I'm going to tell Denver. I'll call her tonight.*

* * *

"Daddy! Daddy! Daddy!" Miranda squealed, hurling herself against her father's legs.

"How's my girl?" Gregory said, bending down to sweep his cute little daughter up into his arms.

"I had a fun day at school," Miranda announced, stroking his cheek with stubby, slightly sticky fingers. "Did *you* have a fun day, Daddy? *Didju? Didju? Didju?*"

No, I didn't! he wanted to scream. *I had an impossible day. The worst!* Although he couldn't discount the world-class blowjob Carolyn had managed to bestow on him. Satisfying at the time, but now he regretted allowing her to touch him, because as far as he was concerned it was over, even though she did not know it.

Just then, Evelyn floated out of the living room into the front hallway of their well-appointed house. His wife always appeared immaculate, not a white-blonde hair out of place, not a wrinkle in the chic Valentino black cocktail dress on her slim, toned body. At forty, Evelyn was a handsome woman. The problem was that she wasn't twenty-something, and that's what Gregory required for sex – a twenty-something girl who worshipped him. A girl who'd put his cock in her mouth and suck him dry. The same girl he'd married twenty years ago, a woman who wouldn't dream of indulging in oral sex now.

"How was your day?" Evelyn murmured, and without waiting for an answer she announced that they had a fundraiser to attend and he'd better shower and dress.

The interaction between him and Evelyn was never personal. They were hardly ever intimate, as he imagined most married couples might be. The sex when it happened was becoming less and less frequent, perhaps once every two months. And it was always the same. Evelyn flat on her back with a pained expression on her face, while he did all the work.

Evelyn never reached orgasm.

Evelyn thought oral sex was perverted.

Evelyn considered penises ugly and disgusting, and never cared to touch him down there.

The truth was that Evelyn hated sex, so who could blame him for getting his kicks elsewhere?

Nobody, that's who.

* * *

Carolyn practically danced around her apartment she was so elated. Fantasy names spun around her in head. *Senator Stoneman and his lovely wife, Carolyn. Mrs Gregory Stoneman. Carolyn Stoneman*. They all sounded so perfect. She was ecstatic.

Today is a magical day, she thought. *Today is the beginning of my new life. I love Gregory so much, and we will be so happy together.*

Picking up her cell phone, she called Denver in L.A.

No answer. Voicemail requested that she leave a message.

Hmm . . . this was not any kind of news to announce on voicemail.

"It's me, Carolyn," she said at last. "And I have something major to share with you. If you want to hear what it is, call me back. I can't wait to talk to you, so hurry!"

She clicked off the phone, a big smile on her face. Gregory couldn't get mad at her for telling one person.

Besides, he'd never find out.

Chapter Eight

Bobby

Frankie had an urge to visit a strip club. Bobby didn't. M.J. was prepared to go either way. He was a crowd pleaser.

"Why'd you want to go see a bunch of fours in Atlantic City when you've got a ten at home?" Bobby said, thinking of Annabelle and how much she was into Frankie.

Frankie was ***not*** thinking of Annabelle. He had banned all thoughts of Annabelle and her dead mother. Fuck it, he was out to have a blast.

"Jeez, Bobby, sometimes you sound like you're fifty years old!" he complained.

"Yeah," Bobby retaliated. "Maybe it's 'cause I'm smart."

"Says who?" Frankie said, pulling a face.

"Says me," Bobby replied, throwing a playful fake punch at Frankie's stomach.

"Can you two pull it together an' decide what's happenin'?" M.J. insisted. "I'm freakin' starvin' here. Let's go Asian."

"Good thinkin', 'cause I'm really into Asian pussy," Frankie leered. "Didja know that Asian girls are screamers. I likee!"

"You likee if it has a pulse," Bobby deadpanned.

"And you don't?" Frankie countered.

"Got a hunch I'm more discerning than you," Bobby said, grinning.

"Yeah, so discerning you only go for the ones you can't have. What's *that* about?"

Bobby decided to ignore Frankie's veiled comment.

"You're such a privileged prick," Frankie muttered, only half-joking.

"Go fuck yourself," Bobby responded good-naturedly.

"Yeah, yeah," Frankie sighed, taking no offence. "If only I could it'd make life so much easier."

"C'mon, guys, we're in a casino," M.J. said. "You got a choice – gambling or food, so somebody make up their freakin' mind."

"Steak," Bobby decided. "I need my strength if I'm spending the rest of the night with this asshole."

Frankie rolled his eyes. "It takes one to know one."

"You think?" Bobby said, checking out a sleek blonde walking past with a much older man.

"I *know*," Frankie responded, his eyes swiveling to take in the blonde's ass.

They finally ended up in Morton's Steak House where the waitress was no slouch when it came to spotting three sexy, obviously single young guys. She zeroed in on Frankie, who threw off that bad boy vibe she'd always found irresistible.

Frankie flirted back. Waitresses weren't his usual style, but this one had an amazing rack, and he wasn't about to waste a night away from Annabelle. Besides, Annabelle was enjoying a little something on the side, so why shouldn't he?

"What's your name, beautiful?" he asked, after ordering a steak, fries, and his favorite onion rings.

Running her tongue along her lower lip in a most provocative way, she leaned into the table. "Patricia," she said. "But my friends call me Tree."

"An unusual name for an unusual girl," Frankie said, turning on the bullshit charm that always worked so well for him. "You're too fine to be slaving away at a job like this. How come?"

"I'm actually an actress," she explained, her expression serious. "Doing this to make the rent until I can afford a move to New York."

Bobby and M.J. exchanged looks. They knew exactly what Frankie would say next.

He didn't disappoint. "Maybe I can help," he offered in his best sincere voice.

Bobby raised a cynical eyebrow. M.J. stifled a laugh.

"Really?" Tree said, wondering if this guy was as full of crap as most of them were.

"Yeah, really," Frankie continued. "I know people. I got connections."

M.J. rolled his eyes.

"What time you get off tonight?" Frankie persisted.

Tree paused for a moment. This guy *was* cute enough with his long hair and bedroom eyes, and maybe – just maybe – he could help her.

"Eleven," she said, licking her lips again.

"Then eleven it is."

"Y'know," Bobby said, after the waitress had moved onto another table, "you should get yourself some new lines."

"Yeah," M.J. snickered. "It's way beyond time, man. 'I got connections' simply don't cut it."

"It's not a line," Frankie protested, feeling boastful. "I can make that girl a lot of money."

"Doing what?" Bobby inquired.

"Something that comes naturally," Frankie replied. "I'll give her a test run an' let you know."

"Let us know *what*?" M.J. persisted, exchanging another knowing glance with Bobby.

Frankie paused for a moment. Should he tell them about his

and Annabelle's money-making venture or should he not? He'd been dying to show off about pulling in the big bucks, but he knew that somewhere within Bobby there lurked a strong moral streak, and he had a feeling that his friend might not approve of his new business.

On the other hand – fuck it. Bobby ran a club where booze, drugs and getting laid took center stage, so who was he to object?

Frankie decided to go for it and reveal the truth. "I've been meaning to tell you guys something," he began.

"If it's about the hookers, we know," Bobby said matter-of-factly.

Frankie was thrown; he wrinkled his forehead. "Huh?"

"What?" M.J. guffawed. "You thought it was a secret?"

"Are you shitting me?" Frankie said, left eye twitching, a sure sign he was disturbed.

"Now who would shit the king of the bullshitters?" Bobby said, laughing.

"You bet your ass we know," M.J. added.

"We were kind of waiting to see how long it took before you summoned up the balls to tell us," Bobby said, winking at M.J.

"Jeez!" Frankie grumbled. "I didn't expect it to be public knowledge."

"It's not," Bobby said. "But girls got big mouths, and now that word is around you'd better be way careful."

"Careful?" Frankie said, his left eye still twitching. "Like why?"

"Like you could get your ass arrested for pandering," M.J. offered.

"What the fuck is pandering?" Frankie snapped.

"Selling pussy," M.J. said.

"We're not selling anything," Frankie insisted. "We're arranging meetings between two consenting adults."

"And pocketing a commission, right?" Bobby said.

"That's pandering," M.J. pointed out.

"Well, shit, nobody can prove anything," Frankie said, getting defensive. "It's a cash-only business, no credit cards, no paper trails. We're not dumb."

"That sounds very organized, only don't ask *me* to come bail you out when you make it all the way to the front page of the *New York Post*," Bobby warned. "You've made enough bucks to buy yourself a Ferrari, so my advice would be to get out while you can."

"Are you fuckin' *crazy*?" Frankie said, eyebrows shooting up. "This is the sweetest deal ever. It's a no-hassle, no break-your-balls walk in the park."

"Yeah, an' you're gonna walk your way right into a jail cell," M.J. interjected. "C'mon, man, you're a freakin' pimp. That kinda shit's against the law."

"Since when did *you* turn into Mister D.A.?" Frankie snarled, not pleased with the way this was going. He'd expected compliments, not criticism.

"Hey," M.J. muttered. "It's your deal, it's sure as shit not mine."

"I'm taking a walk," Frankie said, abruptly rising from the table. "I'll catch up with you later."

"That went well," Bobby said dryly, as soon as Frankie was out of sight.

"Frankie's an asshole," M.J. remarked. "We both know it, so how come we hang with him?"

"'Cause he's *our* asshole," Bobby said, forever loyal. "And that means we gotta look out for him."

"Gettin' him off coke would be a start," M.J. said. "Then maybe *he'd* start takin' things more seriously. This sellin' pussy deal is a big mistake."

"You know Frankie – there's no way he'd listen," Bobby stated.

"Then how about Annabelle?" M.J. suggested. "Maybe we should talk to her."

"Oh, c'*mon*. Annabelle? Are you kidding me? She's worse than Frankie," Bobby said. "And when it comes to our boy, in her eyes he can do no wrong. You *know* that."

Tree headed back to their table, balancing various dishes. She glanced around for Frankie, and was disappointed to see he was gone.

"Where's your friend?" she asked boldly, placing the plates of food on the table.

"I wouldn't sweat it," M.J. said. "He'll be back."

Tree hesitated for a moment. "Can I ask you guys something?" she said, lowering her voice.

"Go ahead," Bobby said, digging into his steak.

"Well . . . it's just that working here I get a lot of horny guys coming on to me. Y'know how it is. They're in town without their wives or girlfriends, and it's like open season on waitresses."

"What do you wanna know?" M.J. asked, hungrily picking up French fries with his fingers.

"Well . . . uh . . . can your friend really help me, or is he handing me a line?"

"You're a smart girl," Bobby said. "Figure it out."

Tree managed a disappointed look. "So he's full of it?" she said.

"Depends on what you expect from him."

"Okay, thanks," Tree said hesitantly. "Then I guess I can trust him."

Trust him to do what? Bobby thought. *Get you in the sack and bang the crap outta you. Yeah, sure, you can certainly trust him to do that.*

Later, Tree returned with the check. Bobby threw down his credit card, and a few minutes later, Tree came back with the receipt for him to sign.

"Isn't it awful about Gemma Summer," she remarked, deciding they were now friends, and it was perfectly okay to make conversation with these guys. As a matter of fact she was beginning to think that she might have picked the wrong one to flirt with. The black dude with the big brown eyes and sexy shaved head was certainly cute. And the other one was a total babe.

"They're saying that Ralph Maestro might've done it," she continued. "What do *you* think?"

"Might've done what?" Bobby asked, just about to sign the check after adding a more than generous tip.

"Shot his wife in the face," Tree said, keeping an eye out for the manager, a man who didn't approve of his waitresses lingering at tables.

"*Whaat!*" M.J. exclaimed.

"Are you saying Gemma Summer got shot?" Bobby asked, shocked to hear the news. "How do you know this?"

"'Cause it's everywhere," Tree said, surprised that they hadn't heard about a newsworthy event like a famous movie star getting shot in her own bed. "It's on TV, the internet – it's every place."

"Holy shit!" Bobby said. "We'd better go find Frankie right now. He needs to get back to Annabelle pronto."

"Who's Annabelle?" Tree asked.

"It doesn't matter," Bobby said, hurriedly scribbling his signature on the bill and jumping to his feet. "We gotta go."

"So you think it's okay if I hook up with your friend?" Tree inquired hopefully.

"I wouldn't bet on it," M.J. said, sliding out of the booth. "Gotta strong hunch he's not gonna show."

And with that, the two of them took off, leaving a somewhat bemused waitress full of hopes and dreams that were certainly not reaching fruition any time soon.

Chapter Nine

Annabelle

Clutching her coat around her to conceal her ripped dress, Annabelle finally managed to leave the hotel suite where Omar Rani – if that was indeed his name – had kept her captive for the last two hours. What had happened to her was unthinkable. She'd been more or less raped and brutalized, treated like an object to be used for one man's pleasure. Omar had been more than rough with her, exhibiting no respect at all. As far as he was concerned, she was bought and paid for, which in his eyes allowed him to do anything he wanted. Her pleas of, *"Stop! No! This isn't going to happen!"* affected him not one bit. She'd struggled, but to no avail. He was relentless. The bastard had treated her like a cheap street whore.

With shaking hands she retrieved from her purse the cell phone she only used when going on an "appointment", and speed-dialed Chip.

"I'm coming out now," she said, stepping into the elevator. "Are you outside?"

"The friggin' doorman moved me on," Chip complained in his usual whiney voice. "I thought you said you wouldn't be more than half an hour."

"Never mind what I said," she hissed as the elevator made a fast descent. "Get here *now*!"

The elevator doors opened and she stepped out into the grand lobby, hoping and praying that she would not run into anyone she knew.

She stood still for a moment, shuddering at the memory of Omar's sweaty hands all over her body, invading her most private places, fondling and handling her as if she was a piece of meat.

Well, screw the fat bastard. There was no way she was allowing him to get away with it. Wait until Sharif Rani heard what had taken place, then the shit would really fly.

Outside the hotel there was no Chip to be seen. Swearing under her breath she had the doorman hail her a cab.

Chip pulled up in the Mercedes just as she was about to enter the cab. For a moment she hesitated, trying to decide whether to stick with the cab or go with Chip.

Chip honked the horn.

Moron. The last thing she needed was attention. Thrusting money at the cab driver, she turned around and headed for the Mercedes.

"Where exactly were you?" she demanded imperiously, sliding onto the back seat.

"Traffic," Chip whined. "It's a miracle I got here as fast as I did."

"You're fired," she snapped, taking out her frustration on her erstwhile driver.

"No way," Chip said, glancing at her in the rear-view mirror. "'S'not my fault this city has more traffic than a nest fulla ants."

She was silent.

"You don't look so good," Chip ventured, narrowly avoiding a meandering jaywalker. "You feelin' okay?"

"Just be quiet," she muttered, seething with anger. "I pay you to drive, not talk."

Chip swallowed a smart reply. She'd fired him once; if she

did it a second time, she might actually mean it. And he didn't want to lose his job. It was some cushy set-up.

* * *

Sharif Rani was in the middle of an important business meeting when one of his many cell phones began to vibrate in his jacket pocket. Excusing himself from the conference table, he took out the vibrating phone, and realized it was his sex phone – the one he used to arrange all his liaisons. Sharif Rani had a very jealous, very young, fourth wife, not to mention a slew of business acquaintances who would love to get something on him. Hence the sex phone, which was listed under one of his minions' names, and used only to set up his 'special' appointments. The caller ID identified Belle Svetlana.

Goddamn it, why was *she* calling him? Belle was only supposed to use this line to confirm his "appointments." And the rest of the week was all taken care of – a different woman every other day – women hand-picked for him by Belle. She knew what he liked.

He contemplated not answering the phone, then decided it was probably wiser to do so in case Belle had to change one of his appointments.

"Yes?" he said, lowering his voice as he moved toward the door of the conference room.

"Sharif?" Annabelle questioned, her voice quivering with the fury she would soon unleash on him.

"What do you want?" he said irritably.

Annabelle was in no mood for a sharp retort. Surely Sharif Rani knew exactly what she wanted? He'd set her up with a sex-mad teenage monster – certainly not a virgin. Now he had to suffer the consequences.

"I . . . can't believe what you did to me," she said, almost tripping over her words, she was so angry.

"What do you want?" he repeated, his tone getting icier by the second.

"I want . . . I want . . ." Trailing off, Annabelle realized that she didn't know *what* she wanted. An apology, yes, that was it – an apology for setting her up with such an uncouth piece of crap, Sharif's so-called son. And another thing – she wanted the boy to apologize too! Boy! Ha!

"Your son is a pig!" she blurted. "He treated me badly. He was rough and rude and disrespectful. You told me he was a fifteen-year-old virgin, and you know that's not true. I want—"

Annabelle was so busy complaining that she didn't hear the click on the other end of the line.

When she discovered he was no longer there, she was enraged. Rani Sharif had hung up on her! The man's manners were appalling. Just who exactly did he imagine he was dealing with?

A little voice in her head whispered, *"Hooker. Whore. Prostitute."*

These were words she did not wish to contemplate. She was none of those things. She was a stylish, rich New Yorker, who'd succeeded on her own without any help from her movie-star parents.

Tears of frustration filled her eyes. Where was Frankie when she needed him?

* * *

Frankie was in a strip club getting a lap dance from a sulky redhead with huge fake breasts and a very active tongue. The stripper was busy licking his neck when it suddenly occurred to him that getting pissed at Bobby and M.J. was a waste of time. They were merely jealous that he'd made a success of such a sweet business. And who could blame them? After all, he couldn't stay a deejay for ever, he had to move on. And if moving on meant raking in the big bucks, then more power to him. Bobby and M.J. came from wealthy families, what did they know about having to make it on your own with no help from anyone?

Frankie regarded himself as a true survivor. He'd come up the hard way and made it right up to the top.

There were a few things he regretted along the way. Some dark and ominous memories he did not care to re-visit. Some very dark memories he pushed to the back of his mind whenever they came up.

The coke helped him to forget the bad things. The coke always put him in a mellow mood, made it easy for him to achieve anything he set his mind to, made him feel like a winner.

Who would have thought that snorting a flurry of white powder could have such a life-affirming effect?

His habit was expensive, but he considered it worth every dime. It wasn't as if he was into crack or heroin or any of the hard stuff.

He liked cocaine.

Big fucking deal.

The stripper was becoming restless. She was executing her best moves and he wasn't responding. She was dangling her pastie-covered nipples dangerously close to his mouth, while thrusting her pelvis against his crotch. Her tongue was still working hard on his neck – heading toward his left ear – although actually touching the customer was strictly not allowed. She didn't care. This was one stripper who was working all the way toward a hefty tip.

Frankie suddenly got up, sending her flying.

Sprawled on the floor, she was about to spew a tirade of insults, when he groped in his pocket, took out several twenty-dollar bills and threw them at her.

"Another time," he muttered. "Not in the mood."

* * *

Since Frankie was not answering his cell, an upset Annabelle texted him and then called up Bethany – one of the girls who sometimes worked for her. "Can you come over?" she asked, feeling in need of company. "Frankie's in Atlantic City and I'm by myself."

Bethany, a lounge singer who'd been around a couple of years too long, was happy to oblige. She arrived half an hour later carrying a bottle of champagne – Cristal, of course – and a carton of orange juice.

"I thought I'd make us Mimosas," Bethany announced, heading for the kitchen.

"Fantastic idea," Annabelle said, putting on a brave face although she still felt used and abused and furious.

"Is everything all right, Belle?" Bethany asked curiously.

"No, it's not," Annabelle said, following Bethany into the pristine kitchen which never got used because Annabelle didn't cook. She'd been raised in a household where they had people to do the cooking – and anything else that needed doing.

"Is it Frankie?" Bethany asked, full of sympathy, but ready for some juicy gossip all the same. "Have you two had a fight? I mean he's a hot guy, but I'm sure he's not the easiest—"

"Why would it be Frankie?" Annabelle interrupted, immediately switching to defensive mode.

Bethany opened the fridge and scooped out some ice. "'Cause it's usually a man," she said, selecting two tall glasses from the kitchen cabinet and popping out a couple of ice cubes. "Men are all such bastards. I can never understand why we put up with their shit. They eat, fart, sleep and snore. And let me assure you, my vibrator gives me better sex."

Obviously she's never slept with Frankie, Annabelle thought.

"Actually, I've sworn off men," Bethany continued. "Unless they're paying. Now I'm all about my career – *that's* what's important to me."

"Well," Annabelle said, heading back to the living room,

"talking of paying, have you ever experienced . . . uh . . . a client who . . . uh . . . treated you badly?"

"Don't call them clients," Bethany said sharply, sitting down on the couch. "The word makes us sound like whores, and we're not. We're professional career women making a lot of money doing something other women do for free."

"That doesn't answer my question," Annabelle said, not interested in Bethany's analysis of the call-girl business.

"Your question, hmm . . ." Bethany said, giving her a piercing look. "I didn't think you went out on jobs, Belle."

"I don't," Annabelle answered quickly. "I'm asking for one of the other girls. She got . . . abused."

"Abused, how?" Bethany asked, raising a penciled eyebrow.

"The uh . . . guy was very rough with her. He practically raped her."

"Had he paid?" Bethany inquired, all business.

"Yes."

"Then it's not rape, is it?" Bethany said, sipping her Mimosa. "It's a done deal."

Annabelle was getting more aggravated by the minute. Why couldn't Bethany understand? "But let's say she didn't want it," she said, pressing on. "How about she changed her mind – wasn't happy with the look of him."

"The real question is," Bethany said wisely, "did she take the money?"

"I told you – yes."

"Then as I said, it's a done deal, no rape involved. Closed case. Now," Bethany continued brightly, "do you have any Peach Schnapps? If we add it to our Mimosas you'll be one very relaxed cookie. And then you can tell me all about who pissed you off."

An hour later, still upset and verging on slightly drunk, Annabelle managed to get rid of Bethany. It wasn't easy because Bethany was on her third Mimosa, and although Annabelle had thought she needed company, she'd realized she was better off alone.

Nursing a pounding headache, she made it into her bedroom and flopped down on the bed.

What if Sharif's no doubt illegitimate fat slob of a son had given her a disease? Or even worse, gotten her pregnant?

She'd carried condoms in her purse, but the horny little bastard had prevented her from reaching them.

She could sue. Yes, sue Sharif Rani and his whole fucking family. He probably had a whole slew of sons from different women. White, black, Arab, American, Asian.

Yes, but how could she sue without giving the game away? Her game . . .

She could just imagine Mommy and Daddy's movie-star faces if they ever found out what kind of a business their dear little daughter was running . . .

After a while she fell into a half-sleep.

Frankie would solve everything.

Frankie always did.

Chapter Ten

Denver

Mario is a total, all that I could ask for – and then some. He's way hot, from the tip of his beautifully shaped toes to his deep olive skin. And about his abs . . . well, all I can say is gimme more! They are world-class!

I have a thing about abs – I guess I feel about them the way most men feel about boobs. Kind of obsessed.

Maybe I shouldn't have jumped into bed with him the night of our first drink together – an occasion I can hardly classify as a date. But what the hey – two Cosmos and it's all bets are gone with the wind!

And yes, we were wild. We headed back to his place pronto. Leaped into bed with a feverish discarding of clothes. Thankfully he made a grab for a handy condom because I certainly wasn't thinking in a rational fashion. Then we were hitting it all the way and then some. It was *sooo* good.

Now he's asleep, and I'm checking out his body first, his house next.

You can find out a lot about a person from the way they live, and since Mario wasn't expecting me to come back to his small house on Fountain, I'm impressed that it's so clean and tidy. Not much mess at all, just a couple of dirty dishes in the sink, and a crumpled shirt scrunched up on the bathroom floor. Everything else is kind of neat.

Too neat?

I can only observe that he's a hell of a lot neater than Josh, who was a basic slob when it came to cleaning up after himself.

As for the bed activity . . . double, triple WOW!! Not to mention BINGO!!

Mario made me come on the first try, and that's not always a given. Sometimes it could take weeks before Josh got me to the point where I scored the big O.

Hmm . . . maybe that was one of the reasons why we both got in such a rut. Boredom ruled. And when boredom enters a relationship . . .

The absolute truth is that Josh might have ended it, but believe me, I was more than ready.

"Hey –" Mario called out from the bedroom. "Where are you?"

"Robbing your apartment," I called back. "Only I can't find anything worth taking other than two Santana CDs and a signed photo of Derek Jeter. What are you doing with *that*?"

"It's a long story," he chuckled, emerging from his bedroom unabashedly naked.

I was glad that I had prudently commandeered his terrycloth bathrobe – obviously stolen from a *Vanity Fair* event because it had *Vanity Fair The Hollywood Issue* emblazoned on the back. Yes, forcing him to walk around naked was an excellent move.

My eyes checked out his delightful buff bod – it was quite a sight.

"C'mere, you," he said, lazily reaching out. "Back to bed immediately."

I liked the way his mind worked. Back to bed and it was only one hour previously we were at it like a couple of randy high-schoolers on prom night. But who am I to argue? Mario Riviera was exactly the distraction I've been looking for.

Well, hardly looking – hoping might be a better description.

He's athletic.

I tried not to disappoint.

He's adventurous.

So am I.

He's insatiable.

Unfortunately I'm getting slightly exhausted. It's been an extremely long day and I'm not used to all this wild and wonderful sexual activity. My thighs ache, my nipples are becoming overly sensitive, and a night's sleep in my own bed is beginning to seem like an excellent idea.

But oh . . . my . . . God! Before I can even think about it we're back in bed and he's making me come again.

I tingle and vibrate all over, it is *that* satisfying.

"You're easy," he said, grinning down at me.

I noticed his teeth, perfect and exceptionally white. They reminded me of Mark Consuelo's teeth. In case you're wondering, Mark Consuelo is the extremely handsome husband of Kelly Ripa. And in case you're wondering, Kelly Ripa is the on-air partner of the ageless TV star Regis Philbin.

"Easy?" I replied, grinning back. "Is that an insult?"

"Nope," he said lightly. "You enjoy sex as much as I do. And here's what I like about you – you're not one of those girls who's into playing games."

Was this a positive or a negative?

I didn't bother asking because I was feeling quite comfortable with this man I hardly knew. And it's ridiculous, because he could be a rapist, a serial killer, a thief, or . . .

Stop that thought. I've always had a very active imagination, and sometimes it gets me into big trouble.

"I think I should be going," I ventured. "It's way past my bedtime."

"We've *had* bedtime," Mario pointed out with a lascivious grin. "Now I'm starving. How about we go grab a burger?"

Yummy! Food! I have to admit that I'm hungry too. Great sex always gives me an appetite.

Before I could say yes, my cell started playing Beyoncé's "If I Were A Boy" from the confines of my purse.

I reached for it and answered.

Mistake.

It was Ralph Maestro. And it's two a.m. Crap! Why did I pick up?

Because it's my job. And Mister Shark Teeth makes himself unavailable after ten p.m.

"Hi," I said, somewhat gingerly. "Is everything okay?"

"I have to speak with you," Ralph said, sounding brusque as usual.

"It's two in the morning," I pointed out, although surely he must know?

"I need you to come over right now," he said, before clicking off.

"Who was that?" Mario asked, slipping into nosy reporter mode.

"A jealous lover," I answered vaguely, grabbing my jeans while scanning the floor for my thong which was obviously nowhere to be found.

"I don't believe you."

"Of course you don't," I responded, deciding I had no choice but to go commando. "And nor should you."

Mario threw me a long, quizzical look. "You're different from most of the girls I come across," he said.

"We live in L.A. so thank God for that," I replied crisply.

"You're direct," he said. "An' I kinda think I like it."

"In that case," I answered succinctly, "thank you for the memorable sex, but I'm afraid I must be on my way."

He burst out laughing. I joined him.

Then he leaned forward and kissed me on the lips, a long juicy kiss – *sooo* nice.

"I'll call you," he promised.

"Sounds like a plan," I replied, slipping on my shoes. "Don't wait too long."

And then I was out of there, in my car, and on my way to the Maestro estate.

* * *

Ralph Maestro was smoking a very large cigar, puffing on it and blowing thick smoke throughout the living room.

He was wearing a heavy silk maroon bathrobe, trimmed with black piping. On his feet were matching slippers. Once again I did not think that he looked like a man in mourning.

This must be my night for men in bathrobes, only I prefer the simple white version on Mario. And I certainly prefer what's underneath.

"Hi," I said, holding back an I-hate-cigar-smoke cough.

"You look as if you just got fucked," Ralph remarked. Not a man who thinks before he speaks.

I decided to take the high road and ignore his sexist comment.

"What can I do for you, Mr Maestro?" I asked, attempting to maintain a professional client/lawyer relationship, while wondering if I looked as glowing as I felt. Apparently so.

"You can get on a plane and fly to New York," he answered matter-of-factly.

"And why would I be doing that?" I responded. I've learned never to be surprised by the things clients request, although flying to New York at two a.m. is a new one.

"Because," Ralph said, speaking slowly, "you know my daughter, and I can't reach her. So it's up to you to go get her and bring her back here."

"It's up to me to do *what*?" I asked, frowning, because it was a ridiculous request.

"You're not deaf, are you?"

"Excuse me?" I said, thinking he was a rude pig, and that maybe he *had* shot his beautiful wife.

"For crissakes, girl, I'm not asking you to fly to the moon," he said irritably. "Annabelle should be here with me, and you're the only person I can think of to bring her back."

"Mr Maestro – Ralph," I said hesitantly, "I haven't seen or spoken to Annabelle in years, so I hardly think she'll—"

"I've already discussed this with Felix," he said, interrupting me as if anything I had to say didn't matter. "And he agrees that Annabelle should be here. He also agrees that you're the one person who can persuade her to come."

"But—" I started to say.

Ralph was not in a listening mood. "There's an e-ticket on your laptop," he said, all business. "United. Seven a.m." He handed me a computer printout. "This is her address and phone number. I've left a message on her answering machine that you're on your way."

And with those words he blew a plume of vile cigar smoke in my face and waved a dismissive hand in my direction. "Goodnight," he said, putting an end to any further discussion.

Beyond furious, I left the Maestro estate. Who the hell does Ralph think I am – an errand girl?

This is total bullshit and I cannot believe that Felix agreed I should do this.

Screw Ralph Mister Movie Star Maestro. And screw Mister Shark Teeth. I'm a lawyer, not a freaking escort service.

Why should I fly to New York to bring Annabelle Maestro home for her mother's funeral?

Why does it have to be me?

Chapter Eleven

Carolyn

After calling Denver and connecting with her voicemail, Carolyn wished that she'd asked Kerri where she was going and maybe tagged along. Her adrenalin was surging, and she didn't feel like spending Saturday night alone in her small apartment.

What was Gregory doing? Was he thinking of her? Was he thinking about their baby and their future together? Was he as happy as she was?

She simply couldn't wait for them to be together out in the open for everyone to see. She imagined his wife's face when he told her. Evelyn was a cold fish and quite obviously didn't love him, so why would *she* care.

Gregory had told her many times that he and Evelyn never made love, that they had no shared interests, and that he would have divorced her long ago if it wasn't for the children.

Carolyn knew it was a clichéd situation – married man with a wife who didn't understand him – but she believed him all the same. Gregory was different, he had integrity, and she loved him with all her heart.

Thinking about it, she wished it hadn't been necessary for her to yell and threaten in the office earlier. But being pregnant was not something to be taken lightly, and she'd been forced to jolt him into understanding that now their situation had to dramatically change.

He got it. He finally got it.

Now all she had to do was wait a little bit longer.

* * *

"Jesus, Evelyn, who *are* these people?" Gregory hissed in his wife's ear.

Evelyn adjusted a ruby and diamond Cartier earring and responded *sotto voce*, "*These people* are reformed criminals who are making our city a much safer place."

"What the hell does *that* mean?" he growled, none too pleased that she'd dragged him to yet another of her boring do-good events.

"You see that man over there," she said, pointing out a bearded Latino man in an ill-fitting suit, with a fierce tattoo on his neck and a single gold stud earring.

"Yes, I see him. So what?"

"He's a former gang member who has come over to our side. He currently counsels young boys about how *not* to get trapped into gang-life."

Listening to Evelyn speak, Gregory was struck by how incongruous she sounded. What the hell did she know about gang-life? His wife, the do-gooder. She always had a cause. She always regarded herself as holier-than-thou.

"Come," Evelyn said, gripping his arm. "I'll introduce you to him."

Gregory had no desire to be introduced to a former gang member. He had other things on his mind – like what was he supposed to do about Carolyn? Whiney, pregnant, cock-sucking Carolyn.

Evelyn steered him across the room, and in her best Lady of

the Manor voice said, "Ramirez, I'd like you to meet my husband, Senator Gregory Stoneman."

Ramirez threw him a hardfaced look.

Gregory recognized the look. It was a *fuck you, white asshole* look. This guy was no reformed gang-banger. He was a smart criminal forging connections.

"It's a pleasure to meet you," Gregory said, placing a politician's fake smile on his face. "My wife tells me you're doing very worthwhile work for our city."

"I'm tryin'," Ramirez responded, his eyes darting around the room. "It ain't easy, but I'm tryin'."

"Excellent," Gregory said, waving over a waiter. He needed another drink.

"Yes," Evelyn said, twisting a thin diamond bracelet on her delicate wrist. "We need more funding for the centers Ramirez plans to open across the city. Right now we only have one, and it's such important work, keeping young boys off the street. I'm hoping to put together a special concert to raise money. Ramirez seems to think we can get some of those rapper people involved."

Rapper people! Evelyn existed in another world. Even *he* knew the correct term was rap artists.

"Anythin' you can do to help," Ramirez said. "Maybe you can drop by tomorrow, see for yourself the work we're doin'."

Yes, Gregory thought, *that's exactly how I plan on spending my Sunday.*

"I might do that," he said. *And then again I might not.*

Ramirez had his eye on Evelyn's bracelet.

Damn! Gregory thought. *I hope he doesn't know where we live.*

* * *

Nellie Fortuna resided in the apartment next to Carolyn's. Nellie was old – in her late eighties – and apparently she had no one left; they'd all died on her. No relatives. No friends. No one.

Long ago and far away, Nellie Fortuna had been a beautiful eighteen-year-old movie starlet living in a Hollywood mansion with a withered old producer – who happened to be a millionaire. Way back in the 1930s, millionaires meant something, whereas today you had to be a billionaire to be relevant. Anyway, that's what Nellie said – she was very talkative and quite a character.

Carolyn tried to stop by at least once every couple of days to make sure the old dear was still alive, and to feed her rather mangy cat, Gable. Apparently, back when Nellie was at the peak of her career, she'd been the lover of many silver-screen icons, including Clark Gable – whose faded picture sat proudly in a silver Art Deco photo-frame on her mantelpiece. The photo was inscribed *To Dear Nellie, Love from Clark.*

It could have been a fan photo, or it could have been the real thing.

Nellie assured Carolyn it was the real thing.

"Every tom-cat I ever owned I named Gable," Nellie would often say. And then she'd smile and become all dreamy-eyed. "He was quite the man . . . I'll never forget *that* one."

When she had the time Carolyn enjoyed listening to Nellie's stories of old Hollywood. They were filled with all the sparkle and glamour of yesteryear, and Nellie spun her tales with such relish.

"These gals today, they all look the same," Nellie would grumble. "And their outfits! Downright disgusting! Now in *my* day . . ."

With Gregory on her mind, Carolyn knocked on Nellie's door and was relieved – as she always was – to find the old lady alive and well, sitting in front of her TV watching the E! Channel, her favorite.

"Just checking on you," Carolyn called out. "Can't stay."

"Hello, dear, you look so pretty today," Nellie said, as always alert and astute. "You've got quite a gleam in your eye. Could we have a new boyfriend?"

Carolyn couldn't stop smiling. "Well, not exactly new," she said softly. "More like, I don't know . . . committed."

Gable the cat padded over and began languorously rubbing himself against her leg. She bent down to stroke him and he purred loudly.

"I think I know," Nellie said, nodding wisely. "It's that nice young man, your boyfriend – what's his name? Ah yes, Matt. He's asked you to marry him, hasn't he?"

"No," Carolyn said, shaking her head. "Matt's history."

"There *is* someone though, isn't there?" Nellie persisted, continuing to probe. "Who is he?"

Carolyn wished she could tell her. Wished that she could sing it from the rooftops. *"I'm pregnant with Gregory Stoneman's baby! I'm pregnant pregnant pregnant!"*

"Just an old friend," she said, keeping it vague.

"Ah, old friends," Nellie mused. "I had plenty of those. Old co-stars. Old lovers. Old married men who couldn't keep it in their trousers. Ah yes, old friends . . ."

"Have you fed Gable?" Carolyn asked, quickly changing the subject. Nellie loved to ramble on about her many affairs, and today Carolyn wasn't in the mood to listen.

"Yes, dear, all done," Nellie said. "But thanks for dropping by anyway – you know how much I appreciate it."

"My pleasure," Carolyn said, making a quick exit. On her way out she decided it would be a nice gesture to invite Nellie Fortuna to their wedding.

Senator Gregory Stoneman

&

Ms. Carolyn Henderson

Invite you to witness their joining in matrimony . . .

Yes! Yes! Yes!

* * *

"No!" Gregory said sharply as he and Evelyn were in the car on their way home. "I will not visit some rat-infested center filled with gang-bangers because *you* think it's a good idea."

Evelyn remained calm as she always did. "Gregory, dear," she said, her voice smooth as silk, "visiting Ramirez at his center will enhance your reputation. The voters will appreciate such a goodwill gesture, they always do. Have your little assistant alert the press. It's an excellent photo opportunity."

Why did she always refer to Carolyn as his "little" assistant? Carolyn was at least five foot eight, hardly little. It was Evelyn's way of putting her down. Not that she suspected anything, but Evelyn was less than flattering about any other female. At a White House dinner party he'd been seated next to Gwyneth Paltrow, and later Evelyn had called her a skinny little nothing. Note the use of the word "little." It was Evelyn's ultimate put-down. What she really meant was that these people were less than her – small and unimportant.

Evelyn was a snob. She'd only married him because politically he was destined to go places, especially with Evelyn and her powerful family behind him.

Had she ever loved him?

Probably not.

But they had two fine, healthy children, and his career was progressing in the right direction and generally life was on track.

But now "little" Carolyn Henderson was determined to screw everything up. And what was he supposed to do about *that*?

One thing was patently clear – he had to do something – and fast.

Chapter Twelve

Bobby

Back in their hotel suite, M.J. ran around packing up their overnight bags while Bobby had Frankie paged. He'd tried reaching him on his cell phone, but to no avail; he'd also attempted to contact Annabelle so that he could alert her that they were on their way back to the city. She didn't answer her phone either.

By this time M.J. had switched on the TV and they'd gotten the full gruesome story of Gemma Summer's murder.

"I can't believe we didn't hear about it earlier," Bobby said, perplexed. "I feel so bad for Annabelle – she must be frantic."

"You think it's possible her old man did it?" M.J. asked. "He always scared the crap outta me."

"He might be movie-star dumb – but not dumb enough to shoot her in their own house," Bobby mused. "Like who would do that?"

"Yeah," M.J. ruminated. "Dumb, or maybe he's so arrogant he thinks he can get away with it."

"The media's gonna get off on this one," Bobby said. "It's their dream scenario. Two movie stars and a murder."

Should he call Lucky? He seemed to remember that when she'd owned Panther Studios, Ralph Maestro and Gemma

Summer had both appeared in movies her studio had produced. She must've known Gemma, maybe even been friends with her.

At that moment, Frankie burst into the suite looking disheveled. "You had me paged?" he questioned, long hair flopping in his eyes. "What the fuck is *that* about? I was all set to make a killing at the crap table."

"I guess you haven't heard the news," Bobby said, his tone somber.

"What news?" Frankie questioned, thinking, *Oh, shit. They've found out. Goodbye, weekend of freedom with the guys. Too fuckin' bad.*

"Annabelle's mother's been shot," Bobby said flatly. "We just heard about it."

"Jeez!" Frankie said, striving to put a shocked and surprised expression on his face. "What the fuck happened? When? How? Is she dead?"

"Yes, she's dead all right," Bobby said. "Take a look at the TV. You should call Annabelle right away."

"Yeah, man," M.J. said, joining in. "We gotta get your ass back to New York."

"You know Annabelle hardly ever carries a phone," Frankie said, pissed that this definitely meant a fast exit.

"Then try your apartment," Bobby said. "I bet she's there."

"Yeah, yeah," Frankie said, making a show of moving toward the TV and pretending to catch the news for the first time.

"There's a buzz goin' around that her old man could've done it," M.J. interjected. "The whole scene is way brutal. Whaddya think?"

"Never met her parents," Frankie said. "An' believe me – Annabelle wasn't close to them. They hardly ever spoke."

"You need to be with her," Bobby said. "We're packed up and ready to go, so I suggest we hit the road."

"Sure," Frankie said, albeit reluctantly.

Bye bye, rendezvous with the sexy waitress from Morton's. Too bad. He could have fucked her, then recruited her.

* * *

A few hours later, Bobby pulled his BMW up outside the building where Frankie and Annabelle resided.

Frankie took his time getting out of the car. It was late, past midnight, and the last thing he felt like doing was listening to Annabelle bitch about her parents. He knew that's exactly what she'd do. Bitching about Mommy and Daddy was one of her favorite rants. It was always about how self-absorbed they were, and how they'd never taken any notice of her when she was growing up. Usually he told her to quit complaining – but tonight the circumstances were different, and with the tragedy and all, he would be forced to sit and listen for hours. It was sympathetic boyfriend time, of that he was sure.

"You want us to come up with you?" Bobby asked, not really meaning it, but making the effort all the same.

"Yeah, man, maybe we should," M.J. said, equally half-hearted. They both knew what a drama queen Annabelle could be, and tonight she'd be out-of-control, probably hysterical.

Frankie decided it wasn't necessary. "I can take care of her."

"Well . . ." Bobby said. "Be sure to give her our love, and tell her how sorry we are. We'll check in with you first thing."

"Got it," Frankie said, finally moving away from the car.

Once Frankie had vanished into the building, Bobby said, "Maybe we should stop by the club, surprise everyone."

"Right," M.J. agreed. "I wouldn't mind checkin' on how many waiters we got runnin' out the back with a shitload of steaks stuffed down their pants."

M.J. had a thing about the staff stealing. If he had his way he'd install hidden cameras everywhere, from the kitchen to the workers' restroom.

Bobby's attitude was more laid back; he'd learned from Lucky that in the hotel and club business you had to make allowances. It was a fact of life that the barmen would replace Grey Goose Vodka for a cheaper brand, the waiters would steal, and the kitchen workers would take home whatever they could. As long as the stealing was not excessive, it was better to live with it and not stress out.

Bobby wondered if Zeena would be in the club, surrounded by her usual group of sycophants.

He hoped she was, then he immediately hoped she wasn't.

Dammit, the crush he had on her was ridiculous. She might be a famous, talented superstar – but she treated him as if he didn't exist, and he wasn't used to being ignored.

He was, after all, a Stanislopoulos, and his mother was Lucky Santangelo. He deserved respect. And he planned on getting it.

* * *

"Another Bellini," Zeena ordered in her slightly accented, deep-down husky voice.

The toy boy on her left jumped to attention. He was a Peruvian model, all of nineteen, and he was Zeena's latest plaything. She paraded him around like a trophy, and the boy was quite beautiful with his sleepy bedroom eyes, pouty lips and flushed cheeks.

Zeena called him Puppy. She called all of them Puppy; she came up with a new one every month.

Out of the corner of her exotically made-up eyes she noticed Bobby Stanislopoulos Santangelo enter the club.

So good-looking. So trying hard to play it cool. So longing to get into her pants.

She wondered how surprised he'd be to discover that twenty-five years ago when she was a mere fifteen, his father, the great Dimitri, had deflowered her on his magnificent yacht in the South of France.

A smile played around her scarlet lips. Ah . . . Dimitri . . . What a man, what a lover . . .

Like father, like son?

Should she take the time to find out?

Perhaps. It might amuse her. Then again it might not.

Bobby was gradually approaching her table. He was late tonight – usually he was around much earlier. Watching him, she had to admit that he had a certain style, although style wasn't everything. Seasoning was preferable. If they weren't nineteen, then Zeena liked them to be older and extraordinarily powerful. Extreme youth and excessive power – in Zeena's world those were her two most potent aphrodisiacs.

She continued to observe as Bobby slowly made his way over, stopping at each table. She watched as every female in the club clung onto his arm, trying to persuade him to sit down at their table, saw how he extracted himself with a polite shake of his head and a few kind words.

Finally he presented himself at her table.

"Zeena," he said, playing the perfect host. "Nice to see you. Anything you need? Anything I can get you?"

"If Zeena needs anything, Bobby," she drawled, toying with the back of Puppy's long hair, "Zeena will ask a waiter."

Bobby nodded. At least she remembered his name tonight, which wasn't always the case.

"Yeah. Sure," he said. "But I'd like to send over a bottle of Cristal for you and your party."

"Only *one* bottle, Bobby?" she said, with a sly tilt of her head.

Christ! She reminded him so much of Serenity, even though she was at least twenty years older. She had the same pissy attitude.

"Or two," he said, determined to stand up to her.

Puppy smirked.

Yeah, Bobby thought, ***keep on smirking, dude, you'll soon be last month's model.***

Zeena gave him a very direct challenging stare before flipping back her sheet of glossy black hair which fell below her waist. "Five bottles, Bobby," she said, indicating the group of hangers-on who surrounded her. "Zeena's friends are thirsty."

Bobby kept his cool, trying not to think about how spectacular she looked tonight in some kind of chocolate-brown spidery dress that barely covered her breasts. He could see her nipples. Yes, he could definitely see her nipples. "Two bottles on the house," he said evenly. "The rest I'm afraid we'll have to charge you for."

She arched a painted eyebrow. "You can't possibly be serious?"

He stood his ground. He might be suffering from some kind of insane crush, but business was business. "House rules," he said pleasantly.

"Ah, Bobby," she sighed. "Are you aware that Zeena can go anywhere in the world and get everything for free?"

"Lucky you," he said, testing her.

Would she get up and leave? Or would she stay? What did he want her to do?

He honestly didn't know.

"Yes," she murmured with a sarcastic twist. "Zeena is extraordinarily lucky." A long beat. "How about you, Bobby? Are *you* lucky?"

This was the longest exchange of words they'd ever had, and since it was obvious she was staying, he thought about making his move, even though she still had one hand caressing the back of Puppy's neck.

Puppy was glaring at him – in spite of the glare, he was giving off quite a gay vibe. What was *that* about?

"I . . . uh . . . like to think a person makes their own luck," Bobby said, clearing his throat.

"Keep on thinking that way," Zeena replied. "Naïveté is *such* a special quality."

And without further ado, she pulled Puppy's face toward hers and indulged in a long tongues-down-each-other's-throat intimate kiss.

Bobby backed away from the table. Screw Zeena and her full entourage of hangers-on. She was playing with him, and he didn't like it.

Or was that exactly what he *did* like?

Chapter Thirteen

Annabelle

"Wake up, babe," Frankie crooned. "C'mon, sweetie, open up those sexy eyes."

Annabelle rolled over in bed. Someone was shaking her shoulder, someone was pulling her away from *the* most delightful dream she'd ever experienced. In her dream she was lying on a bed in a luxurious hotel room overlooking the ocean. With her were Chace Crawford and Brad Pitt. Chace was busily kissing her neck, while Brad was patiently awaiting his turn – but Brad was beginning to get antsy . . . he started roughly shaking her shoulder, and . . .

"Oh my God!" Annabelle exclaimed, awaking with a start and seeing Frankie standing over her. "What are *you* doing here? You're supposed to be in Atlantic City."

"I came back as soon as I heard," he lied, sitting down on the side of the bed. "You didn't think I was gonna let you go through this alone, did you?"

Annabelle rubbed her eyes, reluctant to leave her dream, but happy that Frankie was concerned enough about her degrading experience with Sharif Rani's son to forgo his weekend with the boys and race to her side. "Frankie," she murmured, reaching up to touch his cheek with her fingers. "It was so awful . . ."

"I know, baby," he said soothingly. "It's a terrible thing, but let's be honest about this – it wasn't as if you were close."

"Close!" she exclaimed, struggling to sit up. "Close! I was in the same room, goddamn it. How much closer could I get?"

"Calm down," Frankie said, realizing that she was in shock and had no idea what she was saying.

"What time is it?" Annabelle demanded, glaring at him. "'Cause whatever time it is, I want you to get on the phone to that sonofabitch and ream him a new asshole. Did I tell you he hung up on me? He actually clicked off his phone. Can you believe it?"

So . . . Ralph Maestro had hung up on his own daughter. Maybe Ralph *had* shot his wife, and was now filled with guilt. After all, they were Hollywood people – who knew what kind of brutal acts they were capable of.

Frankie's mind went into overdrive. If Ralph Maestro *had* murdered his wife, was convicted and eventually sent to jail – who would inherit everything?

As their only child, Annabelle – of course. This whole murder thing could end up having a silver lining.

Frankie immediately imagined himself living in L.A., residing in a mansion, throwing wild parties by the pool and mixing with big-time superstars. Movies, sports, the music biz – he'd get to know them all.

It bugged him that whenever he'd suggested taking a trip to L.A., Annabelle had always shut him down. "I don't ever want to go there again," she'd informed him many times. "Living in L.A. were the unhappiest days of my life."

Now everything had changed.

"Well?" Annabelle asked, a determined look in her eyes. "Are you going to phone him or not?"

"Hey," Frankie said, shrugging. "The thing is – I don't even *know* the dude, so what would I say?"

"For God's sake!" Annabelle snapped, green eyes blazing.

"Of course you know him. Just tell him that we're *never* doing business with him again."

"Huh?" Frankie said, quite confused. Annabelle was taking this harder than he'd expected.

"I . . . hate . . . him," Annabelle said through clenched teeth. "And for your information, I don't care how much money we'll lose. It's no big deal, we'll make it up elsewhere. There are plenty of other billionaires in the sea – we'll put out a fishing net and haul in a few."

She was delirious, that much was obvious.

"Listen, babe," he began. "I know this is hard—"

"Hard!" she exploded. "How about taking a look at my bruises? I'm covered in them."

"Huh?" he mumbled, getting more confused by the minute. Annabelle had totally lost it.

"Bruises, Frankie," she said, narrowing her eyes. "Bruises from a big fat moron who was *no way* fifteen. And bites – he bit me on my thigh! Sharif Rani should be ashamed of himself, setting me up with his so-called son. Illegitimate, I'm sure, 'cause he sure as hell wasn't the innocent young Arab boy Sharif led us to believe. He was a big fat hairy American rapist!"

Oh shit! Annabelle wasn't even talking about her mother's murder. She was carrying on about her afternoon meeting with Sharif Rani's son. Jesus Christ! Did she even *know* her mother was dead? Hadn't anyone told her?

"Have you heard the news?" he ventured.

"Didn't you read the text message I left on your phone?" she said shortly. "'Cause you don't seem to care that I got beat up and *raped*! What's the matter with you?"

"I'm here, aren't I?" he said, regretting that he hadn't checked his messages. He'd been too busy losing at blackjack, picking up a pretty waitress, and almost enjoying a lap dance.

"Babe," he said, finally realizing that *he* was the one who had to tell her. "There's something you should know."

"What?" she said, furious that he wasn't reacting in a stronger fashion.

"It's your . . . uh . . . mother."

"What about her?"

"Jesus, I don't know how I'm supposed to tell you this," he muttered. "So I guess there's no other way but to give it to you straight." He stopped and took a deep breath. "Your mother was murdered earlier today. Shot in the face."

There was an eerie silence.

"I . . . uh . . . thought you knew," he added lamely, watching her closely to see how she reacted.

Annabelle stared at him in disbelief. What was he saying? What was he talking about? Was she still dreaming? Had her dream turned into some ridiculous nightmare?

"I'm so sorry, babe," he said. "It's a total bummer, I know."

"When?" she said at last, catching her breath. "When did this happen?"

"Sometime this morning in L.A. I dunno much, only what I saw on TV. Soon as I heard the news I got in the car an' came racing home."

"This morning," she repeated dully, her expression blank. "How come nobody contacted me?"

"I'm sure somebody must've. You checked your messages?"

She shook her head. Suddenly everything seemed surreal. Her mother had been murdered. Her mother, the world-class beauty. The woman everyone loved. The heroine of countless movies. The Oscar-winning actress with the undeniable talent.

Her mother. The untouchable Gemma Summer. A woman she'd never been close to. A woman who'd allowed her only child to be raised by a series of disinterested nannies. A woman who'd spent most of her daughter's childhood away on location shoots – unless there was the need for a *People* or *Vanity Fair* cover story – in which case a cute little five year old added to the appeal of the picture. Then, after the age of eight, there were no more photo sessions. Eight was too old to be considered cute any more, although sometimes her father took her to the Lakers games and they were photographed sitting courtside. But even he stopped doing that when she hit puberty.

Ah yes, puberty. Her South African nanny had taught her the facts of life. Her mother had decided she needed a nose job at fourteen. And a young Mexican gardener who worked on their estate had taught her how to give head.

At school she'd perfected the art of the blow-job, becoming the most popular girl in her class. Sex was her way of getting plenty of attention. She excelled at it.

There was also shopping, for her parents didn't stint when it came to giving her money. They handed her a bunch of credit cards and gifted her with a Porsche on her sixteenth birthday. Anything to keep her out of their way.

So there she was, a popular girl, a rich girl, a spoiled girl, with nobody around to stop her from doing anything she wanted.

And what she wanted was to get away from her self-absorbed movie-star parents. Fly the coop, and lose the tag – *"This is Annabelle. Her mother is Gemma Summer and her father's Ralph Maestro."*

Moving to New York was the best thing she'd ever done. Very few people knew who her parents were, and who she really was. That's the way she liked it.

Gemma Summer. Mother. Dead. And she'd never even got to know her.

"Check the messages on the phone at the SoHo apartment," she said, her throat constricted. "That's the only number Ralph's got."

Frankie did so, and sure enough there were a slew of messages, including a terse one from Ralph himself, saying that he was sending one of his lawyers to New York to bring her home.

Frankie informed Annabelle, who stubbornly shook her

head. "I refuse to go back to L.A.," she said flatly. "Why should I?"

"'Cause it's about your mom," Frankie said, reasoning with her. "You gotta do it, babe. There'll be a funeral, an' you have to be there. I'll come with you. Don't you worry about it, I'll be beside you all the way."

Chapter Fourteen

Denver

My flight to New York was uneventful, apart from the fact that I spotted Denis Leary pacing up and down, waiting to board the plane. Since I'm such a huge *Rescue Me* fan, I contemplated going up to him and telling him what a clever and entertaining show it was – but then I realized he already knew that, and I would probably come across like some half-baked starry-eyed fan – or even worse – a stalker. So I controlled myself, and instead studied the L.A. edition of the *New York Post* and *USA Today*, both of which featured screaming headlines about Gemma Summer Maestro's brutal demise.

It made me realize that by the time I reached Annabelle, she would already know the shocking news – in fact, she might even be on a plane heading for L.A. We could be crossing in the air, which meant that my trip to New York was pointless.

I wondered how Annabelle would take the news of her mother's murder. It was such a shattering and terrible event. To be shot in the face in your own bed . . .

For a second I tried to put myself in Annabelle's place. What if it was my mom? Thank God that was impossible. Or was it? Who knew what lurked just around the corner. We all understand that fate has a way of playing unexpected tricks.

My thoughts moved on to Mario. Should I have called or texted to tell him I was heading out of town? Or would he perceive that as coming on too strong too soon?

Crap. I shouldn't be thinking such thoughts. It's not as if it's a relationship. Mario is not my boyfriend, nor do I want him to be. I am happy on my own. Quite content, thankyouverymuch.

Although . . . sometimes I do miss that spooning thing in bed, the kind of deal you only get when you're with a proper boyfriend.

Once off the plane I checked my BlackBerry. There were several messages and texts. My dad, saying he'd read my name in the papers and what was happening with the case? I'd not had a moment to call him. Felix, reiterating that I should bring Annabelle back A.S.A.P. per Ralph's instructions. And yippee – a call from Carolyn informing me that she had something major to tell me.

Carolyn has been my best friend for ever. I hope that her news is good – like she's gotten back together with Matt and they're planning on getting married. Carolyn should be married, she's that kind of girl. Smart and sensible and nurturing, any man would be lucky to have her.

I myself am not the marrying kind. I have no desire to be tied down to one man for ever. I possess no maternal instinct, although I do love kids – other people's that is. And the last thing I am is nurturing. No, I have to admit that my career is all-important to me, and right now it definitely comes first. Which is why I'm in New York and not languishing in bed with Mario, experiencing even more exceptional sex.

Carolyn and I haven't seen each other in ages, and I miss her. I am so looking forward to her upcoming trip to L.A. She's promised to stay for ten days, and I have all kinds of plans. I'm thinking we could sneak in Vegas for a couple of days, and maybe visit a spa retreat. We both work so hard that her visit will be a great excuse to do nothing else except chill out. I've already warned Felix I will be adding to the Christmas vacation time with a few leftover days I've been saving up. He didn't take it well.

As I stood outside the airport shivering while I searched for a cab, I wondered if sex with Mario was as exceptional as I'd thought. Maybe it just *seemed* great because I hadn't had it in a while. Or maybe Josh was *really* bad in bed.

Poor Josh . . . not my problem any more.

I finally spotted a cab and grabbed it before someone else did.

"Where to?" asked the driver, a surly white man with incongruous dreadlocks and a missing front tooth.

Good question. I hadn't booked a hotel because all I planned on doing was meeting Annabelle, persuading her to fly to L.A. with me, and catching the next flight back.

I checked my BlackBerry for the address in SoHo Ralph had given me, and instructed the driver to take me there. Then I tried the phone number Ralph had also given me, and connected with voicemail, which seemed reasonable as I'm sure Annabelle wouldn't be answering her phone at a time like this.

I left a message: "Hi, this is Denver Jones. I don't know if you remember me, but I'm now an associate at the law firm employed by your father, and I'm here to assist you back to L.A. for the funeral." Lamely I added, "I'm very sorry for your loss."

I wondered if she *would* remember me. After all, Denver Jones is not exactly an everyday name. We'd shared some fun times until she'd dropped me. But that was a long time ago, we were kids then, and I'm sure she's nicer now.

On impulse I called Mario. Didn't mean to, but somehow my phone decided to go there.

"Hey –" he said.

"Hey –" I responded. "Guess where I am?"

"I know where you *should* be," he said, sounding quite pleased to hear from me.

"And where would that be?" I answered coyly, horrified at myself, for I am not a coy girl. There's just something about Mario that brings out the girl in me. Maybe it's those world-class abs. More likely his world-class cock.

"In my bed, next to me," he said.

Giggle. Giggle. *Oh crap,* I'm falling to pieces before my very eyes!

"I'm in New York," I managed, slightly breathless.

That piece of news aroused his interest. "You are? What you doing there?"

Should I tell him?

No. He's a TV reporter, can't let him know too much.

"A couple of personal things I have to take care of," I answered, making it sound as vague as possible.

"I thought you were on the Ralph Maestro case," he said suspiciously.

Was he fishing?

Probably. He's a journalist, after all. He has to be curious.

"I am," I answered carefully. "I mean, my firm is. But right now there's nothing to do."

"Unless Ralph Maestro is arrested," he stated.

"And why would they arrest Ralph Maestro?" I asked, my tone becoming a tad frosty since I had planned on having an intimate conversation about our amazing night of sex, not a discussion about the Maestro case.

"Word is they got nobody else in mind," Mario said. "You should take a look at the blogs, they're all over it."

"That's ridiculous!" I exclaimed, jumping to my client's defense.

"Yeah?" Mario said, taking a long steady beat. "You sure?"

"I have to go," I said, suddenly anxious to get off the phone.

"When you coming back?"

"Maybe later. Maybe tomorrow."

"Quick trip."

"It is."

"So . . . Denver," he said, his voice turning sexy and seductive. "Dinner the instant you return? Yes?"

I loved the way he said my name. I managed a casual, "Sure," and quickly clicked off.

Mario Riviera could be trouble. I'd only spent one night with him, and already I was thinking about him far too much.

* * *

An hour of horrendous traffic jams and death-defying driving later, my cab driver deposited me outside a building in SoHo.

I checked my watch. It was almost four-thirty New York time, and bitterly cold. Pulling my not-nearly-warm-enough jacket around me, I studied the row of push buttons by the door, and spotted *A. Maestro.* After pressing the buzzer I waited . . . and waited . . . and waited . . .

No answer.

I'm sure my instincts are right and Annabelle is already on a flight to L.A.

Damn Ralph Maestro and his stupid instructions. I could be in my sunny office in Century City right now instead of freezing my ass off in front of a locked building in SoHo.

As I was contemplating my next move, a tall youngish man emerged from the building all bundled up in a long khaki army coat, striped scarf, and one of those knit caps that Jake Gyllenhaal's always photographed in.

I felt like ripping the cap off his head, I was that cold. Nobody had prepared me for a New York winter, and I was not dressed for the part.

"Excuse me," I said, jumping right in. "Do you happen to know an Annabelle Maestro?"

"Who?" he said, stopping for a moment.

"A. Maestro," I said, indicating the row of bell-pushes. "She lives here."

"Oh," he said, wrinkling his forehead. "You must mean the redhead on the top floor. Seen her a couple of times in the last year. She doesn't come here much."

"I thought she lived here."

"Nah. From what I hear she has a boyfriend uptown. I guess she bunks with him."

"Would you happen to know where?" I asked, rubbing my hands together with the hope of generating some well-needed heat.

"Sorry, can't help you," he said, smiling at me, and began striding briskly off down the street.

Before the main door closed, I slipped inside. At least it was warmer in the vestibule, and I could figure out what my next move should be.

I was standing by a row of mailboxes, and I did a quick check to see what *A. Maestro* held. The guy in the army coat was right, Annabelle obviously didn't spend much time here. Her mailbox was overflowing, and since it wasn't locked I shuffled through her mail to see if I could spot anything with the boyfriend's name on it.

Nothing except junk-mail, bills and several magazine subscriptions – *Vogue*, *InStyle*, *Harpers*. Yes, this was definitely Annabelle's mailbox. And then, right at the bottom of the pile I discovered a copy of *Rolling Stone*. It was addressed to Frankie Romano at Annabelle's address. Bingo! Must be the boyfriend.

What to do next?

I decided to call Ralph Maestro. Mr Friendly.

Naturally I was informed by a snippy-sounding assistant that Mr Maestro was taking no calls, and when I assured her it was important and concerned his daughter, she came back with a sharp, "No exceptions," and hung up on me.

Very pleasant.

Next I called Felix and told him what I knew.

"Stick around," Felix said. "I'll find out where she is and get back to you."

Ha! Stick around! Apparently he didn't realize the weather in New York was below freezing.

Reluctantly I left the building, trudged down the block and discovered a grungy little coffee shop. When I say grungy I mean it wasn't all clean and sparkly like a Starbucks or a Coffee Bean. This place had character – it also had the guy in the army coat sitting at a table drinking a mug of coffee while tapping away on his laptop.

"Hi," I said, on my way to the counter.

He barely glanced up.

So much for my powers of attraction. Well, I suppose I wasn't looking my best with unwashed hair pulled back into a messy ponytail, bloodshot sleep-deprived eyes, and a red nose.

I'd almost gone from Mario's bed to the airport, and sleeping on the plane is not my fave thing. I prefer to stay alert, just in case.

I walked up to the counter and ordered a cappuccino and a piece of appetizing apple-pie from a heavy-set, middle-aged man who appeared to have strayed out of a scene from *The Sopranos.* He was unshaven, with badly dyed black hair pouffed into a Donald Trump-style bouffant, a pallid complexion, and heavy-lidded eyes.

On impulse I asked him if he happened to know a Frankie Romano.

The man thought for a moment, then said, "Yeah, Frankie. He don't come around no more."

"Do you know where I might find him?"

"The kid's a deejay – he got some cushy job playin' records for a livin'. Used to be in here every mornin'."

"Is there any way I can locate him?" I asked, probably sounding too much like a lawyer.

"Why? You pregnant?" The man burst out laughing at his incredibly sexist remark.

Army Coat glanced up from his laptop. He'd removed his knit cap, revealing a mop of blondish curly hair.

"Actually," I said, holding onto my dignity, "Frankie has inherited money. That's why I need to find him, so I can make sure he knows."

Mister Shark Teeth – neé Felix – had taught me to always mention money when tracking someone down. The word has a magical way of opening up doors.

"The kid's gonna be happy 'bout that," the man behind the counter said, scratching his chin. "I think we got a card or sompin'. Yo – Mara," he bellowed. "Get your fat ass out here."

Mara appeared from the back, an illicit cigarette dangling from her lips. She was obviously the man's wife, and she too looked the part. Scads of heavy make-up, ample hips and a sour expression. HBO would cast her in an instant. "What?" she snapped.

"This girl's lookin' for Frankie Romano – remember the deejay kid, used to be in here all the time. 'Dint he give you his card 'cause you was thinkin' of using him for your cousin's weddin'?"

"Too expensive," Mara sniffed. "What did the little pissant think, that we was made of money?"

"Yeah, yeah," the man agreed. "But ya still got his card, doncha?"

"Chucked it," Mara said, shooting me a flinty glare – like how dare I even ask.

"Sorry, girlie," my Mafia Don said. "The pie's on me. Enjoy."

I took my pie and cappuccino and retreated to a table in the corner. Two minutes later the guy in the army coat leaned over – as I said before, the place was tiny – and handed me a slip of paper.

"What's this?" I asked, noticing that he had very appealing brown eyes fringed with long thick lashes.

"Frankie Romano's number," he said.

"How did you—"

"Overheard your conversation so I Googled him. Frankie Romano, deejay. Parties. Events."

"Oh . . . wow, thanks," I said appreciatively. "I really need to get in touch with him."

"You're not a New Yorker, are you?"

"How can you tell?"

"I dunno, kind of the way you're dressed."

"What's the giveaway?" I asked curiously.

"Thin jacket. No boots. No scarf. No gloves. You must be freezing."

"I am," I confessed, noting that the brown eyes went nicely with the curly blondish hair. "In fact, the moment I saw you I wanted to rip that warm-looking cap right off your head," I added jokingly.

Army Coat grinned. He had crooked teeth, not perfect like every guy in L.A., but just crooked enough to work.

"It's yours," he said, gallantly handing me his cap.

"No, I can't accept it," I protested.

"Sure you can. It's not as if I'm giving you a diamond. Besides, your hair looks like it's in dire need of rescue. Bad night?"

"Actually it was a great night," I said, thinking of Mario. "But then I had to get on a seven a.m. flight and come straight here."

"From?"

"L.A. Can't you tell?"

"No," he said, shaking his head.

"Really?"

"Yeah."

"How?"

"No fake tan amongst other things." He grinned again, and offered his hand. "Sam – and you are?"

"Denver."

"Interesting name. Different."

"My parents thought so."

"What are you really here for, Denver?" he asked, adding more sugar to his coffee and vigorously stirring.

"Business."

"What kind of business?"

"Wow! You're curious."

"Yeah, I've been told that before," he said, with a wry smile. "It's 'cause I'm a writer – makes me want to know everything."

Alarm signals went off in my head. Writer or journalist? Nosy reporter lurking around Annabelle's building, or merely a neighbor?

"What kind of things do you write?" I inquired.

"Screenplays," he said, taking a gulp of coffee. "And you – what's your gig?"

"I'm an associate at an L.A. law firm," I replied, toying with my apple-pie while thinking that the poor guy should move to L.A. where everyone and their brother is attempting to write a screenplay. He's got no chance of getting anything off the ground in New York.

"And why are you really looking for Frankie Romano?" he asked, leaning forward.

I did not feel inclined to change my story. "He's inherited money," I answered vaguely. "I'm here to see he knows about it."

"Hmm . . ." Sam said, looking skeptical.

"I need to find a bathroom," I said, deciding to end this line of conversation.

I got up and I approached my Mafia Don at the counter. "Is there a ladies room I can use?" I asked sweetly. After all, he had given me a free slice of pie.

"For you, honey, anythin'," the man said, having apparently taken a shine to me the minute I'd mentioned money. "Mara," he yelled, turning his head. "Female customer comin' back to use the john."

He opened a partition on the counter and ushered me through. I thought for a moment he was going to pat me on the ass, but fortunately he restrained himself.

I didn't need to pee. What I did need to do was call this Frankie Romano guy and find out if he knew where Annabelle was so I could get her back to L.A.

Mara greeted me in the back hallway with a scowl and cigarette breath.

"In there," she muttered, directing me toward a tiny dark toilet. "An' don't go throwin' nothin' down the toilet bowl," she warned. "I don't want no clogged system."

And with those sweet words she shut the door on me.

I took out my phone, and punched in Frankie Romano's number.

Chapter Fifteen

Carolyn

Sunday morning, Carolyn got up late. Usually her alarm awoke her at six a.m. but today was different. Today was Sunday and she could luxuriate in her bed for as long as she felt like it. Too bad that Gregory couldn't luxuriate next to her, but soon . . .

She tried to imagine what their Sundays would be like when they were together. Long and leisurely. She'd cook breakfast while he read the newspapers and checked out the political shows on TV. She knew he enjoyed doing that, because a few months ago he'd arranged for her to accompany him on a business trip to New York, and they'd spent the entire weekend together. Total bliss, although if she was honest with herself, sometimes his sexual appetite veered toward the selfish side. He loved getting oral sex from her, he claimed it was the best he'd ever had. But the sad thing was that he never reciprocated, which was a big disappointment.

She was sure that once they were living together, things would change. She'd tell him in the nicest possible way what she required in bed, and of course he would comply. Why wouldn't he?

Now, lying under the covers, she wished she could phone him, if only to say good morning and hear his voice.

But no, he'd given her strict instructions never to call him at home on Sundays. "I spend all day with the children," he'd told her. "No interruptions, not unless there's a worldwide emergency."

Respecting his request, she curbed the urge to contact him, and called Kerri instead, saying that she could indeed go to the mall. They arranged to meet at noon.

Finally she got up, took a shower, studied her stomach in the bathroom mirror from all angles to see if she was showing yet, and realized it was far too early to notice anything, not even the tiniest of bulges.

Pregnant! She was embarking on an exciting journey.

* * *

Anything to get out of the house and away from Evelyn's cloying presence. The woman was stifling him, Gregory felt it more and more each day.

Sitting behind his sturdy mahogany desk in his study, he contemplated calling Katy, the English journalist he'd recently met at a press conference. Katy was young, full of ambition, and she'd definitely thrown out all the right signals.

Then he thought that calling her on a Sunday might seem too eager. Perhaps it was best to wait a day or two, then have Muriel set up a lunch for next week. Katy had said she wanted to interview him. So be it.

He still had the problem of a long boring Sunday ahead of him. Both his children were staying with their maternal grandparents for the weekend, and that left Evelyn.

Within minutes his problem was solved by Ramirez Ortego calling on his private line.

How the *hell* had Ramirez gotten his private number?

Evelyn, of course.

"Senator," Ramirez said. "Thought I'd follow up on last night's conversation. If you can make it today, my people would be most happy to see you."

Before he could think of a reason to say he couldn't make it, Ramirez gave him the details of where to come.

He wasn't that angry, because at least it was a legitimate excuse to get away from Evelyn and leave the house. He was sure his dear wife would have no wish to accompany him, and he was right about that. After telling him she was too busy to go anywhere, Evelyn said, "Did you call your little secretary and tell her to alert the press?"

"I do not plan on bothering my *assistant* on a Sunday," he said, pointedly emphasizing the word assistant.

"Too bad," Evelyn said, elegant in a cream pantsuit and day-time pearls. "It's such an excellent photo opportunity."

"Yes," he answered dryly. "Me hanging out with a bunch of gang bangers. What a photo!"

"No, dear," Evelyn corrected. "You helping out at a community center, making sure our fine city stays safe."

God, his wife was so full of shit.

It occurred to him that now he had a legitimate reason for calling Katy, the English journalist. He could ask her if she'd like an exclusive on his visit to the community center, because he was in desperate need of a diversion. He couldn't get his mind off Carolyn's baby announcement, and how the hell was he supposed to take care of *that* problem? He sure as hell wasn't allowing her to ruin everything he held dear. If Evelyn found out, she'd make absolutely certain he was punished in every possible way. She'd immediately take away his children, she'd attempt to ruin his reputation, and the ensuing scandal would no doubt put paid to his career.

He needed to get Carolyn out of his life, and that had to be done soon. But how? That was the question.

Damn Carolyn, and damn Evelyn too. Bitches of a different caliber, but bitches all the same.

* * *

Kerri was an avid shopper with a passion for shopping malls. Carolyn hated shopping and loathed large shopping malls.

Kerri raced from store to store with all the enthusiasm of a new puppy. Carolyn trailed behind.

"I *sooo* love this," Kerri cried out, happily trying on a selection of high-heeled pumps in myriad colors. "What do you think?" she asked Carolyn, while tottering around the shoe store in a pair of yellow stilettos that made her legs appear even shorter than they were.

"Beige might be a more useful color," Carolyn suggested, trying to be diplomatic. "Beige goes with everything. Or maybe black."

"Boring!" Kerri squealed. "That's one thing nobody's ever accused me of being. Boring? Nooo!!"

Carolyn could believe it, since Kerri never stopped talking and always had something to say. Lately it was all about her adventures on the internet.

"There's some unbelievable sites," Kerri assured her with a knowing wink. "All you have to do is post your photo and a brief description of yourself. Then before you know it – just like the song – it's raining men!"

Carolyn nodded, feigning interest, although she could imagine nothing worse than trolling for a man on the internet. Besides, she had her man now, and Gregory Stoneman was all the man she could ever want.

* * *

The street where Ramirez's community center was located was smack in the middle of a slum. As Gregory searched for somewhere to park his expensive car he regretted that he had not called his driver. The least Evelyn could've done was warn him. Although knowing Evelyn, she talked a good game, but she'd probably never visited the neighborhood, so she'd had no idea where she was forcing him to go.

At least Katy was on her way. Katy with the British accent, trim figure, and small but quite appealing tits. He'd called her, told her where he would be, and she'd jumped at the opportunity to cover his visit.

"Can I bring my photographer?" she'd asked.

"Why not?" he'd said.

He had plans for Katy once Carolyn was out of the picture. A man could not live with just Evelyn for his sexual gratification, he had to have more, and Katy seemed to be a likely candidate.

Finding a parking space next to an empty lot, he reluctantly left his car, hoping it would still be there when he returned.

Walking back to the center half a block away, he passed a couple of grizzled old winos slumped against the wall of a crumbling building, swigging from a shared bottle of cheap booze. A Mexican woman scurried past pushing a battered buggy with two babies inside, while a toddler – sucking its thumb – trailed behind her. A couple of suspicious-looking Latino youths lounged on the steps of the center. They scowled at Gregory as he made his way past them and entered the building, which was actually an old abandoned warehouse.

He entered into a cavernous room filled with groups of people of all colors. Hurriedly he looked around, spotted Ramirez, and purposefully marched toward him.

Ramirez extracted himself from conversation with an obese woman in full African dress, a white preacher, and a jumpy-looking teenager, and stepped forward to greet him.

"You came," Ramirez said.

"You didn't think I would?" Gregory replied, noting that the place smelled of rotting garbage with faint overtones of urine.

"Politicians," Ramirez said flatly. "They promise a lot and do nothing."

"What is it that you expect us to do?" Gregory asked, a fake concerned expression firmly stuck on his face.

"Money," Ramirez said, gesturing around. "This place is a shithole. We need all the funding we can get to make it better, put in heating, get some chairs for people to sit on, and a fridge that works. Make it a place that kids want to come to an' hang out. We gotta get 'em off the street, it's the only way to bring about change."

"Evelyn's the fundraiser in the family," Gregory said smoothly. "You should talk to her."

"You can help us," Ramirez said, ignoring the reference to Evelyn. "A word in the right place would go a long way to getting us a grant."

"I'll see what I can do," Gregory promised, wondering when Katy would show up. It better be soon, because he wasn't hanging around.

"But *you're* the man who can make *sure* it happens," Ramirez continued. "Come with me – you should meet some of my helpers, see how hard everyone works."

"Fine," Gregory said, realizing there was no immediate escape.

* * *

Carolyn was sitting in the Food Court eating Panda Express Chinese from cardboard cartons with Kerri. As usual Kerri was talking non-stop.

"I went out with this one guy," she announced, nibbling on a greasy spare rib. "And like at first he seemed perfectly normal.

I mean, he wasn't exactly Zac Efron, but he could've been a contender."

Carolyn nodded, desperately trying to appear interested in yet another of Kerri's dating misadventures.

"We went on a couple of dates," Kerri continued, licking barbecue sauce off her fingers, "then he informed me that since we'd been on two dates and he'd paid, it was time we had sex. Can you imagine? Just like that he comes out with it."

"Shocking," Carolyn murmured, taking a sip of water.

"No!" Kerri exclaimed. "I haven't *gotten* to the shocking bit yet."

"Go on," Carolyn said, managing a surreptitious glance at her watch.

"He wanted sex with me *and* his former girlfriend! Apparently she was waiting at his apartment all ready to party." Kerri rolled her expressive eyes. "Can you imagine? How gross is *that*!"

"I presume you said no."

"Like . . . duh! Do I look like an idiot?"

Carolyn glanced at her watch again. "I should be getting home," she said, starting to fidget. "Do you mind if we leave soon?"

"Really?" Kerri said, her face registering disappointment. "We haven't covered half the stores."

"I've got some work to finish up, and I promised to look in on Nellie," Carolyn explained. "She's all alone – it must be hard for her with no friends or family."

"You're so good to do that," Kerri sighed, stuffing a piece of sweet 'n' sour chicken in her mouth. "I always mean to drop by an' see how she's doing, but I never find the time, although I do pick up her meds every month."

"I expect your dating schedule keeps you on the go," Carolyn said, slightly tongue-in-cheek. "*How* many dating sites did you say you're on?"

"A lot," Kerri answered with a cheery grin. "And you know what – we've got to sign you up too. You'll enjoy it! It's *sooo* much fun."

No, Carolyn thought. *I will not enjoy it at all. I have found the love of my life, and soon he will be all mine.*

Chapter Sixteen

Bobby

There was a group of guys who met up and played softball in the park on Sunday mornings. They had a set routine, nine or ten guys would assemble, and each week – after the game – one of them would host the rest of the day at their apartment. Hosting meant getting in plenty of deli food, making sure there was an abundance of snacks, a full supply of European beer, and most important of all – every sports package on the latest wide-screen blue-ray high-def TV.

They called themselves "The Sunday in the Park" gang. Bobby and M.J. were the founders.

Bobby treasured his time with the guys – no women allowed – it was strictly a males only day. Frankie was not a member of the club, since bonding with the guys was out of his comfort zone. He preferred hanging out with Annabelle, catching the latest action movie, playing pool, and dropping into a cardgame or two.

Bobby was relieved, because although he and M.J. reluctantly accepted Frankie's drug use, the others wouldn't be so happy. In their book, doing coke on a permanent basis was for losers, okay for a party once in a while, but snorting it up your nose numerous times a day was a definite negative. There were times Bobby tried to talk to Frankie about his excessive use of cocaine, but Frankie was never in a listening mood, so every time their conversation ended up going nowhere.

The "Sunday in the Park" gang consisted of two hedge-fund guys, a computer genius, a drummer with a rock band, an investment banker, a well-known chef, a tennis pro, and an actor who starred on a daytime soap. The camaraderie between them was special. The youngest member was twenty-three – that would be the chef. And the oldest was thirty – the investment banker. Everyone left their troubles at home and enjoyed a relaxed no-pressure day. No one was married, and no one was close to doing the big deed, although the subject of women was always up for discussion. One of them always had a dating story to tell – and the other guys felt free to offer advice. "Didja fuck her?" was the most popular question on their agenda.

This Sunday was Bobby's day to host, but he was concerned about Frankie and Annabelle. He kept on wondering if he should drop out and spend some time with them. Annabelle was a pain, but he'd known her since high school, and he kind of felt sorry for her – especially now.

He called Frankie, who mumbled something about being asleep and would check in later.

"How's Annabelle doing?" Bobby wanted to know.

"Later, man," Frankie answered with a big fat yawn.

So much for spending time with them. Frankie obviously had everything under control.

Outside in the park it was crisp and icy, but the freezing weather spurred Bobby to play his hardest, and by the time he got back to his apartment he was feeling invigorated and ready for anything.

For a moment, laying out cold cuts, cartons of potato salad and coleslaw on the kitchen counter, it crossed his mind that it might be nice having a girlfriend around to help out. There'd never been anyone special, never anyone who'd lasted more than a couple of months. He simply wasn't that interested in the girls he came across – the beautiful models and actresses, the party girls and young society girls – most of them searching for a rich husband. Oh yeah, great for a few weeks or months of fun sex, but that was it.

Not that he was concerned. He was just about to hit twenty-six – too young to even think about getting married, but would a steady girlfriend really be such a bad thing?

Frankie had a steady girlfriend, Annabelle, and all Frankie wanted to do was cheat on her, so come to think of it – what was the point?

Bobby held Lucky and Lennie up as a shining example of what a great relationship should be. They were both extremely independent, but they were also loving and volatile, passionate and crazy, and after years of marriage – still madly in love. *That's* what he wanted. A relationship filled with fire.

Zeena had fire. She might be years older than him, but he knew that if he was with her, things would never be dull.

What did age matter anyway? Madonna was over fifty and smokin' hot. Demi Moore had married some dude a good fifteen years younger than her. Not to mention his mom's best friend – the very sexy and gorgeous Venus – married to Billy Melina, a movie star many years her junior.

Fuck it! He promised himself that the next time he saw Zeena, he was definitely going for it.

* * *

The next time came sooner than he thought. Stacking dishes in the kitchen after all the guys had departed – including M.J. – he was just about to check in with Frankie again, when his doorbell buzzed.

Thinking that one of the guys had left something behind, he flung open the door, and there she stood, Zeena herself.

"Bobby," she drawled, wandering past him into his apartment as if she'd visited a dozen times before. "Zeena was in the neighborhood. Decided to see for herself how the heir to a shipping fortune lives."

Shocked and startled, he was also instantly pissed off that she knew about his background. He kept a low profile, stayed out of gossip columns, never discussed his heritage with anyone except M.J. So how exactly had she found out? And what was she doing in his apartment?

Not that he minded.

How could he mind when the object of all his most recent fantasies was standing in his living room clad from head to toe in black leather? She had on a tiny leather mini-skirt, fishnet stockings, thigh-high boots, and a black turtleneck cashmere sweater, paired with a slouchy leather silver-studded motor-cycle jacket. Her coal-black hair fell in a straight curtain way below her waist, and her exotic make-up emphasized her almond-shaped eyes.

There was a slight whiff of dominatrix in the air, but Bobby didn't care. She was here, in his apartment, and it was up to him to make a move.

What did she expect from him? That was the question. He was so used to being the one in control that this was a whole new experience.

Extracting a pack of Gauloises from her oversized Prada crocodile purse, she shook out a cigarette and proceeded to light up with an Art Deco silver cigarette-lighter.

The way she touched the flame to the tip of the cigarette was extremely sexual. Bobby decided against telling her that there was a no smoking rule in his apartment.

She inhaled deeply, then watching him closely with her cat-like eyes, she slowly exhaled.

"Here we are," she finally said, a plume of strong-smelling smoke drifting in the air between them. "Alone together. Isn't that what you've been waiting for, Bobby?"

"No young studs today?" he asked, trying to keep it light. "No entourage hanging on your every word? What's up with that?"

"Disappointed?" she murmured, her tone mocking him. "Were you hoping for a threesome? Or perhaps you're gay." A long-drawn-out sigh. "Ah . . . such beauty." Another long beat. "*Are* you gay, Bobby?"

God! She reminded him of Serenity – all sarcasm and bitchery spewing forth from a mouth he was desperate to kiss.

Was that what turned him on?

Apparently so, because he could feel himself growing hard, and he had the strongest desire to grab her and simply go for it.

He should do it. Because that's why she was here, no other reason.

Miz Superstar had come visiting to see exactly what he had to offer. And he had every intention of showing her.

Chapter Seventeen

Annabelle

Somehow or other, Frankie and Annabelle had become involved in a huge fight before they'd both finally fallen asleep somewhere in the early hours of Sunday morning.

In the midst of their fight, Annabelle had picked up a bottle of vodka and begun purposefully swigging straight from the bottle. Since she had a low tolerance level it didn't take long before she was totally drunk.

Frankie laid out several lines of coke and snorted it right in front of her. He didn't usually indulge with her watching, because Annabelle didn't do any kind of drugs – she preferred the lure of alcohol. But he'd felt like getting totally high.

Their fight had escalated. She'd called him a useless druggie with no balls.

He'd called her a fucking princess with no conscience.

She'd yelled that he was nothing more than a pimp and had no idea how to handle anything.

He'd yelled back that she was a selfish cold-hearted bitch with no emotions, and all she cared about was herself.

Those were just a few of the insults exchanged.

Eventually Annabelle had staggered into the bedroom, still clutching the now half-empty bottle of vodka. Slamming the door in Frankie's face, she'd fallen on the bed and immediately started sobbing, the news of her mother's brutal murder finally sinking in.

Frankie had felt a strong urge to walk out, but since he had nowhere to walk, he'd ended up sleeping on the couch.

They'd both slept their way into Sunday afternoon, and it wasn't until four o'clock that Annabelle surfaced with a killer hangover.

She lay in her bed quite still for a moment, mulling over the events of the previous day, whereupon the enormity and horror of what had taken place in Los Angeles suddenly overcame her, and once again she began to sob, deep body-racking sobs that enveloped her whole being.

Her cries awoke Frankie, and forgetting about their ferocious fight, he hurried into the bedroom, because if there was one thing that really got to him, it was the sight and sound of a crying female. The very thought evoked bad memories. His brute of a father used to beat the crap out of his mom on a weekly basis, and it was up to him from as far back as he could remember, to comfort her.

He'd always felt guilty about taking off, because who was left behind to console her when he was gone?

No one, that's who.

Frankie had moved on, and was busy chasing a new life.

"Hey, babe," he soothed, holding her close. "It's okay, everything's gonna be cool."

"No, it's not," she sniffled. "My mother's dead – and you know something, Frankie? I barely knew her."

"Not your fault," he said, handing her a tissue.

"Maybe it is," she said, sitting up and dabbing her eyes. "Maybe I should've stayed and *forced* her to take notice of me."

"There's no way you could've done that," he assured her. "According to you, she was always on a movie set or posing for pictures in magazines. She was a busy woman."

"I should've tried harder," Annabelle lamented, filled with a cold, empty feeling of loss and sorrow.

"No, babe," Frankie said, playing good boyfriend to the hilt. "You did the best you could."

"Do you really think so?" she asked tremulously.

"No doubt, babe, none at all."

Annabelle spent the rest of the afternoon watching all the coverage and stories on TV about her mother's demise. It was as if she'd finally realized what had actually taken place, and now she couldn't get enough details.

A couple of times Frankie tried to suggest that she call Ralph, but she waved him away and remained sitting in front of the TV.

At least she seemed to have forgotten about her bad experience with Sharif Rani's son, which was a relief because Sharif was their star customer, and to lose him as a client would be a disaster.

As soon as he'd calmed Annabelle down, made her a cup of green tea, fed her a couple of Advil, and persuaded her to stay in bed until she felt better, he called their assistant, Janey Bonafacio, to check on everything.

Janey did not come in on weekends, she worked from home on the computer he'd bought her.

"I'm so sorry," Janey wailed over the phone. "How is Annabelle holding up? Even more important – how are *you*?"

Janey was one of the few people in their lives who actually knew who Annabelle's parents were. Frankie had sworn her to secrecy, warning her that if she revealed anything to anyone about Annabelle or the business they ran, she would be out of a job. Since Janey would allow nothing to come between her and her beloved cousin, she'd agreed. Her son Chip, however, had not.

Frankie had never considered Chip a threat. As far as he was concerned, Janey's son was simply around to do everyone's bidding. At least he could drive a car and was family – that had to count for something. Besides, Chip would never dare defy his mother.

Frankie instructed Janey to doublecheck on everyone's "appointments," and make sure that things were on the right track. "Annabelle's gonna need a few days off," he informed her. "We might have to fly to L.A. so it's up to you to make sure you got it all under control. No fuck-ups. There'll be a hefty bonus in it, Janey, so make Frankie proud."

"Should I come in today?" Janey asked, anxious to get as close to Frankie as possible. "I could be there in an hour."

"Not necessary," he said, equally anxious to get her off the phone. "I'll get back to you later. Gotta go now – my other line's buzzing."

* * *

Chip Bonafacio aspired to far greater things than driving a car for a bunch of whores, picking up Second Cousin Frankie's dry-cleaning, and generally doing whatever that snooty bitch, Annabelle Maestro, requested.

Oh yes, he knew who she was all right. He'd made it his job to find out as soon as he'd started working for them, even though his mom had attempted to tell him as little as possible about the business Annabelle and Frankie were running.

What did she think? That he was a total moron?

Yeah. Apparently so.

Janey thinking he was dumb worked for him. He still lived at home – too lazy to move out – and his mom did everything for him. She cooked and cleaned and did his laundry, handed him money whenever he needed it, and kept her nagging under control, although sometimes she begged him to show an interest in something – anything. *Yeah. Right.*

When he wasn't running his ass off for Frankie – a man he envied and hated at the same time – he preferred to slack off, watch TV, download porn, bet on football, screw whatever girl he could get his hands on, and drink as much beer as humanly possible.

It never occurred to his mom that he knew everything that was going on, including the identities of some of the better-known women he ferried to their dirty little assignations. Everyone acted like he was invisible, but he was smarter than they thought, and he was keeping his own black book filled with all the info he'd gleaned.

Gemma Summer Maestro's murder struck him as the break he'd been waiting for. The gruesome story was splashed across the front page of every newspaper and every internet site in the country.

Chip was sure that he was dangerously close to scoring some major bucks.

Chip Bonafacio had big plans for his future. And they did not include his fat, addicted-to-Frankie, dumb-ass, annoying mom.

No fucking way.

Chapter Eighteen

Denver

"Hi," I said, relieved because I was finally getting an answer from Annabelle's boyfriend's phone. "Is this Frankie Romano?"

"Who wants to know?" said a suspicious-sounding male.

"My name's Denver Jones," I said quickly, pressing on regardless. "I'm a lawyer working for Ralph Maestro, and I'm here in New York trying to contact his daughter, Annabelle."

"Why?" he asked guardedly.

"Well . . . I'm sure you heard about the tragedy –"

"Who hasn't?"

"So you can understand that I do need to speak with Annabelle. It's quite urgent. Can you give me a number where I can reach her?"

"Where'd you get *my* number?"

"You're listed," I answered shortly. "Frankie Romano, deejay – right? Annabelle's boyfriend."

"What makes you think I'm her boyfriend?"

For God's sake! He was more cagey than the CIA! I was cold and tired and I'd been trying to reach her for hours. Thank goodness for Sam, because he'd taken pity on me and let me come back to his apartment and hang out while I tried to reach

Annabelle's boyfriend, who was now behaving in a most irritating fashion. Why had I ever left Mario's bed, 'cause that's exactly where I wanted to be right now, cuddly and warm and having great sex. Instead of which I'm in a strange man's apartment – well, not so strange actually, kind of very attractive in an Owen Wilson kind of way – freezing my ass off and wondering how late the planes continue to take off for L.A.

"Can you help me find her or not?" I said, fast losing patience.

"Is Ralph sending a private jet?"

"Excuse me?" I said, realizing that not only was this guy an asshole, he was a pushy asshole.

"The man's gotta have his own plane," Frankie insisted.

"He doesn't," I said firmly, although I had no idea whether Ralph did or not. And if he did have a plane, he certainly hadn't volunteered it.

"Is it possible to speak to Annabelle?" I asked, getting impatient. "I've left several messages, none of which she's responded to."

"Annabelle's unavailable."

I played what I hoped was my trump card. "I *do* know her," I explained. "We went to school together in L.A. Tell her it's Denver Jones, I'm sure she'll remember me."

"Y'know what," Frankie said, unimpressed. "I'm gonna havta call you back."

Damn! I need to get home. This trip is not working for me. And how come Felix hasn't called me?

I gave Frankie the number of my cell and said, "Please make it soon." Then I clicked off.

"Problems?" Sam asked, strolling into the room carrying a mug of something hot.

"Annabelle's boyfriend sounds like a total jerk," I muttered.

By this time I'd revealed exactly why I was in New York to Sam. After my first attempt to reach Frankie when we were still in the coffee shop, I'd slumped back at my corner table, wondering exactly what I was supposed to do next. Completely at a loss, I'd finally told Sam the truth about why I was there and how I couldn't return to L.A. without Annabelle in tow.

Sam had turned out to be an extremely sympathetic listener. After an hour he'd suggested that I might like to sit it out at his place while I continued to try to reach either Annabelle or Frankie – whoever answered their phone first.

Gratefully I'd accepted his offer, and now here I was, seething with frustration, sitting on the couch in his very nice roomy apartment – waiting for Annabelle's asshole boyfriend to call me back.

"Drink this," Sam said, handing me the mug he was carrying.

"What is it?" I asked, wondering if he was planning on slipping me a roofie and ravishing my poor cold body. Not that anyone would want to ravish me, the way I look. I bet my nose is redder than Rudolph's!

"It's hot chocolate with a side of the rape drug," he said straight-faced.

Wow! It's as if he can read my mind.

"I *am* a lawyer," I reminded him, quite sternly.

"I know," he said. "That's why I'm giving you all the info upfront." He paused, and smiled slightly. "You *know* that's what you were thinking."

"No, I wasn't," I replied, stifling an embarrassed grin.

"Yes," he said, giving me a full-on knowing look. "That's exactly what you were thinking."

I smiled back at him. Suddenly I felt very comfortable in the apartment of a man I'd only met two hours earlier.

I sat on his couch sipping hot chocolate, praying that Frankie Romano would call me back soon and put Annabelle on the line so that I could get the hell out of here and back to L.A.

Although . . . things weren't so bad. Sam was quite attractive in a lean and lanky way, and I had to admit that we were definitely on the road to a major flirtation.

Was I being unfaithful to Mario?

Hell, no! It's not as if Mario is my boyfriend, and it's not as if I'm about to jump into bed with Sam.

Although . . . the thought had crossed my mind.

From a total dry patch to a couple of hot contenders, and all in the course of two fun-filled insane days. This was kind of crazy.

"You hungry?" Sam asked, moving over to an open-plan kitchen. "I could fix us some eggs, or if you're really starving there's a spaghetti joint around the corner."

"Why are you being so nice to me?" I asked, jumping off the couch and following him across the room.

"Oh," he said vaguely. "Could be 'cause you're smart and appealing and I took an instant like. You're also gorgeous."

Gorgeous?!! Was he talking to me with my bed-head, red nose and shivering body?

"Hmm . . ." I said. "Have you recently returned from a desert island where you were deprived of female company?"

"Can't take a compliment, huh?" he said, teasing me.

"Never been adept at that."

"Well, you *are* gorgeous," he said. "You've got that Julia Roberts thing going for you."

"*Pretty Woman* or *Erin Brockovich*?" I asked caustically.

"The hooker or the smart babe," he mused. "Now that's what I'd call a great combination."

"Will you *stop*," I said, although I couldn't help smiling.

He laughed, and leaned his elbows on the counter-top. "I recently got dis-engaged from a total bitch."

"You did?" I asked, perching on the edge of a high stool, relieved that the conversation was taking a new direction.

"Right on I did. Caught her screwing my best friend. How cliché is that?" He shook his head as if he couldn't quite believe it had happened to him. "If I wrote it," he added wryly, "I'd get laughed off the page."

"I wouldn't laugh."

"How's that?"

"'Cause it's always the best friend," I said airily. "Never fails."

He gave me a look. "Personal experience?"

"Absolutely not," I said firmly.

"How about you?" he asked, striving to keep it casual. "Are you in a relationship right now?"

"Absolutely not," I repeated. And after a meaningful pause I couldn't help asking, "Are you?"

"Absolutely not," he said, mimicking my voice. Then he burst out laughing.

I think I could like this guy. Infectious laugh, Owen Wilson looks, a writer, *and* he has a sense of humor.

Of course I suspect that he doesn't possess killer abs like Mario, but are abs *really* that important?

No. They just look nice on the page.

"So," Sam said, flexing his long tapered fingers, "what did we decide? Spaghetti or eggs?"

He'd just used the *we* word, as if we were a couple, which we are most definitely not.

"If spaghetti means venturing outside," I said, pantomiming a mock shiver, "then my vote is for eggs."

"A fine choice," he said, opening up a cabinet door and taking out a frying pan. "Forgive my ego, but I'm a master chef with eggs."

"You are?"

"Oh yeah. Scrambled? Over easy? Poached? Or how about an omelet?"

I glanced at my watch – it was almost eight. Was there any chance of finding Annabelle and getting her on a plane tonight? Hardly likely.

"Scrambled's great," I said.

"Soft? Hard?"

"Excuse me?"

"The eggs."

We both grinned. I felt as if I'd known him for at least a week.

"Soft," I murmured, all thoughts of Mario definitely leaning toward the back-burner.

"That's the way I like 'em too," he said, opening the fridge and removing a cardboard carton of organic eggs.

"Y'know," I ventured, "as soon as we've eaten I should start finding a hotel."

With his back to me he casually said, "You can stay here if you like."

Oh crap! I'd probably sounded as if I was hinting. How pathetic!

"That's okay," I answered quickly. "I, uh, love staying in hotels."

"Really?" he said, not believing me for a minute.

Was I sounding more pathetic by the minute or what? *"I love staying in hotels."* Truth is, I hate hotels, ever since I'd gotten bitten by bedbugs in a hotel in Phoenix when I was tracking down some information on a cheating wife for Felix.

The sound of Beyoncé's "If I Were A Boy" filled the room. My BlackBerry was in action, so I hurriedly groped in my pocket and extracted it.

"Tomorrow morning," Frankie Romano said, all business. "Ten a.m. at our apartment in SoHo. Do you know where that is?"

Duh . . . yes.

"Book two first-class tickets on the two o'clock United flight to L.A. An' make sure you have a limo to take us to the airport, and one at the other end. We'll need a suite at the Beverly Hills

Hotel, and a car and driver on twenty-four-hour alert. See you at the apartment." And without waiting for me to say a word, he hung up.

Mission accomplished.

Or so I thought.

Chapter Nineteen

Carolyn

Since Carolyn was playing the kindly neighbor, Kerri felt that she should at least make an effort and go with her to Nellie's apartment.

Carolyn had not intended to visit Nellie again so soon, but as she'd used her as an excuse to leave the shopping mall, she'd had no choice since Kerri had opted to accompany her.

Once there, the two of them sat around making idle conversation with the garrulous old woman for over an hour. Nellie was all agog about the murder of the famous movie star, Gemma Summer Maestro. She had all sorts of theories about what could have happened. And when she'd exhausted the various scenarios she'd conjured up, she began delving back in time and reminiscing about the Fatty Arbuckle scandal that had taken place in Hollywood many decades earlier. Next she started speaking about Marilyn Monroe and her connection to John and Bobby Kennedy. "I knew Marilyn," Nellie revealed with a secretive smile, indicating that they might have been close. "She was such a luminous beauty. Big-boned though. It didn't matter – every man she ever met fell in lust with her. It was a sight to see."

After ten minutes of Marilyn and the Kennedys, Nellie returned to the subject of Gemma Summer's murder.

At that point Carolyn decided it was best not to mention that when she was a kid she'd attended several birthday parties given for Gemma's daughter, Annabelle, at the Maestro mansion. For some misguided reason her mom had forced her to go, claiming it was the polite thing to do since the entire class was invited. She was ten – how could she argue?

At every party she'd hovered awkwardly in the background watching while circus clowns performed, live elephants paraded across the manicured lawns, and a line of ponies ferried the children around in circles. There was also a huge party tent with tables loaded with hot dogs, hamburgers, pizzas, cookies and cakes. Carolyn remembered there being enough food to feed the homeless for a year.

Gemma Summer had only appeared when cameras were rolling. Carolyn recalled thinking that she had not seemed like a very hands-on mother, but then Annabelle was hardly the easiest of daughters. Annabelle was always boasting and showing off, flashing her privileged life in front of all the other kids.

Fortunately for Carolyn, when Annabelle turned thirteen, the parties stopped. Or at least to Carolyn's relief the invitations stopped coming. It was then that she'd palled up with Denver, and they'd formed an unbreakable friendship.

Denver had not called her back, which was surprising in view of the cryptic message she'd left on her voicemail.

God! She had to tell someone her exciting news soon or she'd burst!

* * *

"In every way we can, we gotta break the cycle of fatherless kids gettin' caught up in gangs," Ramirez lectured, his long pockmarked face a stern mask, his tone loud and harsh. "When there's no father in the house, an' the mother's strung out on drugs or mebbe she's taken two jobs to keep the family goin', *that's* when these boys choose a new family – the family that operate on the streets. An' I should know. I was one of them."

The group of people standing around him verbalized their approval.

"The street gangs have a *need* to keep their army goin'," Ramirez continued, raising his voice. "So they start recruitin' kids as young as eleven an' twelve. By the time they're sixteen, those *children* are hardened criminals with no future. We all have to help stop this. It's our civic duty. An' we can do it, people."

"Hear, hear," piped up Katy, the English journalist who'd turned up just when Gregory was contemplating a fast exit.

Gregory had already noticed that she looked petite and quite fuckable in a pair of knee-high UGG boots, tight jeans and a fuzzy blue top, but she came with an unfortunate appendage, and that appendage was her husband, who also happened to be the photographer.

Gregory was aggravated – he could not believe his luck. One pregnant assistant, and now the girl he had in mind for his own personal pleasure turned out to be married!

On second thoughts he decided she wasn't so hot. Too young and chirpy. Her high excited voice with the clipped British accent would soon become annoying. And she quite obviously bit her nails – a disgusting habit.

Ramirez droned on, while Gregory reconciled himself to the fact that there was no escape until this lecture on gang-life reached its conclusion.

Katy seemed fascinated, while her husband – a tall, skinny jerk in even tighter jeans than his wife's – snapped away.

Gregory endeavored to keep a concerned expression on his face. Not easy. Was Ramirez ever going to shut up?

* * *

It's me again, where are you? Carolyn texted to Denver. *Call me as soon as you get this. I have major news.*

She checked her message machine one more time to make absolutely certain that Gregory had not tried to contact her.

It was a wasted effort. Of course he would not phone her – Sunday was family day. Although, in view of her condition she'd hoped for at least a short message. Surely that wasn't asking too much?

Yes, it was. He was most likely busy with his kids, and oblivious to all else. Gregory was a wonderful father, and one of these days he'd be a wonderful father to the baby she was carrying.

Escaping from Nellie's apartment had not been easy. The old woman loved to talk, so between her and Kerri's non-stop chatter, it had been an exhausting day. She couldn't wait for Monday when she would be back in the office with Gregory a mere few yards away. Meanwhile she had nothing to do except daydream about their future together.

Nothing wrong with that.

* * *

After Ramirez's neverending lecture, rescue finally appeared in the form of two Latino males in their early twenties who marched straight up to Ramirez – shoving people out of the way – and began harassing him in Spanish, yelling and waving their arms around in a threatening fashion.

Although it was apparent that Ramirez was attempting to keep his cool, after a few moments he snapped and began yelling back.

Jesus Christ! Gregory thought. *What the hell is going on?*

He took a quick look toward the entrance, wondering if he should just go – get out before this escalated. He didn't speak Spanish, but the anger taking place between Ramirez and the two men was palpable.

Katy was open-mouthed, while her husband continued to snap photos – until one of the men flashed him the universal *fuck you* sign and spat the words, "Quit with the mothafuckin' camera or I'll shove it up yo' mothafuckin' white ass."

Nice to know they spoke English.

The agitated man returned his attention to Ramirez and the argument continued.

Katy moved toward Gregory. "Do you speak Spanish, Senator?" she whispered.

"No, I don't" he responded, getting a pleasant whiff of her floral scent. "Do you?"

"They're fighting about some kind of drug deal," she said in a low voice. "They're claiming Ramirez owes them money and that he should pay up or else."

"How is he responding?"

"He's telling them to get out."

"But they're not listening."

"No." She shook her head. "I think the one with the red bandanna might be his brother."

Gregory took a second look at the man with the red bandanna tied across his forehead. He was clad in the usual uniform of oversized T-shirt, baggy pants sitting so low they looked ready to fall off, and untied yellow, black and silver sneakers. A large gold medallion hung from a long chain around his neck, while his forearms were covered in various tattoos. He did indeed resemble a younger version of Ramirez, but whereas Ramirez radiated a certain amount of calm, this young male's face was twisted with bitter anger.

Katy's husband had packed away his camera and now he grabbed his wife's arm. "Let's go," he said abruptly. "Who knows where this is heading."

"Senator Stoneman," Katy said, quite wide-eyed, "you should leave with us."

"Yes, yes, I think that's an excellent idea," Gregory agreed, silently cursing Evelyn for allowing him to get trapped in such a potentially volatile situation. "Lead on, I'll follow."

The moment they got outside, Katy's husband bundled her into his truck which was conveniently double-parked. He barely gave her a chance to bid Gregory goodbye before taking off, leaving a bemused and somewhat annoyed Senator standing alone on the overgrown sidewalk. Gregory was not at all pleased. What a waste of a perfectly good Sunday.

As he started off down the street, hoping and praying that his car was parked exactly where he'd left it, a commotion erupted from the front of the center, and the two Latino males who'd been arguing with Ramirez came racing out and began running down the street. A beaten-up old car roared into view.

Gregory turned to look. Suddenly shots rang out. He felt something graze past his head, knocking him backwards.

Then he was falling . . . falling . . . and everything turned to black.

Chapter Twenty

Bobby

"I'm getting a strong vibe that this is all a game for you," Bobby said, coming to the realization that he'd fallen right into Zeena's cleverly planned trap.

She'd arrived at his apartment with every intention of luring him into bed, and naturally he'd gone for it. Why wouldn't he? She was major hot and he had a thing for her. It was a no-brainer. Except why – after the act – did he feel like a girl who'd given it up on the first date? Gotten fucked way too fast.

Man, he was so mad at himself.

"A game?" Zeena questioned, casually propping herself up on one elbow, long dark hair draped around her broad shoulders. Totally naked and beyond fit, she was all sleek burnished skin, sinewy muscles and lean loose limbs.

"Yeah, a game," he repeated. And then, determined to make a point, he added, "But you know what, Zeena, I'm not one of your toy boys – the kind of guy you can have your fun with then shove aside."

"Did I say you were, Bobby?" she drawled, arching a perfectly plucked and penciled eyebrow. "And *I* should point out," she added succinctly, "there is nothing *little* about you. But I'm sure many women have told you that."

"I'm serious," he said, trying to shake the feeling that she'd used him for her own pleasure and amusement.

"So young," she sighed, slowly licking her lips. "Sad that Zeena always gravitates toward the young ones."

"How come you're pulling the age card?" he said, irritated because her cavalier attitude was beyond annoying. "What are you – fifteen years older than me? Today that's nothing."

"Actually," she opined, leaning across him to reach her crocodile purse she'd placed on the floor beside the bed, her exceptionally large hard nipples brushing against his chest, "you're more mature than my usual conquests."

Conquests! Was she referring to him as a conquest? Goddamn it! Who exactly did she think she was dealing with? He was a Santangelo. He'd better start acting like one.

Removing a pack of Gauloises from her purse she let forth a low throaty chuckle. "Poor Bobby," she said mockingly. "So handsome, so rich, but you need to work on your self-esteem, and maybe your lovemaking technique could use some improvement."

Shaking his head in wonderment, he realized she was Serenity all over again – a dismissive bitch on wheels trying to screw with his self-confidence. Nobody had ever complained about his lovemaking technique before. As far as he knew he was an accomplished lover, considerate, not too fast, and he was pretty certain he made all the right moves.

What kind of head trip was she trying to pull?

"I thought you came," he said shortly.

"Zeena always comes, Bobby," she said, lighting up her cigarette. "She makes sure of it."

Now he was really pissed. "What're you saying? That you don't need me? That you can do it all by yourself?"

"Any woman who depends on a man to give her an

orgasm is either a fool or in love," she responded, blowing lazy smoke-rings in his direction. "Zeena discovered that a long time ago."

Great, just great. He'd performed to the best of his ability and she was putting him down. Was this her idea of after-play? Most women opted for a smooch and a few kind words. Zeena preferred to go for the jugular.

He should've known.

"I guess we're done here," he said, staunchly refusing to let her get to him any more than she already had.

She stretched like a particularly athletic cat, throwing her muscled arms high above her head and making a purring sound.

"Zeena is in no hurry," she assured him. "Whenever you're ready, perhaps we should try again."

And with that she stubbed out her cigarette on his glass-topped bedside table, turned to him, trailed her long fingers down his chest and murmured, "How long do you think that will be, Bobby? Zeena can get very impatient."

* * *

Later, when he awoke, he had no idea when Zeena had left, because it was now early Monday morning, and there was no sign of her.

Although when he sat up and took a look around, he discovered a few signs. The cigarette stubs on his bedside table; the brandy glass half-filled with Cognac – the imprint of her blood-red lipstick still on the glass; the smell of her musky scent wafting in the air like some kind of olfactory reminder.

Was he surprised?

No. He should've guessed she would leave silently in the middle of the night without so much as a goodbye.

She was the man.

He was the woman.

Fuck! It was an infuriating situation.

Every time she'd suggested that they make love, he'd complied. Well, it wasn't happening again. He was about to man-up, stop with the girlish infatuation and redeem his balls.

The second time they'd fucked she'd made him feel as if he was auditioning for the role of the perfect lover. Any moment he had the feeling that she was about to call out, "Sorry, not good enough. Next!"

Zeena. What a frigging ball-breaker!

And yet . . .

No! He was not signing up for a second round. No way.

His phone rang and he jumped to answer it. Maybe it was Zeena calling to tell him that she'd had a fantastic and unforgettable time, that he was the best lover she'd ever had, and when could they do it again?

It was M.J.

"Wassup?" Bobby mumbled, once again surveying the pile of cigarette butts on his glass-topped table. Miz Superstar could at least have requested an ashtray. But no, that wasn't her style. Zeena lived to screw with people, she was into testing them – just to see exactly what she could get away with.

"We got an eleven o'clock with the Russian investors for the Miami and possibly Moscow deals," M.J. reminded him. "Don't tell me you forgot?"

Bobby squinted at his watch. "It's not even eight, M.J. What's with the panic?"

"No panic, man. I was thinking that before the meeting we should drop by an' see Annabelle, pay our respects."

"Yeah, you're totally right," Bobby agreed. "I'll call Frankie, give him a heads up we're coming over."

"Do that, an' while we're talkin' – what happened to you last night? I thought you were joining us at Nobu?"

"Got hung up."

"Anyone I know?"

"An old girlfriend stopped by."

"Didja—"

"Don't even ask," Bobby said quickly. "Let's just say it was a very long night."

Clicking off the phone, he made his way to the kitchen where he grabbed a bunch of paper towels, returned to the bedroom and cleaned up Zeena's mess of stubbed-out cigarettes.

Who *did* that kind of thing? It was gross. Why ***hadn't*** she asked for an ashtray? She certainly hadn't been shy about asking him to go down on her. Actually not so much asking, more like an imperious command.

"Let Zeena see what your tongue can do, Bobby," she'd murmured, as if his cock was a non-starter.

Jesus! She'd made him feel so damned inadequate.

He'd gone down on her for almost half an hour and she hadn't come. She was holding back purposely, he knew it.

Then they'd started to fuck again. He was no slouch, but this woman's energy was endless; she was one unstoppable bundle of yoga moves and impossible positions. By the time they were finished he felt as if he'd gone several rounds with Mike Tyson at his peak.

She'd requested handcuffs.

He didn't have any.

She'd requested a vibrator.

He didn't have that either.

She'd told him she enjoyed being spanked with leather gloves.

Too bad. Leather gloves were not his thing. Come to think of it, nor was spanking or vibrators or handcuffs. Weren't they dirty old man fetishes?

"Next time Zeena will come prepared," she'd sniffed.

What made her think there would be a next time?

After the sex marathon he'd fallen asleep and woken to her absence.

Now it was morning and she was gone.

Get over it, he told himself. *Forget about Miz Kinky Superstar. She's a bad drug, and you know it.*

He was over her.

Oh yes, he was definitely over her.

Chapter Twenty-One

Annabelle

"We're flying to L.A. tomorrow," Frankie informed Annabelle. "We're headin' over to the SoHo apartment first thing an' meetin' your dad's lawyer. How about that?"

Annabelle threw him a baleful look. "I thought I told you—"

"No!" he interrupted sharply. "You gotta be there for your mom's funeral, you'd never forgive yourself if you weren't. So that's it, babe. I made the decision, an' we're goin. The lawyer's put together all the arrangements for us to travel in style."

Annabelle was about to argue further, but then she decided against it. Frankie was right, she should go to her mother's funeral. Besides, after watching the devastating story unfold on TV she was anxious to find out the real truth.

Could it be possible that her father *was* a suspect?

No. Impossible. Movie-star Daddy would never harm Gemma, he'd loved and adored his beautiful wife to the exclusion of everyone else – including his own daughter.

Annabelle had often reflected on the few times she'd been alone with her movie star dad. He'd never complimented her or asked about her life – it was always about how exquisite and talented Gemma was, how loyal and sweet-natured. "You should try to be more like her," he'd once said in a gruff voice. "Your mother is the perfect woman."

Annabelle had immediately taken that to mean that she was the imperfect daughter.

No wonder she couldn't wait to get away. Far, far away.

Now she was going back, because Frankie was right – she'd always have something to regret if she didn't.

California, here I come, she thought sourly.

"Why are we going to the SoHo apartment?" she asked, trying to make up her mind what outfits she should pack.

"'Cause that's where your family think you live," Frankie explained. "And if they find out about Park Avenue, that could open up a shitload of questions 'bout how you can afford it."

"Perhaps I should tell Daddy Dearest about our highly successful business," she said, a spiteful gleam in her eyes. "That way he might finally notice me."

"C'mon, babe," Frankie groaned. "Ralph can't be *that* bad."

"Wait until you meet him. Mister Movie Star is not easy, you'll see for yourself."

"Yeah, but you're forgettin' that I get along with everyone," Frankie boasted. "Mister Movie Star Daddy's gonna like me plenty."

"We'll put it to the test," Annabelle said, opening up her jewelry drawer and selecting a few choice pieces to take with her. "And I'm telling you now," she added, "I am absolutely *not* staying at the house."

"All taken care of," Frankie said triumphantly. "Suite at the Beverly Hills Hotel. Twenty-four-hour limo on tap. Am I a comer or what?"

"Ralph agreed to everything?" she questioned, surprised that her controlling father hadn't insisted they stay at the house.

"He wants you in L.A., doesn't he?"

"I guess so," she said, dreading the fact that she would have to spend time with her father. "By the way, what about our business? We can't just take off."

"I got it all under control, babe. Janey's steppin' in to make sure everything runs smooth as syrup."

"Oh, that's just great," Annabelle sneered.

"She's practically doin' that anyway," Frankie said.

"Not really," Annabelle argued. "It's you who recruits the girls, and it's me who usually deals with the clients."

"I'm gonna have Janey move in here while we're away."

"Guess I'd better lock my closet," Annabelle said caustically. "I'm sure she'd love nothing better than to play dress up."

"Why're you always so down on her?" Frankie said, his left eye starting to twitch. "She's doin' an okay job."

Annabelle had her doubts. She didn't care for Janey and it showed. She and Frankie had a thriving business going on, they were raking in big bucks galore, and she didn't want anyone screwing things up. Leaving Frankie's cousin in charge could be a major mistake.

"Maybe you should stay here with Janey," she suggested. "Y'know, just in case any problems come up."

"No way," Frankie said, frowning. He had no intention of missing out on a trip to L.A. "Janey can handle everything. Besides," he added, sidling close and stroking her arm. "My best girl ain't goin' nowhere without me, an' that's a Frankie Romano promise."

* * *

"I wanna speak to the person in charge," Chip Bonafacio insisted, his shifty eyes darting this way and that.

It was early Monday morning and he was standing at the reception desk of a huge glass and chrome building – home to one of the biggest tabloids around – *Truth & Fact*.

The girl sitting behind the desk – a trashy bleached blonde with strawlike hair extensions and badly applied fake eyelashes, was giving him a hard time, even though he'd told her he had a major story to sell.

"Do you have an appointment?" she asked for the third time.

"I keep on tellin' you – I don't *need* an appointment," he said impatiently, well aware that the acne he so dreaded was sprouting up all over his chin. Aggravation always accelerated his condition, and this skank was giving him a hard time.

"Yes, you *do*," she said, glaring at him. "Everyone does."

"Even George Clooney?" he said, challenging the douche.

"You're not George Clooney," she answered scornfully, wondering if she was going to have to call security to get rid of this loser.

"What's your name?" he snapped.

"My name? Why do you want *my* name?"

"'Cause when they buy my story for a million bucks, I'm gonna make sure your skinny ass gets fired."

"Oh yeah?" she said, in full sneer. "Like *you* got a story worth selling."

Chip took a step back. "Gonna risk it?" he asked, giving her what he considered his most effective stink-eye. "I drove up in a Mercedes, I'm not some bum off the street, y'know. I got connections, I know important people."

The girl tapped her talon-like nails on the glass-topped reception counter. Like her eyelashes, they were fake, and last night at a party with her wanna-be rapper boyfriend, one of them had fallen off. Her head was pounding from too many Appletinis the night before, and she was not enjoying this exchange. She was certainly not enjoying this jerk's threats about getting her fired. What if he was legit and *did* have a hot story? Would she get the blame for not letting him through?

Deciding *not* to risk it, she made a snap decision. "Mr Waitrose isn't in today, but his right hand is," she said, avoiding eye-contact. "You can go on up, sixth floor. Someone'll meet you at the elevator."

Chip was elated. That shit about taking down an employee's name actually worked! He'd watched Frankie do it a dozen times, and it had always worked for him. Now he, Chip Bonafacio, was also the man.

Good freakin' goin'.

* * *

Before leaving their apartment in the morning for the SoHo loft, Annabelle got on the phone with several of the girls who worked for them on occasion. She wanted to make sure they all knew that dealing with Janey was only a temporary measure while she was away on a quick business trip to L.A.

Next she called Janey and gave her explicit instructions on how to behave toward the girls when they came by the apartment. "No gossiping," she warned. "No driving them crazy with inane chatter. And *no* asking for autographs. Understood?"

"As if," Janey whined, conveniently forgetting the time she'd asked a fairly well-known lingerie model to sign her centerspread in *Playboy.* Janey hated dealing with Annabelle, Frankie was her main guy.

"As long as we've got that straight," Annabelle said, thinking about Frankie's suggestion the previous night that he give Janey the combination to their safe. She'd told him absolutely no way.

"C'mon, babe," he'd said, trying to persuade her to give in. "What's she supposed to do with all the cash the girls deliver?"

"She can hide it under her fat ass," Annabelle had said, with no intention of budging on this one. "I'm sure she's got plenty of room."

Frankie's cash-only policy was well in place. Sometimes the

clients paid ahead of time – like Sharif Rani – but usually it was the girls who collected the cash, and then later they dropped off the commission. It wasn't the best way of doing business, but Frankie adhered to his no paper trail policy. That way, he figured, they could never get caught.

His naïveté was impressive.

Chapter Twenty-Two

Denver

I am not a tramp and I am certainly not a slut – words men like to use to put women down. I simply happen to enjoy sex, and quite frankly – why the hell shouldn't I? If one takes the proper precautions there is nothing wrong with a fast one-nighter.

Okay, so it was *two* fast one-nighters – and not so fast at that.

Hey, if I was a guy, nobody would blink.

As I've mentioned countless times, I'm coming off a major dry spell, and I happen to have met two interesting and sexy guys. Mario of the fab abs, and Sam – who's a little bit quirky and seems like a really nice guy. The abs might not be quite as fab as Mario's, but everything else is in primo working order, and yes – the sex was once again memorable.

I can't recall exactly how it happened. Well yes, actually I can. After I'd gotten on the phone and made all the arrangements for Annabelle and Frankie's forthcoming trip, Sam decided I needed to chill out, so he'd cracked open a bottle of red wine, and we'd giggled that wine and scrambled eggs didn't exactly go together, but it was an unusual mix.

No, I did not get drunk, just slightly . . . happy. And when he kissed me it was mutual and warm and nice. Kissing is an art, and Sam kind of had it down.

We kissed for a long time before he ventured further, and that was okay because he was a good kisser. Hey – we're both adults, and the kissing progressed to a place where neither of us cared to stop. And there was absolutely no reason why we should.

Sam had moves that reminded me of that ode to awesome lovemaking by the Pointer Sisters – "Slow Hand." Adele or Duffy should definitely rush into the studio and re-make that one – they'd score a mega-hit.

Anyway, I digress. Let me put it this way – Sam was also a winner in bed. Totally different style from Mario, but a winner all the same. Sam's touch was measured, more tactile, in a way more loving. Now I know that sounds ridiculous, since I've only known him a few hours, but I feel the connection big-time.

Am I out of control?

No way. I'm a normal, healthy American female, acting like a normal, healthy American male. Good for me!

It's Monday morning and I'm psyched. Today I get to accompany Annabelle and her pushy boyfriend to L.A.

Sam is in the shower. I considered joining him, but since we're not exactly a couple I squashed the thought.

Josh and I used to shower together. It saved on energy, and we probably had our best sex with cascades of water raining down on us. I wonder if Josh now showers with Miss Stylist-to-the-stars? Probably not. I was the one who always instigated it.

Now why was I thinking about Josh?

I do occasionally. No reason.

Jumping out of Sam's comfortable and cozy bed, I reached for my BlackBerry. There were numerous messages, none that required urgent attention. I smiled at a cryptic text from Carolyn, and immediately texted her back. *In New York. Back to L.A. today. Can't wait to hear your news.*

Sam came strolling in fresh from the shower, a towel knotted casually around his waist. "It's all yours," he said.

Did he mean the shower or what I knew was lurking under the towel?

I mentally slapped myself. I was having too much fun when I should be concentrating on work. Besides, I was anxious to get back to L.A. and find out exactly what was going on. *Was* Ralph a suspect in his wife's murder? Or was the media simply conjuring up a series of meaningless headlines to sell papers, magazines and TV shows?

"Thanks," I said, not feeling at all awkward about the previous evening's activities, even though I was wrapped in a bedsheet with nothing but my yesterday's clothes to put back on.

I headed for the bathroom and closed the door. Sam had laid out a toothbrush still in its package, and a small travel tube of Crest. I added thoughtful to his list of attributes.

Wow! I couldn't wait to tell Carolyn about my two guys. Superstud Mario – all hot passionate Latino sex. And Sam – laid back, smart, and considerate.

Standing under a torrent of soothing warm water felt delightful. I was anticipating my meeting with Annabelle. What would she be like now? Still the same spoiled, entitled human being? Or maybe she'd evolved. And how about Frankie Romano? On the phone he'd sounded way cocky with his list of demands. Would I hate him on sight? I had a thing about men who considered themselves superior beings. Frankie sounded like that kind of guy.

I peered at my reflection in the bathroom mirror. Not good. Julia Roberts indeed. Ha! More like Julia Child! Anyway I did the best I could to make myself look presentable for my upcoming escort duties.

After I was dressed, I emerged from the bathroom to find Sam busying himself in the kitchen making pancakes.

"Are you sure you're a writer and not a chef?" I quipped, thinking how fine he looked in a faded denim shirt and jeans. He was barefoot, and his curly hair – still damp from the shower – was ruffled and quite sexy.

"Yesterday was a big surprise," he remarked, throwing me an appreciative look. "I wasn't expecting a beautiful woman to fall into my local coffee shop."

I felt myself blushing. And I am *so* not the kind of girl who blushes.

"I wasn't exactly expecting to spend the night with such an . . . uh . . . interesting man," I managed.

He raised an eyebrow and half-smiled. "Interesting? Is that all you can come up with?"

"It's short notice, give me time."

"You can have all the time you want."

"Thanks," I said, slightly flustered, "but I've got to get two people on a plane to L.A. so you'll have to give me a rain check."

"It's only nine," he said, handing me a glass of what looked suspiciously like freshly squeezed orange juice. "Sit down and enjoy your pancakes."

"You sound like my mom."

"Gee, thanks," he said wryly. "My life's ambition has always been to sound like someone's mom."

It suddenly occurred to me that I should definitely have breakfast with this man that I'd spent the night with, because I'd probably never see him again. And I liked him. Besides, I had nowhere else to go. I could hardly stand outside Annabelle's front door for an hour.

"Can I get syrup with my pancakes?" I asked. "The real thing, not some low-fat substitute."

"Do I look like a guy who'd give you a substitute?"

"No," I said, sitting down on a stool, watching him flip a pancake.

"Then relax and enjoy," he said, transferring the pancake to a plate and handing it to me, following up with a glass bottle of organic maple syrup – the expensive kind. No Aunt Jemima for him.

I poured on the syrup and took a bite. "Delicious!" I exclaimed. "Who taught you to be such a whizz in the kitchen?"

"Remember the bitch fiancée I was telling you about . . ."

"You're kidding?"

"She was – *is* – a professional chef."

"Well, at least she left you with something."

"That's a matter of opinion."

"You sound bitter."

"Not at all," he said easily. "I'm a great believer in things happen for a reason, and if I was still with her I wouldn't be spending the morning with a refreshingly bright and beautiful L.A.-based attorney."

Hmm . . . that's the second time he's called me beautiful. Flattery will definitely get him wherever he wants to go.

"You're pretty free with the compliments," I remarked, gulping down my orange juice – which was indeed freshly squeezed.

"Only when they're deserved," he said, flipping a second pancake onto my plate.

"Are you trying to make me fat?" I joked. "I'm already enormous by L.A. standards."

"You have an incredible body," he said.

Wow! The compliments were coming fast and furious. Enough already.

"Do you mind if we put on the TV?" I said quickly. "I need to see what's happening with the Maestro case."

He handed me the clicker. "Go ahead."

The Today Show was all over it. Matt, Meredith, Al and Ann were in the middle of one of their group discussions. The theme was Hollywood justice. The question was – how come celebrities always manage to walk? They didn't mention Ralph by name, but the implication was, it was a big possibility that he could've done it.

"Give me your cell phone," Sam said, leaning over me.

"Excuse me?"

"I'm putting all my information in it so you'll have no excuse not to stay in touch."

I couldn't think of a good reason to object. Besides, I wanted all his various forms of communication – address, cell, home phone, e-mail. I'd just spent the night with the guy, so why not?

Obediently I handed him my phone, and in return he handed me his. Obviously it's the latest form of intimacy – downloading all your information into someone else's cell phone.

"So . . ." I ventured, "I'll be going soon."

"I have something for you," he said.

Oh dear me, I hope it's not payment for our night of lust. How humiliating would that be if he thought I was a hooker masquerading as a lawyer!

Did I mention that I have a very active imagination?

"What is it?" I asked tentatively.

"No arguments," he said, reaching down and handing me his knit cap and striped scarf.

"Wow!" I managed, graciously accepting his gift.

"At least it'll keep you warm on your way to the airport."

"Thanks, Sam," I said, quite touched that he was concerned about my welfare. "That's very thoughtful of you."

He grinned, crooked teeth fully on display. "Don't mention it," he said, before leaning over again and giving me a warm hug.

I reached up and hugged him back, inhaling his masculine scent and quite loving it.

What a shame he doesn't live in L.A. This could be the start of something . . .

Or not.

Chapter Twenty-Three

Carolyn

Waking up lying on an unmade bed in an unfamiliar room, Senator Gregory Stoneman struggled to remember where he was and what exactly had taken place. His mind was a jumble of thoughts. Jesus Christ! Had he been *shot*? Shouldn't he be in a hospital? What the *hell* was going on?

His head was throbbing as he attempted to sit up and get his bearings.

A scowling but pretty young girl in cut-off jeans and a tight orange tank-top loomed into view, gazed down at him and yelled over her shoulder, "Yo – Benito! The old dude's awake."

Benito, the energetic Latino male with the red bandanna cutting a swathe across his forehead, sprang into the room.

"Yo, man," Benito muttered, wild eyes darting around like a caged rat. "You had some kinda shit-ass fall. We took you in so's we could help."

"What are you talking about?" Gregory said, reaching up to examine the side of his head with his hand. His temple felt sore, rough to the touch, and extremely tender. "I didn't fall," he said, filled with a sudden flash of anger. "If I recall correctly, somebody took a shot at me."

"Accident, man," Benito said, shifting on his colorful sneakers. "Bullet skimmed past – you got nothin' but a dumb-ass graze."

"Excuse me?" Gregory said, his fury building.

"Listen, man – nobody want trouble, an' you don't want no bad publicity up in yo shit, that's why we help you."

"You didn't *help* me," Gregory said outraged, sitting up all the way. "It was no doubt *you* who shot me. I'm calling the police."

"Told ya," the scowling girl brayed triumphantly. "He gonna turn yo mothafuckin' ass in."

"Shut the fuck up," Benito snarled, turning on her. "He ain't callin' no fuckhead cops."

"Why am I here?" Gregory demanded. "Why didn't you take me straight to the Emergency Room?"

"'Cuz I tole ya – you ain't got nothin' but a scratch," Benito explained. "You one lucky sombitch. Gun went off by accident. But if the cops get a smell, I go back inside, an' I ain't goin' back again 'cause a some dumb-fuck accident. You unnerstan'?"

"No," Gregory said grimly. "I certainly do not understand."

Benito bounced around on the balls of his feet. The large gold medallion sitting on his chest began flying across his baggy T-shirt.

"*Accident*, man," he repeated, taking a reassuring grope of his crotch. "Ya gotta unnerstan'. I did you bad, now you be here, an' I be puttin' it t'you like I'm sorry, that kinda shit. An' anythin' you want me t'do – anythin' – then we gonna be even."

Suddenly Gregory felt everything fall into place. He understood. He got it.

God had heard his pleas for help and handed him the solution to his biggest problem of all.

Benito was standing before him. His savior.

* * *

Most people dreaded going to work on a Monday morning since it signaled the end of the weekend, and five long working days loomed ahead. Carolyn, however, couldn't wait. To her, Monday morning meant five exciting days working in close proximity to Senator Gregory Stoneman. *Her* Senator Gregory Stoneman, because soon he would be all hers.

She couldn't help wondering if he'd told Evelyn yet. Had the opportunity arisen? And if not, why not? The time had come for him to quit with the weak excuses. The time had come for him to be strong and stand up to Evelyn once and for all. That's exactly what he'd promised to do.

She was smiling as she entered the office. She greeted Gregory's newest male intern, and nodded at his other executive assistant, Muriel – an older woman who took care of arranging his speaking engagements and social events.

"Morning, everyone," she said brightly. "Isn't it a gorgeous day?"

Muriel, drab in a sludge-brown pantsuit that emphasized her pear-shaped figure – glanced at her as if she was out of her mind. "It's actually extremely cold," Muriel said, tight-lipped. "And this afternoon the weather forecast calls for rain and maybe even snow."

"Ah yes," Carolyn answered cheerily. "But right now the sun is peeking through the clouds, and later, if we're lucky, we might see a rainbow."

"Always the optimist," Muriel said, making optimist sound like a dirty word.

There was not much love lost between the two women. Muriel had worked for the Senator for ten years, and when Carolyn had come aboard, she'd felt slighted. Muriel had always resented Carolyn, especially when she'd begun to suspect that there was more than a professional relationship between "the new girl" as she always referred to Carolyn, and her boss, the esteemed Senator.

"Senator Stoneman will not be in this morning," Muriel

said, delighted that it was *she* imparting the information and not Carolyn telling her.

"What do you mean he won't be in?" Carolyn asked, the smile slipping from her face. "How do you know?"

"Mrs Stoneman called me at home."

"And said what?" Carolyn asked, her mind racing in all directions.

"She told me that he won't be in until this afternoon."

"Why did she call *you*?"

"Is there a problem with that?" Muriel snapped, stretching her scrawny neck.

"Uh . . . no," Carolyn said. "I simply wondered why she didn't call me."

"I've known the Senator's wife for many years," Muriel replied with a superior smirk. "We often speak on the phone."

"That's – uh – fine," Carolyn said, determined not to let the fact that she was ruffled show. "Did she give you a reason why the Senator is coming in late?"

"No," Muriel said, satisfied that she'd ruined the "new girl's" day. "I've already cancelled all his morning and noon appointments, no need for you to bother."

Furious that Muriel had taken it upon herself to cancel appointments that she should have been dealing with, Carolyn retreated to her small but pleasant office.

Had Gregory told Evelyn, and that's why he wasn't coming in until later? It was a possibility. Evelyn might be hysterical, so it stood to reason that he was busy handling the situation. Perhaps they were already meeting with a divorce lawyer.

Experiencing a shiver of excitement, Carolyn decided that Gregory had finally done it, she was sure. After their talk on Saturday when she'd revealed that she was pregnant, he'd obviously realized that it was time to take action. There could be no more stalling.

Good for Gregory. She couldn't wait to see him.

* * *

Late Sunday afternoon, Gregory had returned home with a plaster covering his grazed temple and a raging headache. Evelyn was in the living room entertaining several of her women friends to a game of canasta. She'd hardly looked up when Gregory had walked into the house. Later on, she'd noticed the plaster, and with an extreme lack of interest had asked him what had happened.

"Ran into a door at that damn slum you sent me to," he'd said shortly, and that was that. She hadn't even bothered to inquire what had transpired between him and Ramirez.

That night he'd hardly slept. His mind was on high alert, wondering if the scenario he'd arranged with Ramirez's brother Benito would work. It was a crazy insane plan that he'd come up with and he knew it. But had Carolyn given him any choice?

No.

Carolyn was determined to ruin and shatter his life; she'd forced him to fight back. It wasn't his fault, it was all hers.

Benito. A young Latino man with criminal tendencies. A drug dealer who'd been in and out of juvenile hall and then prison from the age of fourteen. A desperate man, for if Benito was accused of shooting at a Senator, they would surely throw the book at him, lock him away for a long, long time. There was the matter of a kidnapping too. Instead of taking him to a hospital or the Emergency Room, Benito had bundled him into his wreck of a car and transported him to the rundown condemned house he called home.

Yes, that was kidnapping all right – a federal offense.

The truth was that Benito had not been shooting at him at all. As Benito was leaving the community center, a car full of rival gang members had driven by, spotted him and started shooting. Benito had immediately retaliated, hence the stray bullet that had whizzed past Gregory's head.

Gregory was well aware that had it been a direct hit he would've been killed. Just like that. Gone in seconds.

But it wasn't a direct hit. And as it turned out, it was a fortuitous happening. A happening of which he planned on taking full advantage.

* * *

For over an hour Carolyn debated with herself whether she should call Gregory's home. After all, she *was* his assistant, and it *was* a workday. Surely she was allowed to call his house?

Unless Evelyn knew about her, then it wouldn't be such a clever move. No. Not clever at all.

But still . . . she was, as always, anxious to speak to him, if only to hear the sound of his voice.

Reluctantly she ventured into Muriel's office. The room smelled of lilac and stale cigarette smoke. Yes, Muriel had a bad habit – she smoked, although she always pretended that she'd given it up. The overpowering smell of lilacs concealed nothing.

"Did Mrs Stoneman give any indication of what time the Senator might come in today?" Carolyn asked.

Muriel glanced up from her desk, brow furrowed. "No, dear, she didn't."

"I see," Carolyn said, adding a cheerful, "Well, I'm sure he'll be in soon."

"Or not," Muriel said tartly.

"Excuse me?"

"Perhaps he's taking the day off," Muriel suggested with a sly smirk. "Perhaps he and Mrs Stoneman are spending some quality time together while the children are at school."

Carolyn couldn't help herself. "Why would he want to do that?" she blurted.

"Their wedding anniversary is coming up next week,"

Muriel said, the sly smirk still hovering on her thin lips. "I would imagine he might be taking her shopping to her favorite jewelry store."

Carolyn backed out of the room. That was *so* not happening. He'd be in soon, and everything would be fine.

Chapter Twenty-Four

Bobby & Annabelle

While Bobby waited for M.J. to pick him up, Frankie called to tell him that if they wanted to see Annabelle, they should come to the SoHo apartment. "We'll be there," Bobby said.

Try as he might, he could not seem to put Zeena on the back-burner. She was on his mind big-time. And how dumb was that? The woman was famous, a freaking superstar, and he didn't even have her phone number.

He hadn't asked.

She hadn't offered.

Which meant that if he wanted to reach her, how was he supposed to do that?

It didn't matter because he had no desire to contact her, did he?

A warning voice in his head stated, *"No way."*

Another voice said, *"Sure. Why not? It's one helluva crazy ride. Why not take it?"*

Obviously his emotions were conflicted. His hunch was that whenever Zeena decided, she would simply turn up at his apartment unannounced, just as she had the first time, and knowing Zeena she'd expect an instant replay.

He realized this was not a healthy situation. The woman was messing with his head, and if he was smart he'd get out now before she appeared at his door armed with handcuffs, vibrators, and God knew what else.

Was he strong enough to turn her away?

He would have to put that one to the test.

* * *

Annabelle fidgeted on the back seat of the Mercedes. She was all packed and ready to go to L.A., but as they headed for the SoHo apartment to meet the lawyer her father had sent, she couldn't help feeling scared. What would it be like, facing Ralph? She hadn't seen him in over a year. In fact, she hadn't seen either of her esteemed parents for that amount of time. Now she would never see her mother again – unless Ralph opted for an open casket, and she suspected he wouldn't go for that, not since Gemma had been shot in the face, her ethereal beauty obliterated for all time.

Annabelle remembered their last meeting. Ralph's latest over-the-top movie was première-ing in New York, and they'd invited her to attend the grand opening. She hadn't wanted to go, so she'd claimed she was too busy with her design business, and instead she'd dropped by the Four Seasons where they were staying.

The three of them had sat down for breakfast in their luxurious VIP suite. As usual Annabelle could remember thinking that they were the most beautiful couple she'd ever seen, so physically perfect in every way. Ralph, tall and craggy-faced – resplendent in silk pajamas, a burgundy robe, and fancy monogrammed slippers. Gemma, a fairy princess in a pale-pink negligée, golden curls surrounding her exquisite face, small diamond stud earrings affixed to her delicate earlobes.

They'd seemed pleased to see her.

"You look lovely," Gemma had said with a faint note of surprise.

"Yes." Ralph had nodded his large superhero head. "New York obviously agrees with you."

She took their words to mean that they would prefer she stayed in New York – out of sight and out of mind, away from the dazzling stardom of her illustrious parents.

Ralph had slipped her a check for ten thousand dollars. "A little extra something," he'd said with a jaunty wink. "Spend it wisely."

Yes, Daddy, she'd thought. *I promise I'll spend it wisely and not return to L.A. to disturb your idyllic life together.*

That was then and this was now. Soon she'd be on a plane back to L.A., her unfavorite place.

"You okay?" Frankie asked, patting her on the knee.

"I'm fine," she replied coolly. "Why wouldn't I be?"

Frankie shrugged. One moment she was hysterical about Sharif Rani's rough son – and the next, she was all together and composed, planning what outfits she would take to L.A. Her mother being murdered didn't seem to factor in to anything. He'd never really understood Annabelle and her mood swings. But who cared? He was too busy trying to be blasé about the trip, although he was definitely psyched they were going. The circumstances might not be ideal – but hey – he was heading for L.A. And he couldn't wait.

* * *

Both Bobby and M.J. felt right about stopping by to pay their respects to Annabelle. The three of them went way back to their high-school days, and although they'd never been that close, there were a few shared memories – especially the infamous prom night when the three of them had gotten way beyond wasted and ended up having a threesome in a suite at the Beverly

Hills Hotel thoughtfully reserved for Annabelle by her loving parents – who wanted their girl to have a memorable prom night with her friends. Oh yes, it had turned out to be memorable all right, although everyone's memories of it were quite fuddled due to the amount of alcohol consumed.

Frankie greeted the guys at the door to the SoHo apartment, where he'd asked them to come.

"Why're you here and not at the Park Avenue place?" M.J. wanted to know.

"'Cause this is where Ralph thinks Annabelle lives," Frankie explained. "He's sending his lawyer to escort us to L.A. Gotta stay cool."

"Right," Bobby agreed.

"We're travelin' first-class all the way," Frankie boasted. "I got it all arranged."

"Wouldn't doubt it," Bobby said.

Annabelle appeared wearing a sleek Valentino jumpsuit, thigh-high Jimmy Choo boots and a short, stylish fox-fur jacket. Her pale red hair was half-pulled back, and large black-out Chanel sunglasses concealed her eyes.

"Hey guys," she said in a world-weary voice.

They took turns hugging her while letting forth with the usual words of, "Sorry for your loss."

"And *I'm* sorry for dragging you to this place – it's such a dump," Annabelle grumbled, staring around the light and airy space which was by no means a dump.

"We're only here for fifteen minutes," Frankie said sharply. "Stop bitchin'."

Annabelle raised her sunglasses and threw him a dirty look. Frankie was starting to get on her nerves. Why couldn't she have hooked up with someone like Bobby? He was way hot and so good-looking. The two of them would make a dynamite combination. Plus he was rich. Mega-rich. If she was with Bobby she could stop running hookers and live a life of luxury.

Hmm . . . problem was that after the threesome incident Bobby had never pursued her; it was as if he regretted their history. Besides, he was one of Frankie's best friends, so while she and Frankie remained a couple, things could never progress.

"Anyway, thanks for coming by, guys," she said. "It's nice of you to make it all the way down here."

"No problem," Bobby said, thinking that she didn't seem at all upset by the tragedy that had recently taken place in L.A. Her attitude was one of remarkable calm. Frankie was the edgy one, darting around the apartment with an over-abundance of restless energy, coked out to the eyeballs.

Bobby tried to imagine how he would react if anything ever happened to *his* mom, the dangerously beautiful and forever full of life Lucky Santangelo. He would surely kill, set out to wreak vengeance, do *something* – for he was a Santangelo, after all. He would certainly not sit around in any kind of a calm state like Annabelle. One thing was for sure – no Italian blood ran through *her* veins.

"Where's the lawyer?" Annabelle asked, impatiently glancing at her watch. "Shouldn't he be here? It's almost ten."

"I forgot to mention," Frankie said. "The lawyer's a she – says she knows you."

"Knows me?" Annabelle questioned. "How can she possibly know me?"

"Dunno," Frankie said, cracking his knuckles. "It doesn't matter, she'll be here soon. All we need to know is that she sounds like she's on top of everythin'."

"Great!" Annabelle complained, her mouth turning down into a petulant pout. "Now we'll have to contend with one of Ralph's uptight watchdog bitches. Can't wait!"

"I guess we'll take off," Bobby said. He wasn't about to hang around listening to Annabelle and Frankie bicker.

"I wish you were coming with us," Annabelle sighed. "I'm

going to need all the support I can get, and you've always been such a good friend to me, Bobby."

"You're a strong girl, you'll get through it," he assured her. "All you gotta do is keep it together. Don't let anyone or anything get to you."

"Right," M.J. agreed. "You'll be back here before you know it."

"I suppose . . ." she managed, her voice trailing off as she reached out to touch Bobby's arm.

He automatically jerked away, sensing that Frankie would not approve of the way she seemed to be drawing close. Body language was a dead giveaway, and Annabelle was definitely leaning in his direction.

"We'd better get goin'," M.J. announced. "Big meeting with a group of Russian investors. *Mood*, Moscow – I can see it now!"

"Sounds exciting," Annabelle murmured. "If it all comes off, I'll fly in for the big launch. All of us in Russia together, what a trip that would be!"

"Yeah, go hit it out the park, guys," Frankie said, joining in. "We'll both be in Moscow to celebrate with you. Caviar, vodka – gotta feelin' Moscow's my kinda town."

"You got a feelin' everywhere's your kinda town," Bobby joked, as he and M.J. headed for the door. Annabelle waved them a reluctant goodbye.

Frankie opened the front door to let them out, and as he did so – Denver appeared.

The sight of her brought all three of them to an abrupt stop.

Chapter Twenty-Five

Denver

"Bobby!" His name slipped out of my mouth before I could stop myself. "Bobby Santangelo?" I added, pretending to be confused, although I wasn't, not at all. I was transported back in time to my gawky thirteen-year-old self, with the biggest crush on a boy in a higher grade who had no idea I even existed.

Bobby Santangelo Stanislopoulos was every pre-pubescent girl's big crush. Handsome, charismatic, a basketball champ who also excelled at football – he hailed from an exciting and glamorous family. Along with his best friend, the also very handsome M.J., Bobby was a true star who could get any girl he wanted. And he did, oh yes, he did. Over the years he went through girls at an alarming rate, including one drunken prom night where legend had it that he and M.J. had gotten involved in some kind of insane sex romp with Annabelle. It was the talk of the school for weeks. Annabelle had walked around with a knowing smile, although I remember taking note that she was never one of the lucky ones who actually got to date Bobby. I think it must have pissed her off big-time.

Now here I was, on my way into Annabelle's apartment. And

here *he* was – the childhood crush of my dreams – Bobby Santangelo Stanislopoulos. Crazy that I even remember his full name.

"Do I know you?" he asked, giving me a puzzled smile. It was glaringly obvious that he had no idea who I was.

Recovering my composure, I rallied to the occasion. "Uh . . . actually, not really," I managed, striving for a cool vibe. "I'm representing Ralph Maestro."

"Annabelle's dad?"

"Right. I'm here to escort Annabelle to L.A. And . . . uh . . . well, strangely enough I went to school with Annabelle, and you were at the same high school. So . . . I guess I do know you, but not really."

His smile widened. Perfect teeth. Of course. Would I have expected anything less? I wondered what his abs were like.

"You've got a fantastic memory," he said pleasantly. "I'm a dud at remembering anything."

"I guess it's 'cause I'm a lawyer," I retorted. "It's a trick of the trade. I never forget a face." *Especially yours.*

"A lawyer, huh?" he said, dark eyes checking me out. "You look too young to be a lawyer."

If that's a compliment, I'll take it.

"I do?" I said, noting that he looked even better than he did back in high school.

"It's not a bad thing," he said. "I'd be kinda flattered if I was you."

We exchanged a long look. Y'know, one of those looks that lasts a few seconds too long – but in a good way.

"Well . . ." I began, and just as we were about to continue our mildly flirtatious conversation, the skinny guy with the longish hair and sharp features interrupted.

"You *are* the lawyer Ralph sent – right?" he questioned. "You're here to take care of everything?"

"You must be Frankie Romano," I replied, my ever alert eyes

noticing a thin residue of white powder under Frankie's left nostril. *Wonderful. I got me a druggie to hike back to L.A.*

"'S'right," Frankie said, giving me a second once-over with his ice-chip blue eyes.

Obviously this was a morning for full inspection. I was so glad I'd washed my hair and made an effort to look half-decent. Of course I also had that just-got-laid-two-nights-in-a-row glow, so I felt confident that I looked kind of okay – in spite of the wrong clothes for a New York winter.

M.J. threw me a curious glance. "Hey," he said.

"Hi," I answered with a brief nod.

This was all too surreal. A total jolt from the past.

"Come on in," Frankie said. "These guys are on their way out."

"Short but sweet," Bobby said, throwing me a friendly wink.

"Right," I answered, adding a hasty, "By the way, if you ever need a lawyer – young but killer – look me up. Denver Jones. I'm with Saunders, Fields, Simmons and Johnson." And then, before I could stop myself, I slipped him my card.

What am I doing? I am *so* embarrassed! It's so unlike me to troll for business. Oh God! The cold weather is turning my brain to pure mush!

Bobby and M.J. drifted off, and I followed Frankie into a large, light, but strangely unlived-in-looking space.

Annabelle was sprawled on a lime-green couch sipping Diet Coke from the can. The TV was tuned to *The View*, and Elisabeth Hasselbeck and Joy Behar were picking at each other – arguing about something political.

Annabelle appeared ready for a fast getaway. She was dressed all in black – expensive black – *very* expensive black. Her sleek pale-red hair was smoothed back, and her eyes were covered with oversize black-out shades. Glamour personified. Would I have expected anything else?

She gave me a look, and then did a fast doubletake. A surprised – actually kind of shocked expression crossed her face – or what I could see of her face, considering the enormous shades and all.

"Denver?" she questioned, her voice rising. "Oh . . . my . . . God! It *is* you."

I had not expected her to recognize me, let alone remember my name. We hadn't seen each other in years, and I'm sure I look totally different from the rather serious teenager with the drab brown hair, several extra pounds, and braces on her teeth. Or at least I hoped I did.

Suddenly I was fifteen again, the plain, smart girl, as opposed to one of the in-crowd.

"Yes, it's me," I said, trying to gather myself. "Long time no see."

"Damn right," Annabelle said, jumping to her feet. "How about you – you're lookin' great. Some transformation."

The last thing I expected to come out of Annabelle Maestro's mouth was a compliment.

For a moment I was totally thrown. Annabelle had *never* said anything nice to me in all the years I'd known her.

"Uh, so do you," I managed, remembering the last shopping expedition we'd gone on together; that was the time she'd informed me I was way too fat to get into any of the designer jeans sold at Fred Segal – the mecca of one-stop shopping for rich Beverly Hills girls with money to burn.

At the time I was a healthy size eight, while Annabelle was an unhealthy size zero.

"Are you really a lawyer?" Annabelle asked, actually sounding vaguely interested.

I nodded.

"That's amazing!" she exclaimed, sitting down again and placing her Diet Coke on the coffee-table. "I'm so proud of you."

Now why would she be proud of me? After our brief year of one-sided friendship she'd barely acknowledged my existence.

"Your father's very happy you're coming home," I said, sounding horribly phony. "And may I take this opportunity to say how sorry I am about your mom."

Annabelle lowered her shades and threw me a stony stare. "So," she said flatly. "Did the old bastard do it? Did Mister Movie Star finally crack and blow away all that fucking perfection?"

I was stunned into silence. The venom in her voice was palpable.

Frankie saved the day. Quickly grabbing my arm, he dragged me over to the window. "Take no notice of anythin' she says," he muttered. "She's in deep denial, doesn't know what she's talking about. Ignore her."

Concerned boyfriend had spoken. A piece of work if ever I've seen one.

I wished he would wipe his nose; the residue of white powder was such a giveaway.

Glancing out the window, I noticed Sam trudging down the street, laptop under one arm. He was probably on his way to the coffee shop, which he'd revealed was his favorite place to write. I wondered what he would make of this scene.

Annabelle shifted off the couch once more. "Are we leaving or what?" she asked, her tone of voice verging on being quite irritable. "The sooner I get this over with, the better I'll feel."

Frankie shot me a look. "Is the limo downstairs?"

"Ready and waiting," I replied, totally on top of the situation.

"You wanna tell the driver to come get our luggage."

"Sure," I answered pleasantly.

From lawyer to assistant in one fell swoop. I couldn't wait to deliver these two.

Annabelle and Frankie. A match made in heaven.

Or not?

I guess that's up to me to find out on our long trek west.

* * *

It didn't take me a great deal of time to realize Annabelle had not changed one bit. She might be older, but she certainly wasn't any wiser. She had no clue about how to treat people – starting with our limo driver. The moment she got in the limousine she began complaining about his driving skills. According to Annabelle he drove too fast; his stops were jerky; the heating in the car was overpowering; the TV did not function properly.

Bitch. Bitch. Bitch. All the way to the airport.

I was amazed that she had no questions about her mother's murder, how Ralph was doing, funeral details – nothing.

Frankie seemed used to the constant stream of complaints. He chose to more or less agree and then ignore.

Clever strategy.

At the airport I'd arranged for special services to meet us curbside. Annabelle handed the woman her heavy Louis Vuitton carry-on bag, then proceeded to act as if she didn't exist.

Fortunately, checking-in was swift, although when we got to security, Annabelle managed to create an annoying drama.

"Do I *have* to take my boots off?" she whined. "The ground is filthy."

"Everyone has to," I explained, wishing she'd shut up. Who the hell did she think she was? "And you've also got to remove your belt and take off your jacket," I added, annoying her even further.

"Shit!" snapped Annabelle as a line of pissed-off travelers waited impatiently for her to wriggle out of her thigh-high boots – an act that seemed to take forever.

Frankie had already shot ahead of her, leaving me to manage the situation.

Thanks, Frankie, I love you too. She's your girlfriend, you should be dealing with her crap.

By the time I got them both to the VIP lounge I'd had enough. I left them in the hands of our escort, and ducked out to make a few quick calls.

First Felix, my boss. I didn't care that it was early in the morning in L.A. I merely wished to report that we were thankfully on our way.

"Good girl," Felix said.

I hated it when he called me *girl* – so damn patronizing. Maybe it was time to change law firms, move on. I don't like to sound immodest, but I have managed to earn myself a stellar reputation, and sometimes I don't think Felix treats me with the respect I deserve.

Next I called my dad. I knew my family must be wondering what the hell had happened to me – because part of our family tradition is a phone call a day.

"Why did they send *you* to New York?" Dad wanted to know. "They should've sent an assistant."

I heartily agreed, and informed him I'd be there for our usual Thursday-night dinner.

"You'd better be," he said.

Thursday-night dinner is a family tradition. Everyone gathers at our parents' house. It's quite a mob scene, what with my three brothers, their various wives and girlfriends, and several nieces and nephews. Actually it's great, because in all the craziness of working in L.A., Thursday night represents stability and a safe haven. Josh and I used to love our Thursday nights with the family.

Thinking of Josh, my thoughts immediately switched to Sam and Mario. I really hadn't taken the time to go over the recent events in my personal life. The last couple of days had been quite something. Sex with two totally different guys. Hmm . . . Adventurous little me!

On impulse I texted Mario. *Getting on a plane. How about dinner tonight?*

Then I texted Carolyn. *Keep on missing you. On my way back to L.A. Will call when I arrive.*

Done with my phone calls I returned to the lounge where Annabelle had spread herself across a couch, and was downing her third vodka on the rocks.

Lovely. A coke addict and a drunk. What a perfect start to the day.

Chapter Twenty-Six

Carolyn

"Where are you?" Carolyn asked, relieved that Gregory had finally called. "I've been frantic. Is everything all right?"

Since he'd failed to come into the office all day she'd started to become quite concerned. It wasn't like Gregory to take a day off.

"Everything's fine," he assured her. "Why wouldn't it be?"

"You know why," she replied, keeping her voice low as she spoke into her cell phone.

"Yes, of course," he said, clearing his throat. "But surely you must realize that I have to tread slowly?"

Tread slowly? What did *that* mean?

She couldn't resist getting in a dig. "Muriel said she thought you'd gone jewelry shopping with your wife."

"Oh, for God's sake!" he exclaimed. "Please don't tell me that you actually believed her."

"I wasn't sure what to think."

"You know me better than that."

"Yes, I do, but when you didn't come in today . . ."

"Stop speaking nonsense," he said crossly.

"It's not nonsense," she said, holding her phone tightly. "I was concerned."

There was a brief silence. "Does anybody know we're talking?" he said at last.

"Excuse me?"

"You didn't say my name aloud, did you?"

"No."

"You're alone in your office?"

"Yes," she said, slightly puzzled. "And I don't understand why you're calling on my cell. How come you didn't call the office line?"

"Because from now on, everything between us has to remain private." He cleared his throat again. "There's no reason for anyone to know anything. I'm cementing our future, Carolyn. Remember that."

"Does this mean—"

"It means I'm taking care of everything my way, so start trusting me, and stop asking so many questions."

She experienced yet another shiver of excitement. The man she loved was taking care of everything, which meant that before very long their secret would be out in the open, and everyone would know – including Muriel and her tight-assed, disapproving attitude.

"I do trust you," she said softly. "But I couldn't help worrying."

"I have a surprise for you," he said.

"You do?"

"Something you deserve."

Her smile returned with a vengeance. "What is it?" she whispered excitedly.

"Listen to me very carefully," he said, his voice tense. "Then I want you to follow my instructions to the letter."

"Sounds mysterious," she said.

"It's not mysterious. It's exactly as I said before, we have to be diligent and tread extremely carefully."

"I know that, you keep on telling me."

"Then I hope you're listening."

"I am."

"Okay, Carolyn, please listen once again, for this is exactly what I want you to do . . ."

Chapter Twenty-Seven

Bobby

"Is it just me or, are the two of them the weirdest fuckin' couple in the world?" M.J. asked as he and Bobby headed for the meeting with their potential Russian investors, a meeting they were both anticipating would lead to a major expansion of their club business.

"Hey, whatever turns you on," Bobby answered, still thinking about Zeena.

"Annabelle's like cold as a fuckin' ice truck," M.J. muttered. "Doesn't she get that her mom's been freakin' *murdered*? How about showin' an inch of emotion?"

"She's always been like that," Bobby remarked. "Remember high school?"

"Remember an' regret," M.J. said, grimacing.

"Regret what?"

"Y'know, that prom-night deal."

"Nobody was scoring off anyone," Bobby pointed out. "It was mutual, we were all so out of it."

"Yeah, but the way I remember it – I'd sooner it never happened."

"Too late now, ten years later," Bobby said, reaching for his vibrating cell. He paused for a moment before answering, wondering if it might be Zeena requesting a repeat performance.

Was he even into a repeat performance?

Maybe.

Maybe not.

One thing was for sure – he was definitely confused.

Fortunately, or not so fortunately, it wasn't Zeena, it was Lucky.

"You're up early," he said.

"What else is new?" Lucky replied briskly.

"What can I do for you, Mom?"

"Come back to live in L.A."

"Huh?"

"Just messing with you," Lucky said lightly. "But I do have a proposition I think will interest you."

"You do?"

"Something you've been ragging me about."

"What?" he asked, interest peaking.

"Last night I threw out the sonofabitch who runs the main night-spot at The Keys. He's been getting sloppy. Yesterday I found out for sure that he's been running drugs *and* laundering money. Can you believe it? *So* not a brilliant move to do that kind of crap on *my* property."

"Right."

"I told the asshole if he didn't want his balls served up for breakfast along with two fried eggs and a rasher of bacon, he'd better get the fuck out. Instantly."

Bobby began to laugh. Lucky had such a way with words.

"What did the asshole say?"

"You honestly think I gave him a chance to say anything, Bobby? You know me – I abide by the rules: never fuck with a Santangelo."

"Oh yeah, Mom, I know the rules."

"The moron should've taken note of my rules," Lucky said. "He's gone."

"Just like that?"

"Yes," Lucky said firmly. "Just like that."

"An' now . . ."

"Now I finally might require your services to take over the club. Something you've been begging to do ever since I opened The Keys."

"Hey – not begging, Mom," Bobby corrected. "I'm a Santangelo, remember? Santangelos do not beg."

"Then how about asking?"

"That was a couple of years ago. We'll be gettin' off the ground in Miami soon. M.J. an' me, we got a cool franchise thing in place for *Mood*. We're meeting with a syndicate of Russian investors this morning, so I'm not sure . . ."

"Yes or no, Bobby?" Lucky said impatiently. "You want in or not? Do not play games with me because we both know who's gonna end up winning."

"I gotta talk to M.J."

"Do it. And if your answer is yes, I'll expect you here tomorrow to cut a deal."

"Tomorrow? In Vegas? Isn't that kinda soon?"

"This is business, Bobby. And this is a one-time offer. Call me back within the hour."

Then she was gone. Lucky Santangelo. Businesswoman. World-class beauty. Ball-breaker. Unstoppable force of nature. Mom.

"Wassup?" M.J. wanted to know.

"You're never gonna believe this," Bobby said, slowly shaking his head.

"Try me."

"The Keys. If we want to take over the club concession, could be that it's ours."

* * *

The Russians were a cagey group of billionaires. Three men, and one of the men's wives – an older woman with sinister slit eyes, a Botoxed face, bright red lips and a sneering attitude.

The men were all bald with protruding guts, yellow teeth and disagreeable personalities. Bobby hated every one of them on sight. He'd inherited Lucky's immediate judgment, and Dimitri's acute business sense.

The Russians proposed a deal so ridiculously one-sided that Bobby and M.J. couldn't wait to walk out of their over-decorated offices.

"Y'know," Bobby said as they hit the elevators after the disappointing meeting, "Lucky always told me – when one door closes, another is bound to open. An' I think we're lookin' at an open door all the way to Vegas. What's your take on it?"

"I think if you can get together on a deal with Lucky, then we're sure as shit gettin' on a plane," M.J. said, full of enthusiasm. "You know me, I love L.A., an' as for Vegas – yeah, we can definitely make it work."

Bobby nodded. He'd always wanted Vegas – after all, it was his heritage. Grandfather Gino, along with Bugsy Siegel, was one of the pioneers, way back in the late forties. Gino had built one of the first big Vegas hotels, he'd started his empire in Vegas, and Lucky had followed suit, building two magnificent hotels of her own.

For once Bobby thought about using the Stanislopoulos plane. He didn't usually take advantage of such a luxurious perk, but it was Vegas, and if using the plane made it easier to get there fast – so be it.

M.J. loved the idea. "Never been on the Stanislopoulos plane," he remarked.

"That's 'cause I never use it," Bobby replied.

"Man, if I had a plane at my disposal . . ."

"It's a company plane. It's for the Board of Directors."

"And you," M.J. pointed out.

"And Brigette," Bobby said quickly. "She can use it whenever she wants."

"How is Brigette?" M.J. asked. "She never comes by the club any more. I miss seein' her."

Bobby experienced a twinge of guilt. He'd promised Lucky he'd watch out for Brigette, and yet he hadn't called her in weeks. Last time he'd spoken to her she'd mentioned something about getting together with someone new. Bobby knew he should've followed up the way Lucky would've, but what the heck – he had other things on his mind. And Brigette was a big girl – she could look after herself. Or could she?

No. Everyone knew that Brigette attracted losers – they flocked in her direction like ants racing toward a bowl of honey.

"I'm calling Brigette," Bobby decided. "See if she's into makin' the trip with us. Business plus fun. May as well make the most of it."

"Cool," M.J. responded. "An' since we're takin' your plane, how about I bring my girlfriend?"

"*What* girlfriend?" Bobby asked with a note of surprise.

"A girl I've bin seein'," M.J. answered casually.

"For real?"

"What?" M.J. quipped. "You think I'm makin' her up?"

"You've never mentioned you're seein' someone."

"You've never asked. An' if you'd turned up at dinner last night you would've met her."

"Who is she?" Bobby asked curiously.

"Someone kinda special," M.J. replied with a self-satisfied smile. "I think I might've finally found The One."

Bobby raised a cynical eyebrow. "*Now* you're telling me."

"Wanted to be sure, man. Nothin' wrong with that."

"Bring her," Bobby said. "I'll let you know what I think."

"All due respect, bro, but when it comes to this one – I don't give a shit *what* you think."

* * *

"Yes," Brigette said.

"Yes?" Bobby repeated.

"Why not? It sounds like a fun trip," Brigette said. "And we haven't used the plane in ages. I'll bring Kris."

"Who's Kris?"

"My new friend."

"You're sure you want to—"

"Yes, Bobby, you'll get along. I faithfully promise you that Kris is not one of my losers."

Sure. He'd heard that before. But at least he'd get a chance to judge for himself, and no doubt Lucky would want to meet the new man in Brigette's life.

So . . . the trip was a go. The plane would be ready to take off at eight a.m. M.J. was bringing his new girlfriend. Brigette was bringing her latest love. And Bobby? Well, Bobby was flying solo.

Chapter Twenty-Eight

Annabelle

Returning to L.A. brought back a rush of memories for Annabelle. As she stepped off the plane she stood still for a moment and inhaled the still familiar L.A. smell – a mixture of smog and jasmine. Taking a deep breath she braced herself for the homecoming – such as it was.

Fortunately they would not be staying at the family house. Frankie had been smart enough to arrange for them to have a suite at the Beverly Hills Hotel.

Ahh . . . the Pink Palace, as the luxurious hotel was called back in the day. Many the times Annabelle had skipped school and hung out at the downstairs snack bar in the hotel, scoffing hamburgers and milk shakes and the hotel's famous Neil McCarthy chopped salad. She'd often hit on a random male who was into spending time with a fifteen-year-old truant – and that had been a blast, especially when she'd eventually revealed who she was.

One old producer she'd hit on had practically crapped himself when she'd told him her dad was Ralph Maestro. She'd been blowing him at the time in his poolside suite, and his cock had all but vanished up his own asshole.

Good times!

Now she was returning to the Pink Palace with her boyfriend, Frankie, and who knew what surprises lay ahead.

Denver checked them both in and accompanied them to their suite. "Your father is expecting you at the house for an early dinner," she informed Annabelle.

"With you?" Annabelle asked.

"No, not with me."

"But you must be there," Annabelle wailed, clinging onto Denver's arm. "I can't go unless you come too. You're my support system. I need you."

"I'm not invited," Denver explained.

Frankie threw her a piercing look. "*She's* inviting you," he said, putting his hand on her arm and guiding her toward the door. "Don't we all want this to go as smoothly as possible?"

"I'm one of Mr Maestro's lawyers, not a babysitter," Denver argued.

"Do this for her," Frankie insisted. "She's vulnerable right now, needs all the help she can get. An' you're one of her oldest friends."

"Bullshit I am!" Denver said hotly.

"It doesn't matter. Just do it," Frankie said, giving her a gentle exit shove through the door.

Annabelle was busy exploring the suite. Fortunately it was to her liking. After testing the bed she ordered a dozen more pillows and a fresh duvet. Then she inspected the marble bathroom and ordered three dozen large bath towels and extra toweling robes. After that she made an appointment at the La Prairie spa.

Meanwhile Frankie took a walk around the hotel. It surpassed his wildest dreams. The grounds were a magnificent tangle of bougainvillaea, wild roses and exotic palms of all varieties – he'd never seen anything like it. The weather was balmy and clear with a slight cooling breeze. The pool in all its Olympic glory was surrounded by private cabanas. He immediately booked one, charging it to the room. Then he made his way to the famous Polo Lounge and checked that out. He thought he spotted Justin Timberlake sitting in a booth with a delicious-looking blonde.

Shit! This was his kind of town, his kind of action. Frankie could definitely see himself setting up shop in this town. Frankie Romano – purveyor of Grade A flesh princesses to a parade of horny guys who preferred paying for it rather than playing the dating game. Horny, *famous* guys who would soon become his asshole buddies. Frankie imagined Cruise, Clooney, Snoop Dogg – yeah – maybe even Timberlake.

Frankie grinned to himself. L.A. was where he belonged. And with a little help from Annabelle he was going to make sure they were here to stay.

* * *

Simon Waitrose leaned back in his beaten-up leather swivel chair situated behind a crowded desk, and stared at the shifty-looking youth who'd recently slunk into his office. "What have you got for us, Chip?" he said.

Chip Bonafacio blinked several times in quick succession. This Simon Waitrose man with the English accent and shrewd eyes made him uneasy – he reminded Chip of the infamous Simon Cowell on TV. Direct, challenging and rude. But Chip wasn't visiting Simon's office to make friends. No. He had a story to sell, and he'd already made a tentative deal to get paid a shitload of money. All he had to do was produce proof that the story he was selling was the truth and nothing but.

He'd already had two meetings at *Truth & Fact*, one with Simon's right hand – an abrasive woman with buck teeth and an unfortunate squint – and the second with Simon himself, who'd informed him that if he could produce solid proof that Annabelle Maestro was involved in running call girls, then he'd get his pay-out.

Solid proof. What constituted solid proof?

Well, for one thing, his timing couldn't be better. With Frankie and Annabelle out of town, and his mom staying at their Park Avenue apartment, he'd had a perfect opportunity to search out whatever he could find. First he'd had to put his mom out of action. She was a nosy one, always butting into his business.

No problem, he had a plan, and late Monday afternoon he'd activated it – slipping two Ambien into her tea – a move which soon sent her to the Land of Nod, leaving him free to roam around the damn apartment, searching for anything he could find to collaborate his story.

And search he did – starting in the master bedroom, where he found nothing but designer clothes, shoes and handbags. Annabelle Maestro obviously spent money as if it was going out of style.

He'd moved on to Frankie's crap, discovering two-hundred-and-fifty-dollar ties with the price tag still affixed; Hugo Boss jackets; Brioni suits; expensive sports clothes and a dozen matching black cashmere long-sleeved sweaters.

Between the two of them they must've blown a fortune.

Chip felt distinct twinges of envy. He did all the goddamn work, driving the whores wherever they needed to go, while Miss Nose-in-the-Air Maestro and her coked-out boyfriend reaped all the benefits.

Well, fuck 'em both. Chip was exposing their twisted game, and to hell with the consequences. Soon he'd have his own big bucks to splash around.

The locked drawers in the library room gave up all the proof and photos he'd ever need.

"Here's your proof," he said, trying to sound macho as he thrust a manila envelope across Simon's messy desk.

"And what exactly do we have here?" Simon said, opening the envelope and tipping the contents onto his desk-top.

"Plenty," Chip boasted. "All juicy stuff."

"Juicy, eh?" Simon questioned. "It had better be, because wasting my time pisses me off."

"Wouldn't want to do that," Chip responded with a feeble chuckle.

"No, mate, you wouldn't," Simon said, sorting through the items from Chip's envelope. He held up a photo of Annabelle with her famous parents and scrutinized it. She was about fifteen at the time the photo was taken. "Pretty girl," he remarked. "Got something more recent?"

"Keep lookin'," Chip said.

Simon picked up another photo. This one was of Annabelle with Frankie and two of the girls who occasionally worked for them – one a vaguely well-known singer, one an actress on a weekly series – both of them recognizable faces.

"Those two are workin' girls," Chip said. "I've driven them to many appointments."

"You have?"

"Yeah. They're into scorin' extra bucks – they get around eight grand a pop. In cash."

"Proof?" Simon said.

"You'll see," Chip replied. "I got photos of 'em with their masks on – I got hotel receipts. I got dates, times, client names. Everything's there."

"Okay then," Simon said, leafing through more photos. "Looks like we've got ourselves a big kick-ass story. And here's the good news: if I rush it through, we'll make it for the front page of Wednesday's edition – just in time for Thursday's funeral."

Chapter Twenty-Nine

Denver

My freaking luck, Annabelle has decided that I am her best friend in the world, and Felix seems to think that this is excellent news. Anything to keep number one client Mr Ralph Maestro happy – including sacrificing me for the benefit of the case.

Not that there is a case as such, because while I was freezing my ass off in New York, two suspects were pulled into the mix. Swift work by the Beverly Hills Police Department. I was impressed.

Suspect number one – usurping Ralph from that prime position – is a stalker/fan who apparently had done all his stalking (letters, gifts, threats, declarations of love/hate) from New Orleans – so nobody had taken the threats seriously. But after Gemma's highly publicized murder, the stalker/fan's sister had come forward to reveal that said stalker/fan had set off for L.A. two days earlier, intent on meeting the woman of his dreams/nightmare.

Suspect number two – dropping Ralph even further down the ladder – was a mysterious man the paparazzi had caught Gemma lunching with at a secluded restaurant in the hills above Malibu. The photos were taken the day before her murder, and nobody – including Ralph – knew who the man was.

Was Gemma having a secret affair? Was she cheating on

Ralph? Was the perfect movie-star couple not so perfect after all? The internet gossip sites were in overdrive.

But back to me and my new best friend, Annabelle Maestro.

"I have a life," I informed Felix. "Why do you think it's so important that I go to this dinner tonight with Annabelle? Ralph doesn't even like me, he treats me as if I'm your assistant. I'm an excellent lawyer, Felix, I deserve respect."

Felix Saunders, AKA Mister Shark Teeth, talked me down in his slightly supercilious fashion. It was all about how important client/lawyer relationships were, how the client depends on his lawyer not only as legal counsel, but as a loyal friend and confidant.

Eventually I caved in, because the truth is I wouldn't mind observing the interaction between Annabelle and her famous dad. As a keen watcher of human behavior, in a perverse kind of way I was sort of looking forward to it. One of the things I do in court is to always keep a sharp eye on the jury and their reactions to even the smallest piece of information. I find that when it comes to the crunch, it always pays off.

Mario had texted me back. *Dinner on. Can't wait!*

I contemplated phoning him, then decided against it. Another text would do. Brief and to the point. *Sorry. Dinner off due to work. How about tomorrow night?*

I didn't really care that much. Mario was a diversion – certainly not the start of something meaningful.

Carolyn had sent me another text while I was on the plane. *We must talk!! So much happening!!*

She was due to arrive in L.A. for the Christmas vacation in two weeks. I was looking forward to catching up, spending all my time with her doing plenty of girly things that I never seem to find the time to do on my own. I envisioned a lazy and relaxing day at the Korean spa. A mindless shop at The Grove. Plenty of movies. Maybe even a long weekend in Palm Springs with my main gay friend Teddy – hairstylist supreme. Carolyn was a true friend, the kind of person who would always be there for me no matter what. I could tell she was really psyched about something, and I couldn't wait to hear her news.

* * *

While we were waiting at the entrance to the hotel for the limo, Annabelle grabbed my hand and said, "Thanks for doing this, Denver. I do know it's not part of your job description, and I truly appreciate it."

Annabelle. Appreciating something. Definitely out of character.

Then she added, further confusing me, "Did you know that at school I always used to envy you? Your life seemed so normal compared to mine. You had parents that actually came to school events, and they seemed to *care* about you. I was majorly jealous."

Was she freaking kidding me? Annabelle Maestro, jealous of me! Absolutely no way.

Before she could say anything more, Frankie loped over, having just introduced himself to a famous basketball player who was standing by the entrance waiting for his car.

"Jeez!" Frankie exclaimed, pleased with himself for having spotted another celebrity. "That Rick Fox is one tall motherfucker. I invited him to stop by *Mood* next time he's in New York. Gave him my card."

"Who's Rick Fox?" Annabelle asked blankly.

"Who's Rick Fox!" Frankie chortled. "A former Lakers great! Everyone knows who Rick Fox is. He used t'be married to Vanessa Williams, a total babe."

Just as Annabelle was about to ask who Vanessa Williams was – and I would've explained because I'm a huge *Ugly Betty* fan – the limo pulled up and we all piled in.

Ten minutes later we arrived at the house, and a stony-faced

Ralph Maestro greeted us at the door to his imposing mansion. He gave me a brief nod, shook Frankie's hand, and leaned forward to honor Annabelle with an awkward hug. No words were exchanged as we followed him into the house.

I glanced at Annabelle. Her perfectly made-up face gave nothing away.

Ralph led us into the enormous living room, dominated by a huge portrait of himself and Gemma hanging over the mantelpiece, a fake logfire burned brightly, and a waiter hovered behind an exceptionally long bar.

"Order your drinks," Ralph said in a strained voice. "Have whatever you want."

I noted his tan had faded since last we met. Perhaps visiting a tanning salon was not the best idea during these difficult times. But surely Ralph had people who came to him?

While I was pondering the disappearing tan, Annabelle requested a Martini, and Frankie went for a Jack on the rocks. Frankie was obviously under the impression that Jack (note: Jack as opposed to Jack Daniel's) was *the* hot Hollywood drink. And it seemed he was right, because Ralph ordered the same thing.

I opted for a glass of white wine. Wimpy drink, but at least I could make it last while everyone around me got wasted. And getting wasted was definitely on the agenda, for Annabelle downed her Martini in three fast gulps, then immediately requested a second one.

Oh wow! Here we go. Hold on tight, 'cause I've got a strong suspicion it's going to be a bumpy night.

* * *

Imagine being at a dinner where it is quite apparent that everyone hates everyone else, but for the sake of appearances, politeness rules.

One would think Ralph was hosting a dinner for several avid fans who'd won an evening to be spent with the great Ralph Maestro. He was stiff, uncomfortable and distant.

Frankie on the other hand did not shut up. On his usual coke-fueled high (oh yes, it hadn't taken me long to figure out his numerous visits to the bathroom were not to pee) he carried on about the hotel, the city, the weather, and what an honor it was to finally meet the amazing Ralph Maestro.

"I've seen every movie you ever made," Frankie enthused, eliciting a glare from Annabelle, who'd had no idea he was such a fan. "*Brain-dead*, *The Great American Train Wreck*, *Jolt*, *Finding Mr Lee*. I grew up watchin' your movies. You and Bruce Willis, you guys kicked it like nobody else."

I had a strong feeling that Ralph had been prepared to dislike Annabelle's boyfriend, but the accolades were coming so fast and furious, that Ralph's enormous ego couldn't resist. He nodded, accepting the praise as if it was his due.

Annabelle and I listened in stunned silence as Frankie proceeded to talk about every one of Ralph's many movies in detail.

After a while it seemed Annabelle couldn't take it any longer. "Excuse us," she said, standing up and throwing me a pointed look. "We'll be right back."

Hmm . . . I guess that means I'm going with her, leaving Frankie to shove his nose all the way up Ralph's ass – an act he's obviously enjoying.

Annabelle led me into an ornate guest powder-room decorated in over-the-top shades of turquoise and gold. "I'm in dire need of a cigarette," she muttered, groping in her Balenciaga purse for a pack of Marlboros. "Isn't this torture?"

"I imagine your dad is still in shock," I said lamely. "Besides, Frankie is kind of monopolizing the conversation."

"Frankie can be such a dick," Annabelle said, dismissing her boyfriend with an abrupt wave of her hand. "Who knew he worshipped Ralph? I certainly didn't."

"You had no clue?"

"Nothing. Nada. We never even talked about my family, and now this show of adulation. Quite frankly, I'm pissed."

"Don't blame you."

"Oh, Denver," Annabelle said, suddenly clutching onto my arm. "I'm so grateful you're here. I honestly couldn't go through this if you weren't around to support me."

"That's nonsense," I said, swallowing fast. "You'd be fine."

"No, I wouldn't."

"Yes, you would," I insisted. What was going on here? Why was I all of a sudden Miss Indispensable?

"Anyway," Annabelle continued, "you *are* here, and as long as we stay together I'll be able to cope. The funeral's on Thursday, and right after I want to be on a plane back to New York. Can you arrange it?"

Crap! So add travel agent to my job description.

Back at the dining table Frankie was quoting lines from *Brain-dead*, and Ralph was finally looking bored. Ignoring Frankie who was in full quote, Ralph fixed Annabelle with one of his steely stares and said, "I expect you to go through your mother's things while you're here. The housekeepers will help you. Be sure you watch that they don't try to take anything."

"You want *me* to do it?" Annabelle said, not at all happy at the prospect.

"*Yes*, you," Ralph said sharply. "There's nobody else that's family, therefore it's your responsibility. Be here at ten in the morning."

"But—"

"Annabelle," Ralph said, his voice ice cold. "You're her daughter. It's what she would have wanted."

"I don't think so," Annabelle mumbled.

"Well, I do," Ralph said, big movie-star face staring her down.

End of discussion.

We finally got out of there at nine-thirty.

"Time to party," Frankie said, rubbing his hands together in anticipation of a wild Hollywood night. "Where's *the* place to hang?"

I had definitely had enough of Frankie Romano for one night. "Beats me," I said with a quick shrug. "I'm going home to bed."

"No way!" Frankie exclaimed. "We're hittin' it tonight. I gotta know what's goin' on in this town. Gotta catch the vibe."

"Sorry," I said – not sorry at all. "You're on your own."

"Yes," Annabelle said, agreeing with me. "You're on your own, Frankie. After dinner and all that tension, I'm exhausted."

"Jesus Christ!" Frankie complained. "What's *wrong* with you two?"

"The driver will steer you in the right direction," I offered. "Right after he's dropped us at the hotel where I'll pick up my car, and Annabelle can go get a good night's sleep."

"What are both of you – fifty?" Frankie sneered.

"Twenty-five actually," I said, loathing him more every minute. "But don't sweat it, I'm sure you're capable of having fun on your own."

Annabelle stifled a giggle. It wasn't often Frankie didn't get his own way.

Back at the hotel, Annabelle and I scooted out of the limo, and Frankie took off to go God knew where.

Annabelle didn't seem to mind. "You're right, he can look after himself," she said. "I'll see you in the morning, Denver."

"You will?"

"Ten o'clock. We'll drive over to the house together and deal with my mother's things."

"Look, Annabelle," I said, feeling quite awkward. "I'd really like to help you out, but here's the thing – I have to be at my office tomorrow. I'm way behind on everything. Got a thousand things to take care of."

"Not to worry," Annabelle said with an airy wave of her hand. "I'll have Ralph fix it with your boss. Just remember this – while I'm in L.A., you're all mine."

Talk about getting caught in a trap. It seemed I had no choice in the matter.

Chapter Thirty

Carolyn

Tuesday morning, Carolyn awoke early. She was too revved up to sleep. Gregory had promised her a surprise, and the thought of what it might be was driving her crazy. She was sure it was something she'd like, something to do with their future together, something amazing.

Humming softly to herself she decided she had time to go for a run before work. Slipping into a pale-blue tracksuit and Puma sneakers, she left her apartment and bumped straight into Kerri.

"Am I glad to see you!" Kerri exclaimed. "Got a big favor to ask."

"Ask away," Carolyn replied.

"Well, you know how I always pick up Nellie's meds once a month."

"I know you do, and she really appreciates it. It's so thoughtful of you."

Kerri gave a modest shrug. "Guess it's my twelve good deeds for the year. But here comes the favor. I can't do it today – got a way hot date, an' he's meeting me from work. So since Nellie is out of her sleeping pills *and* her heart meds, can you pick them up for me an' drop them off at her apartment?"

"Of course I can," Carolyn said. "No problem."

"Everything's pre-paid," Kerri explained. "I gave the prescriptions to the pharmacy yesterday, they'll be ready after five."

"Done," Carolyn said.

"You're such a doll," Kerri said, leaning forward and giving her a quick hug.

"We should take turns doing it anyway."

"I'm down with that."

"I should've thought of it before."

"Hey, you're doin' your bit, always lookin' in on the old dear, makin' sure she's breathin'."

"We both do what we can."

"How about an early breakfast tomorrow?" Kerri suggested. "I can give you all the filthy details from what I hope is gonna be a night of crazy mad lust!"

"Sounds good," Carolyn said. Then she couldn't help adding, "I might have some exciting news of my own."

"Awesome!" Kerri said. "Are you seein' someone?"

"I could be . . ." Carolyn replied, almost tempted to spill everything.

"That's my girl. You can tell me all about him tomorrow. Same time, same place. My treat."

Carolyn nodded. "Make sure to take note of every single detail."

"Oh, I will," Kerri said, beaming. "Doncha you worry 'bout *that*!"

* * *

Later in the day, Carolyn breezed into Muriel's office and said, "I'm leaving early today."

"Why is that?" Muriel inquired, tightly wound as she sat ramrod straight behind her desk.

"The Senator knows," Carolyn continued. "I mentioned it to him last week."

"He didn't tell me."

"Does he tell you everything?"

"Where are you going?" Muriel asked, tapping her pen on her desk-top.

None of your business, Carolyn was tempted to say. But she didn't, she remained cool.

"Dentist," she said shortly.

"In the middle of the day?"

Carolyn shrugged. "The Senator said it was okay, and since it seems he's not coming in again, my timing appears to be right on."

"Personal appointments are supposed to take place after office hours," Muriel said primly. "Surely you're aware of that?"

"Yes, I am aware of it," Carolyn replied. "But exceptions happen."

"For *some* people," Muriel sniffed disapprovingly.

Carolyn couldn't help going for the comment she knew would get to Muriel. "Well," she said, "I guess I'm *some* people. See you later, Muriel."

Escaping from the office without further interrogation, she made her way down to the underground parking lot. Things were about to change, it was exciting and she couldn't wait.

She got into her 2006 Pontiac and sat quietly for a few moments contemplating her future. She was filled with all kinds of anticipation. Gregory *had* been mysterious, but extremely firm. He'd said he had a surprise for her. What could it possibly be?

When they'd spoken on the phone the previous day he'd given her strict instructions and told her to follow them without question. "Do not tell anyone anything," he'd warned. "If you do, it will ruin everything."

As if she would. She was hardly likely to confide in

disapproving Muriel or the new male intern who wore patent leather shoes a size too large and an ill-fitting button-down Oxford shirt.

Gregory's words echoed in her head. *Take the main highway over the bridge and follow Route 105. Turn off at exit 10, and drive approximately fifteen minutes until you reach the abandoned Shell station. Wait there until I contact you.*

She had a hunch she knew exactly what he had planned. He was arranging to meet her somewhere quiet, out of sight of prying eyes, and then he was taking her to view a house.

Yes! What else could the surprise be?

It was a no-brainer. Gregory was planting the seeds of their new life together.

She was sure of it.

Chapter Thirty-One

Bobby

M.J.'s new girlfriend, Cassie, was a miniature version of a younger Janet Jackson. Heartbreakingly pretty with a pocket Venus figure, she was only eighteen and trying hard to crash the music business.

Bobby took M.J. to one side while they waited for Brigette to arrive at the private airport. "Holy shit! She's a baby!" he exclaimed. "Jeez, M.J., she's almost the same age as Max. What're you thinkin'?"

"I'm thinking that I've finally found The One," M.J. responded. "Nothin' wrong with that – you should try it sometime."

"We're taking her across state lines," Bobby pointed out. "Is it even legal?"

"Hey, bro, she's eighteen not twelve," M.J. snapped. "An' I'd kinda appreciate it if you'd quit with the comments an' get with the program."

"Fine," Bobby grumbled. "Baby snatch, what do I care?"

He and M.J. had been friends since eighth grade. M.J. had always been a player, girls loved him, but as far as Bobby was concerned his friend was way too young to start settling down; it wasn't cool. Bobby had to admit that M.J. and Cassie made a great-looking couple, and Cassie seemed sweet – although sweet wasn't usually M.J.'s type. He liked them sassy and sexy.

Brigette arrived late as usual – a trait she'd inherited from Olympia, her deceased mother. Olympia had been Bobby's half-sister, and even though Brigette was ten years older than him, he was indeed her uncle – a fact they laughed about a lot.

"You're late," he said, announcing the obvious.

"I know," she said with a big unapologetic grin.

Bobby was pleased to note that Brigette seemed happy – it must be the new boyfriend's influence.

A tall, athletic blonde emerged from Brigette's limo. A female blonde with short cropped hair, broad shoulders, a healthy tan and a wide smile.

Brigette grabbed the woman's hand. "Bobby," she announced, beaming, "I want you to meet Kris. She's the woman who put a smile back on my face. Isn't she amazing?"

* * *

All the way on the flight to Vegas Bobby kept thinking about what Lucky would have to say about this unexpected turn of events. Brigette changing tracks was quite a surprise, although when he thought about it he wasn't that shocked. After all, Brigette had experienced quite a parade of losers and psychos – all of them men – so maybe with a woman she'd have more luck. She was certainly happy enough and she looked fantastic. She and Kris were joking around like a couple of teenagers.

Kris was a pro tennis player and quite successful. "We met in the Hamptons at the P. Diddy All-White Party," Brigette revealed. "I was with an out-of-work actor who'd decided I was just the ticket to pay all his bills – including his ex-wife's alimony – and Kris had recently broken up with her long-time girlfriend."

"We'd been together eight years," Kris chimed in. "She

wanted a marriage license and a baby. All I wanted was out."

"Neither of us were looking—"

"Until we looked in each other's direction," Kris interrupted.

"And then," Brigette added with a shy giggle, "it was a lightning strike. I knew immediately that Kris would change my life – and although we've only been together since the summer, she has."

Kris squeezed Brigette's hand and then concentrated on Bobby for a moment. "I'm so happy to finally meet you," she said. "I know her family means a lot to Brigette, so when the opportunity came up to make this trip together – we both said a resounding yes! I can't wait to meet the rest of the family."

"You will," Bobby said, glancing at M.J. and Cassie, who were all over each other.

It seemed he was the odd one out. By himself. No significant other.

All he had was the hots for a famous superstar who'd used him for stud service. Nice.

* * *

The last thing Bobby expected to see as the eight-passenger extra-long silver limo took them from the airport to The Keys complex, was a huge billboard of Zeena on the strip heralding a one night only appearance at the Cavendish Hotel. She was due to appear the following night.

Jeez! Was there no escape?

The Cavendish – a successful boutique hotel – was located right next to The Keys, and the owners – a lesbian couple – were good friends of Lucky and Lennie.

It occurred to Bobby that tomorrow night he and his group would be sitting ringside at the Cavendish watching Zeena perform. It was a hunch, but if he knew Lucky she'd already set it up as a fun thing to do. When guests visited Vegas, Lucky always made sure they were treated to the best entertainment going.

So . . . if that was the case, what was he planning on doing?

He'd go, of course. Watch Zeena perform. No big deal, she wouldn't even know he was there. He'd be sitting in the audience like any other fan.

"Oh, look!" Cassie exclaimed, leaning out the window and checking the billboard. "Zeena's appearing here tomorrow night. I love her! M.J., can we go?"

She could have asked him to strip naked and run down the street, for M.J. was in the land of the besotted.

"Sure, sweetie, I'll try to get tickets," M.J. promised.

"Lucky's probably already got 'em," Bobby remarked.

"Or if she hasn't, why don't *you* call Zeena?" M.J. suggested. "She's always eyeballin' you like you're her next steak dinner."

It threw Bobby that M.J. had noticed and not mentioned a word until now.

"You think?" he said, playing it major cool.

"C'mon, bro," M.J. said, riding him. "You know as well as I do that Zeena's got a thing for you. She wants your body, man. She wanna ravish your fine ass."

"Didn't notice."

"Yeah, sure," M.J. said, winking at Cassie. "*You* didn't notice, but everyone else in the club did."

"Wow!" Cassie exclaimed, clapping her hands together. "Zeena is awesome!"

"And bi-sexual," Kris added, joining in the conversation. "I must say – I do like a woman who can't quite make up her mind."

If they only knew, Bobby thought.

Before he could think about it further, their limo began pulling into The Keys complex.

Chapter Thirty-Two

Annabelle

Breakfast in the Polo Lounge with a hungover Frankie took care of Annabelle's morning. She pushed Eggs Benedict around her plate while tapping her foot impatiently on the floor.

"Can't wait to get back to New York," she muttered.

Frankie raised his retro Ray-Bans revealing bloodshot eyes. "*'C'mon*, this place rocks, babe," he said, full of enthusiasm. "You shoulda come with, last night. I'm tellin' you – it was a major scene. You really missed out."

"I'm sure I did," Annabelle answered primly, clearly forgetting about her own crazed teenage years, "I'm well aware of the L.A. scene. Decrepit old dudes on the make with Viagra fever, and moronic underage girls flashing their lack of underwear. Lovely!"

"Sounds like our kinda town t'me," Frankie quipped, gulping down a glass of fresh orange juice. "Y'know babe, we could clean up here. Far as I can tell, it's ours for the taking."

"Why would we want L.A. when we've got New York?" Annabelle said, frowning.

"Expansion, babe. That's what business is all about."

"But Frankie," she argued, determined to change his mind,

"surely you understand that we need to be hands-on? We can't run our business from another city."

"Then we should consider spending more time in L.A.," he said, getting off on the thought. "We'll bring in someone like Janey to run things when we're *not* here."

"Sure," Annabelle murmured sarcastically. "There's a Janey lurking around every corner."

"I'll find someone," Frankie insisted. "You know me, I can sniff 'em out."

"I don't understand why you can't be satisfied with what we've got going," Annabelle said, wishing he wasn't so damn stubborn.

"'Cause I want more, babe," he explained. "Nothin' wrong with that."

Annabelle pushed her plate away. Frankie was starting to bug her again. Why was he so set on L.A. when he knew she hated it?

She glanced at her watch. Where was Denver? Thank God she had someone she could depend on to get her through this mess.

Annabelle's memories of Denver at school were fuzzy. She vaguely remembered that they'd hung out for a while, but Denver hadn't been up for clubbing and shopping – she'd always put schoolwork and her family first, plus she'd never had money to burn. Come to think of it, Denver had been a total drudge.

It didn't matter because she was here now, and Annabelle needed her for support since it was becoming painfully obvious that Frankie could not be depended on.

"Isn't that Mel Gibson?" Frankie asked, lowering his voice as the famous actor strode past their table. "Jeez! The dude looks great."

"Who cares?" Annabelle said, tossing her hair back. "And what was all that fan crap going on with you and Ralph last night? Have you any idea how dumb you sounded?"

The word "dumb" did not sit well with Frankie. "What's crawled up *your* ass this morning?" he demanded.

"Apparently not you," Annabelle responded, refusing to look at him.

"What does *that* mean?"

"It means we seem to be growing apart," she said, gazing off into space.

Frankie was silent for a moment while his mind computed what was going on. His girlfriend was getting all snarky on him, and he didn't appreciate it. He realized she was upset about her mother – even though *she* didn't seem to know it – but that was no reason to take it out on him. They were finally in L.A. and they should be enjoying every minute, instead of which they were at each other's throats.

He decided to save the day, turn on the Frankie Romano charm, lure her back into the best relationship she was ever likely to experience.

"Y'know what?" he said. "We're both tense, it's been a helluva few days. But you do know how much I love you – right, babe?" Leaning over, he nuzzled her neck exactly the way he knew turned her on. "Tonight I'm takin' you for dinner, just the two of us. An' then . . ."

"Frankie . . ." she began to say, making a half-hearted attempt to push him away.

"Don't even bother arguing," he said firmly. "You're right, we need some alone time. Leave it to me, babe, I'm gonna arrange everything."

* * *

"Do you have a boyfriend?" Annabelle asked as the limo whisked them toward the Maestro mansion.

"Uh, not exactly a live-in," Denver replied, unwilling to reveal any details of her love-life to Annabelle.

"Very wise," Annabelle nodded as she lit up a cigarette. "But then you always were the smart one. Who needs a man cluttering up your apartment, or do you have a house?"

"No house."

"Apartments are better."

"I suppose so," Denver said, hating this conversation that was going nowhere.

"I have a fantastic apartment in New York," Annabelle boasted.

"I know, I saw it."

Annabelle quickly shut up. She was talking about her stunning Park Avenue spread, not the SoHo dump. Denver probably wouldn't even understand the difference.

They rode the rest of the way in silence until they reached the Maestro estate. As they waited for the gate to open at the end of the driveway, a couple of stray paparazzi fell out of the shrubbery and began snapping away.

Annabelle immediately covered her face with her hands. "Oh God!" she worried. "I can't be photographed. People in New York have no idea who I am. This is impossible."

Denver decided not to point out that at the funeral they'd be inundated with TV crews, photographers and press. It would be media frenzy.

Once they reached the house, Lupe, the Maestros' housekeeper, answered the door. She escorted them up the main staircase to Gemma's sumptuous dressing room – a room almost as big as Denver's entire apartment.

Annabelle plopped herself down on a fancy pink love-seat and with an exhausted sigh said, "I simply can't do this – you'll have to do it for me."

Suddenly Denver was overwhelmed with a rush of bad memories. Annabelle whining to her in high school, *"I can't do this history test, you'll have to do it for me." "I can't make it to the cafeteria today, you'll have to get lunch for me." "I can't go to Carolyn's party, you'll have to tell her for me."*

Denver found herself in bad memory hell and she didn't like it. Once upon a time she'd been desperate to be one of the cool girls – so desperate that she'd done everything Annabelle had asked. But things were different now, and all she wanted to do was to get back to her office and catch up on her work.

"Guess what!" she exclaimed, tapping her watch. "I forgot a very important meeting I'm supposed to be at this morning. I'm so sorry, I have to go."

"But I need you!" Annabelle wailed. "You can't leave!"

"Don't worry, I'll send my assistant Megan over. Megan is super-competent, she'll handle everything. You'll love her." And before Annabelle could object further, she was heading for the door.

Annabelle was livid. She could not believe she'd been deserted in her time of need. Denver Jones should be kissing her ass, not running out on her. Fine friend she'd turned out to be.

* * *

Sitting in a private cabana at the Beverly Hills Hotel, Frankie surveyed the action. There was not much going on; however, it was still early. There was plenty of time for a parade of movie stars to appear and hang out. Preferably Jessica Alba and Megan Fox in the smallest Brazilian bikinis.

A lounger had been laid out for him by the pool, so after slathering on some sun protection, he took himself outside the cabana, first ordering a Bloody Mary.

Last night he'd gotten caught up in quite a scene. Talk about pussy heaven – L.A. was *it*. Girls galore. Girls in backless, almost topless, short skimpy outfits. Girls with long blonde hair and obvious fake tits. Girls with long dark hair and obvious fake lips – desperately trying to emulate their Goddess Angelina. Too bad none of them succeeded.

Frankie had hit a couple of happening clubs. At the second club he'd taken a seat at the bar and surveyed the action. After slipping the barman his card, he'd inquired if there were any owners around.

Eventually Rick Greco – the guy who ran the club and was also a part-owner – had appeared and introduced himself.

Frankie thought there was something vaguely familiar about Rick, but he couldn't quite place him.

"Sorry, dude, we're not lookin' for any deejays," Rick said, giving him a friendly pat on the back.

"Don't sweat it, 'cause I'm not lookin' for a job," Frankie responded. "I'm in town for my girlfriend's mother's funeral. Gemma Summer. You probably read about it. Big case."

"Shit," Rick said, duly impressed. "That's some bummer." A short pause, and then – "Her daughter really your girlfriend?"

What did the jerk think – that he'd made it up?

"'S'right," he said, casually surveying the room. "Annabelle Maestro. We live together in New York."

Rick snapped his fingers for the barman. "Can I buy you another drink?"

"Sure," Frankie said amiably. "Why not?"

And so they'd got to talking, and Frankie had decided that Rick might be an excellent connection – especially when Rick revealed he was a former teen idol who'd been big on TV in the nineties.

"Y'know, I thought I recognized you," Frankie said, flashing back to his early teen years. "Weren't you on that show with the smokin' hot mom an' the two obnoxious asswipe kids?"

"That was me," Rick said, basking in the memory of his former glory. "We had a three-year run. It's something I'll never forget."

Frankie took a second look at the man perched on the barstool next to him: Rick was in his late thirties now, but there were still traces of the former teen idol. Cow-like brown eyes hidden behind wire-rimmed glasses. Sandy brown hair groomed into a semblance of style. And clothes that certainly favored the nineties – a buttoned-down pink shirt, skintight Levis, and pointy-toed cowboy boots.

What a douche, Frankie thought. *This town is ripe for a takeover, and I am just the man to do it. But I need help, and this schmuck could be it.*

"So . . . Rick," he ventured. "You an' me should get together."

"Yeah, really," Rick said, nodding. "I'd like that."

"How about tomorrow?" Frankie suggested. "We could do lunch around the pool at the Beverly Hills Hotel. I got a business proposition you might find interesting."

"Why not?" Rick said. "I'm always open for new ideas."

Frankie smiled. He was king of the freaking connections. He'd been in town less than twenty-four hours and already he was in action.

Life was good.

Life was *very* good.

Chapter Thirty-Three

Denver

I received a text from Sam and read it on my way to the office.

Miss my red-nosed Los Angelino. Our time together was special. You're special. Who am I supposed to make pancakes for now?

A smile spread across my face. I couldn't help liking that he missed me. Well, he must do, to send a text like that.

I contemplated my reply. Had to hit exactly the right note, couldn't sound wimpy. I finally came up with – *Hmm . . . memories of special pancakes. I'm certainly in the mood for more.*

Ambiguous. Just right.

I was still smiling when I entered the office.

Mister Shark Teeth soon wiped the smile off my face with a tart lecture about the importance of client/lawyer relationships.

I stood firm. Told him enough was enough, and that I was no trained babysitter.

He finally accepted the fact that I was done, and then informed me that we would both be attending the funeral on Thursday as a show of respect. I agreed, even though it would mean missing my family dinner.

I finally made it into my office and summoned Megan – my own personal intern who unfortunately was not the competent assistant I had promised Annabelle. Megan was the daughter of a business associate of Mister Shark Teeth, and she was about as dense as they come. I'd tried to teach her a thing or two, but getting through to her was like slogging through the desert at noon in ski-clothes.

Megan was a Valley Girl with nothing but shopping, clubbing and boyfriends on her mind. Her heroes were Lindsay Lohan and Paris Hilton. She worshipped Zac Efron and considered George Clooney and Brad Pitt to be two very old men.

Actually, after thinking about it, she's probably the perfect person to hang out with Annabelle. Two spoiled brats together.

I sent her off to the Maestro mansion with a brisk warning to behave herself and try to represent the firm in a suitable fashion.

Megan was thrilled to escape boring office duties.

After she'd left, I sat at my desk and reviewed the work I had piling up. A shoplifting case involving a TV has-been and a small boutique. And an aggravated assault case between a rapper and a fine upstanding member of the paparazzi. Nothing too exciting, but since both cases involved fairly well-known people, I would try to make the most of them.

In a way I regretted the fact that Ralph had not been accused of his wife's murder. It would've been one hell of a case to help defend. Felix would've done an excellent job, and I would've been right there beside him watching and learning.

After a while I called the vet to inquire about my dog, Amy Winehouse. Amy did not take kindly to being boarded at a kennel, so whenever I traveled I boarded her at my vet, because they treated her like the queen she thought she was.

"I'll pick Amy up later today," I informed the receptionist.

"Uh, Miss Jones, your friend came in with his cat yesterday morning, and when he spotted Amy he said he'd take her. He told me you knew about it and everything was arranged."

"My friend?"

"Mr Meyer."

For a moment shock and fury overcame me. Mr Meyer. *Josh* Meyer. My ex live-in.

"What?" I managed.

"Amy seemed pleased to see him," the receptionist said. "Her tail was wagging like crazy. Is it okay that I released her?"

No, it's not okay, you stupid cow. Josh always wanted to keep Amy and I told him not a chance in hell. Hanging onto Amy was my way of punishing Josh, letting him know that he couldn't always get his own way. And now he's just taken her. Well, screw him. This is war.

"Uh . . . actually, in the future, please do not release my dog to anyone but me," I said, trying not to lose my temper.

"I'm so sorry," the receptionist wailed. "I do hope—"

"It doesn't matter," I said, cutting her off. "I'll deal with it."

After slamming down the phone, I called Josh on his cell. Fortunately he had not changed numbers, but unfortunately I didn't get him, I got his damn voicemail.

"This is Denver," I said, employing my best ice-cold voice. "You took Amy, and I do not appreciate it. You know we agreed the dog would stay with me – so what the fuck, Josh. Call me as soon as you get this."

I clicked off steaming at his audacity. How dare he kidnap *my* dog.

* * *

By five o'clock Josh had still not called back.

Sonofabitch!

Dognapper!

Major asshole!

I realized a confrontation was in order if I wished to retrieve Amy. I knew where Josh worked, taking care of the limbs of some of the biggest sports stars in the city, but I figured going to his home would be a better bet to get my dog back. So a few minutes after five I took off and drove to his house in Hancock Park. Yes, after we split, Josh had purchased a house – something he'd never considered doing while we were together.

I hadn't visited his house before, although I have to admit that after I found out he'd bought it, I did do a couple of drive-bys. Not that I cared, but my curiosity got the better of me, and I'd wanted to see what he'd been saving up for.

From outside, the house looked nice. It was set back from the street with a well-kept green lawn and plenty of trees. The house itself featured Old Colonial-style architecture, quite impressive.

I parked on the street, marched up to the front door and rang the bell.

A frighteningly skinny short woman with long golden curls and a tough expression opened the door. She was in her late twenties, with the obligatory fake L.A. tan. She was dressed designer casual from head to toe.

"Yes?" she asked, one hand on her bony hip. Her tone was as friendly as a bucket full of shit.

"Hi," I said, attempting to peer past her. "Is Josh around?"

She narrowed her flinty over-mascaraed eyes. "Who wants to know?"

"I do, actually."

"And you are?"

"Denver." No sign of recognition crossed her pinched face. "Denver Jones," I added, because I am sure he must have told her about me. Still nothing. "Josh's ex."

The information finally hit her pea-brain. Am I being unfair? I don't think so. She's an idiot, I can just tell.

"He has my dog," I said evenly. "I want it back."

"That's a relief," said Miss Skinny. "I can't stand the mangy creature. Dogs bring out all my worst allergies."

As if to prove she was telling the truth, she sneezed twice and glared at me as if it was my fault.

Lucky Josh, he'd found himself a winner.

"Where is Amy?" I asked, tightly wound.

"Amy?" she questioned vaguely.

"My dog."

"Oh, that thing. I locked it in the shed at the back."

My fury was slowly building. I wanted to smack her. "Why did you do that?"

"I told you. Allergies," Miss Skinny said, stifling a yawn. "Plus the stupid dog never stops barking. How do you stand it?"

"Amy is barking because you've locked her up," I said. "Where's Josh?"

"On his way home, I guess."

"Then I'll take my dog and leave."

"Does Josh know?"

"Does Josh know what?"

"That you're taking the dog."

"Yes," I said shortly. "It's all arranged."

"Well then," she said. "You'd better come in, 'cause I'm not opening the shed door. The dumb dog'll probably bite me."

I wish!

I stepped into the interior of the house, which was a mix of styles. It was also one big mess. Racks of clothes stood around the living room, and various piles of accessories littered every table. Miss Skinny Stylist to the Stars, had certainly marked her territory. The only sign that Josh lived there was a huge flat-screen TV and his comfortable old chair, the chair I'd never been able to persuade him to dump.

Ha! He'd never dumped the chair, but he'd had no problem dumping me.

Not that I cared. Honestly, I couldn't care less.

In the distance I could hear Amy barking. Suddenly Josh came bounding into the house.

Josh Meyer. My ex. The man with whom I'd once spent several precious years.

I looked at him. He looked at me. For a moment it was as if time stood still and we were back together and nothing had changed.

"What's going on here?" Josh asked, breaking the spell. "What are you doing here, Denver?"

I gave him a cold stare. How dare he thieve my dog and then have the nerve to ask me what I was doing in his house.

I observed that he'd put on weight, at least ten pounds, and I couldn't help feeling pleased, because I know that I look good, although I probably look like a huge giant standing next to Miss Skinny who wasn't an inch past five feet.

"You took my dog," I said accusingly.

"*Our* dog," he snapped back.

"No. *My* dog."

"You left Amy at the vet. I could see she wasn't happy, so I took her out of there."

"You had no right to do that."

"I had every right. We found Amy together, remember?"

"Yes, and when you left, I kept her. It's what we agreed."

"It's what *you* agreed."

"Your little girlfriend doesn't even like dogs, so why would you take her?"

"There you go, always trying to control everything," Josh sneered. "Amy was *our* dog, I'm *entitled* to take her."

"No, you are not."

"Yes, I am."

"Pul-*ease*!" Miss Skinny said, inserting her non-existent body between us. "Take your dog and go. The two of you are giving me a migraine."

Allergies, migraines – Josh had found himself a real prize.

"Yes, Josh," I said, weary of fighting. "Give me my dog."

Josh's mouth went into a thin straight line – a sure sign he was majorly pissed.

Had I ever really loved this man?

I guess so, but not any more.

"Fine," he said, still tight-lipped.

"Fine," I responded, staring him down.

A few minutes later I was out of there with Amy Winehouse, both of us happy to be on our way.

I had to make a quick stop at the office, and then after that I had a late dinner with Mario planned. He'd already texted me confirming we should meet at *Ago*. I would just have time to go home and change into something suitable for an evening out with Mario, which would probably end up at his place.

Hmm . . . After my Josh confrontation I needed a little loving care, and Mario was the guy to supply it.

I drove straight to the office, left Amy with my favorite parking attendant, and took the elevator all the way to the forty-second floor.

Megan was back and beaming. "I had the *best* time," she enthused. "Annabelle is *awesome*!"

Ah yes, there's nothing like going through a murdered movie star's clothes with the star's daughter to put a smile on a girl's face.

"Mr Saunders asked for you to take a look at these photos," Megan added, handing me an 8 × 10-inch manila envelope.

"What are they?"

"He didn't say. Can I leave now?"

"Sure," I said, ripping open the envelope.

Felix had enclosed a short note.

Denver. View these photos of Gemma Summer. Any thoughts? Ralph is anxious to know who the man is.

Of course Ralph was anxious to know. His beautiful wife had been photographed with another man the week before her murder.

I took a long look at the photos. There were four of them. Gemma looking beautiful, obviously enjoying herself – clinking glasses with the stranger – a man barely visible, just his profile on show. They were taken at a secluded restaurant high in the hills above Malibu. The photographer must have followed Gemma there, then hidden in the bushes to get his shots.

I looked once, twice, three times, and then it struck me.

Mystery Man was Carolyn's father.

Chapter Thirty-Four

Carolyn

The last thing Carolyn remembered was stopping her car outside the deserted Shell station – long since shut down – and waiting patiently for Gregory to arrive. She truly couldn't recall what had taken place next, although she had faint memories of a girl knocking on her window – a young Hispanic girl who'd seemed agitated and maybe in some kind of trouble. Being the Good Samaritan that she was, Carolyn had rolled down her window to see if she could help, and that was it – no more memory.

Now she found herself waking up in the dusty trunk of a moving car, her hands and ankles bound, a filthy rag stuffed in her mouth.

Panic immediately overcame her. Was this a nightmare? Surely she would wake up any minute? But no. She was trussed up in the trunk of a car, and the vehicle was on the move.

Bile filled her throat, but she swallowed it down, fearful that she might choke.

She attempted to move. Impossible.

Her hands were tied behind her back with electrical cord. The cord was cutting into her wrists and hurting her.

Please God, help me.

She was desperate to say the words out loud, but that was impossible too, so she silently chanted them in her head like a comforting mantra, and hoped that somehow He would hear her.

* * *

"You sure she ain't gonna *die* on us?" Rosa, Benito's sixteen-year-old girlfriend asked. Rosa was a pretty girl – her prettiness marred by a thin white scar running the full length of her left cheek – the result of an all-girl gang fight. Her mama had punished her for that one, kept her locked in the house for two whole weeks.

"How many times I gotta tell ya," Benito answered with a vicious scowl. "We just puttin' a scare in the *puta* so she lose the mo'fuckin' baby."

"All she hadda do was get the dude to pull out," Rosa offered. "Works every time."

"An' that's why *you* got a ten-month-old baby livin' with your mama," Benito said, his expression sour. "'Sides, *she* don' wanna dump her baby, it's what the Senator prick wants."

"Some asswipe," Rosa mumbled, swigging from a can of Red Bull, then wiping her mouth with the back of her hand. "Why's you doin' it for him, anyway?"

"I be doin' it 'cuz I ain't gettin' my ass thrown back in th'joint," Benito said impatiently.

"What you supposed t'do with her?" Rosa asked, opening her purse and taking out a CoverGirl powder compact she'd recently swiped from the drugstore.

"Ya think *I* know?" Benito said, blinking rapidly. "How long it take t'lose a fuckin' baby?"

Rosa shrugged, then began carefully examining her face in the compact mirror.

"Dunno," she said at last, discovering a zit that needed

squeezing. "But a girl in school went to some Irish dude – she got an abortion for fifty bucks. Whyn't we take her there?"

"'Cuz it gotta look like an accident," Benito insisted, wishing Rosa would keep her mouth shut for once.

"Why?" Rosa asked, running her tongue over her lips.

"Quit with the fuckin' questions," Benito growled.

He'd been seeing Rosa on and off since she was fifteen, almost six months – a record for him. She was obliging, didn't nag *too* much, and sucked him off like a seasoned trouper.

The downside was she'd had a baby with a rival gang member, and anytime the opportunity arose, the fucker attempted to blast his ass from here to the White House. It was an ongoing feud, and Benito was seriously thinking about dumping Rosa because of it.

But not now, not with the Senator's pregnant bitch trussed up in the trunk of his car. That wouldn't be smart.

* * *

"It's black tie tonight," Evelyn Stoneman reminded her husband over the house intercom.

Another black-tie event was the last thing Gregory needed. But he was well aware how prudent it was for him to attend, because while Carolyn was on the missing list, he had to make absolutely certain that every move he made was accounted for.

Not that anyone had reported Carolyn missing. Considering she lived by herself, that could take days – and by that time she would no doubt be back with no baby growing in her belly. Upon her return Gregory would commiserate with her, make noises about how there should be tougher laws to combat crime. And then – when the time was right – he'd break up with her.

If luck was with him, the shock of being abducted should make her lose the baby fast – perhaps within hours. And when that happened she would be set free, and Gregory would also be set free. It was the perfect plan.

He'd instructed Benito not to harm her, merely to shake her up. Not that Benito was the most trustworthy human being on the planet, but Gregory had been given no choice. The baby had to go, and Benito seemed to be his only way out.

Evelyn appeared at the door to his dressing room clad in a long white Carolina Herrera gown and tasteful diamonds. "You're not ready," she admonished, wagging a beringed finger at him.

"Give me five minutes," Gregory said gruffly, reaching for a crisp white dress-shirt on a nearby hanger. "That's all I need."

* * *

Once again Carolyn felt the bile rise in her throat, and once more she managed to swallow it down.

The car was traveling over rough terrain, and she was unable to protect herself from being thrown around in all directions.

She attempted to calm herself and think rationally. When Gregory arrived to meet her and realized she was missing, surely he would report her disappearance to the police?

Or would he? Knowing Gregory, he might be too cagey to do so – he was always so worried about his precious reputation.

But if her car was still outside the abandoned gas station, then Gregory would know for sure that something was wrong, and of course he'd report it; his conscience would force him to do so.

But what if whoever had her locked in the trunk of their car had stolen her Pontiac and driven it off? Then how would Gregory know she'd been taken?

Tears filled her eyes and began slowly sliding down her cheeks.

How would Gregory know? That was the question.

And who would rescue her?

Chapter Thirty-Five

Bobby

Surveying the club location at The Keys with M.J. and Lucky, Bobby experienced a full-on flash of triumph. Finally he would be taking the place over, changing the name to *Mood*, and creating the most successful late-night venue in Vegas. It was something he'd dreamed of doing ever since Lucky had built The Keys. He'd always nagged her about allowing him to get the club concession, but she'd resisted, saying he had to prove he could do it first. Well, he'd sure as hell proved it. After being open for almost three years, *Mood* in New York was raking in big bucks, and soon he'd be making a deal to open *Mood* in Miami, and now he had Vegas to look forward to.

"Y'know we're gonna be making major changes," he informed Lucky.

"Wow," she drawled. "I'm *so* surprised."

"You want our stamp on it, don't you?" he said, noting that his mom never changed. With her long dark curls, deep olive skin, and blacker-than-night eyes she was still the most beautiful woman he'd ever seen. And the smartest.

"That's why I called you, Bobby."

"No," he argued. "You called me because I'm the only one you can trust not to set up my own deal on your premises."

"Hardly true," Lucky objected. "There are plenty of reputable club-owners I could've brought in. Rande Gerber, Brent Bolthouse—"

"Keep going, Mom," he said confidently. "You *know* you need me."

"I do?"

"Yeah – say it," he urged. "Go on – say it."

"I need you!" Lucky said in a mock-dramatic fashion. "You too, M.J."

"Thanks, Mrs Gol—"

"Lucky."

"Uh, thanks, Lucky," M.J. muttered. Bobby's incredible mom always managed to make him feel like a kid again.

"Do you realize, M.J., that I've known you and your family since you were twelve?" Lucky said, smiling at M.J. "Your father looked after Gino when he had that aneurism problem. And your mom is *the* most delightful woman."

"Yeah, an' I bet you didn't know that M.J.'s *still* got a crush on you," Bobby quipped. "Only now he has a girlfriend, so I gotta hunch you're probably safe."

"Who wants to be safe?" Lucky teased, mildly flirting.

M.J. glared at Bobby; he was beyond embarrassed. "Whyn't you tell your mom who's got a thing for *you*?" he said, frowning.

"And who would that be?" Lucky asked, faintly amused.

"Zeena," M.J. blurted. "She's got the hots for Bobby, big-time."

Bobby threw M.J. a dirty look. "Bullshit," he said.

"That's quite a coincidence," Lucky said, "because tomorrow night we're seeing her show. I hear it's amazing, so I got us all tickets."

"Never mind about Zeena's show," Bobby said, determined to get off the subject of the predatory superstar. "Aren't you interested in hearing what *kind* of changes I'm gonna make?"

"I have a strong suspicion I can guess," Lucky said, smiling. "But go ahead – tell me anyway."

Bobby launched into his plans for *Mood* in Vegas. He had many ideas, and the first order of business was to do away with the illuminated staircase, the indoor fountains and expensive art. His plan was to create a replica of *Mood* in New York. "It's gotta have a cooler, more laid-back vibe," he insisted. "Right now it's screaming Vegas."

"Business has always been good," Lucky pointed out. "Getting people into the club was never the problem."

"It's not about how much money you rake in," Bobby insisted. "It's more about the crowd."

"And the crowd should be?" Lucky questioned.

"No tourists – unless they're young an' way hot. No fat asses. Like I told you when you first opened – you gotta make the club a happening place for the locals to hang after they get off work. So . . . sexy girls in sexy outfits. Rich dudes with their Ferraris and Bentleys parked outside. Visiting celebs. Everyone with a cool attitude. *That's* the vibe we'll be going for."

"Okay, guys," Lucky said, readily agreeing. "I think I get the picture."

"You do?" Bobby said, surprised that she wasn't putting up a fight about the changes he intended to make.

"Sure I do, so how about we go work out a deal? Then we can relax and have some fun."

Bobby grinned. "You got *my* attention."

* * *

Later it was his half-sister, Max, who really got his attention. She came to his room at The Keys, surprising him, hammered on the door and burst inside.

He hadn't seen Max in a few months, and at the age of seventeen she'd blossomed into a total beauty – but she still hadn't lost her wild streak. Max was the mirror-image of Lucky at the same age. Tall and lithe with a mass of unruly black curls, sun-burnished olive skin, full lips and plenty of attitude. The only difference was their eyes. Lucky's were dark and intense, Max's were a brilliant emerald-green.

The moment he opened the door, she threw herself at him, wrapping her long legs around his waist and hugging him tight.

"Whoa!" he said, laughing as he attempted to disentangle himself. "Not appropriate, you're way too old."

"Ha!" Max exploded with a wild giggle. "I flew here for the day just to see you. The least I expect is a decent greeting."

"Brat!" he said affectionately.

"Womanizer!" she responded, green eyes sparkling. "You're like *so* totally lame, Bobby. Why didn't you tell me you were coming? I had to hear it from Mom. So I jumped on a plane, an' here I am."

"Nice to see you too," he said, still laughing.

"But I love you anyway, big bro," she added with an infectious grin.

"You love me, huh?"

"Yup."

"Nice to know."

"And you love me, right?"

"Sometimes," he teased. "When you're not pissing me off."

"C'mon, Bobby," she said, mock-frowning. "Stop jerking me around."

"Who's jerking you around?"

"You! You! You!" she yelled.

"Calm down."

"Where's M.J.?" she asked, switching moods and opening the mini-bar. "I'm supposed to haul his rockin' ass back to L.A."

"An' why's that?"

"'Cause my b.f.f., Cookie, is desperado to jump his sexy bones."

"Your friend Cookie is way too young to jump anyone's bones."

"Pul-*ease*!" Max said, rolling her eyes. "What century were *you* born?"

"S'great to see you too, kiddo," Bobby said, grinning. "Still with the same smart mouth."

"Anyone ever tell you you're beginning to sound like Grandfather Gino?" she offered, extracting a packet of M&Ms from the mini-bar.

"An' that's a bad thing?"

"Here's the deal Bobby," she sighed, stuffing a handful of M&Ms into her mouth. "I think it's way time I came to New York an' moved in with you. Cool plan?"

"No," he said, shaking his head. "Not a plan at all."

"Why?" she demanded. "You just announced that you loved me. And I'd behave myself. Honestly, Bobby – you can do your thing an' I'll do mine."

"Thanks," he said dryly. "Does that mean I have your permission?"

"Ha! Ha! *Please*, Bobby?"

"Sorry. The answer is no."

"Why? Why? Why?"

"'Cause you've got to go to college," he lectured. "You know that's what Lucky and Lennie are expecting you to do."

"Not gonna do that," she said stubbornly.

"And your reason is?"

"'Cause Mom didn't go, an' then you went for two minutes an' like immediately dropped out. So why have *I* gotta suffer? It's not fair."

"A proper education means a lot, Max."

"Crap!" she muttered, flinging herself down on the couch, long bronzed legs stretched out in the shortest of skirts.

"No," he said crisply. "Fact of life."

"Man!" she complained. "You're getting as lame as Mom. I

guess I'll havta take off on my own with no help from you."

"And go where?"

"You'll see," she said airily. "No college for this girl. I crave adventure with a capital A. And for your information, nobody – an' I mean *nobody* – can stop me."

Bobby shook his head. He felt sorry for Lucky and Lennie – they had big trouble on their hands.

"What kind of adventures did you have in mind?" he asked.

"Oh, y'know," she answered vaguely. "Screwing a lot of guys – my choice. Kind of living on the edge."

"The edge of *what*?" he asked, trying not to laugh.

"You just don't get it, do you?" she said, throwing him a dirty look. "I'm my own person, I'm not Lucky's little girl or your baby sister or Lennie Golden's kid. I'm *me*."

"Nobody's arguing with *that* sentiment."

"Cool, 'cause I'm totally unique, and I plan on doing my own thing."

"And when's this gonna happen?"

"Sooner than anyone thinks," she said mysteriously.

"Yeah?"

"Bet on it, big brother," she said, green eyes flashing danger signals.

"Now you sound like Lucky."

"An' that's a bad thing?" she said, mimicking him.

"C'mon, baby sis," he said, reaching for her hands and pulling her off the couch. "We got a big dinner to get to. Brigette and her new friend, M.J. and his girl. So you'd better behave yourself. There'll be plenty of time to talk about your future later."

"Believe me, Bobby," she threatened. "we will. And I'm gonna win on this one – you'll see."

Chapter Thirty-Six

Annabelle

"Pack everything up and have it all put into storage," Annabelle instructed Lupe. "I'm too upset to deal with anything now – I'll get into it another time."

"Yes, Miss Anna," Lupe said obediently. Somehow she'd never been able to master saying Annabelle's full name. "Miss Gemma's jewelry," she added, full of concern. "What I do with it?"

Annabelle presumed that all of her mother's expensive jewelry was secure at the bank or tucked away in a safe hidden in the house. Frankly she didn't care. Gemma's jewelry wasn't to her taste.

"Leave it," she answered vaguely. "I'll go through it tomorrow."

Right now she was anxious to get out of there. Being back in the house was a total downer – it was making her feel physically sick. All the bad memories of her teenage years had come flooding back with a vengeance. She needed to escape from her childhood home and do something to take her mind off the upcoming funeral.

By the time she got downstairs, Megan was standing just

inside the front door. "Denver sent me," Megan announced. "Your housekeeper let me in. I'm Megan, and I'm here to help out."

Annabelle took a quick look around; fortunately Ralph was nowhere in sight.

"Come," she said, quickly sizing the girl up and deciding that she seemed a likely candidate for a fun day of retail activity. "We're going shopping."

* * *

Frankie made sure he was seated at a prime table near the pool where he could see everyone. It occurred to him that he could've ordered lunch in the cabana, but an excellent table right at the front was more impressive. Besides, who needed to be hidden away? Frankie had an urge to be seen.

He'd already spied a girl so perfect for their L.A. operation were they to get it off the ground. She was tall and stacked, with a kick-ass body that reminded him of Ursula Andress stepping out of the sea in an early Bond movie – a movie he'd watched on TV countless times. He could easily recall getting off on the fact that Bond was such a bad-ass – his kind of guy. And as for Ursula . . . well, she was the fantasy woman who'd guided him through many a lonely teenage night. He'd experienced his first orgasm with the delectable Ursula.

The girl in question was with a decrepit old dude who looked about ready to croak any minute. The dude had white hair – surprisingly a full head of it – and a shaggy white beard. The girl wore a bikini so small that she might as well not have bothered. Occasionally Frankie caught her glancing in his direction. He sensed she was dying to get laid – the old fart did not look capable of managing a sneeze, let alone anything else. Frankie had his card at the ready should she come over.

Rick Greco arrived ten minutes late wearing all white.

"Thought you mentioned we were meeting in the Polo Lounge," he said, obviously put out. "I was waiting around upstairs."

"Nope," Frankie answered, not getting up, a power move. "It was always by the pool. I'm a New Yorker, gotta catch the rays."

"Yeah," Rick said, pulling out a chair and sitting down. "How about our weather? This is December. Not bad, huh?"

"That's exactly why I wouldn't mind movin' here," Frankie allowed, chewing on a breadstick.

"Really?"

"I get off on the climate," Frankie said. "Not t'mention the scenery," he added, indicating the girl in the bikini who was now sitting by the edge of the pool, dangling her long legs in the water.

"You can do a lot better than her," Rick said with a ribald chuckle. "You've already seen the pussy that hangs at my club."

"Right on!" Frankie said.

"But let's not forget you've got a girlfriend, right?" Rick reminded him.

"Yeah, Annabelle," Frankie said, signaling for the waiter – a man he'd handsomely tipped earlier to make sure he got non-stop service. "But I'm here to tell you, Rick, my lady is *very* understanding; she's into lettin' me do my own thing."

"Now *that's* the kind of girlfriend to have," Rick said, rubbing his palms together.

"You got that right," Frankie agreed, ordering himself a Mimosa, while Rick settled for a vodka on the rocks.

He's a daytime drinker, Frankie thought. *All the easier to manipulate. I'm gonna make my mark with this one. I'm gonna take over this freaking town. Everyone's gonna know who Frankie Romano is.*

* * *

Annabelle had a satisfying time spending the day shopping with Megan. They hit all the best places – including Annabelle's favorite, Fred Segal, and Megan's not-to-be-missed Kitson on Robertson Boulevard. Then they covered all the large department stores – Neiman Marcus, Barneys, and Sak's, ending up at Maxfield on Melrose Avenue, where Annabelle dropped a cool eight thousand on a couple of hot outfits.

By the time she'd said goodbye to Megan and got back to the hotel, she was loaded down with shopping bags and feeling pretty damned pleased with herself. Shopping always gave her an incredible high.

Frankie had his coke. She had her black Amex. A fair exchange.

She was about to phone Janey, to check that everything was running smoothly, when the hotel spa called the suite to remind her of her afternoon appointment.

Abandoning her call to Janey, she took off, quite prepared to be deliciously pampered.

* * *

In the middle of lunch Frankie received a call from Bobby. "'Scuse me," he said to Rick as he turned away to take the call.

"Guess where we are," Bobby said, sounding hyper.

"Atlantic City, gettin' it on with my waitress," Frankie joked. "What was her name again?"

"No man, we're in Vegas," Bobby said, laughing.

"You *gotta* be shittin' me."

"I'm here with M.J. and his girlfriend."

"M.J. has a girlfriend?" Frankie said, surprised. "What's she like?"

"Young, black and pretty. He's in love."

Frankie wasn't interested in hearing about M.J.'s love-life, he had bigger things on his mind. "How come you're here?" he said. "I just saw you in New York, didn't look like you were goin' anywhere."

"Got a call from Lucky asking if we wanted to take over the club concession at The Keys."

"That's some surprise, but it's what you always wanted, right?"

"Sure is. And I was thinkin' that you an' Annabelle might be up to takin' a twenty-four-hour Vegas break. I'll send the plane for you."

"You're finally using your plane?" Frankie said, shocked that Bobby was doing so. "What's got into you?"

"I needed to get here fast."

"Jeez," Frankie said, mind racing as usual. "Vegas sounds like a plan."

"Doesn't it."

"Yeah, but the drag is we gotta be here for the funeral on Thursday."

"No problem. We'll all fly back to L.A. together early Thursday. Lennie's away, so Lucky's asked me to escort her."

"Lucky's goin' to the funeral?"

"It seems Gemma did a couple of movies for Panther when Lucky ran the studio. She liked her."

"I'll talk to Annabelle," Frankie said, all revved up. "But you can bet your ass *I'll* be there, with or without her."

"Then I'll go ahead and make the arrangements. Check in with me later."

"For sure," Frankie said, snapping his phone shut.

Rick was looking at him expectantly.

"My best friend, Bobby Santangelo," Frankie explained, keeping it casual while thinking that Bobby couldn't have called at a better time. Rick was already impressed, so this should nudge him right over the edge. "He's . . . uh . . . sending his plane to fly me to Vegas."

"Is that *the* Bobby Santangelo?" Rick asked. "Lucky

Santangelo's son? The dude who owns *Mood* in New York?"

"Bobby's my closest friend. We're thinkin' of partnerin' up."

"Nice."

"Isn't it," Frankie said with a self-satisfied smirk. And then, after a long beat, "So Rick, how about you an' me talk a little business? I wouldn't mind openin' up a place in L.A."

* * *

"How was your day?" Frankie asked when he and Annabelle finally met up in the suite around five.

"Shitty," Annabelle complained, deciding not to mention the shopping spree and her relaxing time spent at the spa.

"It must've been tough, sorting through your mom's things," Frankie said, going for the sympathy vibe. "I feel for you, babe."

"It was," Annabelle agreed with a put-upon sigh. "You can't even imagine."

"Not to worry, 'cause tonight I've planned a romantic dinner. An' tomorrow I'm flyin' you to Vegas for the day. Decided you needed a break."

Annabelle's eyebrows shot up. "Vegas?" she questioned. "What's in Vegas?"

"Bobby for starters. An' I managed to convince him to send his plane for us."

"What's Bobby doing in Vegas?" she asked, thinking that things were looking up.

"Takin' over a club. An' he'll be at your mom's funeral with *his* mom, so we'll all fly back together early Thursday. How cool is that?"

"Yes," Annabelle said, secretly delighted. "You're so right, I do need a break."

"Sure you do," Frankie agreed, not certain if he was pleased or disappointed that she was coming to Vegas.

Before they left for dinner, Ralph called. Annabelle was busy putting the finishing touches to her make-up in the bathroom, so Frankie picked up the phone.

"I'm expecting you both for dinner at the house," Ralph said brusquely.

"You are?" Frankie said, almost speechless for once. "Didn't realize that. We were just on our way to grab a bite at *Spago*."

"Fine," Ralph said, a man of quick decisions. "I'll meet you there." He clicked off before Frankie could object.

Not that Frankie would object; he was in awe of Ralph Maestro, although he was certain that Ralph joining them at *Spago* would not fly with Annabelle. She'd be major pissed.

After thinking about it for a few minutes, he decided the smart thing was not to mention that Ralph had called. Play it dumb, and when Ralph showed up, look surprised.

Annabelle emerged from the bathroom wearing one of her new outfits.

"You look like a star, babe," Frankie commented. "Hot an' sexy – now *that's* my kinda girl."

"I stopped on my way back to the hotel and shopped," Annabelle confessed, pirouetting in her Dolce & Gabbana sleek bronze leather dress. "You like?"

"I'm into the dress," Frankie said, reaching out and grabbing her around the waist. "But what I'm *really* into is the body that's in it."

Annabelle gave a slow smile. Sometimes Frankie knew exactly what to say.

Chapter Thirty-Seven

Denver

The first thing on my mind was trying to reach Carolyn. I had no idea what I was going to say to her, I only knew that we had to speak before I told anyone else of my discovery.

Carolyn did not pick up, so I sent her a text. *Call me immediately. Urgent!* I figured that would get her attention.

Then I started thinking about her parents, Mr and Mrs George Henderson. I didn't know them well, but I did know that Carolyn had always talked about the two of them with love and affection, and whenever I'd gone over to her house when we were younger and Carolyn was living at home, George and his wife, Clare, had seemed perfectly in tune with each other.

George Henderson was a well-respected plastic surgeon – is that how he'd met Gemma?

And Clare Henderson – once George's assistant – worked in real estate. I remembered Clare as a pleasant woman – pretty, but no great beauty.

George, on the other hand, was a very attractive man, tall and lanky with an easygoing charm.

I hadn't seen either of them in at least two years, but Carolyn often mentioned that they were both doing well, George especially. He kept an extremely low profile, never courted publicity, but according to Carolyn had worked on some of the most famous faces in Hollywood. He also did pro-bono work at a children's hospital, and twice a year visited poorer countries around the world to use his skills to help people with horrible disfigurements. I knew that Carolyn was very proud of him.

George Henderson was hardly a likely candidate to be conducting an affair with one of the most beautiful women in the world. But there he was, photographed with Gemma, and any fool could see just by looking at the photos that these two people were totally into each other.

Why was I the only one to have recognized him?

Because his famous clients were hardly likely to step forward, since, according to almost every actress in Hollywood, their beauty was God-given, untouched by a plastic surgeon's scalpel.

Hmm . . . George Henderson. Should I call Felix and tell him that I've identified the man with Gemma? Or should I wait until I've spoken to Carolyn and found out exactly what's going on?

I decided to wait. I didn't want to start something without checking with her.

In the meantime, Mario was expecting me at *Ago*. I could certainly do with a decent meal, followed by some Mario-style sex.

Wow! Am I turning into a sex maniac?!

No. Simply releasing the tension.

Seeing Josh ensconced in his new life with Miss Skinny Stylist was not my favorite way of spending an afternoon. On the plus side, Mario made Josh look like an out-of-shape slacker.

I hurried home, fed Amy, took a quick shower, touched up my make-up, slid into a low-cut top and silk pants *sans* underwear, then I jumped in my car and headed for *Ago*.

Mario was waiting. Well, not exactly waiting – more like sitting at what I presumed was our table, engaged in an intimate conversation with a Hollywood Blonde. I call them Hollywood

Blondes because there is a group of women who look exactly alike. They all have long, thick, glossy blonde hair (extensions help the style to stay just so). Smooth, faintly tanned, unlined faces (a mixture of Botox, self-tan cream, and weekly facials). Long, lean bodies (Pilates, yoga, spinning). And exactly the right size fake breasts.

This one, in her tighter than tight True Religion jeans and lacy loose top, with dangling earrings and a dozen Me & Ro bracelets – including the red Kabbalah string – fit the mold perfectly.

Mario spotted me approaching and quickly stood up, but the Hollywood Blonde had no intention of shifting her finely tuned ass. She stayed firmly in her seat, and attempted to ignore me as if *I* was the intruder.

"Hi," I said. Better to be friendly than bitchy.

Hollywood Blonde threw me a disinterested look, while Mario wrapped his arms around me and greeted me with a warm hug. "Welcome back," he whispered in my ear. "I missed you."

"You did?" I said, falling into his extraordinarily addictive dimples.

"You'd better believe it," he responded.

Hollywood Blonde glared at me, then finally realizing she was a third wheel, she reluctantly stood up. "I guess I should be getting back to my friends," she ventured, obviously hoping Mario would ask her to stay.

He didn't. But that didn't stop her from grabbing his hand, leaning into him and whispering something into *his* ear.

To his credit Mario immediately backed off. "Great running into you, Lisa," he said. "See you around."

"Call me," she purred, once again ignoring my existence – which was basically Mario's fault, because shouldn't he have at least introduced us?

Finally she was gone and I quickly sat down. The seat was still warm from Lisa's True Religion-clad ass.

Mario also sat down, a sheepish grin spread across his face.

I determined not to ask any questions – playing jealous girlfriend was not my M.O. After all, we'd only had one date, it wasn't as if I possessed any proprietary rights.

"Lisa's an old friend," he volunteered.

"Not so old," I retorted, unable to help myself.

Leaning across the table, he took my hand in his. "Jealous?" he asked, still with the sheepish grin.

I might be. But I just had sex with a very attractive stranger in New York. So – jealous? I hardly think so.

"Maybe," I countered, deciding there was nothing wrong with fluffing his ego.

"You don't have to be," he assured me. "Lisa an' I are ancient news."

Too much information. I did not wish to imagine Mario in the sack with Lisa whoever she was. It wasn't conducive to a night of unbridled lust, and I was anticipating a *very* lustful night.

"Thanks for the info," I said crisply. "I'll store it away for future reference."

Flashing his whiter than white teeth, he said, "That's what I like about you."

"Do tell."

"You're acerbic."

"I am?"

"Makes a refreshing change. A lot of beautiful women don't have much to say."

Was he calling me beautiful?

Yes, he was.

Mario was definitely going to get major lucky tonight.

* * *

There's something totally addictive about sex. When you haven't had it in a while, a girl can definitely live without it. But when you're back in action – watch out!

And I was back in action big-time.

After dinner at *Ago* – delicious sole for me, pasta primavera for him, and a bottle of red wine between us – we headed back to his place in a hurry. I followed him in my car, anticipating what was to come.

I would've invited him back to my apartment, but I figured Amy Winehouse had experienced enough trauma for one day. She didn't need the added stress of me and Mario making out.

No sooner were we inside his front door than we both went at it like a couple of sex-starved teenagers. Clothes began falling off at an alarming rate. First his, then mine, until we were both standing naked in the small living room of his modest house. He pulled me close so that my breasts were against his chest, and his hard-on was pressing against my thigh.

"Put your legs around my waist," he ordered, grabbing my ass to assist.

Oh yes, no problem.

But wait a minute – where was the foreplay he'd been so adept at last time? I might be horny (again?!!) but a little attention to turning me on even more might be nice.

And just as I was thinking this, his doorbell rang.

It was past midnight, and straddling him in his living room with no clothes on was suddenly making me feel quite vulnerable.

"Uh, are you expecting anyone?" I asked, unwrapping my legs from around his waist.

"Me? No," he said, equally startled.

"Should we ignore it?"

"It might be important," he decided. "Go wait in the bedroom, I'll deal with it."

He didn't need to tell me twice. I hurried into his bedroom

and slid between the sheets. Then I realized I'd left my purse in the other room and I wished I hadn't, because I needed to check my phone to see if Carolyn had tried to reach me. It was imperative that I reveal George Henderson's identity first thing in the morning, and I *so* needed to speak to Carolyn first.

Suddenly sex with Mario didn't seem so urgent. Whoever had rung his front doorbell had put a damper on things. I had a sudden strong desire to get dressed and go home. But I couldn't, on account of the fact that my clothes were strewn all over the floor in his living room.

Mario returned. Still naked. Still with an impressive hard-on.

I decided to stay until we'd finished what we'd started and then take off.

"Who was that?" I asked. "And don't tell me you answered the door with no clothes on?"

"Protected my modesty with a cushion," he quipped. "A very large cushion."

"I thought size didn't matter," I said lightly.

"You're kidding, right?" he said, leaping into bed beside me and starting to lick my nipples.

Ah . . . now we get foreplay.

"You're adventurous, right?" he said, his voice low and husky. "Ready to try anything?"

"Why?" I asked breathlessly, totally turned on again.

"'Cause *I* am. It's my thing to always embrace the unexpected – it can turn out to be a real trip."

And with those words he threw off the sheet and began moving his magical tongue down my body, spreading my thighs with his strong hands, licking his way to between my legs.

I gave a deep sigh and threw my arms up, covering my eyes. A man who *really* knows how to give head is a gem indeed. And Mario knew a thing or two about how to please a woman. Suddenly all thoughts of taking off were gone with the wind as I lay back and enjoyed the ministrations of his talented tongue.

He paused for a moment. I urged him not to stop. "Whatever you're doing, it's *sooo* good," I murmured. "I'm almost there . . ."

And his tongue returned to giving me serious pleasure.

I couldn't hold back any longer, it was just too damn hot. I let myself go, and experienced an all-consuming, everlasting orgasm of mammoth proportions. "Oh . . . my . . . God," I gasped, my body quivering with delight. "That was . . . orgias-tic!!"

"She has such a way with words," Mario whispered, nibbling on my ear.

Wait a minute – how could he be attending to my ear when his head was still between my legs?

And then it dawned on me. There was a third party in the bedroom.

Chapter Thirty-Eight

Carolyn

"Under no circumstances contact me," Gregory had warned Benito. "I will contact you if necessary."

Benito didn't care. He'd been given a job to do, and once the job was completed he and the Senator had no reason to ever speak again. Unless he got into trouble and needed help – in which case he'd have no problem asking for the Senator's assistance. One thing Benito knew for sure was that he would *never* allow himself to be carted off to the big house again. *Never*. Dead and buried was the only sane alternative to jail.

Meanwhile, this job of taking the Senator's bitch and shaking her up so that she lost her baby was lasting too long. He'd thought it would all be over fast. Grab the *puta*, ride her around in the trunk of his car for a few hours, and bingo – baby gone.

But no – he'd driven around for endless hours outside the city, over the bumpiest roads he could find, until eventually Rosa, sitting next to him in the passenger seat, had started moaning that she was tired and hungry, and that they'd better stop and see if they'd achieved what they'd set out to do.

"I'm openin' the trunk," Benito growled, pulling over to a deserted side street. By now it was night-time, and come to think of it he could go for a burger himself. "You go take a look at her," he commanded.

"Why *I* gotta do it?" Rosa objected, argumentative as usual.

"'Cuz I ain't lookin' between her legs," Benito steamed. "That ain't no man's work."

"It's *your* shitass deal," Rosa said belligerently. "You got us into this."

"Shut your mouth an' *help*," Benito ordered, grabbing a flashlight and jumping out of the car. Running around to the back, he sprung open the trunk and shone the flashlight on Carolyn. She was lying there, still trussed up, and now she was motionless, which scared the crap out of him. The first thought that went through his head was – what if the *puta* went and died on him? If that happened, it meant he'd be heading back to lock-up, or even worse – the executioner's chair.

Immediately he'd slammed the trunk shut, and without saying a word, he'd gotten back in the car and driven to his dump of a house, borrowed from a drug-dealer cousin who was doing time. Once there, he'd parked the car amongst the rotting garbage in the alley at the back, and with some reluctant help from a complaining Rosa, he'd half-dragged and half-carried the Senator's pregnant girlfriend inside before dropping her down on the bed and untying her.

The good news was that she was still breathing. The bad news was that there was no blood in sight, and even he knew that when she lost the baby there had to be blood, Rosa had assured him of that. "'Course," his sixteen-year-old girlfriend had said, like she was some kind of expert. "We dunno how knocked up she is. If the baby's big – we're gonna see it when it come out. My cousin lost her baby, an' that stupid baby was so huge she couldn't even flush it down the shitter."

Benito didn't care to listen. What did Rosa know? Exactly nothing.

After securing the woman's right wrist to the bedframe with

strong electrical cord, he slunk into the other room, switched on the TV, threw himself into a chair and stared blankly at the screen.

His gut told him this was not a healthy scene.

His gut told him that he had to get rid of the woman. She was bad luck, bad karma.

Fortunately she hadn't seen him, but she *had* seen Rosa.

So what? There were a million girls who looked like Rosa with their short skirts, platform shoes, too much make-up and teased hair. Their captive would never pick Rosa out in a line-up, and even if she did, Rosa would not risk opening up her mouth and involving him.

One thing he knew for sure, he had to come up with a new plan, because keeping the Senator's pregnant bitch in his house was no longer an option.

* * *

With Benito settled in front of the TV, Rosa seized the opportunity to slip out to the alley and open the back passenger door of his car. She was looking for the woman's purse. When they'd taken her, first smothering her face with a chloroformed pad, Rosa had grabbed the purse and hurriedly thrown it on the back seat. Benito hadn't noticed, he was too busy trussing up his unconscious victim and attempting to jam her in the trunk of his car.

Sometimes Benito could be so dumb. This taking the woman thing was dumb, but Rosa went along with whatever Benito wanted because he was her boyfriend, and it wasn't easy finding a boyfriend once you had a crying baby at home. Besides, having an older boyfriend like Benito gave her power in school when she bothered to attend. Nobody dared mess with Benito's girlfriend. Everyone knew she was his property and therefore untouchable.

Rosa had decided that grabbing the purse was her bonus for

helping out. She wasn't walking away empty-handed – why should she?

After recovering the purse from the car, she scurried back into the house and stashed it under the kitchen sink. Later, when Benito was asleep, she'd take a look and see what was in it. Hopefully money, 'cause Benito gave her nothing; she had to steal from his pockets when he was sleeping.

"Yo!" he yelled from his seat in front of the TV. "Get me another beer, an' slide your ass in here."

Rosa obliged. She knew what he wanted. Beer followed by a solid blow-job.

It was never wise to fight with Benito.

* * *

Gaining consciousness, Carolyn realized she must have passed out, for when she came to she was no longer tied up in the trunk of a car, she was lying on a narrow sagging bed in a dark room with her right wrist tightly affixed to the bedframe.

Little did she know that this was the same room Gregory had woken up in, only a couple of days earlier.

Waves of fear overcame her as she attempted to sit up. She was desperate to use the bathroom, her stomach ached and she began shivering uncontrollably.

The room was small, cold and damp. There was the smell of cigarette smoke and onions in the air, no carpet on the bare floorboards, and the tattered covering over the one window was tacked up with nails. Through the walls she could hear the noise of a loud TV, and overhead there was the faint drone of a helicopter.

Where was she?

What was happening to her?

She wasn't rich or famous, so why would anyone want to kidnap her?

Panicked, she couldn't be sure how much time had passed since she'd been taken. A few hours? A day? She had no idea, but it seemed like it was night-time, and her growling stomach informed her she was hungry, while her dry mouth craved water.

Overcome with feelings of fear and confusion, all she could do was hope and pray that any minute she would wake up, and this would turn out to be some insane nightmare.

Then the thought came to her. Gregory would race to her rescue. He had to.

After all, she was carrying his baby.

Chapter Thirty-Nine

Bobby

The dinner with Brigette and Kris, M.J. and Cassie, Lucky, Max, plus the two female owners of the Cavendish Hotel, Renee and Susie, went well. As usual, Bobby found himself impressed by his mom's knack of making everyone feel comfortable, even though Max spent most of the evening needling her.

Lucky seemed delighted with Brigette's choice of lover, while Kris was totally enamored with Lucky. Renee and Susie were in lesbian heaven. Meanwhile Cassie and Max were hitting it off big-time.

Why not? Bobby thought, watching the two girls chat non-stop. *They're almost the same age. M.J. is definitely cradle-snatching.*

Finally he got a chance to talk to Lucky alone, just the two of them. "What's up with Miss Wild Thing?" he asked, referring to his little sister.

"Max is driving us crazy," Lucky confessed, making a helpless gesture. "But what can we do?"

"How about letting her make her own decisions?" Bobby suggested. "She's almost eighteen, she's smart enough."

"Not as smart as *you* were at eighteen, and she's still only seventeen," Lucky responded. "It would drive me insane to see her go through the kind of experiences Brigette endured."

"What makes you think that might happen?" he asked.

"C'*mon*," Lucky said. "Max is young and gorgeous, plus she comes from a mega-rich family. You and I both know that every asshole searching out a major score will be after her, which is why I want her safely stashed in college until she's older."

"No chance, Mom," Bobby said, shaking his head.

"Why do you say that?"

"'Cause Little Sis is ready to roll – with or without your permission."

"You think?"

"She's already told me she's not going to do the college thing."

"Too bad, 'cause there's certainly no way I'm letting her run wild. That's not an option."

"Could be you got no choice."

"There's always a choice," Lucky said, her face clouding over. She took a long beat before continuing. "You know what the main problem is? She takes after me when I was her age. And trust me – I never listened to anyone."

"Shouldn't that make you understand where she's coming from?"

"Believe me – I try."

"If I remember, didn't Gino marry you off at sixteen?"

"Oh yeah, he sure did," Lucky said with a dry laugh. "Gino did it 'cause he thought that way he could control me. Naturally it didn't work. I outsmarted him all the way."

"But hey – Mom – you turned out a winner. You've achieved so much. *And* you did it all by yourself."

"Thanks, Bobby, but you still don't get it. Nothing's simple any more – we live in dangerous times."

"Back in the day, wasn't your mom murdered? And your brother, *and* the guy you were engaged to? Are you telling me things weren't dangerous then? Jeez, Mom, gimme a break."

"Sure they were, but like I said – it's a different world now. Besides, I was major street-smart, I knew how to look after myself in any situation."

"Max is smart, too. She got herself out of that whole kidnapping scam a couple of years ago."

"Pure luck. Besides, she had Ace to help her."

"Whatever happened to him? He still around?"

"Kinda, it's an on off thing."

"I guess you know she wants to move to New York."

"Oh yes, I've heard all about that. She's conjured up this fantasy about living with you."

"No *way*," he said. "I love Little Sis, but I'm not about to be responsible for her."

"Believe me – I get it, Bobby."

"Hey, you and Lennie will work it out."

"We'll sure as hell try."

"Hey, lotsa luck with that," Bobby said, grinning. "You're gonna need it."

Lucky smiled ruefully. "Enough about Max, what's going on with my number one son?"

"I'm taking over your club, that's enough to keep me busy."

"I mean relationship-wise, Bobby. What's the deal? Any girl I should know about?"

"Nobody special," he answered casually. A pause, another grin. "I'll just have to keep looking."

The next morning, Max flew back to L.A. Bobby drove her to the airport. Once again, he urged her to think about giving college a try, then he left it at that. There was no point in arguing with her. Max wanted her freedom, and as far as she was concerned, nobody was going to stop her.

Later, he spent the day at the club with M.J. They brought in an architect, a designer and a building contractor. It was all systems go.

Immersing himself in the meeting, Bobby also kept a sharp eye on his watch so he'd be around to welcome Frankie and Annabelle when they arrived at the hotel. He wasn't sure why he'd invited them; it was a spur of the moment decision he was starting to regret. On reflection he realized that he might've thought he needed a wall of people around him to protect him from Zeena, the maneater. Not that he planned on getting sucked in again, but perhaps it was inevitable.

Where were all the nice girls – the smart, intelligent, age-appropriate girls? They certainly weren't hanging out at *Mood*. He'd had it with the models and the party girls and the rich heiresses.

For a moment his thoughts turned to Denver – the lawyer he'd run into at Annabelle's in New York. She'd mentioned that they'd attended the same high school. He hadn't remembered her from then, but he'd liked her style – even though their meeting was brief. She'd given him her card, and it occurred to him that maybe he should call her, she'd seemed normal enough. She'd had a kind of appealing glow about her, and she wasn't stick-thin, she looked as if she might enjoy a steak or two. He should've told Frankie to bring her.

Hey – too late now. What was he thinking, anyway? He was simply trying to protect himself from Zeena.

Or was he? *Bring it on, Miz Superstar. I can deal with anything you got.*

* * *

Like most mega-stars who are known by only one name, Zeena expected everything – and then more. Her demands were calculated and bizarre, and nobody dared argue with her. She strolled through life secure in the knowledge that most people would bow down to her, and she could get away with anything.

Zeena had a penchant for using people. She got off on seeing how far she could push them. It was all a game, and if she happened to destroy someone along the way – too bad.

Men intrigued Zeena, although she was not averse to a woman or two when the occasion arose.

Bobby Santangelo Stanislopoulos intrigued her. He was different from the usual younger men she was attracted to. He had style, he had money, he had presence. And . . . even though she'd criticized him in bed, he certainly knew what he was doing.

So when Zeena discovered that Bobby would be in Vegas the one night she was appearing there, she considered it serendipity.

Renee, the owner of the Cavendish, let it drop that Lucky Santangelo and a group – including Lucky's hot son – would be attending Zeena's one-night charity event.

Zeena feigned total disinterest. "Would Zeena find them interesting people?" she asked.

"You mean you've never met Lucky?" Renee responded. "Oh my God! Lucky is *the* most amazing woman. The two of you should get together – you'll love her."

"Zeena is very particular about who she loves and doesn't love," Zeena purred. "However, I trust your judgment, Renee, so after my show, arrange for this Lucky woman and her group to attend a private dinner with us."

"Done!" Renee said, clapping her hands together. "You won't regret it."

"Hmm . . ." Zeena drawled, reaching for her trademark Gauloises. "I sincerely hope not, because Zeena hates to be bored. Being bored is a mortal sin."

* * *

By the time their meeting was over, Bobby found himself alone. M.J. had taken off with Cassie, Brigette and Kris were at the spa, and Lucky was on the phone in her palatial office dealing with business.

He wondered if he could get out of attending Zeena's concert that night, then he remembered he'd invited Frankie and Annabelle along with everyone else, so there was no escape.

Zeena would be up on stage doing her thing. It wasn't as if he'd have to see her or spend any intimate time with her.

On impulse he decided to make the limo trip to the airport and meet Frankie and Annabelle himself. It was better than sitting around doing nothing, and maybe they'd all stop off at the Wynn Hotel and play a few rounds of blackjack before hitting The Keys.

On his way through the lobby to the front of the hotel, he passed the magazine and newspaper stand. A headline caught his eye on the front of *Truth & Fact*. A headline that stopped him in his tracks.

Holy shit! This was not about to be pretty.

Chapter Forty

Annabelle

There were two flight attendants on the Stanislopoulos plane – Gitta, an attractive Dutch woman, and Hani, an Hawaiian beauty. Both women were pleasant and competent, and both knew how to deal with any situation. They'd been working for Stanislopoulos Shipping and Industries for over ten years – Gitta since she was twenty-five, and Hani a day before her nineteenth birthday. But today they were aware they had a problem, and both were mulling over different ideas about how it should be handled.

Frankie Romano was aboard the plane with his girlfriend Annabelle Maestro. They were on their way to Las Vegas – and therein lay the problem. Gitta and Hani could not decide whether to tell the loving couple about what could be lying in wait for them the moment they stepped off the plane, or whether to maintain a discreet silence.

Gitta opted for silence. Hani thought it best if the couple were forewarned.

At loggerheads, they consulted one of the two pilots, an older married man who harbored a secret crush on Hani.

"You should do what feels right for you," the pilot said,

gazing at Hani – the woman he could never have, on account of a wife and three small children at home.

"Then we tell them," Hani said firmly.

"Not them – *him*," Gitta said, always the diplomat. "*He* should be the one to inform her. Less embarrassing."

"Maybe I could take a peek at this magazine," the pilot suggested.

"We don't have a copy," Gitta answered.

"Gitta thought it best if we didn't bring it aboard," Hani explained.

The pilot shrugged. "If it's one of those tabloid magazines, then it's probably a story based on lies," he said. "Could be best if you *don't* mention it." Hani threw him a stony look which forced him to hurriedly change his mind. "Although," he added quickly, "you could take this Romano guy to one side and warn him."

"I'll do it," Gitta offered. "It'll be better coming from me."

"Why?" Hani argued. "Are you not sure I can handle it?"

"I know you can," Gitta said soothingly. "But should he get excited, I'm an expert at calming people down."

"And I'm not?"

"We both are," Gitta allowed. "Why don't I bring him to the galley, and we'll tell him together."

"Problem solved," the pilot said, relieved that he was off the hook. "Let me know how it turns out."

* * *

"I have a horrible suspicion that I might've been molested as a child," Annabelle mused, picking at a dish of nuts as Bobby's plane zoomed them toward Vegas.

"An' you're only remembering it *now*?" Frankie said incredulously.

"It's all coming back to me," Annabelle persisted.

"Obviously I buried the memory, but now that you've dragged me back to L.A. . . ."

"I haven't dragged you anywhere," Frankie said, narrowing his eyes. Jesus! She was in a pissy mood.

"May I remind you that it was *your* brilliant idea that we fly to L.A. for the funeral, leaving a perfectly excellent business in New York which Janey and her moron son are probably screwing up as we speak."

"Janey's not screwin' up anything," he snapped.

"Have you spoken to her?" Annabelle demanded, removing her sunglasses and glaring at him. "Checked in?"

"Jesus Christ, babe, we just got here," he groaned. "Isn't it time you stopped breakin' my balls?"

"I thought you left your balls with Daddy," Annabelle sniped. "All tied up with a pink satin ribbon and the credits of his latest movie."

"You can be such a bitch," Frankie said, shaking his head.

"Ralph Maestro. Your hero," Annabelle taunted. "And possibly *my* molester."

"Gimme a fuckin' break," Frankie said shortly. "When did you decide to invent *that* story?"

"Oh, you think it's a story, do you?" Annabelle said, bristling with annoyance that he didn't immediately believe her. After all, it could be true. Frowning, she decided she needed to go to one of those regression shrinks who would dig deep into her murky childhood and find out everything.

"It's not that I don't believe you, babe," Frankie said, figuring that he should at least humor her, because once she got into one of her impossible moods, it could so easily turn into an outrageous knock-down fight about nothing. "It's just that I think your mom's murder is affectin' you emotionally."

Unexpectedly, Annabelle's eyes filled with tears. Yes, of course it was. That and Sharif Rani's big fat son attacking her – about which Frankie had done exactly nothing.

There and then she made a life-changing decision: she had to lose her boyfriend. Frankie was a toxic sonofabitch who thought about nothing except snorting coke, scoring money and looking out for himself. Plus she couldn't stand the fact that he'd sucked up to Ralph as if he was the fucking President of America.

The thrill was definitely gone.

Should she tell him now, on the plane, leaving her free to run to Bobby?

Hmm . . . interesting thought. But probably wiser to wait until they got back to New York and things calmed down.

Bobby was definitely a future prospect, but since he was a friend of Frankie's she had to make sure her timing was right. If she dumped Frankie, she was certain Bobby would offer a sympathetic shoulder to cry on.

And from there . . . who knew what could happen?

* * *

"Excuse me, Mr Romano," Gitta said, lightly tapping him on his shoulder. "Might I have a word with you?"

"Huh?" Frankie said, wondering if he'd left a residue of coke on the bathroom counter and this woman in her smart pink and green uniform was about to tell him it was against federal rules to snort coke on a plane.

Shit! What could she do? Arrest him?

No way. He was being paranoid.

"Is there a problem?" he asked, automatically swiping his hand beneath his nose, obliterating any telltale signs of white powder.

"There's something you should be aware of," Gitta said. "I don't think we should disturb Miss Maestro at this time, so perhaps if you can come with me?"

They both glanced over at Annabelle who had fallen into a light sleep, a copy of *Us Magazine* almost slipping off her lap.

It occurred to Frankie that maybe the plane was in trouble. A faulty engine, a locked landing-gear, a fire. Jesus Christ! It could be anything.

Leaving his seat, he followed the flight attendant to the galley, where the second flight attendant – a pretty Hawaiian girl – was standing with her arms crossed. She didn't look panicked, she looked altogether too calm for there to be anything wrong with the plane.

"What's up, ladies?" he asked, thinking that the younger flight attendant was kind of hot in an exotic way.

"This is quite awkward, Mr Romano," Gitta said. "But we've decided that it will be better for all concerned if we advise you of the situation."

The goddamn plane *was* going down. His fucking luck.

"What situation?" he managed. *And where's the fucking pilot?*

"There's a headline story in one of the tabloids," Hani said, crisp and to the point. "It's about you and Miss Maestro."

So . . . their relationship had finally made the rags. What was so awkward about that? Annabelle had never courted publicity, but he didn't mind at all. He imagined the headlines.

FRANKIE ROMANO – STUD AT LARGE

HANDSOME BOYFRIEND OF

MURDERED MOVIE STAR'S DAUGHTER

TAKES OVER HOLLYWOOD

The truth was that being famous had always appealed to him.

"I'm afraid it's not a very reputable story," Gitta continued, bursting his bubble. "The truth of the matter is that it's quite scandalous, which is why we thought we should warn you before you de-planed."

"Not very reputable how?" he questioned, wondering if he'd done anything to rock the boat.

"Well," Hani said hesitantly, "they're calling Miss Maestro a notorious madam, and they're also saying that you are a drug addict, and that you procure girls for the prostitution business the two of you run."

"Naturally we understand that none of this is true," Gitta said, hastily joining in. "But we thought it best to tell you before the paparazzi descend."

"I do hope we've done the right thing," Hani added, wondering if any of the story was true.

Frankie stood quite still. He was in total shock. A headline story in the tabloids about their private business venture. Calling Annabelle a notorious madam, and him a drug addict and a procurer. How could this be?

Annabelle would go fucking nuts. And she'd blame him, because according to his lovely girlfriend, everything was always his fault.

"Where is this lying piece of crap rag?" he demanded, his voice a low angry growl.

"I'm sorry, Mr Romano," Gitta said. "We didn't bring a copy aboard."

"Why the fuck not?" he said, suddenly losing it. "You feed me this shit story, an' now you got nothin' to show me. What the fuck is wrong with you?"

"Mr Romano—" Gitta began.

"Don't Mr Romano me," he raged. "I'll tell you what you can do for me. You can keep your dumb fuckin' mouths shut, an' not mention a word about this made-up crap to my girlfriend. You understand?"

"Whatever you say," Gitta said, throwing an "I told you so" look in Hani's direction.

Hani was not happy with Frankie's reaction. How dare he speak to them in such a rude fashion. The tabloid story was probably true, and then she started wondering how someone as nice and low-key as Bobby Stanislopoulos could be friends with such an uncouth man.

Frankie Romano was a pig. As usual, Gitta was right. They should not have said a word – merely allowed him to find out on his own time.

* * *

Annabelle slept right through the landing. Frankie did not bother waking her. The further he kept her away from the two big-mouthed flight attendants, the better.

His mind was in overdrive, but he realized there was nothing he could do until he got a look at the offending article and read every word.

Bastards! He'd sue the shit out of them and then some. He'd hire the sharpest fucking lawyer in New York. Ralph would pay. Ralph would be as outraged as he was that his daughter's reputation was at stake.

Where the fuck had the tabloid gotten its information?

Christ! He needed to know exactly what they'd printed. The timing couldn't be worse, what with the funeral coming up the next day. Ralph would shit himself.

He had to phone Janey, see if she knew anything. But right now his main thrust was to get Annabelle off the plane, stash her in the limo Bobby was sending to the airport, and go pick up a copy of whichever tabloid it was that had printed the story.

It couldn't be that bad.

Or could it?

Chapter Forty-One

Denver

To say I was furious would be putting it mildly. More humiliated, mortified and degraded. How could I have allowed myself to be caught in such a shocking trap?

I am no prude, but a threesome, without my knowledge? *No! No! No!* Another woman sneaked into the bedroom by Mario – my knight in very tarnished armor? *I think not.*

What a douche! What an asshole! How could I have ever liked him? Me, who has always considered myself to be an excellent judge of character.

And guess who the third wheel was?

Yes, you guessed right – Hollywood Blonde herself, *sans* True Religion jeans and lacy top. Lots of blonde hair on her head, and nothing down below. Men like them fully shaved in Hollywood – that way, they can pretend they're screwing a twelve year old!

Once I realized the situation, I was out of there in a flash. Racing from the bedroom I grabbed my clothes off the living-room floor, and dashed out the front door, a naked Mario in full pursuit, yelling, "Come back! What's up, baby? I thought you'd be into some harmless fun."

Harmless fun! Was he kidding me?

Harmless fun with Hollywood Blonde or any other female for that matter was simply not my scene.

I made it to my car and drove off with a still-naked Mario running alongside hammering on the passenger window. Once home I stood under the shower for a good ten minutes trying to wash all memories of Mario's trickery away.

Now it's Wednesday morning and I am still pissed. I felt like I'd been made a fool of – and I also felt violated and super-dumb for allowing it to happen. The clue should've been Mario coming back to bed without telling me who was at the door. And silly me – for some reason I didn't press him to find out. God! How stupid could I get?

After taking another long shower I threw on a comfortable tracksuit, pulled my hair into a ponytail, and *sans* make-up, ran an eager-for-activity Amy Winehouse around the block a couple of times.

Amy's tail began wagging as soon as we headed back to my apartment.

I quickly discovered there was a reason: my loving ex, Josh, was lurking outside. Exactly who I *didn't* need to see, especially as I was not dressed for an old boyfriend confrontation.

Josh was balancing two Starbucks containers of coffee, and a bag of bagels, and he obviously had every intention of coming in.

Amy Winehouse leaped on him, full of doggie excitement. I threw him a stony look.

"Hi," he said.

"What are you doing here?" I responded curtly, deciding that I didn't even care that he was seeing me in my make-up-less state.

He handed me a coffee. "Peace-offering," he said, going for the friendly approach. "I was out of line taking Amy, and I wanted to apologize."

Josh always had perfect timing. *Not.*

"Can I come in?" he asked, bending down to pet Amy.

"Actually," I began, making a show of consulting my watch, "I need to get ready. I'm running late."

"Five minutes," he implored. "That's all I ask."

I weakened. Not that I wanted Josh to come in, but I have this stupid thing about hurting people's feelings, and he *had* brought me coffee. Besides, I could quite fancy a toasted bagel before facing the rest of the day.

"Fine," I sighed. "Five minutes only."

"She's a hard woman," Josh said, going for his jokey voice which did not impress me.

We headed into my apartment – once *our* apartment.

I indicated the paper bag. "Bagels?" I questioned.

"From your favorite place," he said, quite pleased with himself. "Shall I do the toasting honors?"

"Go ahead," I said, suddenly feeling tired and weary. I had no clue why Josh was visiting, and frankly I didn't care.

Josh went behind the counter that divided my living room from the kitchen area, and popped two bagels into the toaster.

"You bought a house," I stated blankly, sitting down at the counter.

"What did you think of it?" he asked cheerfully, as if we were the best of friends.

"Very nice. Lucky you," I said, unable to keep the venom out of my tone, because what I really wanted to say was – *You bought a house without me, and that's not fair.*

"It's a sound investment," Josh remarked. "Especially in this economy."

"Why? Are you getting married?" I asked in full bitchy mode.

"No way," he said vehemently. "Tori and I, we're merely temporary."

Tori. Of course!

"Does *she* know that?" I asked, mildly curious to find out if he was stringing her along.

Josh decided to ignore my question. Typical Josh. He extracted the bagels from the toaster, slightly burned, exactly the way he knew I liked them. After spreading butter on mine, he put it on a plate and handed it to me.

This was just like old times. If it was Sunday we'd be reaching for the *New York Times* by now and settling in for a long leisurely read.

But it's not Sunday, it's Wednesday, and I have a ton of stuff to get done. Besides, Josh and I are no longer together, so what the hell is he doing in my apartment?

"You look great," he said, scratching his chin while he eyed me up and down. "Have you lost weight?"

Was he saying that last time he saw me I was *fat*? *Sonofabitch!*

"No," I answered shortly, thinking that he'd definitely put on a few pounds. "Still the same old me."

"The same old *beautiful* you," he said, with a strong emphasis on the beautiful.

Man, what was it with the compliments lately? Getting laid definitely sends out mad signals.

I munched my bagel, sipped my coffee, then said, "Thanks for coming by, Josh, but I really do have to get going."

"Yes, sure," he said obligingly, before adding a slightly tentative – "We should do this again, right?"

Wrong! But I nodded anyway.

Later, at the office, I wished I'd told him to screw off. He had a lot of nerve, dropping by my apartment without an invitation. Who exactly did he think he was?

Megan knocked on my office door and entered bearing a huge vase of red roses.

"Somebody likes you," she sing-songed, placing the roses on my desk. "And Mr Saunders has requested your presence, pronto."

I grabbed the note attached to the roses.

Sorry seems to be the hardest word.

Mario.

Yeah, right.

Then I checked my cell for the fifth time to see if Carolyn had replied to my text. She hadn't. Nor was she answering her phone, and when I'd tried her office earlier they'd informed me that she had not come in. I wondered if she knew about George and Gemma. She'd always been close to her father – maybe he'd confided in her.

Hmm, I had to give Mister Shark Teeth the name of the man in the photo with Gemma. No more holding back, it was full-disclosure time.

* * *

Felix was sitting behind his massive desk, a grim expression on his pointy face, lizard-clad feet up on his desk. Today the lizard shoes were dyed a bright shocking pink, so wrong for the workplace.

Before I could say a word he tossed a tabloid magazine across his desk and said, "Have you seen this?"

I picked up the copy of *Truth & Fact* and took a look. The headline was enough to horrify me.

MURDERED MOVIE STAR'S DAUGHTER

RUNNING PROSTITUTION RING

WITH DRUG ADDICT BOYFRIEND

And next to the headline was a photo of Annabelle wearing a slinky evening dress and a seductive expression.

My mouth must have dropped open, because Mister Shark Teeth said, "I presume you did not know about this?"

He presumed right. I was in total shock.

"Uh . . . no," I managed.

"Weren't you with them in New York?" he asked accusingly, like in the short time I'd spent with them I should have found out everything. I mean, I'm smart, but not *that* smart.

"Yes, in time to pick them up and take them to the airport," I explained. "I hardly spent a week or two hanging out with them, so how on earth would I know about their so-called business?"

"A good lawyer knows everything," Felix said, shooting me a critical look.

A good lawyer should not wear shocking-pink lizard shoes. It's totally wrong. Besides, the color hurts my eyes.

"Sorry that my private detective skills are not quite up to par," I said snippily. "However, I do have the name of the man in the Malibu photos with Gemma Maestro."

This perked Mister Shark Teeth's interest. "You do?" he said, tapping his gleaming front teeth with a long thin index finger.

"His name is George Henderson," I continued. "He's a plastic surgeon."

"Are you sure?"

"Quite sure," I answered confidently. "Actually he's the father of a friend of mine, Carolyn Henderson. Carolyn, me and Annabelle all went to the same high school together."

"Seems you know everyone," Felix said, his tone caustic.

"Well, I've lived here since I'm eleven."

"Anyway," Felix said, removing his feet from the desk, "Ralph is expecting us. He'll want damage control on this tabloid nonsense. And let's see exactly how much he knows about George Henderson."

"Are you thinking that I should come with you?" I asked, willing him to say no.

Naturally he didn't. My damn luck.

So, Maestro mansion, here I come – again!

All I needed was Mario hanging around outside and once again my day would be perfect.

Chapter Forty-Two

Carolyn

After enduring a long and restless night listening to the pouring rain outside, and feeling desperate about the situation she was caught in, Carolyn wasn't sure whether she'd actually slept or not. Her stomach ached badly, and she was beginning to be concerned for the welfare of her baby.

Light was peeking through the torn covering on the window, so she assumed it must be morning.

She started thinking about the girl who'd brought her the bread and water the night before. The girl wasn't doing this alone; there was a man involved, a man who didn't want her to see his face. After the girl had blindfolded her, the man had taken her to the bathroom and stood there while she'd urinated. Another humiliation.

Who were these people? And even more important – what did they want with her?

Awash with waves of deep despair, Carolyn attempted to think more clearly and work out a timeline. She'd knew she'd been taken early afternoon on Tuesday, and after that she'd been driven around stuffed in the trunk of a car for endless hours. A couple of times she must have passed out, for when she awoke she was lying on this filthy bed, with her right wrist tied to the bedframe with strong electrical cord.

Now it had to be Wednesday, so people should be missing her. Kerri would know something was wrong when she'd failed to pick up Nellie's meds and then not met her for breakfast. Muriel would surely be suspicious when she didn't come into the office. And as for Gregory . . .

She wondered what he was doing, thinking.

When he'd turned up to meet her at the deserted gas station and she wasn't there, what was his reaction?

It all depended on whether her car was still there. If they'd abandoned her car, and she wasn't in it, then he had to know that something was horribly wrong, and surely he would have immediately called the police?

Or would he?

* * *

Benito spent Tuesday night sleeping in his chair in front of the TV, while Rosa curled up on a beaten-up old couch. She'd tried to go home, but Benito was having none of it. "Yo! You're stayin' here," he'd yelled at her in a threatening fashion. "An' don' go givin' me no shit."

Before going to sleep he'd made her take a peek at their captive to make sure she was still breathing.

The woman – shackled to the bedframe – had stared up at her with fear-filled eyes and begged for water.

For one brief moment Rosa had felt sorry for her. She'd fetched her a mug of water and a couple of slices of stale bread.

After gulping down the water and devouring the bread, the woman had requested to use the bathroom.

Rosa had run to Benito and asked him what she was supposed to do.

"Don' want her pissin' in my bed," he'd grumbled. "Blindfold her, we'll take her."

Why did he keep saying *we*? It really got to Rosa, but she'd reluctantly done as he asked. When she was finished, Benito had come into the room, untied the woman and roughly half-dragged her to the toilet.

As soon as he got her back in the bedroom he'd secured her wrist to the bedframe once again and made a fast exit.

Rosa had realized she was as trapped as the woman on the bed. Why did she have to be involved in Benito's business? It wasn't her shit, it was his.

After ripping the blindfold from their captive's eyes, she'd taken off before the woman could say anything, and joined Benito in front of the TV.

Now it was morning, and Rosa decided she'd better take the woman more bread and water. Didn't want her dying on them, that wouldn't be cool. And because of Benito, she could end up getting half the blame.

* * *

With her mind veering off in all different directions, Carolyn didn't know what to think. One moment she was panicked, the next she somehow or other forced herself to remain calm.

When the young girl came back with a couple more slices of stale bread and a half-bottle of tepid water, she decided that she'd better try and forge some kind of communication between them. She'd read somewhere that if ever you found yourself in a hostage situation, you had to attempt to bond with your captors – make them realize that you were a human being.

"Thanks," she muttered, gratefully swigging the water. "My name's Carolyn."

The girl stood there watching her, a blank expression on her face.

"If it's money you're after," Carolyn said, attempting to speak slowly so this young girl would understand, "my father will pay. I can tell you how to contact him." She paused for a moment. "Or my boss. My boss is a Senator, he's a very important man – he'll pay to get me back."

The girl still didn't say a word.

"I don't know if you're aware of what you're doing," Carolyn said, making sure to keep her voice low and even, "but you and your friend have kidnapped me. Kidnapping's a federal offense. The punishment is extremely severe, and I . . . uh . . . think I should tell you that I'm pregnant, so you're not just kidnapping me, you're—"

The girl suddenly came to life. "I know you're fuckin' knocked up," she blurted. "'Cuz that's th'reason you here." Then, realizing she'd probably said too much, she rushed out of the room.

Carolyn felt waves of sickness overcome her. The only person who knew she was pregnant was Gregory. So how did this girl know?

Then a thought entered her head, a thought so twisted and evil that she immediately tried to dismiss it.

Did Gregory have anything to do with this?

Was it possible?

No.

Yes.

Maybe.

* * *

"No way I'm keepin' the bitch around," Benito announced the moment he awoke, a scowl crossing his face. "This mo'fuckin' shit get me jailtime for sure," he added, vigorously scratching his balls. "Gonna cut her loose."

"What about the Senator?" Rosa inquired, in her mind

planning how she could get out of the house. She had a very bad feeling about what was going down, especially after the woman's chilling words about kidnapping and severe punishment. She wasn't responsible for any of this, it was all Benito. She was just doing what he ordered her to do. Besides, she'd already explored the contents of the woman's purse, and there were prime pickings – including an iPhone and eighty bucks in cash. She couldn't wait to get her hands on everything.

"The asswipe don't know how t'find me," Benito said, full of bravado. "Prick can't do nothin'."

"When you plannin' on gettin' her outta here?" Rosa asked, anxious to know.

"We're gonna dump her on the street tonight," Benito said, stretching his heavily tattooed arms. "Soon's it get dark."

"If she lasts that long," Rosa muttered, wishing he'd stop including her in his plans.

"What?"

"She ain't lookin' too healthy."

"Bitch lose the kid yet?"

"No."

"Fuck!"

"I gotta go home," Rosa ventured. "Spoke to my momma last night, my baby's sick, an' Momma's gotta get to her job. Daycare won't take the baby when it's sick, so I gotta go."

"Ya ain't goin' nowhere," Benito said, still in full scowl. "Not till we get the *puta* outta here."

"You don' understand. I *gotta* go, Benito," she pleaded. "My momma's gonna kill me if I don't take the baby."

"Whyn't ya stop with yo fuckin' whinin' an' start doin' what I tell ya for once?" he demanded.

"But my baby's sick," she repeated, trying to squeeze out a tear or two, almost believing her own lie.

"Don' give a shit."

"What I gonna tell my momma?"

"You ain't tellin' her nothin'," he said, still scowling. "An' why ya always gotta gimme such a hard time?"

"Sorry," she said sulkily, backing off.

"Y'know," he said with a sly smirk, "I got plenty wimmin chasin' me. I can pick any *puta* I want, so's ya better watch it."

"They gonna do you like I do?" Rosa said, standing up for herself.

"It don't take no degree t'suck me off," he boasted, with a self-satisfied chuckle. "It be their pleasure."

"*Hijo de puta*," Rosa muttered, the one Spanish insult she knew.

Fortunately, Benito didn't hear her.

Chapter Forty-Three

Annabelle & Bobby

Had Frankie seen a copy of *Truth & Fact*? That was the question on Bobby's mind. And if Frankie *had* seen it, he must be going apeshit.

Just in case, Bobby stashed a copy of the offending tabloid under his jacket, and impatiently waited to greet Annabelle and Frankie at the airport.

The moment the two of them alighted from the Stanislopoulos private plane, Bobby could tell Annabelle knew nothing. She was all smiles and full of enthusiasm about spending the night in Vegas, hardly the picture of a grieving daughter.

"I cannot wait to see Zeena's show," she said, giving Bobby a warm hug. "Zeena is *such* an amazing performer. I saw her show last year in Miami. She's a true superstar, like Madonna."

Was it his imagination, or did Annabelle purposely rub her breasts against him?

Frankie on the other hand definitely looked as if he knew something was up.

"Gotta take a piss," Frankie said as they approached the limo.

"Why didn't you go on the plane?" Annabelle asked, turning to him with a frown on her face.

"'Cause I didn't havta go then," he said, left eye twitching. "Is it all right with the Queen of Everythin' if I go take a piss?"

"I'll come with," Bobby offered.

"How cozy," Annabelle drawled. "All boys together."

"We'll be right back," Frankie said.

"There's champagne in the limo," Bobby offered. "Make yourself comfortable."

The two of them took off, away from the limo and into the airport building.

"I guess you know," Frankie stated.

"Of course I fucking know," Bobby replied. "It's a screaming headline on every newsstand. They all carry *Truth & Fact.*"

"Jesus!" Frankie exclaimed, as they headed into the men's room. "For real?"

"You've seen it, right?" Bobby asked.

"Not yet. Your two flight attendants warned me it was out there, but they didn't bring a copy on board."

"Prepare yourself," Bobby warned. "It's rough."

"No shit," Frankie said glumly.

"Here." Bobby extracted the copy of *Truth & Fact* he'd kept under his jacket. "Read it and go slit your throat."

Frankie snatched the magazine and began reading. The headline was brutal enough, but he could not believe what was in the story. Times, dates, details of monetary transactions, the names of alleged clients and the girls who worked for them. And even worse were the private photos he and Annabelle had taken just for fun. Photos from their personal collection. *Stolen* photographs. Annabelle joking it up with some of the girls, holding up their masks. Intimate photos of them lounging in bed together. Photos from Annabelle's childhood with Gemma and Ralph front and center.

How the fuck had the stinking tabloid gotten hold of them?

There was only one answer. Someone must have broken into their Park Avenue apartment and stolen them.

Frankie could feel the fury building inside him like a volcano about to blow. Why the hell hadn't Janey informed him there'd been a break-in at the apartment? What the fuck, he paid her enough, so how come she hadn't called and warned him?

Another dumb douche bag. Annabelle was right, he should never have hired her.

"Gotta make a call," he said to Bobby.

"To your lawyer?"

"No. To my half-witted cousin who's supposed to be looking after things for me."

"May I say she's doing a fine job."

"Fuck you," Frankie said, thrusting the magazine at Bobby. "Y'see these photos, they're all filched from our apartment. Annabelle's gonna go freakin' nuts."

"There's nothing you can do, it's out there now," Bobby said, attempting to calm him. "Next week it'll be old news."

"Fuck that shit," Frankie said, burning with anger. "I'm gonna sue the ass off everyone involved."

"It'll cost you," Bobby pointed out. "Once you put yourself in the hands of lawyers—"

"I've got the money," Frankie responded, thinking of the stash in their safe in New York. "I'm takin' this all the way."

"Yeah, but if you ignore it, it'll go away."

"They've crapped all over my reputation, Bobby, an' that kinda garbage stays around an' stinks up my world. So fuckin' ignore it – no way."

"I'm sorry, bro, this is a bad situation."

"Listen," Frankie said, "do me a big one – go with Annabelle to the hotel while I try an' work out my next move. Tell her I got the runs or somethin'."

"Nice."

"Maybe she won't even see it. Right?"

"C'mon, Frankie, get real. Someone's bound to mention it, her father for starters. And don't kid yourself – there'll be a ton of press at the funeral."

"Thanks. You're makin' me feel a whole lot better."

"I'm just saying the way it is. You want the truth."

"Yeah. Right."

"Okay then, take it easy. I'll escort your girlfriend to the hotel. And remember – next week this'll be yesterday's news."

* * *

Annabelle lounged in the back of the limo sipping champagne while considering her options.

Bobby had certainly been happy enough to see her – his greeting had been very friendly and she liked that. She smiled to herself. Once she was rid of Frankie, Bobby would be easy pickings, and why not? Without Frankie hanging around she was a total catch. She'd give up the business and hand it over to her ex as compensation, because ever since the incident with Sharif Rani's son, she was totally over it.

Bobby would certainly be able to keep her in style, she wouldn't have to run a stupid call-girl business. He was – or would be when he inherited everything – a freaking billionaire.

Yes, as soon as they got back to New York she'd tell Frankie to move out. They'd split the cash in the safe, and then they could both get on with their lives.

Thursday was the funeral. Friday they'd be on a plane back to New York. And Saturday she'd give her coke-addicted boyfriend the news.

It's over, Frankie. Have a nice life.

* * *

"Hey," Bobby said, jumping in the back of the limo and settling himself next to Annabelle.

"Hey yourself," she replied, thinking how handsome he was, and what a smart decision she was making about her future. "Where's Frankie?"

"He's got a bad case of the runs, sitting tight in the bathroom. He'll meet us at the hotel."

Annabelle couldn't believe her luck. Alone with Bobby so soon! It seemed the perfect time to start making her moves.

"Y'know," she ventured, lowering her voice so the driver couldn't hear, "Frankie's coke habit is veering out of control. I'm not sure how much longer I can take it."

"He seems okay to me," Bobby said, determined to stay neutral, especially in view of what she was about to discover. Now was not the time for her to start worrying about Frankie's coke addiction; she had bigger problems ready to slap her in the face.

"*You* don't have to live with him," she said bitterly. "*You* don't have to walk in on him snorting that disgusting white powder up his nose, and then swearing he hardly ever does it when I know it's a constant thing."

"Yeah, that must be a drag," Bobby said, trying to sound sympathetic.

"It's more than a drag," she said vehemently. "You know what, Bobby? I can't deal with it any more. I want out."

Damn! This was something he didn't wish to hear right now. Annabelle and Frankie had a shit-storm to face – and the best way to deal with it was to present a united front.

"Have you talked to him, told him it upsets you?" he said.

"Frankie's not responsible like you, Bobby," she said, reaching over and covering his hand with hers. "Have *you* ever tried talking sense into him?"

"He's not *my* boyfriend," Bobby remarked, wondering how he could get his hand out from under hers without it looking obvious.

"Y'know," she mused, "Frankie isn't one of us, he never was. You, me and M.J. – we've always been tight. Remember high school? We were like the Three Musketeers – everyone wanted to be part of our group."

Bobby had no idea what she was talking about. He and M.J. had never hung out with Annabelle – only that one fateful prom night, and after that they'd gone out of their way to avoid her and the group of privileged princesses with whom she spent all her time.

He slipped his hand out from under hers on the pretext of reaching for a bottle of Evian.

"No champagne?" she said coyly, holding up her glass for a refill.

"Can't drink during the day," he said, pouring her more champagne. "Gives me a hangover."

"Poor baby," she crooned. "You'll have to catch up tonight. Oh, and by the way, make sure I'm sitting next to you. I might need your moral support."

Jeez! What was up with Annabelle? Suddenly the prospect of spending the evening with Zeena seemed quite inviting. Anything was better than getting trapped with a needy Annabelle Maestro on the eve of her murdered mother's funeral. Even another sex romp with the maneater.

Chapter Forty-Four

Denver

Wow! Ralph Maestro in a fury is a sight to behold. Big movie-star face all red and wrinkled. Eyes flashing venom. Voice a rough, tough growl. Huge frame overpowering and quite threatening.

He was pacing around his living room, and he was not a happy man. His long-time publicist Pip – a small middle-aged man wearing a white suit and a jaunty Fedora – sat silently in an oversized armchair. Everything, except Pip, was oversized in the Maestro mansion, including Ralph.

Ignoring me as usual, he pounced on Felix like a black panther trapping its prey.

"I am outraged and horrified," he bellowed. "This filth is purely a ploy to embarrass me. What are you doing about it?"

"We're hitting them with an injunction to stop next week's issue," Felix said, calm as usual.

"Next week's issue!" Ralph roared. "Are you telling me there's more?" He turned angrily on Pip. "Did you know this?"

Pip shook his head, his expression hang-dog.

"'Fraid so," Felix said apologetically. "Once these rags get a hold of a story, they hang on until all the blood is drained from the body."

Even I was surprised that there was more to come. I'd read the offending headline story on the way over, and it was pretty tawdry. How much worse could it get? And why hadn't Felix mentioned to me that there was more? It pisses me off when he leaves me out of the loop.

"Have you *seen* next week's story?" I asked.

Ralph's heavy-lidded movie-star eyes swiveled to take me in. "*You*," he boomed in his loud voice. "Weren't you with my daughter in New York? Surely you knew what was going on?"

"I . . . uh . . . merely escorted them back to L.A.," I explained.

"It's her goddamn drug-addicted boyfriend," Ralph thundered. "He's the one that got her into this. I should put a hit out on the cocky bastard."

Pip huddled deeper into his chair. Felix and I exchanged shocked glances. Had Ralph really just said that?

Yes. Unfortunately he had.

Pip cleared his throat. "Be careful what you say, Ralph. Walls have ears, and if Annabelle's boyfriend should end up on a slab in the morgue . . ."

He didn't have to say any more, the implication was quite clear.

"Where are they?" Ralph yelled. "I called the Beverly Hills Hotel and I was informed that they won't be back until tomorrow."

I remembered the text I'd received from Annabelle saying they were off to Vegas to see Zeena's one-night show and would be back in time for the funeral. Annabelle had added a cryptic P.S. stating that she expected me to accompany them to the funeral. Seems I'm a popular funeral date. First Felix wanted me to accompany him, and now Annabelle is insisting that I go with her and Frankie.

I relayed the information about Vegas to Ralph.

"Vegas!" he steamed. "For what? To pick up more dirty little tramps for their degrading business? How do you think this garbage reflects on *me*? I'm a big star, not the father of some goddamn whore. This could ruin my career."

Talk about exaggeration! Ralph was obviously a master.

"They'll be back early tomorrow," I offered, hoping to diffuse the situation.

"That's not soon enough," Ralph announced ominously. Once again he turned to Pip. "Get me a plane," he commanded, as if he was requesting a cup of coffee. "We're going to Vegas."

* * *

One private plane later and we're all on our way to Vegas. No time to go home and change. No time to do anything except call my neighbor – a martial arts expert – and ask him to walk Amy.

Felix wasn't pleased. I had a strong suspicion he too would've appreciated changing clothes – maybe put on a less colorful pair of shoes.

Pip had arranged for Ralph to have use of a studio plane, but once Ralph was aboard he acted as if he owned it.

As soon as we were airborne, Felix brought up the subject of George Henderson.

"Of course I knew she was seeing him," Ralph said, loud and abrasive.

"You mean you were aware it was him in the tabloid photos?" Felix asked, quite put out. "Why didn't you tell the police? Or at least you should've mentioned it to me. I *am* your lawyer."

"Gemma cherished her privacy," Ralph replied, lighting up a foul-smelling cigar. "She didn't want anyone knowing that she might be considering a few nips and tucks."

So *that's* how she'd explained the intimate photos to her husband. Very clever.

"The detectives need to know," Felix said, a tad sharply. He was a stickler for always doing the correct thing.

"They're detectives, let them find out for themselves," Ralph said, puffing on his cigar and blowing noxious fumes throughout the cabin before downing two large Scotches in a row.

Both men decided it should be my job to discover where Annabelle and Frankie were staying in Vegas.

Who's the detective now?

As soon as we landed I called Annabelle's cell. No answer. Next I tried Frankie. He picked up immediately, as if he was expecting my call.

"Frankie?" I questioned.

"Who is this?" he asked, fully suspicious.

"It's Denver."

"What do you want?"

Charming! Such a lovely greeting.

I decided not to mention the tabloid. Too risky. He might lose it – that's if he even knew about it.

"Just checking in about tomorrow," I said casually. "Annabelle told me you're in Vegas for the night. What time will you be returning to L.A.?"

"Dunno," he said. "You'll havta ask Bobby, we're flying back on his plane."

So Bobby had a plane. What was *that* about?

"Where can I find Bobby?" I asked, keeping it light.

"At The Keys."

"Are you all staying there?"

"Gotta go," Frankie said abruptly.

I had my answer.

Yes, I think I would've made an excellent detective.

* * *

On the way from the airport in a white ultra stretch limousine which could've comfortably accommodated fifteen people, I checked my texts and voicemails, while Pip called The Keys and instructed them to have a suite available for Ralph Maestro's use.

There were still no texts from Carolyn, and I was starting to feel a little bit worried about not hearing from her. Taking off without a word to anyone was not Carolyn's style, so why wasn't she answering me? How often did I say urgent in a text?

I made up my mind that once we reached the hotel I would find a quiet corner and call her office again. If she was away, surely they'd know where she'd gone?

In the meantime I sent her another text.

I had several voicemails to get through, most of them business-related, plus two calls from Mario asking if I got his flowers and when could we get together again.

Uh, how about never?

Then came the surprise – a call from Carolyn's dad, George. Wow! Had he somehow or other found out that I knew he was the man in the photo with Gemma? This was crazy. I quickly listened to his message.

"Denver. It's George Henderson. I'm sorry to bother you, but Clare and I received a very disturbing call from the Washington police. Apparently Carolyn's car, which is registered in my name, has been found abandoned. I can't seem to reach her, and since I know you two are close, I wondered if you have any idea where she is. Please call us as soon as you get this message."

My heart did a skip and a jump. Intuition told me that this was not good news. I slid along the endless leather side seat and finally got near enough to the driver to ask how long it would be before we reached the hotel.

"Five minutes or fifty," the driver announced, flashing me an annoying smirk. "It all depends on our Vegas traffic."

"See if you can make the five work," I said, curt and to the point. "Mr Maestro is in a hurry."

"Sure thing, Miss."

Did I look like a Miss? Shouldn't I be addressed as a Ms. Or at least a Ma'am?

My mind was wandering, it always does that when I'm stressed. I needed to call Carolyn's dad back, and I didn't want to do it from the limo, therefore I'd just have to wait – frustrating as that was.

I attempted to think about other things. Bobby Santangelo Stanislopoulos drifted into my head. So . . . he had his own plane. How did *that* happen?

Then I remembered, not only was he the infamous Lucky Santangelo's son, but apparently the word around school had been that his father was some kind of billionaire Greek shipping tycoon who'd died when Bobby was young, and that Bobby and his niece were destined to inherit everything when they reached a certain age.

Hmm . . . I guess the plane is part of everything.

"Are we almost there?" Ralph growled, sounding more like an angry dog than a worldwide movie star.

"Five minutes or fifty," I replied, trying not to breathe in too many cigar fumes. "It all depends on the Vegas traffic."

"Fuck the Vegas traffic," Ralph fumed. He turned to his brow-beaten publicist, who was ageing by the minute. "Pip," he commanded. "Call someone and get me a police escort. I need to be there ***now***!"

Chapter Forty-Five

Carolyn

Senator Gregory Stoneman carried on as normal. To the outside world he was his efficient, hardworking self, dealing with business as usual. However, inside he was a mess, hoping that an unpregnant Carolyn would soon put in an appearance, and everything would return to the way it was. Well . . . almost to the way it was, minus one baby – not even a baby – a fetus growing inside Carolyn.

She'd given him no choice except to do something about it before it was too late. He'd had no alternative but to think of some way to stop her from ruining his life and the lives of his family – especially of his two precious children, who deserved to be protected at all costs.

Hiring a drug-dealing gang-banger was hardly the perfect way to deal with the situation, but it was the only solution that presented itself to him. And at the time, it had seemed so easy.

Now he was starting to fear that he might have gone too far. Thank God he'd warned Benito not to hurt her, simply shake her up enough to lose the baby, and when that was done, set her free.

But surely it couldn't be taking so much time?

She'd been snatched just after noon on Tuesday, and now it was late Wednesday afternoon, so where was she?

He had a cell number for Benito, but he didn't dare use it. Cell calls could be traced, and it was imperative that he was not connected to Carolyn's disappearance in any way.

As Gregory was mulling this over, Muriel entered his office.

"Senator," she said, a worried expression on her face, "there is a police detective who wishes to have a word with you. Is it all right if I show him in?"

* * *

Rosa managed to get out of the house on the pretext of going to the market and buying food. Benito had a voracious appetite for junk food. He always had a yen for Twinkies and donuts and packets of salty chips which he dipped into big tubs of spicy salsa. Prison had taught him nothing about healthy eating.

Rosa didn't care. She too existed on junk food – it was satisfying and cheap.

Before leaving the house she'd transferred the contents of Carolyn's leather purse into her fake Louis Vuitton bag, purchased from a street vendor for fifteen bucks. The pickings were excellent, the prize being the woman's iPhone. A freakin' iPhone with music and photos and all kinds of other shit. Rosa was in heaven. She already possessed a cheap cell that did exactly nothing. Now she had her own personal iPhone!

The drag was finding out how to work the stupid thing. It seemed complicated. She managed to turn it on and pressed the iTunes icon. So cool! Lists of songs came up, so she tapped "Boom Boom Pow" by the Black-Eyed Peas.

Listening to the song with a smile on her face, she danced

her way toward the corner market, oblivious to what was going on around her. So oblivious, in fact, that she didn't notice the three teenage girls who surrounded her out of nowhere, snatched her purse, grabbed the iPhone out of her hands, knocked her down, kicked her in the face, head and stomach and took off.

The last thing Rosa remembered thinking was, *Benito is going to kill me*. Then everything faded to black.

Chapter Forty-Six

Bobby & Annabelle

"Hey, kiddo, you're on your own," Lucky informed Bobby. "I'm handing over the tickets for Zeena's show, and please don't forget that Renee and Susie are throwing a private dinner after the event, so be sure to make it. Renee is expecting all of you."

"Jeez, Mom, they're *your* friends," Bobby complained. "An' now you're running out on us. What's *that* about?"

"Lennie is stopping off in L.A. for exactly three hours en route to his New Zealand location," Lucky explained. "And I plan on spending all three hours with him. Okay with you, number one son?"

"I guess that's why you've got the greatest marriage in town," Bobby said, wondering if he'd ever have a relationship that good.

Lucky smiled her brilliant smile. "Yes, Bobby, that's exactly why. Lennie comes first."

Which meant that he was stuck. Concert. Private dinner. *Zeena. Zeena. Zeena.*

All his guests couldn't wait to see her show. Brigette and Kris, M.J. and Cassie, and Annabelle and Frankie. What a group!

Why couldn't he fly back to L.A. with Lucky and leave them all to it?

Because he'd invited them, and that would be rude and inconsiderate.

So . . . there was no escape.

He wondered how Frankie was doing. Had he found out who gave the tabloid the story? Had he told Annabelle? Would he have the *balls* to tell her? And when he did so, would he have any balls left? Annabelle was already muttering about splitting with him, so the *Truth & Fact* story could seal the deal.

Deciding to find out what everyone was up to, he called Brigette, who told him that she and Kris were just about to hit the casino floor.

"Kris has never gambled before," Brigette said excitedly. "I'm going to teach her blackjack."

Bobby hoped she wasn't bankrolling her girlfriend's gambling fling – that wouldn't be cool.

Next he reached M.J., who informed him that he and Cassie were going to hang out in the suite until show-time.

"I'll meet you in the lobby at seven," Bobby said. "Don't be late."

"Yeah, man, we'll be on time," M.J. assured him. "Cassie's real excited."

I bet she is, Bobby thought. M.J. was a total catch.

When Lucky had first built The Keys he'd considered buying an apartment in the luxury condominium building attached to the hotel. Now he was glad that he hadn't done so – Vegas was for bachelor parties, getting married in either a lovesick haze or a drunken stupor, and losing money at the tables. Lucky loved Las Vegas but Bobby wasn't such a fan, although the challenge of making *Mood* the hot club in town was quite appealing. He'd already made the decision that he'd commute for the first few months, get the club up and running, then put in a manager he could trust to run things his way.

Bored with his own company, he thought he'd make his way downstairs and join up with Brigette and Kris. It was a better prospect than doing nothing.

* * *

By the time Frankie reached Janey on the phone, he'd developed strong misgivings about her involvement in the tabloid story. She ***had*** to know about it, so why hadn't she called ***him***? Even worse, she wasn't picking up the phone at the Park Avenue apartment where she was supposed to be looking after things. It was only after three attempts that she finally answered her cell.

"What the fuck, Janey?" he screamed down the phone. "Who did this?" And even as he said the words, it suddenly came to him. Janey's lazy, good-for-nothing, devious motherfucking son.

"It's Chip, isn't it?" he yelled. "That moron sold us out."

"It's nothing to do with me. I didn't know anything about it," Janey said, immediately defensive.

"Don't fuck with me, Janey," Frankie warned. "You know you don't wanna do that."

"Well," Janey said reluctantly, "if it *was* Chip, then he must've gone behind my back an' done it."

"Stop feedin' me shit," Frankie said, his left eye twitching with anger. "How'd he get the photos if you didn't help him? There's no way. You're the one with the run of the apartment. You must've helped him."

"He stole them," Janey admitted, starting to snivel. "He had to have gone through everything while I was passed out." A pregnant pause. "Frankie," sob sob, "I got a horrible feeling he drugged me – his own mother! How could he do such a thing?"

"Where is the prick?" Frankie said, imagining exactly what he would do to Chip when he got hold of him. "An' you'd better find out, 'cause when I get back I'm gonna snap his scrawny neck in two."

"Oh Frankie," Janey wailed in desperation. "Please don't say things like that. Chip is family, you know he's a good boy at heart."

"Bullshit! He's a born loser."

"Somebody must've gotten to him, offered him lots of money. He's young, he doesn't understand."

"Do you honestly think I give a fast crap in hell? When I get hold of your demented baby boy, he's gonna understand good. In fact, he's gonna be sorry he was born."

"No, Frankie," Janey pleaded. "Please don't do anything rash. I beg you."

"Shut the fuck up, Janey. I suggest you shift your fat ass an' go find him. Chip is gonna pay for this. Our fuckin' business is ruined, not to mention my reputation."

"I'm so sorry, Frankie," she sniveled.

"You should be, for givin' birth to the little bastard," Frankie said, before snapping his phone shut.

He was still in the airport men's room, and several men going about their business were staring at him.

Shoving the phone in his pocket he stared back.

"Bad day?" one man ventured.

"Fuck off," Frankie muttered, before marching outside, where the first thing he saw was a newsstand – copies of the offending tabloid, *Truth & Fact*, piled high.

With one big sweeping gesture he knocked them to the ground, scattering them everywhere. Then, muttering under his breath, he set off to find a cab.

* * *

The suite Bobby had gotten them in The Keys was pure luxury – even more so than the Beverly Hills Hotel which for Annabelle's taste was a touch too traditional in style.

The Keys suite featured an enormous circular bed covered in

fur throws (fake of course, Lucky was a strong supporter of PETA), a giant flat-screen TV and a full shelf of the latest DVDs, CDs, and bestselling books.

The bathroom was all pale-green marble, with a TV in the ceiling above the tub so that a guest could comfortably lie back, soak and watch their favorite programs.

Annabelle wished they were staying longer. She also wished that she would be sharing the bed with Bobby, not Frankie.

Soon . . . yes, soon . . . she was sure of it.

Where the hell was Frankie, anyway? He was taking his time coming from the airport and she didn't appreciate being kept waiting.

She thought about creating a big fight when he finally arrived and getting it over with. Or was it wiser to wait until after the funeral?

Probably. But Annabelle was into instant gratification, and that meant dumping his sorry ass the moment he hit the suite.

But no, she had to do the smart thing and wait until they returned to New York. If she did it now, he was perfectly capable of running back to New York without her and clearing out the safe. She wouldn't put that kind of move past him, and there was a lot of cash stashed in their safe – a few hundred thousand at least.

Then the thought occurred – why was she even considering splitting it with him? She was the brains behind the business. Why shouldn't she keep everything for herself?

It was an excellent thought. Before dumping him she'd remove the cash and put it in a safe-deposit box at the bank registered in her name only. Frankie would go nutzoid, but there would be nothing he could do about it. *Too bad, Frankie.*

Annabelle realized that she had plenty to think about before making any rash moves.

* * *

Testing his luck, Frankie stopped by a roulette table on his way up to the suite and placed a two-thousand-dollar bet on black. It came up. He let the four thousand dollars ride, and black came up again. Six thousand dollars' profit in a matter of minutes – not bad for a two-thousand dollar initial bet. Maybe his luck was changing and this whole tabloid thing would blow over without anyone noticing.

Yeah, sure, and roses would grow out of President Obama's ass.

Still testing himself, he let the full eight thousand ride once again. And to his shock and amazement, black hit again!

Grabbing his sixteen thousand dollars in thousand-dollar chips, he headed for the cashier station. On the way he spotted Brigette Stanislopoulos sitting at one of the blackjack tables. Next to her was a statuesque blonde.

Never one to miss an opportunity, he made his way toward them. "'Scuse me," he said, tapping Brigette on the shoulder. "Brigette, right? We met at *Mood* in New York a few times. I'm Frankie Romano, close friend of Bobby's. We're all gettin' together tonight."

"Of course. Frankie," Brigette said with a polite smile. "Bobby told me, and I do remember you. You're the superdeejay."

Jeez, she was so damn pretty, a little older than he would've liked – thirty something – but she was mega-rich like Bobby. He'd heard so many stories about Brigette Stanislopoulos and her fatal attraction to losers. If he wasn't with Annabelle, a woman like Brigette with her startlingly bright blue eyes, cascades of blonde hair and extreme mega-bucks, might be exactly what he needed. There was nothing wrong with a little older-woman action. Yes, he could definitely go for the voluptuous heiress.

"This is my partner, Kris," Brigette said, introducing him to the other blonde sitting next to her, another stunner.

Bummer! The heiress had turned dyke. Too bad. Although . . . the potential for a threesome flashed before his eyes, and he was major into what he saw.

Bobby interrupted his fantasy by coming up behind him and saying, "You're back."

"Yeah, I'm back," Frankie said.

"And I see you've met Brigette."

"Listen, guys," Brigette said with a good-natured smile, "much as I'd love to sit around and chat, I'm trying to teach Kris to play blackjack, so can we catch up later?"

"You got it," Bobby said, grabbing Frankie's arm. "Let's go, bro."

They walked across the casino.

"I just won a shitload of money," Frankie said, still slightly dazed by his big win. "Gotta cash in."

"Have you told Annabelle yet?" Bobby asked as they headed for the cashier.

"About my big win?" Frankie said flippantly.

"No. About the story, asshole."

"I'm figuring she's not gonna find out," Frankie said, plunking down his chips at the cashier's counter.

"Then you're a bigger asshole than I thought," Bobby said, shaking his head in wonderment at Frankie's thick skin. "Of course she'll find out. Believe me – it'll go a lot smoother if she hears it from you."

"You don't know Annabelle," Frankie said glumly.

"Yeah, I think I do. So take my advice and tell her."

"Later," Frankie said, stuffing wads of cash in his pockets. "Right now I'm on a roll. An' nothin' stops Frankie Romano when he's hittin' a hot streak."

Chapter Forty-Seven

Denver

Ralph Maestro actually got a police escort. I couldn't believe it! Two motor-cycle cops (very studly motor-cycle cops) appeared out of nowhere, and with sirens screaming, the heavy traffic opened up. Within eight minutes we were arriving at the hotel.

And what a hotel! The Keys was a magnificent structure. Unlike most Vegas hotels, it screamed class and style.

I hadn't been to Vegas since Josh and I spent a weekend at the Hard Rock when he attended a college reunion and insisted I accompany him. Total nightmare. Although for some strange reason the sex was outstanding. I guess Vegas turned Josh on.

Valets, porters, bellboys, and a couple of guys in dark suits surrounded our limo, and when Ralph emerged, everyone went into *let's-kiss-the-big-movie-star's-ass* mode. It was a sight to behold, although Ralph was obviously used to it, for he practically ignored everyone as they escorted him through the lobby to a private elevator and then up to a magnificent four-bedroom suite with a pool table, a full bar, and a white piano in the living room. Outside the suite, a gleaming turquoise lap pool shimmered in the middle of an exquisitely landscaped terrace.

We were staying – what – two hours at the most? But only

the best was good enough for Ralph Maestro, Mister Movie Star Supreme.

I needed to call George Henderson back, and I didn't want to do it from the suite, so I made a quick excuse that I had to buy something in the pharmacy, and ducked out.

Mention the word pharmacy to a man and they immediately back off. Felix was no exception, although he did tell me to make it fast.

Downstairs I searched out a quiet corner near a side entrance and pulled out my phone, but before I could use it, who did I see walking toward me but Bobby and Frankie.

I had nowhere to run. It was too late anyway, as Frankie had seen me and the two of them were heading full force in my direction.

"What the hell are *you* doin' here?" Frankie demanded, left eye in full twitch. "Didn't you just call me from L.A.?"

"I never said I was in L.A.," I answered defensively.

"What the fuck is goin' on?" Frankie wanted to know, moving closer, invading my personal space.

Oh crap. What was I supposed to say? That I'd flown in with Ralph who was ready to kill him. And that if he was smart he'd run for the hills without passing Go.

"Leave the girl alone," Bobby said, throwing me a dazzling smile. "You're questioning her as if you're the D.A."

"I'm not into people playin' mindgames with me," Frankie grumbled. "Why was she pretendin' to be in L.A.? Somethin's wrong, I can smell it."

Bobby gave me a sympathetic look. My eyes couldn't resist focusing on his mouth. Was it possible for a man to have such kissable lips? I guess so, 'cause he sure as hell has them.

"Look," I said, deciding to come clean, "if you must know, I flew in with Ralph Maestro. He's major pissed about the story in *Truth & Fact*, and he's come here to find Annabelle and take her home with him."

Frankie looked like he'd been socked in the face with a wet fish.

"Ralph Maestro is here?" he managed to splutter. "Here, in Vegas?"

"'Fraid so," I answered calmly, sneaking another look at Bobby's lips.

"Fuck!" Frankie exclaimed, completely deflated. "He didn't believe that shit, did he?"

"I rather think he did. Y'know, there are photos, details . . ." I trailed off.

Frankie seemed ready for a total meltdown.

"What's the deal?" Bobby asked. "Should Frankie go see him, try to explain that it's all a big mistake?"

I admired Bobby for trying to help his friend out. On the other hand, what kind of mistake could it possibly be?

"I think if Frankie can manage to stay out of his way, that might be the smartest thing for him to do," I said. "You've got to understand that Ralph is furious. He's out for blood, and it might be Frankie's."

"Annabelle hasn't seen the story," Frankie said, left eye now twitching out of control. "I need to get to her before Ralph."

Bobby leaned in and took my arm. "Maybe you can do us a favor and not tell Ralph you've seen Frankie," he said. "Give Frankie time to figure things out."

"I guess I can do that," I replied, not minding Bobby invading my personal space at all.

"Gotta go," Frankie suddenly said. And before either of us could say a word, he took off like a rocket ship, leaving me alone with Bobby.

"Jeez!" Bobby sighed. "What a crappy situation. I think I need a drink, how about you?"

"Now *that* sounds like a plan," I responded, forgetting about Felix and Ralph and the obsequious Pip. They would just have to manage without me.

"We'll go over to the Cavendish," Bobby said, taking charge. "It's quieter."

Who was I to argue? I was on my way to having a drink with my teenage crush, Bobby Santangelo Stanislopoulos, and nothing was going to stop me.

* * *

An hour later, I realized I still hadn't called George Henderson, let alone reported back to Felix, who was no doubt livid. But sometimes in life you gotta go with the flow, and this was one of those times.

We were sitting out on the terrace bar at the Cavendish sipping mojitos – well, that's not strictly true – *I* was sipping a mojito, while Bobby was drinking beer from the bottle. "Tastes better that way," he'd informed me.

We were talking non-stop, and I found him to be so interesting, not shallow at all. In school I'd convinced myself that he might be the best-looking thing on two legs, but he was a rich kid so he was probably boring and full of himself.

Not so. Not so at all.

He was telling me about his club in New York, and how he planned on taking over the club concession at The Keys. He was full of terrific ideas and loads of enthusiasm. Then he started asking me about myself, and what aspirations *I* had for the future.

Wow! This was a two-way conversation, unusual to say the least. Most men got off on talking about themselves on a first date and that was it. Of course this wasn't a date, merely a friendly drink to discuss Frankie's plight. Not that I personally cared about Frankie, but Bobby – being a loyal friend – seemed concerned.

Ah yes, a date would be a whole different ballgame. And maybe . . .

No! What was I thinking? Bobby probably dated models and

actresses, true beauties with stick-thin bodies and a penchant for throwing up.

"Why are you smiling?" he suddenly asked.

"Um . . . I didn't realize I was."

"Yeah, you had a real Cheshire Cat grin on your face."

"I did?" I said, innocence personified.

"You sure did."

"Actually," I confessed, "I was wondering if you dated girls who threw up."

"Huh?" He gave me a full-on quizzical look. "Why would I do that?"

"Why wouldn't you?"

"You're funny."

"I try to amuse," I said, as I felt my phone vibrating for maybe the sixth time. "Do you mind if I check my messages and make a quick call?"

"Go ahead. Any need for privacy?"

"That's okay. I have a friend in Washington who seems to be on the missing list. I have to call her father back, see if he's found out where she is."

Bobby nodded. He had the greatest eyes, dark and intense. I imagine he's a killer in bed.

George Henderson had left another message for me to call him, but when I did he failed to pick up. So I left *him* a message to say that I didn't know where Carolyn was, and would he please try *me* back again.

Meanwhile, Bobby's cell rang. He stood up and walked away from our table. Apparently he *did* require privacy.

When he returned to the table he had a thoughtful expression on his handsome face.

"Everything okay?" I asked, sipping my mojito.

"I'm guessing I can tell you 'cause I do believe you're on our side," he said, picking up his bottle of beer and taking another healthy swig.

"Tell me what?" I said, delighted that he seemed to trust me.

"Annabelle and Frankie are heading back to L.A. They're being smart, and getting out while they can."

"Wow!" I exclaimed. "Ralph will be even more major pissed."

"You can't tell him," Bobby warned. "This is between us."

"Scout's honor," I answered, without even thinking about where my loyalty should lie.

"You don't look like a Scout to me," he said, grinning.

"I don't?" I said, being all flirty and girlish.

"No, you don't," he said, flirting back.

Oh God! I was enjoying this far too much.

"By the way," Bobby said, "I'm now stuck with a couple of extra seats for Zeena's show tonight. You want to come? You can bring someone if you like."

"Uh, it's just me," I said, adding a quick, "There is no special someone right now."

He gave me a long, lingering look. "Join the club," he said.

And as our eyes locked there was a major commotion and the very famous superstar, Zeena, and her five-man entourage, made a splashy entrance into the bar.

Bobby jerked to an upright position, while I inspected the woman with curious eyes. I'd seen Madonna once in person, and she'd seemed so much smaller than she appeared on stage and TV. Zeena was quite the opposite – a tall, swan-like creature with coal-black hair hanging below her waist, heavily shadowed cat-eyes, and deep ruby-red lips. As she swept by us, the scent of her perfume was overpowering.

Bobby glanced at his watch and immediately called for the check. "I'll take you back to your hotel," he said. "And remember, you know nothing about Annabelle and Frankie taking off."

"I know nothing," I repeated, formulating a story to tell Felix that would keep me in Vegas overnight.

The check came, Bobby threw down cash, and we got up to

leave. As we moved toward the entrance, a deep throaty voice called out his name.

Bobby stopped short and turned around.

"Zeena," he said, as if he hadn't noticed her before. Like how could he miss her? "This is a surprise."

"A surprise, Bobby?" she drawled, her tapered fingers playing with the stem of her wine-glass in a most suggestive way. "How can it be a surprise when you're coming to my show tonight?"

"Yeah," he said curtly. "We're looking forward to that."

And without another word he gripped my arm and steered me out of there.

* * *

Felix was angry, steely-eyed and quite irate, exactly as I'd expected.

"Where have you been?" he hissed in my ear, so close I could smell his peppermint breath.

"Funny thing," I replied, made-up story at the ready, "I ran into my mom's sister and family. They live in Detroit and I haven't seen them in five years."

"We are here on business," Felix reminded me sternly. "This is not family reunion time."

"I understand," I replied, refusing to be intimidated. "Which is why as soon as I could get away, I did. But here's the thing – I had to promise to stay over. Not to worry," I added quickly, giving him no time to object. "I'll catch an early flight to L.A. in the morning. I'll be back in time for the Maestro funeral."

Felix was lost for a snappy reply – not something that happened to him very often.

"Ralph cannot reach his daughter," he said at last. "Since there is no answer from their suite, Ralph wants you to locate her and bring her here without the boyfriend. He'll deal with Frankie Romano later."

"How am I supposed to do that?" I asked, nonplussed. "She could be anywhere. Besides, she never goes anywhere without Frankie."

"Annabelle trusts you," Felix said.

"I know she does," I replied, thinking, ***What does that have to do with anything***? "This place is huge," I added. "How will I find her?"

"Figure it out," Felix said shortly. "You have one hour. After that we're flying back to L.A. And you, young lady, are making a mistake not coming with us." He waved his index finger at me, and threw me an extra-stern look. "A very *big* mistake."

Chapter Forty-Eight

Carolyn

Nobody knew who she was, the Latina girl in the cheap bloodstained top and the tight little mini-skirt. She'd been lying in the street in the pouring rain for a while before a passerby had finally called 911 and the paramedics had come to get her.

The attending doctor in the ER figured she was very young, although after a thorough examination to see if she'd been raped before being beaten, the female doctor ascertained that she'd given birth not that long ago.

The girl was unconscious with serious head injuries, and damage to her face, especially her right eye. The doctor wasn't sure they could save the eye, it was not her field of expertise. They were waiting for the eye specialist to come and examine her.

In the meantime the girl remained unconscious, and until she woke up, nobody knew who she was.

* * *

"Not another damn charity event," Gregory Stoneman said, his face darkening with annoyance. "Night after night, Evelyn, you drag me to these things and yet you know how much I hate them."

"The people who attend events such as this one tonight are the people who keep you in office," Evelyn said, giving him one of her disapproving frowns. "They are the ones who vote for you, Gregory, and you would do well to remember that."

Christ! Evelyn was so sanctimonious.

He could do with a blow-job right now. His cock itched for the feel of Carolyn's tight mouth, the way she held the shaft of his cock with her hands when he came, the way she never said no, *and* allowed him to come in her mouth.

"Are you listening to me, Gregory?" Evelyn said in her imperious queen voice. "You have one hour to be dressed and ready. It's not black tie, a suit will do. Wear your new blue shirt and the gold cufflinks my father gave you last Christmas."

Was she actually telling him how to dress now? God! The woman was insufferable.

Idly he wondered what she'd do if he bent her over his desk and took her from behind, jammed his itching cock right into her uptight backside and let her have it.

She'd scream, that's what she'd do.

Oh, Carolyn, Carolyn. What have I done? Where are you?

A detective had come to his office earlier in the day. The police had found Carolyn's car abandoned, with the driver's door wide open. The detective wanted to know if he had any idea where she might be.

He'd shaken his head and managed a worried expression. Then Muriel had volunteered that Carolyn had left to go to the dentist the previous day, and nobody had seen or heard from her since.

"It's nothing serious, is it?" Gregory had asked, faking major concern.

The detective had maintained a non-committal demeanor. "Please contact us if you hear anything, Senator."

"Certainly," Gregory had said.

Of course it was serious. A missing woman. An abandoned car in the middle of nowhere. It was dead serious.

Why hadn't Benito hidden the car?

But then again, why would he? He was a gang-banger, not a person with any brains.

Gregory experienced a sudden flash of extreme guilt.

"By the way," Evelyn said, toying with one of her cabochon ruby earrings, "I heard from Ramirez earlier today. He requested that you call him or drop by the center. There is something he wishes to discuss with you."

Gregory experienced a leaden feeling in the pit of his stomach. What the hell did Ramirez want?

* * *

Benito could not believe that Rosa was disrespecting him by not coming back to the house after he'd allowed her out to go to the market to buy food. He knew exactly where she was, she'd run home to her baby – a baby fathered by another man, an enemy – member of a rival gang.

Swearing under his breath, he vowed to punish Rosa for doing such a thing. No female disrespected him and got away with it. How dare she put her baby before him! It was an insult. She was lucky he kept her around, the ungrateful *puta*.

Now he was faced with the problem of getting the Senator's pregnant bitch out of his house without Rosa's help. Who had time for this shit? He had things to do, people to see. His lucrative corner drug business did not run itself.

* * *

Rigid with fear, Carolyn feverishly began working on the electrical cord securing her right wrist. Something her captors hadn't reckoned on was that she was left-handed, so although the knots were tough to undo, she reckoned she was making progress.

If only she had a knife or something to cut the damn cord with, it would be so much easier. The noise of the TV coming from the other room was relentless. Whoever was in there certainly enjoyed watching TV – it had been playing most of the day.

She wondered if and when the young girl would reappear. Several hours must have passed and no one had come anywhere near her. Was their plan to keep her shackled to the bed like a dog until she starved to death? She'd already soiled herself; there was no alternative since she couldn't escape from the bed.

Her fear was mixed with a mounting anger. Carolyn was no fool – she was beginning to understand that perhaps love had blinded her to the man Gregory Stoneman really was.

Questions kept running through her head. Why had he asked her to meet him in such a deserted spot?

What was his obsession with the fact that she should tell no one of her pregnancy?

And the worst thought of all – had Gregory arranged to have her taken because she was pregnant with his child?

The more she thought about it, the more convinced she was that Gregory could be involved. It sickened her. What a disgusting human being he must be, to have come up with this plan. And what exactly did he expect the result to be?

Were these people supposed to kill her and the baby she was carrying? Was that it?

Systematically she continued to work on freeing herself.

Chapter Forty-Nine

Bobby & Denver

Seeing Zeena at the Cavendish hotel bar had done nothing for Bobby. In fact, he was pleased to note that observing Zeena in the harsh light of day was quite a shocker. She came across as hard-looking, with her heavy dramatic make-up and long sweep of coal-black hair. Truth was, she might be athletic in bed, but out of bed her famous toned body was downright masculine. She had muscles like a man, and long sinewy arms. There was nothing feminine about her.

And here he was, sitting with a normal, extremely attractive girl, with soft curves, full natural lips, and the most inviting hazel eyes. Denver. Pretty, smart and he was rapidly falling in like.

After he left her, he returned to his suite feeling quite elated. Maybe this could be the start of something. She'd mentioned she was unattached, and since he was too – who knew what could happen?

Zeena. An adventure. An experience. Been there, done that.

With a sudden flash of insight he realized he was over his infatuation.

A shower seemed like a plan. Stripping off his clothes, he padded into the bathroom and switched the ceiling TV to a sports channel. Then he stood under the six powerful showerheads, giving himself up to the cascades of water beating down on him.

He wondered how his wild and wonderful mom would get along with Denver. Lucky would like her because Denver was smart and independent – Lucky's kind of woman. Max would hate her, because Little Sis was insanely jealous of any female he dated. In Max's eyes he was her big brother, and woe betide any woman who came before her in his affections.

The cold water was invigorating. The volume on the TV was so loud that Bobby didn't hear the bathroom door open. When someone slid into the shower beside him it took him completely by surprise.

"Hi, Bobby," a totally naked Zeena drawled in her lowdown husky voice. Then cupping his balls, she added, "Have you missed me?"

This surprising him in the shower move was pure Zeena.

"How the hell did you get in here?" he asked, dumbfounded as he attempted to back away – which was impossible as she had his balls in a disturbingly firm grip.

A throaty laugh. "Surely you know that Zeena can go anywhere she wants? And Zeena can *get* anything she wants. And right this moment, Zeena wants your cock in her mouth. So do not fight it, simply enjoy."

And before he could move or do anything, the superstar was on her knees sucking his dick – which had a mind of its own – because out of nowhere it was ramrod hard. He had no say in the matter.

Zeena did nothing half-heartedly. She was what the guys would describe as a Master Cocksucker – although Mistress of the Blow-Job might be a more apt title.

She sucked him dry and then some, and he put up no defense, or rather his dick didn't. When she was finished she announced she had a show to prepare for, and leaving him dripping in the shower, she was gone as stealthily as she'd appeared.

Holy shit! Thank God he didn't have to explain what just happened to a girlfriend, because if he *did* have a girlfriend – she'd never believe him.

Feeling used and angry at himself, he made it out of the shower and quickly dressed.

Basically Zeena had molested him, and his dick had happily gone along with it.

Goddamn it! Why hadn't he locked the hotel door? Or at least the bathroom door?

But then again – knowing Zeena, locks would present no deterrent. Miz Superstar could probably spring a lock with her snatch!

Still pissed, he left the suite and went downstairs.

* * *

So here I was, stranded in Vegas with nowhere to hang out until my date (yes, I'm calling it a date) with Bobby.

It was almost five, so I had two hours to kill before meeting him. When Ralph and entourage departed, the luxury suite became unavailable, so I was on my own. I quickly made up my mind that a change of clothes was in order, and maybe a comb-out at a hair salon. Plus I'd better book myself a room for the night, unless . . . No! Too soon! Bobby isn't just another guy. He's special.

I hit the shopping mall, searching for something suitable. Nothing too sexy – that would be obvious. More subtle sexy.

Hmm . . . I was in Vegas – subtle sexy was a whole world away.

After traipsing through several stores, I finally came across the perfect dress. A one-shouldered Donna Karan number in soft red silk jersey. Too expensive by far, but hey – I was in a reckless mood. So what if it cost almost two weeks' salary!

The problem was that, once I had the dress, I knew I had to buy shoes to go with it.

Here's the deal. I am not usually an extravagant person, but for tonight's adventure I am planning – obviously – to go all out. And yet . . . I don't understand why.

Yes, actually I do understand. This so-called date with Bobby is taking me back to my awkward teenage years. It's validating the fact that the boy everyone craved back in the day was paying attention to *me*!

This entire episode was so juvenile. I have actually blown off my boss, not to mention an important client of the firm, to indulge myself for once. Crazy behavior! What happened to work always comes first?

I'm beginning to get mad at myself. This was so totally unlike me.

Then I spotted the perfect shoes – strappy gold sandals with ultra-high heels and an ultra-high price tag.

Should I? Shouldn't I?

Oh, man! I am turning into a *Sex and the City* kind of girl, and that's not like me at all.

I purchased the shoes, then headed for the beauty salon where they washed and blow-dried my hair into soft curls, then talked me into having a professional make-up. More crazy behavior!

After the make-up artist and hair stylist were done, I changed into my new dress in the ladies room and inspected my image in a full-length mirror. It was the super-glam version of me. Quite a radical change.

Did I like the way I looked? I wasn't certain. But I *was* certain that with the mini-makeover I was sure to be more Bobby's type, false eyelashes and all.

* * *

M.J. and Cassie both had dizzy smiles on their faces when Bobby met them in the bar downstairs.

"You look happy," he remarked, ordering a beer.

"Yeah, we do," M.J. responded, exchanging an intimate grin with his young girlfriend.

"What?" Bobby said. "You won at blackjack?"

"Better than that," M.J. responded, his grin getting wider by the minute.

"Spill," Bobby said.

"We got married!" Cassie squeaked, her pretty little face all aglow. "Isn't it awesome?"

"You did *what*?"

"Married, dude," M.J. said excitedly. "Would've liked you as a witness, but it was an off the wall kinda let's go ahead an' do it deal."

"Holy shit, M.J.," Bobby said, shaking his head. "Your mom's gonna kill you."

"Not when she meets Cassie she won't," M.J. said confidently. "She's gonna love her."

"You're sure about that?"

"Yeah, man. Can you try to look happy for us?"

"I can't wait to see Zeena," Cassie piped up. "Will we get to see her after the show?"

"Sure," Bobby said, mourning the loss of his best friend, for he had no doubt that after M.J.'s announcement there was no chance of a one-on-one conversation.

"Where's Annabelle and Frankie?" M.J. asked. "They need to hear our news. We got some major celebrating to do later."

"An emergency came up," Bobby explained. "The two of them had to turn around an' fly back to L.A."

"Too bad," M.J. said. "They never got to meet my bride."

Bobby wasn't prepared to deal with M.J.'s craziness right now. Getting married in Vegas indeed. What a cliché! No prenup. No proper wedding. M.J.'s parents were going to flip out.

Soon Brigette and Kris appeared, and they too were all smiles.

It seemed everyone was having a great time except him. Bobby knew that he'd be having fun too if it wasn't for the Zeena incident. In retrospect he should've pushed her out of the shower and told her to get the hell away from him.

But no, he hadn't done that, because his goddamn dick had been too busy getting off on the attention.

Damn! A little control would have been nice.

* * *

Maneuvering my way through the casino in heels much higher than I was used to, I realized that with the clinging red dress, the new hairstyle and the super-slick make-up, I had totally taken myself out of my comfort zone.

Men were paying me a lot of attention, and I didn't like it. The attention was making me feel exposed and vulnerable. And speaking of feeling vulnerable, the red dress did not allow for a bra, so the girls were out there for all to see.

What was wrong with me? Why this sudden need to get all glammed-up?

Because obviously I was competing with the legions of women who I imagined were constantly chasing after Bobby.

Irrationally I started to feel angry. At him! It was all *his* fault. Why had I put myself in this position? It was quite ridiculous. I should've flown back to L.A. with Mister Shark Teeth and Ralph the movie star. I'm a professional lawyer, not some lovesick girl attempting to get noticed.

By the time I reached the bar where we'd arranged to meet, I was ready to tell Bobby that unfortunately I couldn't stay, so sorry.

But all bets were off the moment he stood up to greet me. He had on a blue shirt, open at the neck, dark jeans, a thin leather belt, and his black hair was slightly damp and curling over his collar.

Mario, with his dimples and fine abs, was not even close to looking this good.

"Wow!" Bobby said, pulling me in for a small but intimate hug. "Look at you!"

Was that a compliment? Please let it be a compliment.

"Wow!" I retaliated. "And look at *you*."

"I guess we both clean up pretty good," he said with a wide and quite irresistible grin on his face.

"I guess so," I replied, slightly breathless.

He introduced me to his friends, and after that I was lost in his dark sexy eyes.

I knew, without a doubt, that it was destined to be a memorable evening.

Chapter Fifty

Annabelle

Not only were they flying back to L.A. before Ralph was able to find and confront them, they were suffering the indignity of making the trip back on a commercial flight.

Annabelle was apocalyptic with fury. Frankie had ruined her life! Her well-thought-out plans for a delightfully uncomplicated future with Bobby were totally shattered.

The problem was that her drug-addict boyfriend had screwed them both by hiring his asinine cousin and her dimwitted son. What a pathetic pair! She'd warned Frankie time and time again that the two of them were useless, but he'd refused to listen. Now their story was splashed across the front page of the cheapest tabloid around, and she was being painted as a madam! A madam – how ridiculous was that?

When Frankie had appeared in the suite earlier, she'd been all ready to blast him for taking his time getting there. But before she could say a word he'd handed her a tastefully gift-wrapped package and urged her to open it.

Annabelle needed no encouragement when it came to opening presents. She'd ripped off the wrapping paper, revealing a black leather box. In the box nestled a pair of sparkling diamond earrings.

Hmm, she'd thought. *Maybe Frankie isn't such a loser, after all.*

The earrings were expensive and quite exquisite. For once Annabelle was impressed.

After putting them on and admiring herself in the bathroom mirror, she'd wandered back into the bedroom where Frankie was in a lustful mood. She'd responded, because when Frankie was on his best behavior the sex could be quite outstanding, and lately they'd not been connecting.

He'd slowly undressed her until all she had on were the diamond earrings and her strappy Jimmy Choos. Then he'd sat her on the side of the jacuzzi tub, spread her legs, gotten on his knees and gone down on her.

Giving oral was not Frankie's thing at all, so she'd been quite delighted. The result was an amazing orgasm.

But then, in true Frankie fashion, he'd ruined everything by telling her about their headline story in *Truth & Fact*. And on top of that, he'd informed her that Ralph was in Vegas, intent on splitting them up and dragging her back to L.A. with him, locking her up and probably throwing away the key for ever.

Frankie was exaggerating, but Annabelle did not know that.

When he'd finally gotten up the nerve to show her a copy of *Truth & Fact*, she'd gone berserk. To see herself depicted as a madam and sometime call-girl was quite shocking. She was appalled.

"We gotta get outta here," Frankie had said, sweating and agitated. "Pack up an' let's hit the road."

"But what about Zeena's concert?" she'd asked. *And Bobby*, she'd wanted to add, but didn't.

"Fuck the concert. You want Ralph to find us? We gotta split like half an hour ago."

Annabelle had done as she was told, but not without a litany of objections along the way.

They were now at the airport, and horror of all horrors, they were boarding a commercial jet that didn't have first-class! Even worse, their seats were located in the back of the plane.

Annabelle voiced her objections to the African-American flight attendant who couldn't give a rat's ass.

"Sorry," the flight attendant said, not sorry at all. "This flight is completely booked out. You're lucky to get seats at all."

"Lucky?" Annabelle sneered. "I think not."

The flight attendant moved away. She'd had a tough day and was in no mood to deal with a difficult passenger.

"I hate this!" Annabelle complained in a loud voice. "Who are all these ugly people dragging so much crap aboard?"

"It's called hand-luggage," Frankie said, wishing she'd be quiet. He was trying to figure out their next move, and it wasn't easy. Should they run back to New York? Or should they stick it out and stay around for the funeral?

"Hand-luggage!" Annabelle sniffed. "More like the entire contents of their miserable houses."

"Excuse me," said a middle-aged woman with a bad perm sitting across the aisle. "Aren't you that movie star's daughter turned hooker?"

Annabelle visibly blanched. Was some fat old hag calling her a hooker! How could that possibly be?

"You got the wrong person, lady," Frankie said quickly, leaning forward to shield Annabelle from the woman's prying gaze.

"No," the woman insisted in a shrill voice. "I haven't. I was reading about you two this morning in the hotel coffee shop." She wagged her finger at them. "Naughty! Naughty!"

"You got it wrong," Frankie said gruffly, willing her to butt out.

Their annoying fellow passenger had no intention of doing so. "It's you. I *know* it's you," she said, nudging her husband who was slumped in the seat next to her trying to pretend he had no idea what was happening. "It's them, Fred," she shrieked. "I told you so! Should I get their autograph?"

"Leave it be, Gladys," Fred said irritably.

"Why should I?" the woman argued. "Their autograph could be worth a few bucks on eBay, you never know."

"I doubt it," Fred said, burying his head in the airline magazine.

"Oh," she said dismissively, "*you* doubt everything I say. But I'm telling you, it's them, and I should get them to sign *something*."

Frankie tuned the couple out. He had too much going on to care about the likes of a loud-mouthed old bag who wouldn't quit bothering them.

Annabelle hunkered down in her seat and ordered Frankie to get her a glass of champagne.

"Not on this flight," he said, thinking that she lived in a dream world. "You'll have to wait until we get to the hotel."

In his mind he was formulating a plan. What if he was able to use this story to their advantage? Milk it for free publicity. Turn up at Gemma Summer Maestro's funeral and brazen it out. Annabelle would be the one garnering all the attention. Annabelle would be the star, making Ralph an also-ran. The media got off on big juicy scandals, and this was a huge one. Beautiful daughter of two mega-famous parents – one of them recently murdered – caught peddling the flesh of New York's most elite women.

If Annabelle was the star, then there had to be a villain. He could play the villain, why not? It hadn't gone too badly for the couple from *The Hills* reality show. Heidi and Spencer – or Speidi, as the press had christened them.

Yeah. This story could launch them into the fame stratosphere he'd always dreamed of. So what if it was a fame based on scandal? They'd still be famous.

What they needed to point them in the right direction was a smart manager, a savvy person who would guide and protect them. A person who would get them out there in the right way.

No *Howard Stern Show* or *Access Hollywood* for Annabelle. Her first interview should be with Barbara Walters or Diane Sawyer. After that exclusive, the couch on *The View*, Annabelle explaining her story to the women. Her story would be all about poor little rich girl – or, in Annabelle's case – poor little bitch girl! The women of *The View* would eat it up.

This would lead to an appearance on *Oprah*, and after that, a multi-million-dollar book deal. If it all fell into place, they'd be sitting on top of everything they'd ever dreamed of.

Frankie's adrenalin was fast moving into overdrive. This was an opportunity not to be missed.

Now all he had to do was convince Annabelle.

Chapter Fifty-One

Carolyn

One or two more swigs of cheap Scotch from the bottle, and glancing outside, Benito was satisfied that it would soon be dark enough to smuggle the Senator's bitch out of the house and dump her somewhere – anywhere far away from him.

He'd been sitting around drinking all day, brooding about Rosa running out on him, leaving him with nothing to eat except a few stale crackers and half a jar of rancid peanut butter.

He couldn't believe Rosa had the stones to treat him this way. Little whore. They were all dirty little whores – including the one taking up space in his bedroom and stinking it out. He could smell her – the stench was creeping out from under the closed bedroom door. The sooner he got rid of her, the better off he'd be.

He was sick of being trapped in the house, unable to take care of business, stuck in front of the TV watching all kinds of dumb shit. The boredom was getting to him. What he needed was some porno to change things up.

He moved over to a rickety table standing next to the TV and rifled through his cousin's collection of DVDs stacked on the floor.

Sure enough, between *Rambo I* and *II* and a pile of

wrestling DVDs, he came up with a promising title. *Fat Black Pussies.*

Not that he was into black bitches, he wasn't. But this was no time to be particular.

After slotting the disc into the player, he took another swig of Scotch, and sat back ready to enjoy himself.

* * *

"Any identification on her at all?" Detective Lennox asked the female doctor, a petite brunette.

They were both standing next to Rosa's bed in the hospital. The detective was a tall man, with sparse grey hair and sharp features. In a strange way he reminded the doctor of Clint Eastwood; he had that reassuring, take-charge quality about him.

Dr Glass shook her head. "Nothing," she said, wishing she had more information to give him. "Whoever beat this poor girl even took her shoes. All she had on was her top and skirt."

"Gotta tell ya, the street violence in that particular neighborhood is out of control," Detective Lennox remarked, jotting something in his notebook. "Gangs, addicts, thieves, hookers – the *real* low-lifes – they're out there in force, an' they prey on anyone they can. Nobody's safe."

Dr Glass nodded, and found herself wondering if he was married.

"Y'know something?" Detective Lennox continued. "Even *I* wouldn't walk around there after dark. It's that bad of a cesspit."

"This didn't happen when it was dark," Dr Glass pointed out. "It was daylight when they brought her in."

"Poor kid," Detective Lennox said, handing the doctor his card, while thinking she was an extremely attractive woman. "Do me a favor an' have someone call me when she starts talking."

"You mean *if* she starts talking," Dr Glass said.

"Yeah," Detective Lennox said with a weary shake of his head. "Can't hurt to hope for the best."

* * *

Keeping a sharp eye on the fading light behind the tacked-up curtain covering the window, Carolyn had almost freed herself from the ties binding her wrist. The fear was building. Her heart was pounding out of control, and so many new questions were running through her head.

Did she have an escape plan?

What was she going to do when she finally broke free?

Where was she running to?

Her plan was to escape through the window, since the door was no doubt locked. Besides, on the other side of the door were her captors.

More thoughts – *what if the window had bars outside, or if there was a window lock? And what if the space was too tight for her to climb through?*

There were so many unknowns to contend with, and even if she did manage to get out, what was she supposed to do then? Especially as she had no idea what part of the city she was in.

It didn't help that she had no money, no phone, and her clothes were soiled, filthy and covered in sticky grease – the result of being locked in the trunk of a car. On top of everything else she was starving hungry, thirsty, exhausted and worried for her baby.

But most of all, she was determined.

Determined to somehow or other get out of this degrading and disgusting trap and confront Gregory, for now she was almost sure that he had to be responsible.

If he was, she would make him pay for his betrayal of what she had imagined was their mutual love.

She would make him pay with his career, because she'd finally reached the conclusion that his damn career was the only thing he really cared about.

Senator Gregory Stoneman, she resolved, ***you are in for a nasty shock.***

Chapter Fifty-Two

Bobby & Denver

Bobby was hardly surprised that everyone warmed toward Denver. She was smart and engaging – and damn, she looked hot! A little too hot, because not only was M.J. ogling her cleavage, but Kris had eyes for her too. Brigette didn't seem to notice, nor did Cassie, they were both so psyched to be on their way to Zeena's show.

Bobby was not psyched. The last thing he had any desire to do was sit and watch Zeena perform for two hours. But how to get out of it?

No suitable excuse came to mind.

Renee and Susie, the owners of the Cavendish, met them in the lobby of their hotel when they arrived.

"Zeena's looking forward to seeing all of you after the show," Renee said. "I'm sad Lucky won't be joining us."

"Yeah," Bobby said. "Lucky sends everyone her love."

"Oh my God! I can't wait to see Zeena on stage," Cassie exclaimed, full of girlish enthusiasm. "She's *such* an icon. I've been listening to her music and watching her on TV and in the movies since I was five!"

"Don't tell *her* that," Renee warned. "No artist needs to be reminded of how old they are, especially coming from a pretty little thing like you."

"Hands off my wife," M.J. said, *sotto voce* to Bobby.

"You're safe," Bobby replied, then remembering something Lucky had told him, he added, "Susie might look mild, but if Renee even thinks about straying – watch out!"

"Good to know," M.J. said.

* * *

Bobby's friends seemed nice. I remembered M.J. from high school – he was always the cool dresser with the hot car. His girlfriend was very young but sweet, and she was in a high state of excitement about seeing Zeena's show.

I have to admit that I'm not that into Zeena's kind of music. It's a little too dance-techno for me. I'm more of a John Mayer, Jason Mraz kind of girl. Also I'm very into old eighties soul.

I wondered what kind of music Bobby liked. Rock? Rap? Soul? A combo? There was so much about him I didn't know.

"Hey," he said, holding onto my arm as we headed for our seats, which happened to be front and center. "If you don't like the show we can always duck out and catch up with everybody later."

"No, we can't," I replied, enjoying the feel of his hand on my bare arm. "We're right in Zeena's eyeline."

"She'll never notice," he said, as Brigette settled into the seat next to him.

"Of course she will."

"So . . . uh . . . tell me," he said with a half-smile. "Did you pull that sexy dress out of your purse?"

"Excuse me?" I said, curbing a strong desire to reach up and touch the slight stubble on his chin.

"You flew here for the day, right?"

"Correct."

"Were you expecting to stay?"

"Actually," I confessed, "if you must know, I went and bought this dress after we had drinks together. I got it especially to wear tonight. For you," I added boldly.

"For me?" he said, raising an eyebrow.

"Most popular boy in high school who never even knew I existed," I said lightly. "So I figured tonight I'd make sure you noticed."

"Oh, I'm noticing all right," he responded, his half-smile turning into a full-on grin.

"Excellent," I said crisply. "That means I haven't wasted two weeks' salary."

"Ah Denver," he sighed. "Don't you know, the dress doesn't make the woman, the woman makes the dress."

I blushed. I swear I did. And I *do not* blush.

Oh crap, why hadn't I flown back to L.A. with Felix?

This might be the start of something that could quite possibly rock my world.

Did I want that?

Yes, right now I really did.

* * *

Before Zeena appeared, a female Asian announcer in an electric blue tie and tails outfit, with whip in hand, took to the stage and sternly warned the audience there could be no taking of pictures and to please turn off all cell phones.

Denver wasn't very happy about that. "I'm expecting an important call," she whispered to Bobby.

"Put it on vibrate," he advised. "And if it's a horny boyfriend you can tell him he's too late."

"I'm not expecting any calls from horny boyfriends. And trust me, if they were my boyfriend, they wouldn't be horny, they'd be perfectly content and satisfied."

"Whoa!" Bobby said, and burst out laughing. "High opinion of your skills."

They exchanged a smile as the lights dimmed to complete darkness and then a center spot highlighted a golden cage descending from the ceiling containing Zeena and two live white tigers. The audience gasped as the music rose to a crescendo, playing the superstar's current number one hit single "Power."

Clad in a smokey, see-through catsuit, which emphasized every curve of her sinewy body, the tigers lounging on either side of her, Zeena milked the adoring audience like the true professional she was.

Stepping out from the cage, she left the tigers behind and launched into an elaborate song and dance routine with six African-American male back-up dancers clad in leopardprint leotards, which culminated with them picking her up and holding her aloft like a pharaoh queen.

The audience went nuts. Zeena *was* their pharaoh queen in the flesh. And they were worshipping at the altar.

Two elaborate production numbers later, and Zeena sauntered to the microphone to indulge in some light repartee with her adoring audience. Every word she said was met with sighs and applause and an edgy expectation about what would come out of her mouth next. Zeena was known for saying the most outrageous things.

As usual she had the audience exactly where she wanted them, and that always encouraged her to stretch the boundaries.

Watching her, Bobby was beginning to feel uncomfortable. He wished he could blank-out the earlier sex romp in the shower. Hardly a romp – more like Zeena getting exactly what she wanted – as usual. He promised himself he would never allow it to happen again.

Sneaking a sideways glance at Denver, he saw that she was checking a text message on her phone. Obviously she was as unimpressed with Zeena and her gaudy theatrics as he was.

"If I sound particularly smooth tonight, I'd like to give a shout-out to my special lover, Bobby Stanislopoulos," Zeena crooned into the microphone. "Bobby is a man who knows *exactly* what Zeena needs to make all the sweet sounds you appreciate."

The audience roared its approval.

Bobby could not believe what she'd just said. Lover? Was she freaking *kidding?!!*

M.J. leaned across Brigette with a big grin and gave him a thumbs-up.

Denver stopped checking her phone and concentrated on the woman standing on the stage.

"You see," Zeena drawled, savoring every moment of her bizarre announcement, "when Zeena wants her voice to soar, then Zeena has need for a certain male nectar . . ." A long suggestive pause. "So Bobby . . . may I take this moment to thank you for the late-afternoon shower and the delicious nectar of love that works *sooo* good."

The audience screamed their approval.

Only the incredible Zeena would dare go there.

* * *

I was attempting to read an urgent text from George Henderson, when out of nowhere Zeena mentioned Bobby's name. And she didn't just mention his name – she called him her lover. *Lover?* Wow! She sure as hell had *my* attention.

Miz Superstar then went on to spew forth a slew of euphemisms.

I am not slow, but believe me – I got the picture. So did everyone else in the damn place.

What a full-on drama queen! The thought of her with Bobby made me feel quite nauseous. Oh crap, I sure could pick 'em!

Bobby started pulling on my arm, a distraught expression on

his face. "It's not what you think," he half-whispered, losing his cool and almost stuttering. "She's crazy."

When caught, why do men always say, *It's not what you think.* Isn't that even lamer than, *It's not you, it's me.*

I made a swift recovery. *Never let them see you care.* My mom had taught me that. *Thanks, Mom!*

"Listen," I said, managing to sound quite collected, "I promise it has nothing to do with what Zeena announced to the world, but I have to get out of here. I received a text telling me there's an emergency situation going on in Washington concerning my best friend. I should head straight for the airport right now."

Of course he didn't believe me, why would he?

Zeena had launched into another production number. I had no intention of staying around, so as quietly as I could, I stood up, squeezed past his friends, and made a fast exit.

Bobby jumped to his feet and followed me. I had a feeling he would, but it wasn't going to do him any good. No damn good at all.

Chapter Fifty-Three

Annabelle

Frankie was never happier than when he was in action, and seizing control of a no-win situation invited major action. He refused to allow *Truth & Fact* to besmirch his reputation and walk away the victors. Oh no, he would turn it around as only he could.

When their plane landed at LAX, he informed Annabelle that they were not checking back into the Beverly Hills Hotel. "Not a smart move," he told her. "Ralph will track us down, an' that's exactly what we don't want to happen, so here's my plan . . ."

Annabelle listened as he laid out what he had in mind. In theory it sounded brilliant, but who knew if Frankie was capable of pulling it off?

"Don't you worry about a thing," he assured her, as he checked them into a suite under an assumed name at the Sunset Marquis – a hotel he did not think Ralph would find them at.

"What about my things?" she demanded, still playing the Hollywood Princess. "All my stuff is at the Beverly Hills Hotel. I need my clothes, my make-up."

"I'm taking care of it," he said. "You sit tight an' let me handle everything."

"Oh God, Frankie," she wailed, suddenly seeming quite vulnerable. "We are so fucked."

"No way, babe. We're coming out on top. I'm never gonna let you down."

Annabelle decided he wasn't so bad after all. At least he was there for her all the way, and that was something.

Frankie ran around trying to make his girlfriend comfortable, then as soon as he'd settled her in front of the TV with a bottle of Cristal and a Leonardo DiCaprio movie on pay per view, he made his first call.

One call was all he needed to get connected.

* * *

Fanny Bernstein had a reputation. Fanny Bernstein was not a woman many people dared to argue with. Fifty-ish, she was big and brash with a mass of frizzed dyed-orange hair, enormous boobs which she had no objection to flashing when the occasion arose, diamanté-rimmed eyeglasses and a cavern of a mouth. She called everyone honey or dollface, and if you were on her shit-list she called you cuntface.

Nobody ever wanted to be on Fanny's shit-list – especially Rick Greco, who had remained close to his former manager, even though she had never landed him another job after the demise of his successful nineties sitcom.

When Frankie called Rick – who knew all about the story in *Truth & Fact*, as did everyone else in Hollywood – and asked him who he should meet with, Rick didn't hesitate. "My one-time manager, Fanny Bernstein. Fanny's kicked more ass than you've had hot pussy. There's nobody she doesn't know."

"Can you set up a meeting for me right away?" Frankie said. "And by right away, I mean today."

"Sure," Rick said agreeably. "And if the two of you do business, I'll expect a finder's fee for putting you together. Are we down with that?"

"Put us together in the next couple of hours and you got it."

Exactly an hour later, Frankie was sitting in Fanny's garishly decorated office, taking in the framed photos of Fanny with everyone from President Clinton to John Travolta hanging on her walls. Rick Greco was also present, stinking of a particularly strong aftershave and once again dressed all in white. The two of them were waiting for Fanny to put in an appearance.

Frankie kept on glancing at his watch. Rick had said an hour, so where was this woman who, according to Rick, was about to turn everything around?

"Fanny gets off on making a grand entrance," Rick remarked. "She's eccentric, but I swear to you she's the one person you want in your corner. She's got all the power and clout you'll ever need. Like I told you – Fanny's a dynamo."

The dynamo made her grand entrance twenty minutes later. She swanned into her office clad in a purple caftan which clashed with her orange hair, spangly flip-flops, large cartwheel earrings, and dozens of jangling gold bracelets. Under her arm she clutched a miniature poodle, its fur dyed the same color as her hair.

"Boys," she announced, plopping her considerable ass down in the leopardprint chair behind her mirrored desk. "I'm here, I'm not queer, so what's your fuckin' problem that I had to forego a session with my acupuncturist?"

"Meet Frankie Romano," Rick said. "You might've seen him on the cover of *Truth & Fact* this week."

"Seen him! I've fucked him!" Fanny cackled, breaking up at her attempt at humor. "No kiddies, I haven't," she continued. "That must've been the water delivery guy. You've seen one little prick, you've seen 'em all!"

Frankie shot Rick a dirty look. *This* was the woman he was about to trust with his and Annabelle's future? No way.

He started to get up.

"Sit your ass down," Fanny commanded, taking off her

diamanté glasses and twirling them in a circle. "Learn to take a joke, an' you an' I will be as tight as an ant's crack."

For once in his life, Frankie was speechless.

"I've read the story," Fanny continued. "So tell me, Mister Pimp Man, whaddaya want outta this? Fame? Money? Glory? 'Cause I can get you all of it."

"You're sure about that?"

"Oh dollface, I'm sure as a shitload of sailors on shore-leave headin' for a whorehouse."

And Frankie didn't know why, but suddenly he was convinced.

* * *

The Leonardo DiCaprio movie finished, and Annabelle was bored. Frankie had told her not to go anywhere, but being holed up in a hotel was not to her liking. She sat in the middle of the kingsize bed, propped herself up with multiple pillows, and clicked TV channels, coming across *E.T.*, a program she sometimes watched – probably because Mark Steines was so damn cute.

Mary Hart was sitting outside on a location shoot with Shia LaBeouf, questioning the young actor about his love-life.

Idly Annabelle watched them interact until a slew of commercials hit the screen.

Back from commercials, a somber-faced Mark Steines announced that he had a breaking news story, and as he launched into it, Annabelle realized that he was speaking about her mother's murder. Apparently, there had been an arrest.

Sitting up straight, she immediately called for Frankie. Then she remembered he was out, securing their future.

Damn. She needed to speak with him. And she needed to speak with him now.

* * *

"Simon – you limey sonofabitch," Fanny roared into her pink old-fashioned phone perched atop her mirrored desk. Her words were said with a mixture of cheery affection and thinly veiled venom. "What's kickin' between *your* big balls today?"

"Fanny Bernstein," Simon Waitrose, Editor of *Truth & Fact*, stated. "*My* balls are doing fine. How about *yours*, luv? Still big and bouncy?"

"That's my tits, you horny bastard," Fanny cackled.

"How could I ever forget?"

"You got that right, sleaze-bag. Once seen, never forgotten."

This entire conversation was being played out on speaker-phone. Frankie and Rick were Fanny's attentive audience.

Frankie was impressed that she knew exactly who to call, and that she had the man's home number, because it was three hours later in New York.

"I presume I must've insulted one of your clients," Simon Waitrose went on. "Right, luv? 'Cause why else would the lady herself be calling, interrupting my dinner with a lovely young thing."

"A date with another hooker, Simon?" Fanny said caustically, winking at her captive audience. "Is she one of Frankie Romano's girls?"

"Oh Jesus! Don't tell me Frankie Romano is your client," Simon groaned.

"Yes, dear. So I wanna know who gave you the story? And you'd better e-mail me part two, otherwise there'll be a big fat juicy lawsuit writhing its way up your skinny English ass."

"Damnit, Fanny," Simon objected, "every word we printed is the truth."

"Sure it is, dollface," Fanny sing-songed. "An' *you* don't use Viagra."

"What?"

"E-mail me part two, then we'll talk."

She hung up with a satisfied smirk, opened her desk drawer and removed a stack of faxes which she passed across the desk to Frankie.

"Part two," she said. "Read it, then get down on your knees an' thank me."

"But didn't you just ask him to send you part two?" Rick said, sweating, because Fanny refused to put on the air conditioning. She insisted her office remain at 85 degrees at all times.

"Simon's main assistant resides in my back pocket – if y'know what I mean," she said, with another knowing wink. "Soon as you told me why we were having this meeting, I got onto it. Simon Waitrose deserves to shift his ass for the deal I'm about to offer him."

Frankie was busy reading part two. All of a sudden he had relatives and friends he never knew existed; there were photos of him as a kid and quotes from his dad – the fucking loser who used to beat the crap out of him, and never came looking when he took off at the age of fifteen.

"I don't believe this shit," he said, angrily throwing the faxes back on her desk. "I've never heard of any of these assholes, claimin' they were at school with me. As for my dad – we haven't spoken in ten years."

"Not to worry, dollface," Fanny said. "I'll get it stopped. Simon owes me a big one. And in return, after the exclusives with the respectable media – and I use the word 'respectable' loosely – we'll throw him a bone. A one-on-one sitdown with Annabelle. So tell me, dollface, where *is* your partner in the selling-flesh business?"

"At the hotel," Frankie said. "We're hiding out so Ralph doesn't get hold of her. We've heard he's in a raging fury and wants to bury my ass."

"Ah . . . Ralphie," Fanny sighed, a faraway gleam in her eyes. "Had him when I was fifteen and a virgin. It was a one-night stand. He spotted me at a party, sent his stand-in over to see if my tits were real, then took me upstairs and had his way with me." She guffawed at the memory. "Nice cock. Not big enough for me, though."

Once again Frankie was speechless.

Chapter Fifty-Four

Carolyn

Fat Black Pussies wasn't his favorite porno, but it was still turning Benito on. He started thinking about jacking off since Rosa wasn't around to service him. No food. No pussy. What the fuck was a man supposed to do to keep himself entertained?

Then it occurred to him that there was a perfectly workable pussy lying on his bed. A pussy that was good enough for a Senator. And if he jammed his big fat dick into that pussy – maybe it would shift the baby she was carrying, and everyone could go home happy.

Yeah. He'd blindfold her, fuck her, give her a whiff of chloroform, stick her in the trunk of his car, and drop her off on a street corner far enough away that she could never lead anyone back to his cousin's house.

Screw Rosa. He didn't need her. He'd solved the problem all on his own.

He moved toward the door of the bedroom and opened it an inch. The room was dark enough, but he could make out his victim moving around on the bed.

Then, just as he was about to fling the door wide open and take his hard-on into the bedroom, the phone rang.

Shit! Bad timing! But in case it was business, he closed the door and picked up the phone.

It was big brother Ramirez.

* * *

For one long moment Carolyn was completely paralyzed. Fear crept over her like a shroud of fog, and she found herself unable to move. She'd almost freed herself, then someone had started to open the door. A phone rang, and whoever was there closed the door and went away.

Now she was too scared to run.

Get it together! her inner voice cried out in her head. *At least make an attempt to find a way out of this hellhole. Do it! Do it now!*

Filled with apprehension, she broke the final tie and forced herself to put her feet on the floor. Her shoes were gone, they must've fallen off when she was first taken. But having no shoes was the least of her problems.

Shaking, she got off the bed, rushed toward the window and what she hoped and prayed would soon be freedom.

* * *

"Fuck you!" Benito screamed into the phone. "I ain't listenin' to anything ya gotta say."

"Calm down, my brother," Ramirez replied. "All I'm asking is that you come to the center tomorrow and speak with me."

"Why th'fuck I wanna do that?" Benito yelled.

"Word on the street is that you're a target," Ramirez said calmly. "And I can help you."

"Don' fuck with me just 'cuz ya think ya King of the fuckin' Do-gooders," Benito sneered. "I got news – anybody get near me, they seein' a war on their mo-fuckin' hands. I got an army behind me."

"What good an army do you if someone put a bullet in your head?" Ramirez said, the voice of reason. "No army gonna save you then."

"Fuck you!" Benito screamed again, before slamming down the phone.

His brother drove him loco, always trying to persuade him to come to the center and repent his ways. Last time he'd gone there he'd almost got shot leaving the place. Rosa's fuckin' baby daddy again. It was time he reversed the situation and blew the mo'fuckin' prick away.

He began going over his conversation with his brother. It wouldn't surprise him if Ramirez was trying to set him up. Get rid of him, so that under the guise of Mister Clean, Ramirez could move in and take over his lucrative drug-running business.

Yeah, that was it. Ramirez was jealous, he wanted what was his.

Too bad. Big brother was getting nothing.

* * *

Upon reaching the window, Carolyn frantically dragged the torn covering aside. Outside it was pitch black. She could see nothing.

The fear she felt was all the way in her throat. Her heart was pounding out of control. She felt sick to her stomach and dizzy.

The window itself opened outwards with a rusty handle. There was no lock and she knew it would be tight, but with a little luck she could squeeze through the limited space. She had to.

Random thoughts flooded her brain.

What if her captors came in the room and pulled her back inside when she was halfway through the window?

What if they were so mad they beat her up, or even killed *her?*

As frightened as she was, there was no going back.

Somehow or other, she began her escape.

Chapter Fifty-Five

Bobby & Denver

We were on our way to the Vegas airport, Bobby and I. When I'd told him about my emergency, he'd insisted on flying me to Washington in his plane in spite of my objections. Then he decided he'd better come with me in case I required his assistance in any way.

What was I supposed to do? The text from George Henderson was a desperate cry for help, and although George wasn't asking me to head for Washington, where he and his wife already were, I knew that I had to go. And if the fastest way to get there was on Bobby's plane, so be it.

Carolyn was missing – not in a *"gone away for a few days"* kind of way, but in a sinister *"she's been abducted"* kind of way. And everybody who has ever watched the news knows exactly what *that* means.

Missing girl more often than not equals rape and murder.

According to George, the police had found Carolyn's car abandoned in a remote spot with the driver's door open, one of her shoes lying on the ground. She had not turned up at work, missed an arranged breakfast with a neighbor, and had not been seen since noon on Tuesday when she'd left the office for a supposed dental appointment. When contacted, her dentist said there *was* no appointment.

I had no idea what I could do to help, but Carolyn was my best friend, and I knew I had to be there, if only to lend moral support to her parents.

I called Felix on my way to the airport to give him a heads up.

"I don't understand what's the matter with you lately," Felix snapped, his usual charming self. "Do you not care about your job?"

This hurt, coming from Felix. Of course I cared. In all the time I'd worked at Saunders, Fields, Simmons & Johnson, I'd always put my job first. Just ask Josh.

Once again I wondered if the time had come to think about moving on. I'm sure I could score an excellent position elsewhere.

I then phoned my next-door neighbor to let him know I would not be back for a few days, and could he keep Amy Winehouse for me? "She's fine," he assured me. "Not to worry."

As soon as I was off the phone, Bobby jumped on my case. "Everything okay?" he asked, being annoyingly solicitous – like *that* was going to make me forget Zeena's revealing little speech, a speech I had not mentioned, nor had he.

The not-mentioned speech was standing between us like an elephant in the room, except we weren't in a room – we were in a limo on our way to the airport and Bobby's private plane.

He is *so* not me – what was I thinking?

* * *

Ever since Bobby realized that he had a certain power because of his heritage, he'd managed to gain control over most situations. He'd learned from both his parents, and even though he was a child when Dimitri passed, he'd studied his late father in photos and on videos, and noted the way he acted. Dimitri had always conducted himself with immense charm, compassion and unwavering control. The three C's.

Lucky had her own particular way of handling things, and it always seemed to work for her.

Both his parents were tough, loyal and driven, they both knew what they wanted, and they'd always come out on top.

Bobby desired the same for himself. He realized he'd been born into great privilege, but he'd never allowed himself to get carried away with all the trappings of enormous wealth, and he'd certainly never traded on his exceptional good looks. He'd made a concentrated effort to make it on his own, and he'd succeeded.

One of the things he prided himself on was that he'd always treated women well – making sure to let them down easy when things didn't work out. He'd endeavored to be a good guy.

Now Zeena had managed to make him look like her dumb-ass little plaything. And he was furious. At Zeena. But most of all at himself.

From the moment the words had slipped from Zeena's scarlet lips, Denver had begun to treat him like a vague acquaintance with whom she was being forced to spend time. Sure, she'd agreed to a ride on his plane, but that was out of an urgency to get to Washington, not because she wished to be with him.

He didn't know what to say to her. Should he try explaining? *Uh . . . Denver, here's the deal – Zeena came into my shower unexpectedly, I never invited her, and uh, yeah, she did give me head, but . . . uh . . .*

Shit! Where could he possibly go with this?

The first girl he'd liked in a long time, and Zeena had crushed any hope he had of taking it further.

The limo pulled up at the airport, and a special services escort smoothed their path to the plane.

Once aboard, Denver noted where Bobby was sitting, and

deliberately chose a seat across the aisle. Gitta, one of the attractive flight attendants, asked her if she needed anything.

"I'm fine," she said. "Thanks anyway."

"You know," Bobby said, leaning across the aisle, "there's a bedroom aboard, so if you feel like sleeping . . ." He trailed off. Mentioning a bedroom sounded suggestive in a ridiculous kind of way, almost as if he was coming on to her. Which he wasn't. Not at all.

But he'd like to. Oh yes, he'd definitely like to.

The problem was that Zeena had put paid to any chance of that.

* * *

It's strange. When something dramatic happens in your life, everything else seems unimportant. Two hours ago, I'd been kind of obsessed with Bobby, but right now I couldn't care less. Had I *really* been running around spending all my salary on a sexy designer dress and shoes? Getting my hair done? Enduring the discomfort of stupid false eyelashes and too much make-up? Silly me. I must've had a brainstorm.

Now all I could think about was Carolyn. Where was she? Had she been abducted as George Henderson seemed to believe? How did one even begin to search for her?

I didn't have any answers, and for someone who has a need to be on top of things, that's frustrating.

I started thinking about the recent texts I'd received from her. Fortunately I store everything in my phone memory – just in case. Was there a clue somewhere?

Pulling out my phone, I began going over them. The last text I'd received from her was on Monday. *We must talk! So much is happening!*

What did *that* mean? Was she back with Matt, her ex? Had she met someone new?

It had to be about a man, I was sure of it.

I glanced over at Bobby. He was slumped in his seat, probably exhausted after his late-afternoon blow-job from the scary-looking superstar. Zeena reminded me of Vampira – a superwoman from another planet.

Still clad in my far too revealing red dress and uncomfortable heels, I grabbed the shopping bag that contained my original clothes, undid my seatbelt and stood up.

A pretty Hawaiian flight attendant who'd introduced herself as Hani, rushed to see what I needed. "I'd like to change clothes, Hani," I said. "Is that possible?"

"Certainly," Hani replied with a polite smile. "Follow me."

I followed her into a fully decorated bedroom. A bedroom! On a plane!

There was a queen-size bed, flatscreen TV, a closet, and a full en-suite bathroom complete with a walk-in shower!

I wondered if Bobby had given Zeena a ride on his plane.

No, she probably had her own 747. Mega-rich people lived in a different world.

I didn't care. All I cared about was finding Carolyn.

* * *

Denver shut herself in the bedroom and emerged fifteen minutes later dressed in the clothes she'd worn earlier: loose-fitting beige pants, a crisp white shirt and a slouchy jacket. Her hair was back in a ponytail, and she'd removed most of her make-up.

Bobby thought she looked glowingly beautiful. This girl was a natural beauty, she didn't need all the trimmings. He quickly recalled the great time they'd had in the bar at the Cavendish earlier. The two of them had experienced such a strong connection. He knew it wasn't his imagination, they'd really had major chemistry.

Damn! Why did Zeena have to come along and screw everything up?

"Uh . . . did you find everything you needed?" he asked, feeling totally off his game, which wasn't like him at all.

"I wasn't looking," Denver answered coolly. "Is there a phone I can use?"

Summoning Gitta, Bobby asked her to show Denver where the phone was located.

Denver picked up the phone and turned her back on him.

He was dying to know who she was calling. She'd said she didn't have a current boyfriend, but who knew?

He tried reversing the situation in his head. Male singing star announcing to the world that he'd just gone down on Denver. Not a happy thought. It was no surprise she'd closed ranks on him.

He made an attempt to look at the positive side. At least she'd accepted a ride on his plane. Maybe there was some way he could make amends.

Then he thought, *No chance in hell.*

He had a strong hunch that Denver was not the kind of girl who forgave easily.

Chapter Fifty-Six

Carolyn

The fear was so overpowering that Carolyn was finding it hard to breathe. Taking desperate short gasps of air, she attempted to pace herself and stay focused, for she knew that whatever distress she was in, it was not going to stop her from doing what she had to do. And what she had to do was get the hell out.

Heart pounding non-stop, she was resolute in her determination to run from this loathsome place where she'd been treated as less than sub-human.

Yanking the window open as far as it would go, she was hit with a heavy sheet of rain. Summoning all the strength she had left, she managed to climb up onto the sill.

Stopping for a moment, she took a deep breath. "One step at a time, one step at a time," she muttered to herself, as somehow or other she managed to fit her body through the small space, almost getting stuck – but with one supreme effort forcing herself out.

As she hit the ground outside, her bare feet sunk into thick mud, and the heavy rain that had been falling all day, started pounding her body, soaking her within seconds.

She had no idea where she was. There were no street-lights

and the night was deadly black. Somewhere in the distance she could hear a dog howling, and the incessant drone of a far-off helicopter.

Forcing her survival instinct to kick in, she began desperately running.

* * *

Muttering and cursing, Benito tried to shake off Ramirez's phone-call and return his attention to the porno taking place on the TV screen.

His fuckhead brother had always tormented him, ever since they were kids living in a one-bedroom slum house with a drugged-out mother and no father in sight. It was Ramirez who'd forced him into gang-life at the age of twelve, and by the time he was thirteen, Ramirez had him out on the street selling drugs.

Ramirez was a hard-core bad-ass who'd suddenly changed tracks and turned into a self-righteous, hypocritical son-of-a-mo'fuckin'-*bitch.* Benito hated his guts.

Staring at the TV screen, he tried to block out memories of when he was a kid.

It took a while, but eventually *Fat Black Pussies* had the desired effect, and his dick began getting hard again – a combination of the raunchy sex he was watching, and the hatred and anger he felt toward his brother.

Soon he decided it was time to show the Senator's bitch who was really boss.

Abruptly he got up and strode purposefully toward the bedroom door.

Chapter Fifty-Seven

Annabelle

"What do you mean, they've made an arrest?" Frankie said, scratching his forehead.

Annabelle had jumped on him the moment he'd arrived back at the hotel, not giving him a chance to tell her about their new manager-to-be, and how full of innovative ideas Fanny Bernstein was.

"Switch on the TV — it's on every channel," Annabelle announced excitedly.

"Who've they arrested?" Frankie asked. "The stalker?"

"What stalker?" Annabelle said, staring at him blankly.

Annabelle Maestro was something else. Apparently she had not been following her own mother's murder case.

"There was mention of a stalker," Frankie told her. "Some over-zealous fan from New Orleans who came to town to worship at Gemma's feet. The cops had him pegged as a person of interest."

"This time they're not saying who it is; all they're saying is that an arrest has been made."

"You must be relieved," Frankie said, pulling a Diet 7up from the mini-bar.

"Maybe it's Daddy Dearest," Annabelle suggested with a wicked chuckle.

"Jeez, Annabelle, if it *was* Ralph, we'd all know about it," Frankie said, quite disgusted that she was not taking this seriously. "And if you're interested in hearin' *my* take on it, even *thinkin'* that Ralph could've done it is pretty sick." A beat. "You might wanna see a shrink about that."

"And *you* might want to see a shrink about your vile coke habit," Annabelle retaliated, once again thinking that maybe she was making a mistake sticking with Frankie.

"Listen, babe," he said, backing down from a fight, "there's someone you've got to meet. The woman's a freakin' powerhouse, an' she's the one who's gonna get us out of this mess."

"Exactly *how* is she going to do that?" Annabelle asked with a look of disbelief.

"She'll tell you how when you meet her," Frankie said, holding on to his patience. "Fanny will explain every move we're gonna make."

"And when am I supposed to meet this so-called powerhouse?" Annabelle asked, faking a bored yawn.

"Tonight. Ten o'clock in the garden restaurant at the Château Marmont."

"Ten is too late," Annabelle said irritably. "We've been on and off planes all day. I'm exhausted."

"We gotta eat, don't we?" Frankie said, exasperated.

"I suppose so."

"Okay, so let's do it."

"I guess," Annabelle said, less than enthusiastic.

"An' babe, I should warn you," Frankie said, thinking it was best to prepare her for the ball of energy that was Fanny, "this woman is some crazy character. But you gotta believe me, Fanny Bernstein is gonna get us everythin' we want."

* * *

One look at Fanny, and Annabelle shifted into her snobby *Beverly Hills, I'm better than you* mode.

Fanny got her number immediately. Rich girl. Bitch girl. Movie star's daughter with all the privileges and none of the attention and love. During her long and illustrious reign in Hollywood as a top manager, Fanny had met plenty of girls like Annabelle.

"Calm down," she was tempted to say. *"You chose to hook up with a coke-addict from the wrong side of the tracks. So get off your high horse, honey, and let's discuss your future."*

Annabelle offered a limp handshake, appalled that Frankie was even thinking of doing business with this hot mess of a woman.

Fanny rejected the handshake and moved in for a hug, repulsing Annabelle even more as she found herself enveloped in Poison, her unfavorite scent.

"Fanny Bernstein," Frankie said. "Meet Annabelle Maestro, the love of my life."

Fanny winked at Annabelle as they settled at an outdoor table. "Doesn't that corny bullshit make you wanna throw up?" she cackled.

Annabelle couldn't help agreeing.

"It's men, dollface," Fanny continued. "They all spew forth the same tired old lines. Y'know what I'm sayin'?" And then, affecting a deep male voice she said, "'Damn, you look beautiful tonight. No, your ass does *not* look big in that dress. Sure I'll buy you a new car. How about sucking my pee-pee, darlin'? I promise not to cum in your mouth'."

Unable to help herself, Annabelle broke up laughing. This woman in the outrageous purple caftan with the huge earrings, orange hair and loud mouth, was hilarious.

"I slipped that one to the Pres," Fanny confided. "The horny bastard ate it up. The truth always gets a big haw haw."

Annabelle didn't like to ask which President she was

referring to. Probably Clinton, not Bush, and certainly not Obama.

Frankie relaxed. He'd been nervous about putting Annabelle together with Fanny, but now he could see why Fanny was so successful; she knew how to play it, and before long she had Annabelle completely under the Fanny Bernstein spell.

* * *

Back in New York, Janey Bonafacio was in a deep state of panic. Not only had her son run off with what she was sure was a formidable payment for selling the story of Annabelle and Frankie's business venture to a tabloid, but she was left dealing with the fall-out – and there was considerable fallout. The phones hadn't stopped ringing. Reporters and paparazzi were staked outside the swanky apartment-house – much to Annabelle's snooty neighbors' fury. Clients were threatening that if their names were revealed, there would be major lawsuits. And some of the so-called celebrity girls, their identities disclosed, had actually turned up at the front door ready to kill Frankie and Annabelle or whoever else was available.

Janey was a nervous wreck. But even though Frankie had spoken to her in such a harsh way over the phone, she still harbored a soft spot for him. He was still *her* Frankie, and because it was Chip who'd done such a reprehensible thing, she felt that in a way it was she who was responsible.

According to one of her neighbors who had a key to her apartment in Queens, Chip had vanished. Packed up all his stuff and taken a midnight run. Which was just as well, because when pushed, Janey had a formidable temper, and she would have felt no guilt taking it out on her good-for-nothing son.

Anyone else would've abandoned the Park Avenue apartment and run for the hills, but Janey remained loyal, hoping that when Frankie got back to New York, he would forgive her.

* * *

"It's settled then," Fanny said, attacking the shared dessert plate set in the middle of the table. "We all know what we have to do?"

Annabelle nodded. She felt a lot more secure now that Fanny had taken over.

"Outfit?" Fanny questioned, just to make sure Annabelle had absorbed her instructions for tomorrow's funeral.

"Black," Annabelle said obediently. "Not pants, a skirt—"

"Of a decent length," Fanny interrupted.

"No jewelry except my Maltese cross. Very little make-up. Dark shades."

"Perfect," Fanny said, her fork heading for another scoop of chocolate cake. "And you, Frankie?"

"Yeah, yeah, I got it," he said restlessly. "Nothin' flashy, keep my mouth shut whatever happens."

"Do not worry, I'll be there to make sure Ralph doesn't turn on you, which is unlikely because the press'll be out in force, and Ralph would never risk besmirching his movie-star reputation by doing anything stupid in front of the cameras."

"How about after?" Annabelle questioned. "Do we go back to the house?"

"We'll play that one by ear," Fanny said, a dribble of chocolate trickling down her chin.

"Done deal," Frankie said.

"Yes, it is," Fanny agreed, reaching for a forkful of cheesecake. "Oh, and Frankie, we'll be doing the *People* magazine interview in the afternoon, so keep your coke intake to a minimum, and no telltale white powder decorating your nose."

"Hey—" Frankie began to say.

"Don't bother," Fanny said, stopping him from speaking. "I've heard every excuse in the book, and I couldn't give a monkey's left ball about what you do on your own time, but when we're working – no drugs. Got it?"

Annabelle smiled. Finally someone who could control Frankie. What a bonus!

Chapter Fifty-Eight

Carolyn

Benito grabbed his crotch as he approached the door to the bedroom and turned the handle. He was good and hard, which meant that the Senator's bitch was in for a treat now. She was about to get the real deal, not some old dude's limp dick. Benito Ortego was a man to be reckoned with.

The bedroom was in darkness, but he planned on blindfolding the woman anyway – a security measure in case she ever tried to identify him. He'd blindfold her, then he'd turn the light on so he could see exactly what kind of pussy he was getting.

As he entered the room he was hit by a freezing rush of cold air coming from the window. Rosa, the stupid douche, must've opened it for some reason. The place was like a mo-fuckin' iceberg.

Groping his way to the bed, he realized with a combination of shock and disbelief that his captive was no longer there.

Shit! The fuckin' bitch had escaped!

* * *

Rosa's eyes flickered open – only one eye actually, because her right eye was throbbing and covered with a heavy dressing.

She attempted to speak, but she couldn't do more than let out a croak since her mouth was so dry.

"Where am I?" she tried to say.

A nurse appeared. "Stay quiet, dear," she said in a soothing voice. "I'll let the doctor know you're awake."

"I want my momma," Rosa whimpered, reverting to the scared teenager she really was.

The nurse paged Dr Glass, who appeared fifteen minutes later.

As soon as the doctor saw that the young girl was conscious and talking, she immediately called Detective Lennox.

"Something came up, I'm on another case," the detective said, not sounding too pleased about it. "I'm goin' to have to send someone else to take her statement."

"You're not coming yourself?" Dr Glass asked, strangely disappointed.

"Missing woman – Senator's assistant," Detective Lennox explained. "By tomorrow the press'll be all over it. The Chief already is."

"I understand," Dr Glass said.

"If things clear up, maybe I'll stop by tomorrow, speak to the girl myself." A pause. "You on duty tomorrow?"

"All day."

"See you then."

Dr Glass returned her attention to her patient.

"I want my momma," Rosa repeated, tears streaking down her cheeks. "I want her to come here *now*."

* * *

"What can I do for you, Ramirez?" Gregory asked over the phone, keeping his voice neutral. He'd made up his mind that it was wise to get the phone call over with, find out what the man wanted.

"It's about my brother," Ramirez said.

"Your brother?" Gregory questioned, swallowing hard.

Had Ramirez found out what was going on?

Was it possible that Benito had ratted him out?

Jesus Christ! The shit was about to fly.

"I need to speak with you about him," Ramirez continued. "Can you come by the center early tomorrow? It's urgent."

Ramirez might as well have said, *"Bring plenty of money, 'cause I'm about to blackmail your dumb white ass."*

Gregory bit down hard on his lower lip. Yes, he was dumb, for what he'd put into motion was unforgivable.

"I'll be there," he said gruffly.

* * *

Stepping on something sharp caused an excruciating pain that shot through Carolyn's foot like a knife. She let out a cry of despair.

It wasn't enough that she was drenched, freezing, and running for her life. Now this.

As her eyes became acclimatized to the dark, she started to get her bearings and realized she was running down an alley filled with overflowing garbage cans, abandoned cars, old furniture, and worn out mattresses. On each side of the alley was a mass of overgrown grass and an abundance of weeds.

A rat scurried across her path. Stifling a scream she kept going, because one thing she knew for sure, she had to get as far away from the house she'd been held in as fast as possible. If her captors discovered she was gone and came looking for her, what then?

It wasn't something she cared to think about.

Chapter Fifty-Nine

Denver

Bobby had suddenly become like one of those annoying big dogs that one is constantly tripping over.

He didn't know how to back off. It was apparent he'd never had to.

"Go back to Vegas and let Zeena blow you from here to the next Lakers game," I had a yen to say. But of course I didn't – that's the not-into-hurting-people's-feelings side of me.

Sometimes I can be such a wimp. Or a bit of a hypocrite, depending on how you look at it. I'd gone off Bobby because he'd gotten head from some scary superstar who'd announced their sex tryst from the stage. But in the last few days I've had excellent sex with two different men – so I'm hardly a vestal virgin!

Still . . . when Bobby and I had drinks together I'd definitely felt the spark of something special happening. So him running straight off and getting blown by Queen Vampira was a bit of a downer to my ego.

But hey, it wasn't as if we'd slept together, or even kissed, so maybe I was making too big a thing of it.

I settled back in my seat and tried to catch a few hours' sleep. I'd need all the energy I could muster when we arrived.

It was late by the time we landed in Washington – three a.m. on Thursday morning Vegas time, and six a.m. local Washington time. I didn't care about the time. I had every intention of meeting up with Carolyn's parents and finding out what was happening.

"They'll probably be asleep," Bobby said.

"Are you kidding me?" I replied, giving him a withering look. "Would *your* mom be asleep if *you* were on the missing list?"

"You've got a point," he said, nodding his handsome head.

I might have gone off him, but that didn't mean I couldn't still appreciate his spectacular looks. *Dammit!*

While we were winging our way to Washington, Bobby had made arrangements – he was obviously a master at that. A car to meet us at the airport. God, I hope it's not another limo. A two-bedroom suite in the same hotel as the Hendersons. That didn't bother me because I had no intention of sleeping, and at least it would serve as a base.

A few minutes before the plane landed, Bobby felt it necessary to say something about the Zeena incident. He'd obviously been building up to the great explanation.

"Uh . . . Denver, there's something I should explain about Zeena," he said, sounding mighty uncomfortable. "Y'see, she's . . . uh . . . a very demanding woman, goes for what she wants whenever she wants it. And . . . uh . . . yesterday what she wanted happened to be me."

"I kind of get that," I said, refusing to help out.

"Yeah, well, I was taking a shower, and she suddenly appeared out of nowhere. Now I know I should've told her to get out, but—"

"Hey," I said, quickly stopping him from making any more excuses. "You don't have to account for anything to me. We hardly know each other, Bobby. It's none of my business."

"But it is," he insisted. "We spent time together earlier, and it was so great." He took a long beat. "You've got to understand that the Zeena thing meant nothing to me."

"Apparently it meant something to her," I said, still refusing to let him down easy.

"I've come up with this crazy idea," he said.

"What?"

"Why don't we forget about what happened, and consider returning to square one?" he suggested, dark eyes sincerely locked onto mine. "How does that sound to you, Denver? 'Cause it sounds real good to me."

God! The man was irresistible. Any other time I probably would've forgiven him in a flash, but my mind was firmly on Carolyn, and getting involved was nowhere near the top of my agenda.

"Look, I get it," I said, weakening. "No hard feelings." Suddenly I found myself stupidly grinning. "Did that sound like a pun?"

He grinned back at me. "Yeah, as a matter of fact, it did."

We exchanged a long and meaningful look. Then he said something very special. "Right now we should concentrate all our energy on finding your friend. I'm here for you, Denver, and I'll do everything I can to help you. But after that, it's a new beginning for us. Right?"

And like a lovesick fool, I found myself murmuring, "Right."

Chapter Sixty

Carolyn

Alarm and fury propelled Benito into action.

His alarm was about the woman remembering the location of his house and fingering him as her kidnapper.

His fury was about her getting away in the first place.

How long had the Senator's bitch been gone? He didn't know. It couldn't be that long.

Had Rosa helped her? Was that why she'd run out on him? Had she left the window open and untied their prisoner?

Shit! Shit! Shit!

She could've already reached the cops and told them where he lived.

He was *not* going back to jail. No fucking way! If the cops arrested him, he'd spill everything in exchange for a deal. Senator Stoneman would be the one taking the rap for this fucked-up mess, not him.

Grabbing his gun, he ran out to his car. Maybe he wasn't too late. Maybe he could catch her and drag her back to the house.

The only way she was leaving was when *he* said so.

* * *

By the time Carolyn ran out of the alley and reached the street, she was in a bad way. Soaked to the skin, her foot leaking blood, she knew she had to get help.

Looking up and down the neglected and rundown street she realized she was in a bad part the city, most likely somewhere in the south-east quarter, a notorious crime-ridden area.

There was no one on the street, most of the street-lights were broken, and the only place she could see open was a bar on the corner.

She limped toward it, the pain in her foot excruciating. The rain continued to pound down, making things even worse.

If only she could get to a phone . . . that's all she needed to be safe. One phone call to the police, and they'd come get her.

* * *

His car wouldn't start, sending Benito into a rage. This was no time for his piece-of-shit car to break down. The pissing rain didn't help.

He tried to start the car again with no success. The battery spluttered for one brief second, then died.

He had to get moving and search for the Senator's bitch, but how was he supposed to do that with no car?

Then he remembered that Rosa's mother had an old Buick. It sat outside her house doing nothing. So fuck it – he'd take it. Too bad.

Pulling up his hoodie to ward off the rain, he set off to cover the ten blocks to Rosa's mother's house.

Taking her precious momma's car would be Rosa's punishment for running out on him. *Puta!*

* * *

Carolyn limped up to the outside of the bar and pushed the wooden door to gain entry.

A big man stood inside the doorway blocking her way. Arms crossed against a massive chest, he yelled, "Get the fuck outta here, ya filthy stinkin' cunt. How many times I gotta tell ya vagrants that ya ain't gotta come around here."

"But I've—"

He wasn't having it. Red in the face and angry, he was not prepared to listen. With one fell swoop he grabbed her around the waist and propelled her outside, shoving her so hard that she fell in the gutter.

"An' don't come back," he shouted, returning to the bar and slamming the door.

Carolyn was in shock. She'd escaped a devastating kidnapping and now she was being treated like a piece of garbage.

Slowly, she picked herself up.

A homeless man walked by pushing a shopping cart. Dressed in rags, he had an American flag wrapped around his head, and a mangy dog trailing behind him.

She ran over to him and begged for help.

"Wanna get a feel of me jimmy-jam?" he guffawed, exposing himself to her. "You'll love me piece of meat, girly. C'mon, help yourself, lick away. No charge."

Quickly backing off, she started running down the street again, avoiding a drunk who spat at her, and two transvestites who totally ignored her when she tried to ask for assistance.

She passed two public phone booths, both with broken phones dangling by the cords.

Finally she realized that until it was light, it was far too dangerous to be out on the street. Spotting the covered doorway of a pawnshop, she ducked inside the opening and huddled in a dusty and litter-filled corner, exhausted and terrified.

All she could do was wait for daylight and hope she would survive the night.

Chapter Sixty-One

Bobby

Bobby was convinced he'd made some headway with Denver regarding the Zeena débâcle. He'd tried to explain exactly what had taken place, and to his relief – after ignoring him for most of the flight – Denver had seemed pretty cool about it. She'd even ended up smiling at him – a *most* positive sign.

He was glad he'd been able to provide his plane to take her to Washington. There were some perks of his multi-million-dollar heritage of which he could choose to take advantage.

He was also pleased that he'd decided to accompany her, although he was sure M.J. and his bride, and Brigette and her girlfriend, would hardly be thrilled to discover their absence. Not to mention the absence of the plane. They were probably all bitching that he'd deserted them.

Too bad. He was in pursuit of a girl he wanted, and for once he was throwing caution out the window. Lucky would definitely approve of his actions. Lucky was a staunch proponent of going after what you wanted.

The bottom line was that Denver was special, he knew it. And if he had his way, they'd end up being special together.

Meanwhile he had every intention of helping her find her missing friend, and since Lucky had connections across the board, he'd called her from the plane, and asked if there was anything she could do to help.

After a few relevant questions, Lucky was her usual brilliant self. She promised to make a few phone calls. Naturally she knew people in Washington, including the Chief of Police. Lucky's intervention didn't mean that they would automatically find Carolyn, but it did mean that everyone concerned would be putting in their best effort.

He decided against telling Denver; it was probably better that way.

Chapter Sixty-Two

Denver

Tentatively I knocked on the door of the Hendersons' hotel room. I'd asked Bobby not to come with me to their room – this was no time for introductions. Reluctantly, he'd stayed in the suite.

George Henderson answered the door. A tall man with salt-and-pepper hair and an easy charm, I could see the pain in his eyes. George had the look of a man who was totally drained.

For a brief moment I wondered if the anguish in his eyes was because Carolyn was missing, or perhaps his sadness had something to do with Gemma Summer's murder.

Whatever. The man was in a distressed state.

Even though I hadn't seen him in a couple of years, we embraced, and in a choked-up voice he said, "Thanks for coming, Denver. It means a lot to me and Clare."

As he spoke, Clare, his wife, emerged from the bathroom. Once a very attractive woman, I was shocked at her appearance. She was thin and gaunt, with dark shadows under her eyes and a mass of tangled, graying hair.

It occurred to me that this deterioration in her appearance

could not have taken place in the last twenty-four hours. This was a disturbed woman. Whatever she was going through, Carolyn's disappearance had only added to the mix.

"Hi," I said, taking a firm step toward her, ready to hug her too.

She backed away like a nervous filly. After an awkward moment, she said, "Where do *you* think my daughter is?"

There was almost an accusatory note in her voice, as if I *should* know, and if I didn't I was of no use to her.

"I'm so sorry, Mrs Henderson," I said quietly. "I don't know where Carolyn could be."

"But you girls talked all the time, I know you did," Clare said, a malevolent gleam in her weary, red-rimmed eyes.

"No, we didn't," I said, shocked at this bitter angry woman who in no way matched up to the soft-spoken woman whom I remembered from my youth. Carolyn and I used to hang out at the Hendersons' house, and sometimes Clare Henderson baked us cookies and drove us to the mall. That woman with the softly-styled hair and kindly demeanor was long gone.

"Perhaps you can bring me up to date on everything," I said, turning to George.

"Oh, he can bring you up to date all right," Clare said, her voice rising. "He can tell you all about the affair he was having with his murdered movie-star girlfriend." She paused to glare at him. "*That's* why Carolyn is missing. It's karma. George's punishment – and mine."

Finished with her rant, Clare collapsed on the end of the unmade bed, sobbing hysterically.

George looked at me despairingly. It was a look that said, *What's done is done. I can't take anything back.*

"I'm sorry," I said in a low voice. "But shouldn't we be concentrating on finding Carolyn?"

"Of course," George said. "I received a call from a Detective Lennox. He'd like us to come over to the precinct as soon as possible. From the sound of him, he certainly seems more cooperative than yesterday when we arrived. I'm hoping they'll have good news for us."

Being summoned to the precinct didn't sound like good news to me. Had they found Carolyn's body? Was *that* the good news?

Suddenly the enormity of what was going on washed over me. My best friend was missing. And there was a strong possibility she could be dead.

Chapter Sixty-Three

Hank Montero – The Wild Card

The recession had hit everyone hard, especially Hank Montero – former actor, stunt-double, property-master, mechanic, and finally house painter.

Hank, a good-looking guy in a rough and ready way, had always managed to pull down a steady income. First as an actor – not successful. Second as a stunt-double – that is, until he got badly injured and was on Social Security disability benefits for a year. Next he'd gotten himself a job as property-master for a TV commercial company, but cash went missing, and unfortunately Hank got the blame. He'd tried being a mechanic, but after he'd taken some rich dude's Ferrari on a joy-ride and smashed the car to pieces against a brick wall, breaking a leg in the process, he'd gotten fired.

Finally, an old acquaintance from a short spell he'd done in prison for grievous bodily harm (he'd beaten the schmuck with the Ferrari – long story) offered him a part-time job house-painting. That job lasted until he screwed the woman whose house he was painting, and the woman's husband had come home unexpectedly and caught him rear-ending his devout Christian wife.

Jobless, he'd jumped on anything that came his way.

Meanwhile his third wife was pissed, his two teenage kids were pissed (a Goth and a slut) and his house was in foreclosure.

Hank Montero was a desperate man when he got an offer that was to change his life.

And change his life it did.

But that was before his insane nineteen-year-old ex-stripper current wife had tried to shoot him in the nuts with his own unlicensed stolen handgun – a move that forced a nosy neighbor to report the incident to the cops. And since they had nothing better to do, two cops had turned up at his house and after ascertaining he had no permit for his gun, and noticing the hefty stash of cocaine that his wife had left in full view on the kitchen table, they'd hauled him down to the precinct.

Which would've been fine. ***If the gun hadn't been the same one that shot the big movie star, Gemma Summer.***

Hank Montero was fucked.

Chapter Sixty-Four

Carolyn

Benito hit the street fast, his anger propelling him through the driving rain until he reached the rundown house where Rosa's mama lived.

Sure enough, her beat-up old Buick was parked right outside. He tried the handle and since the lock was broken, the door swung open easily.

The interior of the car smelled like old cabbage and sweat, and one of the side windows was shattered.

What did he care? He had only one purpose in mind, and that was finding the Senator's bitch.

After hot-wiring the car, he eased out of the parking space and took off.

* * *

Feeling quite desperate, Carolyn shut her eyes and tried to pretend she was safely home, but the noise of cars roaring past kept her on alert. Down the street a bunch of gang-bangers had appeared, and they were conducting some sort of drag race. They were screaming and yelling at each other as their souped-up cars raced up and down the street. She could hear glass breaking, and girls shouting their encouragement in shrill drunken voices.

Would they help her?

No. She didn't think so. Self-preservation told her it was safer to stay exactly where she was until it started to get light.

* * *

The Buick was an even worse piece of shit than his own car. Benito reached the conclusion that if he was hot-wiring a car, he certainly could've done better.

In his mind he blamed Rosa – it was all her fault. Never again would he hook up with teenage pussy, it wasn't worth the trouble.

Sticking near the curb, he crawled along the street in the Buick, keeping a sharp watch for the Senator's bitch.

She had to be close by, she couldn't've gotten that far. Besides, he was feeling lucky. And when Benito felt lucky, nothing stopped him.

* * *

Rosa's mother, Florita, got to the hospital very late, way beyond visiting hours. But after Florita explained to the night-duty nurse that she'd had to find someone to sit with her daughter's baby, and then discovered that her car had been stolen, the nurse let her through.

Rosa sobbed when she saw her mama, genuine tears of regret that she'd never listened to anything her mama had to say, and that she'd always thought she knew better.

Florita, a small compact woman with a ruddy complexion and work-worn hands, hugged her only daughter, tears filling her eyes. *"Mi chiquita,"* she crooned, rocking Rosa back and forth in her arms. *"Mi amorcito."*

Then she'd begun a rant in Spanish all about how Benito was the lowest of the low. He must be the one responsible for this terrible thing. She should never have allowed Rosa to spend so much time with such a ***bastardo***.

Rosa was too beaten-up to argue. She wasn't fluent in Spanish, although she got the gist of what her mama was saying, and she was inclined to agree with her. In Rosa's heart she knew that what Benito had done was criminal and bad. Kidnapping the Senator's woman was wrong, and lying in a hospital bed, Rosa realized she had to tell someone, explain that it wasn't *her* doing.

"Mama," she whispered. "I have something to tell you . . ."

* * *

The more noise the gang-bangers made, the tighter Carolyn squeezed into her corner, terrified that one of them would spot her. She'd often read stories about homeless people being tortured, then set on fire simply for sport. And she was well aware that's exactly what she must look like, a homeless person with nowhere to go.

The fear she felt now was even worse than when she was tied to the bed.

What had she done to deserve this?

Why was she being punished so harshly?

* * *

Benito continued to hug the curb, driving as slowly as possible without the piece-of-shit car stalling, while also keeping a sharp eye out. *She couldn't've got far,* he kept telling himself. He'd seen her lying on the bed less than an hour before she'd vanished.

He should've kept her trussed up like a chicken, but Rosa had said securing her wrist would do.

Rosa – another dumb bitch. He would surely punish her for running out on him.

As he drove down the main street he noticed activity ahead – a group of dudes drag racing. It suddenly dawned on him that he'd ventured out of his comfort zone into a part of town that was ruled by Rosa's baby daddy and his cohorts.

It was *their* territory. *Their* street.

Shit! It wasn't as if he was in his own car, thank God.

No . . . but he was in Rosa's mama's Buick.

Fuck! Better get out of here before they saw him. Better get out *fast*.

* * *

Carolyn heard the sound of tires squealing on the wet street. The noise, the yelling. And then suddenly she heard gunshots somewhere in the distance.

She covered her ears. This had to be her worst nightmare.

Huddling deep into her corner, she prayed for morning.

Chapter Sixty-Five

Bobby

Prowling restlessly around the suite, Bobby wasn't used to being sidelined. He would've preferred going with Denver to see the Hendersons, but as she'd decided it wasn't a good idea, he'd stayed behind.

After ordering coffee from room service, he switched on the TV. The *Today Show* was in progress, with Matt Lauer interviewing yet another politician accused of cheating on his wife with a hooker.

Recognizing the guy's name, Bobby recalled that the man had been outed in the tabloid piece on Annabelle and Frankie. Poor ill-advised bastard, the jerk was actually on TV attempting to defend himself.

The politician's interview ended, and on came the news. The lead story was all about the arrest of a suspect in the Gemma Summer murder case. The newscaster did not name the person who'd been arrested.

Was Denver aware that an arrest had been made? Probably not.

Well, one thing he knew for sure, she'd want to hear the news immediately since her boss was Ralph Maestro's attorney.

Picking up the phone, he got the number of the Hendersons' room. He now had an excellent excuse to go there.

Chapter Sixty-Six

Denver

I must say that I was kind of delighted when Bobby arrived in time to accompany us to the police station. Yes, I'll admit it, I'm relieved that he's here with me. Usually I'm super-confident that I'm able to deal with any situation, but imagining what could've happened to Carolyn was making me queasy.

I'm not a very religious person, but all I could think about was, *Please, God, let her be alive.*

Horrific scenarios kept running through my head. I remembered reading about the girl who was buried alive and found three months later. Another shocking case was the serial killer who'd dismembered his victims and buried them under his house – including several young women. Then there was the famous case of Washington intern, Chandra Levy, whose remains were discovered in a park thirteen months after her disappearance.

Chandra had worked for a politician with whom she'd been having an affair.

For a moment I thought about Carolyn's boss, Senator Gregory Stoneman. Carolyn had often spoken about him in glowing terms. I'd once accused her of having a crush on him, and she'd become most defensive instead of laughing it off.

I thought about her last text – *We must talk! So much happening!* And her text before that – *Call me as soon as you get this – I have major news!*

What was her major news? And what did *So much happening* mean?

I wondered if the police had spoken to the Senator. If they hadn't, then I was going to suggest that they should.

As soon as he arrived, I introduced Bobby to the Hendersons. By this time Clare was a tad calmer.

Bobby, who did not know about George's involvement with Gemma Summer, filled me in on the recent arrest.

I noticed George go on major alert; he was obviously desperate to ask questions, but he refrained from doing so, remaining tight-lipped.

At least *he* wasn't the shooter, merely the lover.

Bobby had a car and a driver waiting downstairs. Thank goodness it was a low-key sedan and not a flashy limousine.

"We'll all ride together," I suggested to the Hendersons. They agreed.

It was too early, L.A. time, for me to call Felix and hear the news about who'd been arrested – my money was on the stalker – but believe me, I couldn't wait to find out everything.

Chapter Sixty-Seven

Hank Montero – The Wild Card

Hank Montero was no virgin when it came to police questioning, but the two Beverly Hills cops who'd arrested him were relentless. They'd kept him in a room all night asking him the same questions over and over. His head was reeling, it was so intense. And Hank Montero did not do well with intense.

It was all his damn wife's fault – Pinky, the nineteen-year-old stripper with the foreign accent and huge bouncy boobs. She'd been after a Green Card, and he'd been cross-eyed at the thought of spending leisurely nights playing with those boobs. But it all turned sour as soon as he married her, what with the house going into foreclosure, and his two appalling kids – the Goth and the slut – both of whom flatly refused to leave home.

After they were married, Pinky had stopped stripping, turned into a nagging shrew, and announced that her boobs were off-limits.

Damn! What was a man supposed to do?

He'd taken a bad-ass job he'd known was wrong, collected the money, stashed it in a safe-deposit box in his name only, and celebrated by screwing their next-door neighbor – a flat-chested Southern bleached blonde, who made up for her lack of boobs by behaving like a maniac in bed.

Unfortunately, Pinky had come home early from her latest job at Hooters, caught him at it, gone for his gun and made a dangerously close pass at shooting him in the balls.

The Southern blonde had run from their house, a neighbor had called the cops, and all would've been fine if Pinky hadn't left a pound of coke on the kitchen table. Yeah, she dealt coke as a sideline for a neighborhood thug. Lovely girl.

The cops had hauled everyone down to the station.

Later, when they'd checked out his gun, they'd discovered it was the same weapon used to kill Gemma Summer.

Big whoopee.

Hank was well aware that they had him in their clutches and they weren't letting go anytime soon.

Unless . . . he could make a deal.

Chapter Sixty-Eight

Annabelle

Following Fanny's orders, Annabelle dressed down, all in black. With her pale red hair, her favorite diamond Maltese Cross nestled at her neck, and a more subtle make-up, the effect was quite startling. She looked a little bit like her famous mother.

Staring at herself in the mirror she was conflicted. Half of her wanted to run back to New York, hide away in her apartment and not speak to anyone. The other half wanted to face the world and fuck 'em all, as Frankie was prone to say.

But could she maintain that attitude?

She wasn't as strong as everyone seemed to imagine. And the thought of facing Ralph – Big Daddy – at the funeral was making her stomach cramp up.

Ralph, in a fury, was a frightening sight to behold. She remembered that as a child, she would run and hide in a closet whenever her father lost his temper.

Annabelle decided she needed more than Frankie and Fanny to bolster her confidence. She needed Denver by her side. Her old schoolfriend was so together, always exuding total confidence. That's what Annabelle needed – a positive person who had nothing to gain by being there for her.

Denver had promised to accompany her to the funeral. But that was before the embarrassing headline story in *Truth & Fact*. Denver probably wanted nothing to do with her now that she'd been painted as a goddamn madam! Besides, Denver was on Ralph's side – she worked for his lawyer.

All the same, she knew that Denver was a good person, and perhaps if she contacted her, they could work something out.

* * *

Frankie had a lot going on. Contrary to backing off, Rick Greco was hot to get into business with him. They'd started talking about creating a new club situation – maybe involving Bobby and M.J. if they were interested.

Fanny Bernstein had turned out to be a star, she knew everyone and was proceeding full speed ahead. Frankie and Annabelle had already signed a letter of agreement giving Fanny 25 per cent of future earnings. Fanny wasn't one to sit around.

"I'll be talking to Bravo, E! and MTV about a reality TV show next week," she'd informed him. "You'll hang out in L.A. until we go to New York for Annabelle to appear on *The View*. Stick with the big picture, Frankie. You'll be shifting to L.A. permanently, so get your skinny ass into moving."

Frankie hadn't revealed that golden nugget of news to Annabelle. Right now she was agitated, so he had to handle her with care. Hopefully, after the funeral she'd return to her usual self, then they could both start enjoying their upcoming success.

Frankie Romano – media star. It had a winning ring.

Yeah! Finally! Frankie Romano was going to be famous!

* * *

Fanny Bernstein didn't just enjoy funerals, she reveled in them. Funerals to Fanny were not a place to mourn the dead, they were a place to cement old connections and forge new ones; a place to see and be seen; to talk about future projects, and make lunch arrangements. Fanny had never come across an opportunity she didn't embrace, and funerals were full of opportunities – especially if the deceased was a famous person.

The Gemma Summer funeral should be a hotbed of new and interesting connections. And Fanny was certain she'd have an excellent seat, because she'd be walking in with her two new clients.

Surprise, surprise, Ralph Maestro. Let's observe your reaction to this ***little play.***

Fanny selected a black ruffled dress, enormous earrings, sparkling silver slippers (high heels hurt her feet), and many silver bracelets.

Eventually she was good to go.

* * *

Preparing for his wife's funeral, Ralph Maestro chose what clothes he would wear.

Gemma was dead. *He* would be the center of attention, every eye would be on *him*. And not all of them for the right reasons, thanks to his dear daughter, Annabelle.

Annabelle Maestro. A rebellious child, an impossible teenager, and now, as an adult, she'd brought disgrace to the Maestro name, humiliating him beyond redemption.

His first instinct had been to separate her from her sleazy boyfriend, drag her back to the house and shake some sense into her – hence his fast trip to Vegas. But when he couldn't find her in Vegas – no doubt she'd fled back to New York – he'd changed his mind.

The solution to Annabelle was to cut her off, disown her – allow her to bury herself in her own filthy profession. He was through.

Lupe buzzed his dressing room. “Meester Saunders is here,” she announced. “An’ Meester Pip.”

“Tell them I’ll be right down,” Ralph said, fixing his tie. A recent purchase. Black silk. Six hundred and fifty dollars.

Yes, every eye would be on him.

Chapter Sixty-Nine

Carolyn

At first light, Carolyn awoke from a half-sleep with a start. She was freezing, every bone in her body ached, her mouth was parched, and her foot was throbbing. Yet she felt elated because she'd managed to survive the night, and now she was almost certain she could find someone on the street to help her, or at least call the police on her behalf.

Gingerly she stood up, barely able to feel her feet. The rain had finally stopped, but it was still bitterly cold.

Was it safe to venture out of her hiding-place?

She still wasn't sure.

* * *

Senator Gregory Stoneman left his house early on Thursday. He'd spent a restless night fretting about why Ramirez wanted to see him. Ramirez had said it was urgent and that it was something concerning his brother, so as Gregory approached the community center he was prepared for the worst.

If it was blackmail he'd pay up. He had no damn choice.

Carolyn was also on his mind.

Where was she? What had Benito done with her? He was

supposed to have taken her for a few hours, shake her up until she lost the baby and then let her loose. It was now two days and there was no sign of her.

What if they'd harmed her? Could he be held responsible?

Jesus Christ! *WHAT HAD HE DONE*?

* * *

Florita swore her daughter to keep her silence when Rosa had confessed how she'd helped Benito kidnap the Senator's woman. Florita crossed herself, sank to her knees, then in Spanish she began begging the Lord for her daughter's redemption.

"You will never see that *desgraciado cabrón* again," she wailed, when she was finished praying. "The moment you leave the hospital I send you to your cousin in Guatemala."

"No, Mama, no," Rosa protested. "What about my baby?"

"For your protection," Florita admonished, wringing her hands. "I look after baby. You stay away. This a very bad thing you have done, Rosa. *Estúpido*. But God will watch over you, *mi amorcita*. He will be your savior."

Rosa nodded. Mama was right. God had punished her for doing a bad thing. Now God would protect her.

* * *

Slowly Carolyn peered down the street, and in the light of day she saw what the neighborhood she'd been trapped in was really like. There were several vacant lots littered with garbage, rusting half-finished buildings, protected by broken construction fencing, packs of stray dogs, and a couple of neighborhood shops – one selling hardware, and the other a small market. Neither of them were open.

Across the street she spotted the man who'd exposed himself to her the night before. He was pushing his shopping cart filled to the brim with useless junk, and singing to himself. When he saw her, he waved as if they were old friends. His mangy dog trotted behind him, a sad little creature.

She thought about approaching him again, but then realized he wasn't capable of helping her.

At least it was daylight and she was still alive, so was her baby. She patted her stomach, and set off down the street. There had to be a police station or a post office, somewhere official where she could get help.

Never again would she ignore a homeless person on the street, for if you didn't have the money to make a phone call or buy a loaf of bread, you were utterly lost.

Chapter Seventy

Denver

On the way to the precinct I opted to sit up front with the driver, leaving Bobby in the back with the Hendersons.

It was already eight a.m. in Washington, which meant it was five a.m. on the West Coast. I didn't dare disturb Felix, but I had no qualms about waking my intern, Megan. Pulling out my cell from my purse, I did just that.

What a surprise, the girl was awake!

Thinking she was an early riser, I said, "Megan – getting up early is a very positive way to start the day. You'll get so much extra work accomplished."

"Actually," Megan replied with a most unbusinesslike giggle, "I'm just getting home."

Oh, great! Was she drunk? I couldn't tell.

"I need a report on the Maestro case," I said briskly. "I understand there's been an arrest. Who is it?"

"Who's what?" Megan asked, her words followed by a couple of random hiccups.

Ah yes, unfortunately my brainy little intern was totally wasted.

"Does the firm know who's been arrested?" I said, all business.

"Dunno," she replied, vague as usual.

"Find out and call me back," I said tersely. "I'm on my cell."

"Will do," Megan said, followed by a series of muffled giggles.

Megan was not alone.

Half of me wished I was in L.A. finding out for myself what was going on. The other half knew I was exactly where I should be, trying to discover the truth about Carolyn's disappearance.

Chapter Seventy-One

Bobby

Detective Lennox was a tall man, lean and weathered, with knowing eyes, and a deep voice.

Bobby thought he looked like a man who knew what he was doing, and Denver's initial reaction toward him was positive. To both of them he seemed like he was in charge.

"Mr and Mrs Henderson," Detective Lennox said, ushering the distressed couple toward his office. "Please follow me."

Bobby and Denver were right behind them.

Detective Lennox stopped for a moment and held up an authoritative hand. "And you are?"

"Friends," Denver said quickly. "I'm a lawyer, Carolyn's closest friend."

"We have no need for a lawyer," Detective Lennox said.

"She's not here in an official capacity," Bobby interrupted, asserting himself. "We're both here to help find Carolyn." Denver threw him an appreciative glance. "This is Denver Jones and I'm Bobby Santangelo," he continued. "We're ready to assist in any way we can."

The detective nodded. The name Santangelo sounded familiar. When word had filtered down from the Chief to treat this case as high priority, he'd heard the name Santangelo mentioned somewhere along the way.

"Well," Detective Lennox said unsurely, "if it's okay with the Hendersons?"

"It is," George said.

They all crowded into the detective's cramped office. There were not enough chairs to go around, so Bobby took up a position by the door.

George Henderson spoke up. "Can you please bring us up to date," he said in a strained voice.

"Yes, I can," Detective Lennox said, linking his fingers together, making an arc. "Since yesterday there has been some progress."

"Progress?" Clare Henderson said, her face lighting up. "Have you found my little girl? Is she all right?"

Detective Lennox cleared his throat. "I'm sorry, Mrs Henderson, we haven't found her, but we do have an excellent lead. We've managed to trace several calls made from her cell phone – they're all coming from the same area."

"What area would that be?" Bobby asked.

"Not a very salubrious part of town, I'm afraid. We suspect that the calls are not being made by Carolyn. Right now we have people checking on the recipients of the calls."

"Have you spoken to Senator Stoneman? And Carolyn's co-workers?" Denver asked, thinking that for a cop he sure used a lot of fancy words.

"We have," Detective Lennox replied, mildly annoyed that this beautiful young woman who claimed to be a lawyer, was speaking to him as if he was an amateur. Of course he'd interviewed everyone the missing girl had worked with! And her neighbors.

"How about her ex-boyfriend?" Denver asked.

"Nobody's mentioned an ex-boyfriend."

"His name is Matt London. I'm sure he's listed."

"Thank you, Miss Jones," Detective Lennox said, his voice tinged with sarcasm. "Always a bonus to get help on the job."

Bobby glanced over at Denver. He had a strong feeling she was going to lose it. Attempting to diffuse the situation, he asked the detective to pinpoint the area the cell calls were coming from.

Detective Lennox said he could not divulge that information, but that he would keep them up to date on everything, and the best thing they could do was go back to their hotel and wait.

Bobby suspected that sitting and waiting was not about to fly with Denver, so as soon as they were outside the precinct, he walked to the corner and called Lucky again.

One thing about his mom, she was a real sport, and even though he was waking her, she promised to call him back once she had the information he needed. "Make it soon," he urged.

"It's me you're talking to, Bobby," she responded dryly.

Back at the hotel, the Hendersons went straight to their room. Bobby turned to Denver and suggested breakfast.

"I'm not hungry," she said listlessly.

"You've got to eat."

"Why?"

"'Cause you should stay strong."

"For what?" she said with a helpless shrug. "So I can identify her body when they find it?"

"Don't think like that," he said, placing his arm around her shoulders. "You're not the kind of girl who gives up."

"How do you know?"

Bobby gave her a long, slow look. "I just do."

Chapter Seventy-Two

Hank Montero – The Wild Card

The Public Attorney assigned to Hank Montero was short, fat and bald. His name was Dewey Find, and he was in the middle of a personal crisis – an acrimonious divorce that was costing him everything he had.

Dewey had loser clients up the kazoo, and quite frankly he didn't give a fast fuck about any of them. His plan was to opt out of the rat race as soon as he'd saved enough money, and flee to Hawaii, where he planned on finding himself an innocent native girl, and living in a hut on the beach for next to nothing.

Dewey existed in a dream world of his own making.

He hated Hank Montero on sight. Hank was all the things he wasn't. Tall, well-built, with a full head of hair.

"Make me a deal," Hank implored.

Yeah, Dewey thought. *You did a bad, bad thing, so I'll make you a deal that'll guarantee you at least ten years behind bars getting butt-fucked by all the guys who used to jerk off to Gemma Summer's movies.*

"Write a confession," Dewey advised his latest client. "Full disclosure. It'll go a long way to helping you receive a much lighter sentence."

So Hank, not the smartest pebble on the beach, did just that.

Chapter Seventy-Three

Annabelle

There is nothing the media likes better than a good old-fashioned funeral with all the trimmings. Gemma Summer's funeral promised to provide everything and more. A church service, followed by an outdoor burial service, with stars and top executives galore. Plus – bonus-time – the exquisite Gemma's celebrated movie-star husband. And her extremely notorious – as of twenty-four hours ago – daughter, Annabelle – recently exposed as a top New York madam who wasn't adverse to turning a trick or two herself.

This all was nirvana to the hordes of press assembled at Forest Lawn Memorial Park – a burial place for mega-stars. Especially as they'd gotten word through an anonymous source (Fanny Bernstein) that Annabelle Maestro would indeed be attending.

The excitement level was high.

Amongst the throng was Mario Riviera, who hoped he might get a glimpse of Denver. He'd certainly blown it on their last date, and he'd been trying to make amends ever since without much success.

Denver could be privy to some inside scoop she might share with him. It was always a coup, getting one over on the rival entertainment shows with information they didn't have, and since he'd recently been promoted to co-anchor on the new show *Hollywood Word*, he was out to prove himself. Why not make use of any connections he could muster?

Mario Riviera was not just a pretty face.

* * *

Leaning toward her new client, Fanny grasped Annabelle's hand. "Stay strong, dollface," she said, full of good cheer. "It'll be over before you know it."

"I'm not on my way to the dentist!" Annabelle said tartly, thinking that sometimes Fanny could be quite irritating.

Along with Frankie they were sitting in a low-key black town car on their way to Forest Lawn Memorial Park in the Hollywood Hills.

Annabelle was apprehensive about facing Ralph. Her father was such a frightening figure, so much larger than life. When she was a child she'd sometimes experienced nightmares starring his massive face. It had been very disturbing.

Even thinking about it now brought back creepy memories. That larger-than-life face, looming over her . . . it was not a pleasant recollection.

Unfortunately, Ralph now knew all about the business she was running with Frankie. She was well aware how furious he must be.

But then she had to believe that Fanny was right, that there was nothing he could do or say to her in front of everyone, especially as there would be a huge media turn-out observing his every move.

Fanny, clad in the black ruffled dress which made her look twice her size, reached for the bottle of champagne she'd thoughtfully brought with her. She handed it to Frankie along with some plastic glasses. "Open," she ordered. "Then pour, dollface. We are in dire need of a tipple to take the edge off." She turned to Annabelle. "Am I speaking for both of us, Princess?"

Annabelle nodded her agreement. A glass of champagne was exactly what she needed to get through the upcoming ordeal. Maybe two or three glasses. Slightly buzzed seemed like a grand alternative to stone-cold sober.

* * *

Accompanied by his lawyer and his trusty PR flack, Pip, Ralph Maestro left his house quite prepared for the circus that was to follow.

There had been much speculation over the past week about Gemma's murder, but now thankfully all the gossip and innuendo had been put to rest. An arrest had been made, and that was that.

The police had not revealed any details, but the general assumption was that the stalker from New Orleans who'd been tracking Gemma was the person arrested. Even Felix didn't know for sure.

Ralph was still steaming about the recent revelations concerning his daughter. Annabelle was not a smart girl, she'd always been jealous of the relationship between himself and Gemma. She'd barely been able to hide the resentment she'd felt toward both of them.

It was sad, but now he was done with her. Annabelle would never receive another penny from him.

* * *

The funeral procession was small and dignified. Gemma had no immediate family, she was an only child and her parents were deceased. Ralph had invited only a few of their friends to be part of the line of black limousines following the hearse containing Gemma's flower-bedecked coffin. Actually not so much friends as heads of studios and important executives. Ralph, like Fanny, was never one to let a career-enhancing opportunity pass by.

Several helicopters containing news crews hovered over the procession.

Even in death, Gemma Summer could still make headlines.

Chapter Seventy-Four

Hank Montero – The Wild Card

As confessions go, Hank Montero's was a winner. With the help of his attorney, he'd worked on it all night. Put in every detail he could recall. One thing about Hank, he had a pretty good memory for details.

Nobody was locking Hank Montero up for a murder he was hired to commit. No freaking way.

Yeah. That's right. He was a paid assassin.

An outside contractor.

Not responsible.

And Hank Montero had no compunction about pointing the finger at the person who'd hired him.

No compunction at all.

Chapter Seventy-Five

Denver

Under different circumstances I would be falling madly, crazily in love with Bobby – and believe me, I am not a romantic, but there is something about him that is so damn irresistible. Not only is he totally drop-dead gorgeous in a very manly way, he's actually thoughtful and kind – and most of all, *nice*!

What I should be doing is backing away big-time, because he's actually too good to be true. But then I remembered Zeena and the blow-job incident, so maybe he's not *that* perfect. Hmm . . .

I shouldn't be thinking about him; all my concentration should be on Carolyn, my vanished friend, most possibly the victim of foul play. She could've been raped and killed and left for dead, and here I am falling in love with a man I'll probably never see again after we part ways.

He lives in New York.

I live in L.A.

No chance of anything happening here.

Besides, I'm sure he has an army of beautiful women falling at his feet, because apart from all his other attributes he's mega-rich.

Not that I care about money, I don't. It's the person who counts.

"Breakfast is the most important meal of the day," Bobby lectured, guiding me through the lobby into the hotel dining room.

"You sound like my mother," I murmured.

He threw me a quizzical look. "I'll let you off the hook with that remark because you're under stress."

A hostess led us to a booth, giving Bobby an extra-special smile along the way.

Seconds later, a waitress came over to the table and handed out menus. Once again, Bobby received a special smile.

That's what it would be like, being with a man like Bobby – women coming onto him all the time.

Why do I always pick the handsome ones? Mario, a classic example with his three-in-a-bed plan.

Sam, the screenwriter I'd left in New York, was a better fit for me. And Josh – when he was interesting. Not now, with the ten extra pounds and the *I think we made a mistake breaking up* attitude.

Men! Life would be much simpler without them. But not as much fun!

"I'm ordering for you," Bobby said, taking control.

"And why's that?" I asked.

"'Cause you're staring at the menu like it's written in a foreign language."

"Sorry. I can't concentrate."

"I know," he said, giving me a long, sympathetic look. "It must be tough."

"Carolyn and I have been best friends since high school," I said, my eyes welling up with unexpected tears. "She's like the sister I never had."

"You can't give up hope," Bobby said, moving nearer and sliding his arm around my shoulders. "The police have found her phone, that's a positive."

"Is it?"

"Yeah, Denver, it is."

I managed to down a glass of apple juice, a few sips of coffee and half a piece of toast.

Bobby went through a plateful of eggs, bacon and sausages like a starving man. Then we both took out our phones and started checking messages.

I had quite a few, several of them from Mario, saying things like *I miss you. Where are you? Why aren't you returning my calls?*

Hey, Mario, it's 'cause you're an asshole.

There was a crisp text from Annabelle. *I know things are different now, but I wish you would come to the funeral with me. I really need you.*

Annabelle Maestro needed me! Wow! Never thought I'd hear *that* coming from the Princess of Beverly Hills.

There was a terse message from Felix, obviously sent by his assistant because no one over the age of fifty has any clue how to text – *I am very disappointed in you, Denver. Work should always come first.*

Screw you, Mister Shark Teeth. As far as I'm concerned, personal emergencies will always take first place.

I contemplated sending him that message. Then I thought, *Why bother?* I'd definitely decided it was time to move on.

Bobby's phone vibrated and he hurriedly answered the call. After talking for a few moments, he clicked his fingers for the check.

"Let's go," he said. "Instead of sitting around waiting, I have a plan."

Chapter Seventy-Six

Carolyn

Carolyn soon discovered that if you had the look of a homeless person, you were regarded as invisible. The few people on the street, scurrying about their business, went out of their way to avoid her. They either crossed the street or hurried on by, pretending she didn't exist.

She knew she must be a frightening sight. She was filthy, with matted hair, her clothes coated with mud, no shoes. She presented a pathetic figure, limping barefoot along the street.

A couple of drunks, sitting against a graffiti-decorated wall, shouted lewd insults at her as she passed by. A gaggle of kids heading for school jeered and laughed in her face. One of the boys picked up a large stone and threw it, hitting her on the forehead, drawing blood.

She quickly ducked into another doorway and took refuge.

When was somebody – *anybody* – going to help her?

* * *

"Good morning," Gregory said, entering the community center. He was disgusted at what he was being forced to deal with. Most of all he didn't want to be here. He didn't want to hear what

Ramirez had to say. He already knew that whatever it was, he wasn't going to like it.

Ramirez was sitting at an old wooden table scribbling notes with a pencil in a dime-store notebook. He glanced up. "You're early, Senator," he remarked.

"Got a lot to do today," Gregory answered, thinking, *Let's get right to it, you blackmailing son of a bitch.*

"Pull up a chair," Ramirez said. "Sorry the coffee machine is broken. Nothin' to offer you. That's the way it goes around here."

"Perfectly all right," Gregory said. He sat down and stared at Ramirez. "What exactly can I do for you?" he asked.

"It's about my brother," Ramirez began, putting down his pencil.

Yes, Gregory thought, *I'm sure it is.* Then he waited for Ramirez to tell him that unfortunately Benito had gone too far with Carolyn, and now that she was dead, he'd better be prepared to pay up, because it was all due to his devious plan.

"He's in big trouble," Ramirez continued, his long pock-marked face quite somber.

"And how exactly can I help?" Gregory asked, playing along.

"My brother is a target," Ramirez said. "He refuses to listen to me. But you – a Senator . . . I was thinking if you offered him a job. Maybe you need a gardener, a pool man, someone to do odd jobs. If he could live on the premises, get off the street . . ."

Gregory kept his face expressionless. This was insane. Did Ramirez honestly think he would hire his brother for no good reason? Why would he do that?

"It would only be for a few weeks, a temporary situation, while I take care of the threat."

"What threat?" Gregory asked hoarsely.

"It's the usual story," Ramirez said. "You'd probably call it gang warfare. My brother – Benito – has a girlfriend who had a baby with a member of a rival gang. This *cholo* wishes Benito dead. It's as simple as that. And if I don't intervene . . ." Ramirez trailed off.

Benito. Dead. Would that be such a terrible thing? Especially as he'd harmed or maybe even killed Carolyn.

Gregory shook his head. "I'm sorry, Ramirez. I can't help you with this."

Ramirez's eyes were like two steely slits. "Can't?" he questioned. "Or won't?"

Gregory felt hostility in the air. He stood up. Now that he was not about to be blackmailed, he needed to get away from this depressing place and forget all about Ramirez and his goddamn brother.

"Can't, Ramirez," he said in a tone that invited no response.

Ramirez also stood. "I see," he said. "But Senator, I must tell you this – if it was a member of ***your*** family in peril – perhaps one of your lovely children – I would do everything in my power to help you."

Was there a threat in Ramirez's words? Was he threatening Gregory's children?

Goddamn it. Why had Evelyn introduced him to this man? These people were toxic. Evelyn should have known better.

* * *

After a while Carolyn emerged from the doorway where she'd taken shelter. The streets were filling up, people hurrying to work, all of them avoiding her as if she had a communicable disease.

All she needed was enough change to make a phone call, but her pleas for help went unanswered.

* * *

"I'm sorry I cannot assist you," Gregory said, walking firmly toward the door. He had an urge to get away from Ramirez and this place as fast as possible, especially as the threat of blackmail was no longer looming over him.

Ramirez followed him to the door. "You are a disappointment to me, Senator," he said. "I thought, like me, you were prepared to help get these kids off the street."

"Your brother's not a kid," Gregory snapped.

Ramirez blinked several times. "And how would you know that?"

Gregory shrugged. "I simply assumed," he said, opening the door and walking outside.

It had started to rain again and Gregory was annoyed that he'd left his umbrella in the car. He had on his new grey suit, and raindrops would ruin it.

As he started to leave, an unmarked police car pulled up outside, and a plainclothes detective emerged.

Gregory immediately recognized the man as the same detective who'd been at his office asking questions about Carolyn.

What was this all about?

Once more he was filled with dread.

Chapter Seventy-Seven

Denver

Bobby was a take-charge kind of guy, and since I'm a take-charge kind of girl it could've developed into a battle of who's going to make the decisions. But I was in a weakened state, so whatever Bobby suggested I went along with.

Apparently he'd obtained information about the area where the calls from Carolyn's cell were coming from. His decision was that we drive around the streets in that part of town, simply to check things out.

Normally I would've said, *"What's the point?"* But since it was a better plan than sitting in a hotel room waiting for news, I went along with it.

Our driver, a friendly guy from Sierra Leone, informed us we were venturing into foreign territory. "You don't want to leave the car," he said, puzzled as to why we would consider going there in the first place.

"Not planning to," Bobby assured him.

But when we were in the thick of the dilapidated and supposedly dangerous neighborhoods, I kept on spotting vacant lots full of overgrown brush and abandoned buildings surrounded by broken fences, and I thought, *Oh my God – what if Carolyn's dead body is lying out there somewhere? We have to do something.*

"Shouldn't we get out of the car and search?" I said to Bobby.

He looked at me as if I was certifiable. "Search where?" he asked, as we drove by a graffiti-covered wall, a bunch of derelicts huddled against it, hiding from the rain under a makeshift awning of old cardboard boxes.

"I . . . I don't know. Anywhere, somewhere. There's all those empty lots. Why aren't the police here with tracker dogs? Shouldn't there be search-parties out looking for her?"

"They can't start searching with nothing to go on," Bobby said gently.

"Then *we* should do it!" I burst out.

"Hey," Bobby said, "I know you want to do everything possible, but this is a big city. She could be anywhere."

I slumped back against the leather seat. "I know," I said softly. "But doing nothing makes me feel so helpless."

"You want to go back to the hotel?" Bobby asked, reaching for my hand and squeezing.

I'm not psychic or anything like that, but something told me we should keep looking.

"No," I said. "Let's drive around some more."

Chapter Seventy-Eight

Annabelle

Several people gave eulogies at Gemma's funeral. Her long-time agent. A studio head. Her most recent co-star. A celebrated director she'd worked with many times. Her best friend – an older woman who could barely contain her tears. And finally Ralph Maestro himself.

Ralph cut an imposing figure standing at the podium – larger than life in every respect, cleverly concealing his anger regarding the fact that his daughter had dared to put in an appearance with her low-rent boyfriend. The two of them had balls of steel. He was outraged that they'd had the nerve to turn up.

Commonsense prevailed. The press were out in force, so he'd said nothing to Annabelle. At Pip's urging he had not ignored her. He'd greeted her with a distant kiss on each cheek – Hollywood-style – and walked away to mingle with other mourners.

Ralph spoke about his beautiful wife with great sincerity. His eulogy was touching and gentle. The audience of friends sitting in the neo-Classical Hall of Liberty at Forest Lawn Memorial Park were filled with compassion for this bereaved movie star, destined to be a lonely man.

But of course, this being Hollywood, everyone knew that

Ralph Maestro would not be lonely for long. Women were already surmising about who would have first shot at Ralph Maestro. He was a major get.

* * *

"This is an excellent start," Fanny Bernstein whispered in Frankie's ear. "Annabelle's a natural. Did you *see* how our little dollface handled the press?"

Frankie nodded, none too pleased. Yes, he'd seen all right. Who would've guessed that Annabelle possessed acting talent? She'd done a fine job of portraying the inconsolable daughter. She'd expertly deflected any questions about the piece in *Truth & Fact*. And the assembled media had fallen in love with her.

Frankie, on the other hand, found himself ignored. He wasn't important enough for the press, they couldn't care less about him, it was Annabelle all the way.

Frankie's considerable ego had taken a major nose-dive.

Fanny appeared to know everyone, but she didn't bother introducing him – another irritant. Goddamn it, she was supposed to be representing *both* of them, not just Annabelle.

After the funeral he planned on having a serious heart-to-heart with Fanny Bernstein. It was about time she treated him with the respect he deserved.

* * *

After the private service, everyone trooped out to the cemetery to watch as the coffin was lowered into the ground.

Several helicopters swirled overhead. It was a perfect California December day; no clouds in the sky, a warm but slight breeze.

Annabelle wondered if they should go back to the house with all the other mourners.

Fanny said they should.

In a strange way Annabelle was highly elated. People were being so nice to her, they were talking to her about how she resembled her mother and how lovely she was. They were asking whether she'd ever consider a career in the movies. Nobody – not one person – mentioned the damn tabloid.

The studio head handed her his card and suggested she call him. Her mother's best friend said they must have lunch. Gemma's most recent co-star, a handsome actor with a Johnny Depp swagger, inquired if she was single.

"Yes," she answered quickly, hoping that Frankie wasn't lurking anywhere nearby.

Hollywood. Beverly Hills. Los Angeles. Suddenly Annabelle felt she was finally home.

Goodbye, New York. L.A. was her future.

Chapter Seventy-Nine

Bobby

They'd been driving up and down the mean streets for over an hour.,

"We should head back to the hotel," Bobby suggested, feeling Denver's pain. "This wasn't such a brilliant idea."

"Maybe ten more minutes?" Denver said hopefully, her eyes glued to the side window, scanning the street.

"No," Bobby said firmly. "This is a useless exercise. I'm sorry, Denver."

She nodded, eyes still watching. "I guess you're right," she sighed.

"Hotel?" their driver asked, a man who couldn't wait to get away from this area. His passengers had to be from out of state – they obviously didn't realize how dangerous these streets could be.

"Yeah," Bobby said. "The hotel."

The driver put his foot down, a happy man.

Suddenly, Denver let out a cry to stop the car.

"What?" Bobby said, startled.

"For God's sake! Stop!" Denver yelled at the driver.

The poor man didn't know what to do. One passenger wanted to return to the hotel – now the pretty woman wanted him to stop. And even though it was daylight, stopping was not safe. He tried to explain to the woman, but she was having none of it.

"Stop this car," she commanded. "Now!"

"What have you seen?" Bobby asked. "C'mon, what is it?"

"I . . . I don't know," Denver stammered as the car pulled into the curb. "Back half a block, there was a person on the street . . ."

"A person on the street," Bobby repeated blankly, shaking his head.

"No, really . . ."

"What person, Denver? Someone you know?"

"I . . . yes . . . *I think it was Carolyn!*"

Chapter Eighty

Carolyn

"What are you doing here, Senator?" Detective Lennox inquired.

Gregory stepped back out of the rain into the entrance of the community center.

Slumming. What else would I be doing here?

"I am concerned about the welfare of the youth in this city," Gregory said, launching into smooth politician talk. "Ramirez Ortego and I often meet to see what I can do to help. Getting these kids off the street is of major importance."

Ramirez shot him a look.

Detective Lennox sighed. "Can we go inside? I'd appreciate it if you would come too, Senator."

Gregory experienced a leaden feeling in his stomach. What now? Had the detective discovered Carolyn's body, and somehow linked it to him and the Ortego family?

Stay calm, he reminded himself. *Do not panic.*

Ramirez and Detective Lennox obviously knew each other, for as the three men walked inside, Detective Lennox placed his hand on Ramirez's shoulder in a familiar fashion.

"I came here to tell you myself, Ramirez," he said gently. "I didn't want you hearing it on the street."

Ramirez's face was a mask. "Is it Benito?" he said. "Is it my brother?"

Detective Lennox nodded. "I'm sorry, Ramirez. I'm really, really sorry."

* * *

Carolyn did not think she could make it any further. Every street she turned onto was another desolate row of broken and empty buildings. And every person she attempted to approach turned their back on her.

She was cold and alone. Her foot was blowing up, and in spite of the freezing cold she felt feverish and dizzy. If she didn't get help soon she would give up, find a corner and curl into a ball. No food. No water. A sharp pain in her lower abdomen.

Was she losing the baby? Was that blood she felt trickling down her leg?

She couldn't go on. It was too much.

She leaned against the wall of a boarded-up shop and gasped for breath.

A car drove past. A decent-looking car.

Would they stop for her? Feebly she waved.

No. They wouldn't stop. Nobody would.

She crumpled to the ground on the wet pavement and closed her eyes.

"Carolyn?"

It was the voice of an angel she was hearing.

"Oh my God, Carolyn!" the voice said. "It *is* you!"

Chapter Eighty-One

The Shocker

In Hollywood, expecting the unexpected is an everyday occurrence. Scandals take place on a daily basis.

Phil Spector shoots a woman in the face. O.J. Simpson slashes up his wife and her male friend. Britney has a public meltdown. Lindsay Lohan runs around smashing up cars and wearing no panties. Heath Ledger overdoses. Jessica and Jennifer and Cameron break up with yet another boyfriend. Michael Jackson dies amidst much speculation.

There is always something going on. The Hollywood community is rarely shocked.

But once in a while, something happens that is so off the chart that people are actually stunned.

The Gemma Summer funeral presented such an event.

Everything went off smoothly. The ride to Forest Lawn Memorial Park. The heartfelt eulogies. The lowering of the coffin ceremony.

And then came the big finale, witnessed by everyone present.

Several police cars. A scattering of cops. And two detectives. Detective Preston – a tall African-American man. And Detective Lee, a younger Asian woman.

The two detectives approached Ralph Maestro as he walked away from the grave site, their expressions determined.

Immediately alarmed, Pip, loyal PR flack that he was, stepped in front of his important client.

"Move," Detective Lee said in a surprisingly deep voice.

"Ralph Maestro," Detective Preston said. "You are under arrest for your involvement in the murder of your wife, Gemma Summer Maestro. You have the right to remain silent. Anything you say can and will be used against you in a court of law. You have—"

"This is an outrage!" Felix Saunders exploded, as the detective finished reading Ralph Maestro his rights.

Ralph remained stoic, his larger-than-life movie-star face devoid of any emotion. After all, this was Hollywood and he was a star.

Nothing was going to happen to a big celebrity such as himself.

Nothing at all.

Chapter Eighty-Two

Denver

Wow! So much happened in such a short period of time that I'm kind of dazed.

Discovering Carolyn wandering the streets was a total fluke. Amazing!

I have to thank Bobby for working behind the scenes and finding out everything he could. Guess it's pretty useful, coming from a family who can pick up a phone and call the Chief of Police.

We rushed Carolyn to the emergency room with me holding her in my arms all the way there, and Bobby taking care of reaching the Hendersons and Detective Lennox.

A Dr Glass met us at the ER and whisked Carolyn off, while I hugged the Hendersons and tried to make sense of the whole thing.

Bobby was there for me all the way – fielding everyone's questions, getting me coffee, watching over me. It's kind of a strange feeling, having someone look after me. I've always been so independent, so sure I could handle any situation. But right now I realized that having Bobby around was pretty damn comforting.

When we picked Carolyn up and bundled her into the car,

she'd looked so pathetic and wrecked, and she was quite hysterical. God knows what kind of ordeal she'd been through.

Detective Lennox was waiting to question her, but Dr Glass had not given him the go-ahead, which I think kind of pissed him off as he paced up and down drinking endless cups of coffee out of Styrofoam cups.

Finally Dr Glass appeared in the waiting area. "Carolyn's going to be fine," she assured us – paying special attention to Mrs Henderson, who looked kind of wrecked herself. "She's suffering from exhaustion, severe dehydration, and she has a nasty cut on her foot which will need stitches. We're giving her a tetanus shot just to be safe. However, you will all be happy to hear that the baby is fine."

"Baby?" Mrs Henderson said, confused.

"Baby!" I gasped, equally confused.

"Carolyn is almost two months' pregnant," Dr Glass revealed. "I thought you all knew."

So *that* was Carolyn's exciting news. Finally!

Bobby took my hand and squeezed it.

Hmm . . . who knew that mere hand-holding could send chills down a girl's spine?

"You surprised?" Bobby asked.

"You bet!" I replied. "Now I need to find out who the father is."

He gave me a slow smile.

Oh man! Those whiter than white teeth. Those lips. Those dark, intense eyes.

Should I be getting turned on at a time like this?

I think not.

But screw it. Carolyn's safe. So what was wrong with concentrating on Bobby?

Nothing.

"Why?" he said sensibly. "Isn't it up to her to tell you when she wants you to know?"

Smart too. Questioning her right now was not a good idea.

I suddenly realized how tired I was. Emotionally drained and ready to go home and crawl into bed with Amy Winehouse beside me.

There was nothing more I could do here. The Hendersons needed time with their daughter; I would just be in the way. Besides, if all was okay, Carolyn would be coming out to stay with me in a week or so.

I asked if I could see her. Dr Glass said no, only family for now.

Bobby kind of read my mind. "How about I fly you home?" he suggested. "Your friend is safe, there's nothing more you can do here."

"But you live in New York," I murmured. "I can easily catch a commercial flight."

His dark eyes bored into mine. "I'm taking you home," he said, his tone inviting no argument.

I said my goodbyes to the Hendersons, wished them well, and made them promise to have Carolyn call me as soon as she was up to it.

We both shook Detective Lennox's hand, and then took off, me and Bobby Santangelo Stanislopoulos.

Sitting in a car on the way to the airport I felt a shyness overcome me, and that's not me at all.

Oh God! In the midst of all the drama was I falling in . . .

No! No! No!

"Whereabouts do you live in L.A.?" Bobby asked.

"Why? You planning to have your plane land on my street?" I answered flippantly.

"Maybe," he said, grinning. "That way I can get rid of you sooner."

"Get rid of me? How dare you!" I joked.

"Y'know," he said, giving me a long, lingering look, "you're even prettier when you're mock-angry."

I swallowed hard. Usually I would come up with a smart retort, but Bobby had me flummoxed.

The plane was waiting. Naturally. It seemed Bobby snapped his fingers and things happened.

Hani and Gitta were on board to greet us, clad in their smart uniforms.

Hmm . . . I think I could easily get used to this style of travel.

I glanced at my watch. It was almost noon, Washington time. Three hours earlier in L.A. The Maestro funeral would soon be underway and I would not be there to participate.

Too bad.

Or not.

The moment the plane took off I fell into a deep sleep, curled into a tight ball. Someone – I think it was Bobby – put a blanket over me and a pillow behind my head, but nothing was about to wake me. I was totally beat.

When I did surface a couple of hours later, Bobby had news.

Apparently Ralph Maestro had been arrested for ordering his wife's murder. It was all over the internet.

Unfortunately – or fortunately – I'd missed the whole thing.

I couldn't wait to get home and find out everything.

As soon as we landed, Bobby had a car waiting – of course – and we set off for my apartment.

I was major conflicted. Was I going to invite him in? What kind of state had I left my apartment in? Where were we headed? Could this possibly turn into something?

Yes! Yes! Yes!

But fate always has a crazy way of intervening, and standing outside my apartment was Sam – the screenwriter I'd spent one night with in New York.

"Hey there!" Sam exclaimed, full of enthusiasm. "I just sold my screenplay to Universal, so here I am!"

And yes, there he was – complete with overnight bag.

Awkward.

Very awkward.

Especially as Sam was acting as if we were a couple. Or at least that's what Bobby seemed to think, for he gave me a quick peck on the cheek and took off fast. There was nothing I could say to stop him.

Bye bye, Bobby, nice knowing you.

Completely thrown, I invited Sam in, gave him a drink and hearty congratulations, and then told him he couldn't stay.

Sam got the message – he wasn't slow.

Over the next few days I found out a lot. I discovered that Ralph Maestro was not merely a movie star, he was a man with connections. Important and powerful connections. So although he was arrested and charged with hiring Hank Montero to murder his wife, Ralph was released within hours. Felix Saunders saw to that. A five-million-dollar bond, and the big movie star was back in his enormous mansion, a confident man. Confident that when the case finally came to trial, perhaps in four years – the same amount of time it had taken to get famous record producer Phil Spector into court for trial number one – he would walk free. For in Ralph's mind he was guilty of no crime.

The beautiful ethereal Gemma Summer, his loving wife, had screwed around on him, and to Ralph that was an unforgivable sin. He revealed to Felix and the investigating detectives, that one day, while sharing a beer with his former stunt double, Hank Montero, he'd happened to mention that any woman who cheated on her husband deserved to be shot.

How was he to know that Hank – a man who'd fallen upon hard times – would take him literally?

"It was a stupid joke," Ralph informed them all. "A careless remark seized upon by an unbalanced psychopath."

Felix nodded. He understood. Felix understood everything.

Later there were questions about the money Hank claimed Ralph had paid him.

"The man was down on his luck," Ralph said without a flicker of guilt. "I gave him a few thousand dollars to tide him over. If you can't help your fellow man, what use are you to anybody?"

I had looked into his face and seen raw evil in Ralph Maestro's piercing eyes.

But Felix was a master – he knew he would have no trouble getting Ralph exonerated from all charges.

Felix was a killer lawyer.

And Ralph was a killer client.

Shortly after, I quit the firm of Saunders, Fields, Simmons & Johnson.

Perhaps my dad was the one with the right idea. Suddenly, prosecuting criminals instead of defending them seemed a lot more palatable.

Carolyn was on her way to stay with me for Christmas and hopefully she'd tell me everything – for so far, her kidnapping remained a mystery. I was also dying to find out who the father of her baby was. We had a lot of catching up to do.

I wasn't sure what my future held, but one thing I did know for sure: I planned on making all the right choices.

As for Bobby, well, harking back to high school, he was the handsome jock, and I was the studious girl he never noticed. I'd always known it couldn't possibly work out.

Now I could get back to concentrating on my career.

I was free. I could do absolutely anything I wanted.

The Epilogue

Six Months Later

At first Annabelle was dazed – not even shocked because instinctively she'd sensed her father was guilty all along. Oh yes, she'd joked about it, but deep down she'd always harbored a gut feeling that somehow or other Ralph was responsible for her mother's brutal demise.

Ralph Maestro and Gemma Summer.

The perfect couple.

Perfect no more.

Of course she was sure that Ralph would be acquitted, if he ever went to trial. This was Hollywood, after all. Movie stars could and did get away with murder.

In the meantime, Annabelle refused to allow her father's newfound notoriety to slow her down. Oh no, not at all. Fanny was in charge, and anything Fanny suggested was right on the money.

The top shows wanted her. *Oprah*, *Larry King Live*, even *The Jay Leno Show*. She appeared on them all.

It turned out – exactly as Fanny had predicted – that in front of the camera Annabelle was a natural. Charming. Sweet when she wanted to be – wicked when she didn't. Amusing. Literate. She was a talk-show host's dream guest.

Then, exactly as Fanny had also predicted – along came the offers to put her name to a book. It was a multimillion-dollar deal. *My Life – A Hollywood Princess Tells All.*

A fast publication. A phenomenal rise to the top of the best-seller lists. And soon Annabelle Maestro was a bona-fide star in her own right.

* * *

Frankie finally called it quits on their relationship. He did not appreciate Annabelle's shitty attitude; she was lording it over him as if she was the second coming of Angelina Jolie. One thing Frankie knew for sure – he was not cut out to be background material.

Fanny was pissing him off too. Everything she did was for Annabelle to shine – nothing for him. The reality show featuring the two of them as a couple never happened. Instead Annabelle was offered her own show based on her dumb book.

That was it for Frankie – he didn't give a fast crap. He had other things to get off the ground. Besides, he and Annabelle had grown apart months ago.

When Frankie said goodbye, Annabelle said good riddance.

Both of them had moved to L.A. and the Hollywood lifestyle suited Frankie just fine. He and Rick Greco were in business together – a business Frankie knew only too well. Persuading out-of-work actresses to sell their perky little bodies on the side for mucho bucks was easy pickings. So far, business was booming. Frankie was one very happy Hollywood pimp.

* * *

Carolyn recovered in record time. Determined to put her ordeal behind her as quickly as possible, she decided to leave Washington and return to L.A. with her parents.

Evelyn and Gregory Stoneman visited her in hospital. What a treat *that* was. Carolyn could hardly believe that Gregory had the balls to turn up with his wife.

"We're so sorry, dear," Evelyn had crooned, thrusting a box of expensive chocolates at her. "Poor Gregory was worried sick."

Worried sick, was he? Carolyn thought. *I bet he was.*

She did not know for certain if Gregory was involved in her kidnapping, but he sure as hell couldn't look her in the eye.

The love she'd once felt for him was long gone.

"Have the police found out who did this terrible thing to you?" Evelyn continued, while Gregory studied the floor and didn't utter a word.

What a coward! Carolyn thought. In case she suspected something, he'd turned up with his uptight wife to protect him, a woman she barely knew.

Carolyn was sickened. Senator Gregory Stoneman was not the man she'd thought he was. In fact, now she realized that he'd never had any intention of leaving his wife and starting a new life with her. The man was a lying, cheating *married* sonofabitch.

But still – in spite of everything – when questioned, she'd been unable to implicate him in her kidnapping.

When Detective Lennox had asked her what she was doing outside an abandoned gas station in the middle of nowhere, she'd stated that she was lost. No word that it was the place where Senator Stoneman had instructed her to meet him.

What a coincidence it all was. And how strange that the girl who'd shoved a chloroformed soaked pad in her face had known she was pregnant.

The girl's words continued to haunt Carolyn.

She was released from the hospital within twenty-four hours, none the worse for her terrifying ordeal apart from several stitches in her wounded foot.

She left Washington with Gregory's baby growing inside her

and no regrets. She would have his baby, and that would be his punishment, for there was no way she'd ever allow him in her child's life.

Senator Gregory Stoneman was dead to her. And that's the way it would always be.

* * *

Zeena's illustrious career continued to soar – as did her collection of young men. She'd recently appeared at the Maracanã Stadium in Rio, and along the way she'd discovered nineteen-year-old twins – male underwear models – who played as a team in more ways than one. Then along came Minda and Miranda, two stunning Brazilian Supermodels.

Zeena was quick to realize that mixed doubles was perhaps the most daring and exciting game of all.

Satisfaction guaranteed. That was for sure.

Once in a while Zeena's thoughts drifted back to Bobby Santangelo Stanislopoulos whom she considered to be the one who got away. Yes, sometime in the future she was sure that they were destined to reconnnect, and when they did, maybe she'd tell him about her teenage adventure with his father, the great Dimitri.

Maybe.

Maybe not.

Zeena never planned ahead.

* * *

Dr Glass and Detective Lennox tentatively began dating. The two of them were extremely busy people who did not have time for romance. Both divorced, they were taken by surprise when their casual relationship developed into something more.

* * *

Mario Riviera received a welcome promotion. From co-host on the half-hour daily show *Hollywood Word*, he was upped to weekend host, anchoring a solid hour on Saturday and Sunday by himself. Apparently the viewers appreciated his flirty and audacious attitude, not to mention his spectacular abs and appealing dimples.

Obviously Denver Jones did not appreciate any of it, for she failed to reply to his numerous texts, and never even thanked him for the flowers he'd sent her.

Too bad.

Miz Jones was missing out.

* * *

Rosa returned from Guatemala a changed girl. Spending time in a not-so-affluent country with her impoverished cousins had taught her a thing or two.

While she was away she missed her baby, and she determined to be a better mother. She also missed her momma, and promised herself she would stay home more, help out, and stop cutting school. Sleeping around was over for Rosa; she'd learned a serious lesson when she'd heard that Benito had been shot to death. His demise sent shivers down her spine; even more bad news, the shooter – now incarcerated – was her baby-daddy.

Rosa was still only sixteen, but the realization that she had to change her lifestyle was strong within her.

She often thought about the woman Benito had kidnapped, and after checking through old newspaper stories on the school computer, she found out who the woman was and that she'd been rescued.

The news filled her with relief, but she still felt guilty about her involvement. Her momma had sworn her to secrecy, warned her she was never to tell anyone. But the information was too much for her to keep to herself; she had to tell someone.

One day, after school, she went to see Ramirez at the community center he ran. She had never met him before, but she knew he was Benito's brother, and according to reputation – a good man.

Nervously, she told him the whole story. He listened intently to every word.

When she was finished, Ramirez hugged her tightly and assured her she had done the right thing.

Rosa felt cleansed at last.

* * *

Ramirez thought long and hard about Rosa's revelations.

He could go to the police, Detective Lennox in particular, because they'd known each other for some time and shared a mutual respect.

Or . . . he could keep his silence and use Rosa's story to his own advantage.

Ramirez had a choice, and it wasn't long before he decided which way to go.

Once more he called the Senator and requested a meeting. Senator Stoneman informed him he was too busy to meet at the present time.

Ramirez told the Senator that of course he understood, and perhaps he would call the Senator's wife to discuss all the improvements he wished to put in place at the community center.

Gregory Stoneman sensed an implied threat, and agreed to another meeting with Ramirez.

Within weeks, work started to completely renovate the community center. The money Ramirez had been begging for suddenly began to flow.

As far as Ramirez was concerned, it was an extremely satisfying solution.

* * *

As for Senator Stoneman, he lived in abject fear that one day the truth would be revealed about his involvement in Carolyn's kidnapping. There was no doubt in his mind that before Benito got himself shot, he'd confided in his brother, for although Ramirez had not said it in so many words, it was quite obvious that he knew.

And Carolyn seemed to know too. The look of disgust and disappointment in her eyes when he'd visited her in the hospital was not something he'd forget in a hurry. If she ever talked, his career would be over.

However, Gregory was a survivor *and* a politician, so with a bland smile on his face, he kept on going with the ever-perfect Evelyn by his side. And when Ramirez wanted something more from him, he obliged.

Senator Gregory Stoneman definitely knew what was best for his survival.

* * *

M.J. moved to Vegas with his new bride to oversee the relaunch of *Mood* – Las Vegas. When Cassie landed a gig singing in the lounge at the Cavendish, M.J. was delighted. He wanted her to get a shot at stardom if that was her dream, and since she was so young, experience was everything.

It might have been a quickie Vegas wedding, but after six months of being together every day, they were both convinced they were in it for the long run.

* * *

Janey Bonafacio was never able to track down Chip, nor could Frankie. Janey was relieved that Frankie had finally forgiven her for allowing Chip to run riot in their New York apartment, stealing photos, documents and all the cash from their safe.

Frankie had not discovered the money was gone until he and Annabelle had returned to New York for Annabelle's appearance on *The Today Show*. When he'd found out they'd been robbed, he'd gone totally crazy.

Annabelle was more pragmatic. "There's nothing we can do," she'd said. "We're lucky Bobby fixed it so we didn't get arrested for running call girls."

This was true. Bobby and his family's connections had saved the day. Bobby was a true friend.

After a while Janey had headed to L.A. to be near her beloved cousin.

"What Chip did wasn't your fault," Frankie had informed her. "You may as well come work for me in L.A. I need someone I can trust. I'm back in business!"

Janey was only too happy to oblige.

* * *

Chip Bonafacio relocated to Tucson and managed to stay out of sight. Neither Frankie or his mom had any idea where he'd gone.

He changed his name, rented a penthouse apartment, hooked up with a pole dancer named Daisy, and bought himself a brand new motorcycle. Man, he was rolling in cash and he loved it.

However, his newfound affluence was not to bring him lasting joy. Three months after the *Truth & Fact* article ran, he was killed in a head-on collision with a delivery truck.

Daisy quickly gathered up all the cash he had left – which was quite substantial – and hurriedly ran out of town.

* * *

Hank Montero had not led a charmed life. He'd had the looks to become a movie star like his old pal, Ralph Maestro. Way back they'd attended an acting class together on Hollywood Boulevard. The class was run by a tightly-wound English woman who'd ended up sleeping with Ralph. Naturally, because she and Ralph were sleeping together, she'd given him all the best roles in the student productions – the shows that casting directors got to see.

Because he was front and center, Ralph was soon discovered, and Hank was left behind.

A couple of years later when Ralph was a known name, he'd had the studio hire Hank as his stunt double. Not a bad gig – until Hank had fallen off a goddamn building and broken nearly every bone in his body.

After that, things started to slide downhill – and when, many years later, Hank had finally looked up his old pal Ralph Maestro and begged for a loan, Ralph had said he'd think about it.

Think about it, for crissakes! Ralph was a freakin' movie star with money comin' out his ass! Hank was major pissed.

But two months later, to his surprise, Ralph had called him. They'd met at a bar on Hollywood Boulevard – a place they'd used to frequent back in the day.

Ralph had a proposition. It wasn't a proposition that Hank particularly embraced, but he was desperate for money, and what the hell. The way Ralph explained it, the bitch had it coming.

Ralph set everything up. Gave him the place of entry to his house – assured him there would be no alarm on the side door he told him to enter by, and that the dogs would be secured. Ralph issued instructions on where to go and exactly what to do once he got in. Ralph laid it out so there could be no mistakes.

Except nobody had taken into consideration Hank's third wife, the coked-up Pinky, and her out-of-control jealous streak.

Who would've thought she'd grab his gun (the same weapon

Ralph had told him to dump in the L.A. River immediately after shooting Gemma – which of course he hadn't done) and attempt to blow his ass off? And who would've thought the goddamn nosy neighbor would call the cops? And who would've thought Ralph Maestro would walk away clean, while *he*, Hank Montero, received a minimum sentence of nineteen years in prison, because the jury of his so-called peers did not believe that Ralph Maestro had hired him to take care of business.

No indeed, Hank Montero had *not* led a charmed life.

* * *

The opening of the revamped *Mood* in Vegas was destined to be a lavish affair. Bobby wasn't into organizing a huge party, but Lucky was, and so was M.J. Between the two of them they planned to make it the grand club opening of the year.

Invitations were sent out ahead of time.

Bobby personally mailed one to Denver. He wasn't sure if she'd respond – after all, he hadn't heard from her since he'd left her in L.A. with an obvious boyfriend lurking on her doorstep.

Damn! He'd been looking forward to getting to know her, spending time with her, taking it slow and easy.

She'd told him she didn't have a boyfriend. Apparently she did.

He decided to phone her and see if she was coming to the opening – with or without her boyfriend. Preferably without.

Over the last few months he'd taken out a few girls, and they were always lacking that certain something Denver possessed. He'd thought about her a lot.

She picked up on the third ring.

"Hey –" he said. "It's Bobby."

Without taking a beat, she said, "The same Bobby who ran off and left me with an ex-boyfriend on my doorstep? Not even an ex – a one-nighter from my past. Thanks a lot."

"I was being respectful," he said, feeling an immediate connection.

"And not even a phone call," Denver chided.

"Hey, whattya mean – a one-nighter?" he said lightly. "I didn't tag you as a one-nighter kind of girl."

"You didn't tag me at all," she said boldly, delighted to hear from him.

When she'd received the invitation to the opening of *Mood*, she'd kind of hoped he would call. But then she'd thought, *Why would he?* Over the last few months she'd been busy getting her new career off the ground, and she hadn't thought about Bobby that much.

Well, sometimes . . . when she was out on a boring date and started remembering their camaraderie and the closeness they'd felt.

Christmas had come and gone, and so had Carolyn – her pregnant friend who flatly refused to reveal who the father was. Carolyn had given up her job in Washington and moved back to L.A. to spend time with her mother – Clare Henderson was in the throes of divorcing Carolyn's dad.

Denver had a new job working for the city. She was an Assistant D.A. and she loved it. Prosecuting the bad guys was far more satisfying than defending fat cat movie stars with friends in high places.

"So," Bobby said, "if that guy was a one night only, does that mean you're free?"

"Well, I'm certainly not charging for it," Denver quipped.

"Nice," Bobby said, laughing.

"Where are you?" she added.

"In a plane on my way to Vegas."

"Your plane?"

"It's not my plane," he said patiently. "It's the Stanislopoulos company plane."

"But aren't you Bobby Stanislopoulos?" she teased.

"I guess so, Miz District Attorney."

"How'd you know about my new job?" she asked curiously.

"You think I haven't been keeping tabs on you?"

"Hmm . . ." she said, experiencing a warm shiver of delight. "Really?"

"What's it gonna be?" Bobby said. "Am I stopping in L.A. or are you jumping a flight to Vegas?"

"Well . . ."

"Hey, Denver – I've heard of foreplay, but this is ridiculous."

"Yeah," she said softly. "It sure is."

"So . . . I guess I'm coming to L.A. – right?"

"Looks like I can't stop you."

"Looks like you don't want to."

Denver clicked off her phone, unable to wipe the smile off her face.

Beyond the Epilogue

Denver

Four hours after Bobby's phone call we were in bed together and it turned out to be everything I'd ever dreamed of.

Okay, so here's my checklist.

Abs: Perfect.

Technique: Perfect.

Lovemaking: Beyond.

Overall performance: I don't *think* – I *am* crazy in love. And yes, Bobby Santangelo Stanislopoulos is exactly as I'd imagined him to be.

After his phone call – which somehow or other I'd been expecting – he turned up at the door to my apartment, and it was pretty incredible to see him again.

He stood outside – tall, dark, and major sexy.

I reached forward, took his hand and pulled him inside.

He moved toward me, slammed the door shut with his foot and immediately began kissing me. Long, slow, tongue kisses which took kissing to a whole new level.

"I haven't stopped thinking about you," he said, his voice deep and husky.

"Me too," I managed, touching his face.

"What?" he teased. "You haven't stopped thinking about you either?"

"Hey . . ." I giggled.

Oh God! I am *so* not a giggler.

Then his hands were pulling my T-shirt over my head, and I began unbuttoning his shirt, because we both craved flesh and I wanted him more than I'd ever wanted anyone.

Bobby was King of Foreplay – unfastening the front clip on my bra, brushing my nipples with his fingertips, nudging my breasts together and working on them both at once.

I was breathless with the anticipation of what was to come – half-wishing he would move faster and yet at the same time wishing he would never stop caressing my breasts.

I felt him hard against my thigh, and I slid my hand down to feel him. Then I knew I had to taste him, make that intimate contact I didn't do with just anyone – in fact, no one since Josh, because call me old-fashioned, but giving oral sex should be saved for someone special. And Bobby was special.

Oh yes . . .

Finally we made it to the bedroom, threw off the rest of our clothes, and started to make love in a leisurely fashion, because we both knew that without a doubt there was more to come, so there was absolutely no reason to rush.

I have no idea what will happen next.

Bobby lives in New York.

I live in L.A.

But one thing I know for sure – some things are meant to be – and this is only the beginning.

About the Author

There have been many imitators, but only Jackie Collins can tell you what really goes on in the fastest lane of all. From Beverly Hills bedrooms to a raunchy prowl along the streets of Hollywood; from glittering rock parties and concerts to stretch limos and the mansions of the power brokers – Jackie Collins chronicles the real truth from the inside looking out.

Jackie Collins has been called a "raunchy moralist" by the late director Louis Malle and "Hollywood's own Marcel Proust" by *Vanity Fair* magazine. With over 400 million copies of her books sold in more than 40 countries, and with some twenty-six *New York Times* bestsellers to her credit, Jackie Collins is one of the world's top-selling novelists. She is known for giving her readers an unrivalled insiders knowledge of Hollywood and the glamorous lives and loves of the rich, famous, and infamous! "I write about real people in disguise," she says. "If anything, my characters are toned down – the truth is much more bizarre."

Visit Jackie's website www.jackiecollins.com, and follow her on Twitter at JackieJCollins and Facebook at www.facebook.com/jackiecollins

POCKET
BOOKS

Jackie Collins

MARRIED LOVERS

Three high-powered Hollywood couples, two hot affairs, one underage Russian ex-hooker, a passionate murder – and the players' lives are changed forever.

Cameron Paradise, a stunning twenty-four-year-old personal trainer, flees Hawaii and her champion-surfer husband, **Gregg**, in the middle of one of his abusive tirades and makes her way to L.A. Tall, blond, with a body to die for, it doesn't take Cameron long to find a job at an exclusive private fitness club where she encounters L.A.'s most important players.

Although she could have any man who walks through the club's doors, she is more focused on saving money – so that she can open her own studio one day – than getting caught up in the L.A. scene of wild parties and recreational drugs. Until she meets **Ryan Lambert**, an extremely successful independent movie producer.

Ryan is married to pampered **Mandy Lambert**, the daughter of **Hamilton J. Heckerling**, a Hollywood power-player son-of-a-bitch mogul. Ryan has never cheated on his demanding Hollywood Princess wife . . . until he meets Cameron.

ISBN 978-1-84739-448-4
PRICE £7.99

POCKET
BOOKS

Jackie Collins

LOVERS & PLAYERS

Dangerous sex, family secrets, irresistible power, mega money and two murders equal one reckless week in New York . . .

In **Lovers & Players**, the Diamond family rules. Red Diamond is an abusive and much-loathed billionaire. His three sons: Max, Chris and Jett are summoned to New York, for a family meeting which rocks their world.

Diahann, a beautiful black ex-singer, works as Red's housekeep – a job her daughter, Liberty, does not approve of. A waitress who is a would-be singer herself, Liberty has dreams of her own and while she pursues them, Damon P. Donnell, married hip-hop mogul supreme, pursues her.

Young New York heiress Amy Scott-Simon is engaged to marry Max. At her bachelorette party she runs into Jett. Jett has no idea who Amy is. And she doesn't realise who he is. A one night fling leads to major complications.

As the lives of these characters intertwine, power, money, fame and love are the ties that bind – emotionally and otherwise – in this highly charged love story about family relationships and deadly choices.

ISBN 978-1-84739-439-2
PRICE £7.99

POCKET BOOKS

Jackie Collins

DEADLY EMBRACE

The mistress of sexy fiction is back . . .

Madison Castelli – the beautiful, talented and street-smart journalist – is distraught after finding out her father has been hiding secrets from her all her life, and is possibly involved with the mob. To get away from it all, she flies to L.A. only to find herself held hostage by masked gunmen.

Michael Castelli is being accused of murder. But has he been set up as pay-back for a deed in his past? And could his daughter's life or death situation be connected?

Michael is determined to find out and exact his revenge. And what Michael Castelli wants, Michael Castelli usually gets . . .

ISBN 978-1-84739-437-8
PRICE £7.99